THE NEIGHBOR WAGER

THE NEIGHBOR WAGER

USA TODAY BESTSELLING AUTHOR

CRYSTAL KASWELL

Entangled Publishing, LLC
644 Shrewsbury Commons Ave., STE 181
Shrewsbury, PA 17361
rights@entangledpublishing.com

Amara is an imprint of Entangled Publishing, LLC.

Visit our website at www.entangledpublishing.com.

Edited by Lydia Sharp
Cover art/illustration and design by Elizabeth Turner Stokes
Interior formatting by Britt Marczak

ISBN 978-1-64937-572-8
Ebook ISBN 978-1-64937-530-8

Manufactured in the United States of America

First Edition February 2024

10 9 8 7 6 5 4 3 2 1

AMARA
an imprint of Entangled Publishing LLC

ALSO BY CRYSTAL KASWELL

For all my Orange County girls

PROLOGUE

River

Ten Years Ago

Lexi Huntington is the sun, and I'm a planet in her orbit, powerless to resist her gravity.

Or is she the moon and I'm the tides?

The shore, pounded by the waves the tides create?

No. The sun. That's the better metaphor. It fits her—she's as bright and brilliant as the ball of fire in the sky.

I scribble the phrase in my sketchbook.

She's the sun, and I'm a planet in her orbit.

There's no rhythm to the words—not yet. They need shading. Shaping.

Artistic ability runs in the family, but I lack Grandma's skill with words. Pictures are more my speed. Princesses with golden curls. Fire mages with white-blonde hair. Acrobatic monks with flaxen locks.

Of course, I draw a lot of curvy blondes. I have inspiration from the girl next door.

After I sketch the scene, I fall back onto my bed, study the glow-in-the-dark star stickers struggling to hold onto the popcorn ceiling. As with everything in Huntington Hills, our house is a bit gaudy.

Grandma curses the nineties architecture but, deep down, she loves the neighborhood. She loves the town. She loves living next door to the family who owns a third of Orange County and half the city.

Thankfully, my room is a refuge. It's small—only a desk, a bed, a bit of floor space, and a big window overlooking our backyard and the next-door neighbor's—but it's mine. The white desk is covered in multicolored sketches. The bed still rocks Spider-Man sheets (under the plain red bedspread, of course). The Roy Lichtenstein posters blend perfectly with the shelves packed with graphic novels. One entire bookshelf is filled with modern classics. Another with adaptations of classic literature.

That's sort of what I'm doing now, trying to turn my thoughts into a story, the way Grandma does. The visuals I adore—castles with grand towers, knights slaying dragons, waves crashing into cliffs—and the words she adores.

My cousin Fern and I are working on a project for Grandma's birthday. A small graphic novel, where a butt-kicking adventurer destroys evil and finds love. It combines all of our passions.

Only, Fern is more of a reader than a writer. Which means I'm here, picking up the slack, struggling with how to write the perfect sentence.

Would the love interest say this?

She's the sun and I'm the planet, powerless to resist her orbit...

Sure, why not?

It's what I would say, anyway.

I rush back to my desk, pull my large sketchbook—a different one—from on top of my art textbooks, and I draw. Three panels where the love interest, an adventurer, stares at the sky, professing his love for the princess. But not to her, not yet. He's practicing first.

The second I finish and drop my pencil, I hear it: music next door.

The Huntingtons are having a party.

That isn't a notable event. The Huntingtons have a party every week, it seems. But I know this isn't any old party.

This is Lexi Huntington's Sweet Sixteen.

The Lexi Huntington's Sweet Sixteen.

Only three days after my birthday. That's fate. Kismet. Destiny. Whatever word you use, it means the same thing:

We belong together.

Sure, right now, the stars don't align, but one day, they will. I have patience. I can wait for the right moment.

Tonight, I only want one thing: to offer her a gift. It is her birthday, after all. Who wouldn't want a four-panel birthday card? I've been working on it for the past two weeks, making sure every line and color is perfect.

I stand, stretch, change out of my wrinkled Star Trek shirt into something more appropriate for a Huntington party: cargo pants and a short-sleeved plaid button-up. For me, this is as formal as it gets.

I can't see what's happening inside, but outside my window, the party is already humming. At least a dozen people gather by the Huntingtons' enormous pool, sipping punch and admiring the fake waterfall on the other side of the backyard. And it's quite the backyard.

The Huntington estate sprawls over half our block. Their pool is as big as our house. Their house is the size of a department store. The rest of their backyard is, well, the parking lot of a department store.

Obscene for the neighborhood, but then the city is named after their great-grandfather.

Usually, I resent the inequality of it. But it's hard to complain about anything that keeps me this close to the sun.

For a few minutes, I study the party from above, as if locked away in a tower. The fashion, the posture, the music. Something popular on the radio. One of those girl-power pop artists

Grandma loves.

Grandma...

Grandma doesn't want me to go.

Grandma doesn't appreciate my crush on Lexi. She thinks Lexi will end up hurting me.

But has the sun ever hurt the earth? Okay, never mind, that's a bad metaphor. I suck at metaphors. That isn't the point. The point is I don't believe Lexi would ever hurt me.

Which means I need to sneak out, now. I press my ear to the door, to make sure the coast is clear, then I grab the envelope I packed for Lexi, and I sneak into the carpeted hallway. I creep down the stairs, into the mid-sized living room.

Thankfully, Grandma isn't sitting on the worn-leather couch. She isn't watching TV or sipping red wine or reading. She's not in the messy kitchen, either.

"She's in her office," my cousin Fern says, stepping into the kitchen from the backyard.

Fern is more of an older sister than a cousin, really. My mom bailed when I was a teenager, so I grew up here with Grandma, and Fern spent summers in the room next to mine. She took me under her wing, since I was two years younger and infinitely less cool. Her (really, *our*) older sister looks out for me, too, but she isn't here now because she's taking courses at UC Berkeley.

"Let's sneak out and go to the party," I say.

"You read my mind." Fern grins. "No sneaking *in*, though. We're invited, remember?"

Well, not specifically, but I know what she means. We have an open invitation from Mr. Huntington to *come by anytime*.

Fern checks her outfit—a pair of high-waisted jeans and one of Grandma's button-up silk blouses—and nods her approval. "How's my hair?" She tosses back her dark brown hair as if the natural-looking waves are, in fact, natural. "Do I need a makeover?" She doesn't wait for a response, just dives into her romance novel–inspired daydream. "Can you imagine that scene?

A makeover before a party at the Huntingtons' place? I could slide down the stairs in a backless gown and silver heels, with my hair pinned up on my head."

"A backless gown?" I raise a skeptical eyebrow.

She nods and continues watching the scene in her mind, a far-off, dreamy look in her eyes.

"To a high school party?" I press.

"It's a Huntington party, River. There will be someone in a backless gown."

"Lexi?" My blood pumps faster, imagining Lexi Huntington draped in a piece of silk, the pink fabric cutting a long line down her elegant back.

Fern laughs as I drift into fantasy land. Which is ridiculous. She lives in her imagination even more than I do.

"Come on," she says, pulling me firmly from my mind, back into the small space of the kitchen. "Let's get there in time for the birthday girl to make her entrance."

I take her hand and follow her out of the kitchen. We cross the grass in our tiny backyard, into the side yard, the one that connects our house to the Huntingtons'.

As usual, the tall wooden gate is wide open, allowing anyone and everyone into the party—well, anyone and everyone *invited*.

The music grows louder as we step into their backyard. Now that I'm closer, I can see the people around the pool are mostly adults. Friends of Mr. Huntington. They're in suits and cocktail dresses, sipping clear liquor from martini glasses or bubbly liquid from champagne flutes.

There's a bar back here, right between the massive man-made waterfall and the rose garden, complete with a crystal bowl full of pink punch. Likely alcoholic.

The bartender, a twenty-something guy in a catering uniform, watches Fern approach the table, take a glass, ladle the punch.

He leans in to whisper something to her. She returns an inviting smile.

I look away. I'm not foolish enough to believe my gorgeous, friendly sister is somehow lacking experience with men. She's twenty years old now.

But I'm worried because she spent weeks crying over her last boyfriend. Because, like me, she believes in the magic of love and the idea of destiny. And realizing the person you're with isn't *The One* is soul-crushing.

"Be careful," I say, when she returns with two glasses of bright pink punch.

She laughs. "Take your own advice."

"What do you mean?"

"Lexi Huntington."

"What about her?"

Fern opens her mouth to answer, but then I don't hear a word.

And I don't see anything else in the world.

Because *she* is here now.

Lexi Huntington pushes everything else away.

From right here, ten feet from the sliding glass door, I watch Lexi descend the oak stairs in the middle of the living room. She keeps one hand on the railing. She uses the other to wave to her guests.

She's not wearing a backless dress, but she is wearing pink. A neon pink as bright as her mocktails. As pink as the bikini she wears all afternoon. As pink as the color she paints her nails and the lipstick she wears when she sneaks to the backyard to kiss boys from school.

Not that I watch her do that once she's started. But I can wonder...if it were me with her instead...

For one beautiful moment, I imagine the pink makeup on my skin. My lips. My neck. My collarbone. Like in one of those old movies Grandma loves. In one of the scenes in her romance novels. The physical marking of passion. Not just a sexual passion—an emotional one.

Lexi is drop-dead gorgeous, yes, but I don't want her solely because of her round blue eyes, her soft lips, her curvy figure.

I want her because she's Lexi.

She's the sun and I'm the planet in her orbit, powerless to resist her gravity.

Of course the adventurer in my graphic novel would describe love this way. What other way is there to describe it?

My sister keeps talking, the guests keep mingling, the music keeps playing. But I don't hear a thing. Only the notes Lexi creates in my head. A beautiful melody, as romantic and timeless and easy as a dance.

Fern follows me inside, from the backyard into the main room. For a few minutes, she stands with me, watching Lexi greet her father's friends professionally and her school friends casually. As usual, Lexi slips between modes perfectly. She stays charming and effervescent and inviting.

After Fern finishes her punch, she leaves—probably to go see that bartender—and I stand at the wall, alone, watching the action. Every time Lexi finishes chatting with a friend and goes in search of another conversation, I tell myself, *This is it. I'm going to talk to her.*

Every time, I'm too slow. My heart is thundering and my feet feel like lead.

She starts another round of banter before I work up my courage. The party fills up. Two dozen people mill about the large living room. Then three.

Mr. Huntington, the patriarch of the family, taps a wineglass with a fork to call a toast.

Once the room has quieted, he holds up his glass. "Today is one of the proudest days of my life. My daughter Alexandria Huntington's sixteenth birthday."

As if she's drawn by magic, Lexi floats (really *floats*) to her father. The crowd parts for her. The room focuses on her. The entire world stops for her.

Because with Lexi, we're *all* the planets, powerless to resist her orbit.

She embraces her father with a hug and a bashful smile. "Dad," she says shyly, then releases him, and her smile widens. "You're embarrassing me."

"That's my job, as your father." He raises his glass again. "And it's your older sister's job, too." He points to the back of the room. To the double doors that lead to the kitchen, not that you can tell, given the size of the audience.

Again, the room parts. People move toward the couch on the right or the shelves of classic literature on the left, to make room for a pastry chef holding a massive, three-tier cake.

And right behind the chef?

Lexi's older sister, Deanna Huntington.

Even though she's only two years older than Lexi, the same age as I am, Deanna is hopelessly out of place at the party. *Why am I here* energy radiates from her. It's not just the heavy combat boots or the thick eyeliner or the zippers on her asymmetrical dress. It's something about her.

Like me, Deanna doesn't fit into this big, beautiful world. She's not bubbly or blonde or bodacious.

And like me, Deanna adores her sister. The second she and Lexi make eye contact, all that awkward energy disappears. She's happy to be here, celebrating her sister's Sweet Sixteen.

Deanna follows the pastry chef to the table in the middle of the room. The moment he sets the pastel-pink cake down, Deanna raises her hand to get everyone's attention and starts the birthday song.

Mr. Huntington chimes in first. By the third word, the rest of the crowd is singing along. Happy birthday to Lexi. Happy birthday to the most beautiful, charming girl in the world.

After the song, Mr. Huntington pats Lexi on the shoulder with pride. He looks around the room, taking in all the sentimental glory. I can imagine what he's thinking, because it's written all over his face. His little girls, growing up before his eyes.

With one big breath, Lexi blows out her candles. What's her wish? What could the girl with everything—popularity, looks, success, money—possibly want?

She shoots smiles around the room, noting the many admirers, the perfect pink hue of her cake, the look of wonder on my face—

Wait…what?

Lexi Huntington's beautiful blue eyes fix on me. For a brief moment, the stars align. The warmth of her stare encompasses me. My stomach flutters. My heart pounds so hard I feel it in my throat. My entire body buzzes with delight.

My hours studying the hue and shape of her eyes from afar failed to prepare me for the intensity of her stare.

Then, just as quickly, she smiles at someone else, a broad-shouldered guy in a leather jacket, and all the light flees the universe at once.

Maybe, in Grandma's books, I could get together with someone like Lexi. But here, in Orange County? Why would the Homecoming Queen date the president of the Graphic Novel Club?

Right now, I'm not on her radar.

Right now, I'm no one. Just another face in a room full of faces.

I wait for her to pass slices of cake around the room, then I sneak to the backyard. It takes too long to move through the crowded space. There are too many people eager to order drinks, dance, wish Lexi a happy birthday.

My fingers curl around the paper in my hands. The card. Of course.

It is her birthday. I need to give her this. When I finally make it through the backyard, I move through the side yard, to the front of the house. A quiet spot.

Only the porch isn't empty.

Lexi's sister Deanna is standing at the railing, shifting her weight between her combat boots, sighing with exhaustion as she beams with pride. I hadn't realized she slipped out of the house. I was so focused on Lexi and nothing and no one else in the room.

Deanna is pretty, in her own way. Not pretty like Lexi. Maybe pretty isn't the right word, it's more like... I don't know. I'm terrible with words. All I know is what I see—

She notices me, her head turning toward me, and her expression fades to something I don't like: pity.

She spots the envelope in my hand. It's obvious what it is, who it's for. "I can deliver that if you'd like," she says.

"Will you?" I have no specific reason to doubt her. Only the vague sense she, like everyone else, disapproves of my feelings for Lexi.

"I'm a woman of my word." She offers her hand.

I believe her. Deanna is many things. Honest is one of them. I place the card in her palm.

"Can I give you some advice?" Deanna asks.

"About what?"

"Your lack of combat boots," she says drily. "What do you think?"

I smirk a little. "Well... My wardrobe does lack combat boots." We live in Southern California, though. There's no need for boots most of the year.

We both know she didn't mean the boots.

"Even if Lexi liked guys like you, she isn't like you," Deanna says. "She's sweet in her way, but she's not romantic. She'll never appreciate hand-drawn birthday cards or sunset sails or long walks on the beach."

"How do you know?" I ask.

"Because I'm the same way," Deanna says.

"You and Lexi are the same?" I raise a brow. There's very little the sisters have in common. Besides their last name and their aptitude for achievement.

"With this, yes. We love, but we aren't romantics. We're too practical for that, at least I am, and Lexi..." She trails off, her eyes going distant for a moment, before she continues. "You're better off forgetting about her. Find someone else, study abroad, whatever it takes to get her out of your head."

Her words are a kick to the gut. She wants me to forget about Lexi?

"Good night, Deanna." I take a step backward. To head back home. To my room. The only place where I can safely process and express my feelings. Through art.

"It's nothing personal, River. I like you," she says, and I believe her. She has no reason to lie. Not about this or anything. "I don't want to see you get hurt."

Same thing Grandma said. I shrug as if I don't care.

"Good night." She turns and walks back into the house.

I move down the stairs, through the side yard, to my too-empty house.

Deanna has the same advice Grandma does. It's just as annoying coming from someone who knows Lexi as well as Grandma knows me.

But that doesn't make it less true.

That's the problem.

They're both right.

I need to move on. I'm already going to spend my summer at an art program in New York City, so maybe...maybe that's what I need to forget about Lexi. She hardly knows I even exist. Part of me understands that taking their advice is probably for my own good, but...

How can anyone forget the warmth of the sun?

CHAPTER ONE

Deanna

"Look at that, Dee. Five months, twenty-six days," Lexi squeals as she sends a thumbs-up to her boyfriend's text, then slips her phone into her purse. She steps into the huge elevator and presses the button for the penthouse floor. "Can you believe I've been with Jake that long?"

"Of course I can believe it. I believe in the app, and the app said you two are a match." I follow her into the small space and keep my eyes on the buttons.

Wilder Investments.

And we're meeting with the head, Willa Wilder.

Maybe, since we're meeting with a woman, we have a chance. Women are more willing to invest in products for women. I don't even care that the app isn't *just* for women, it is for women, and that's all that matters today. As long as we have a chance. Any chance.

I can admit it. I'm desperate. We're burning through cash at a rapid rate. Between salaries, office space, and advertisements, we're far, far in the red. Which is normal, for a start-up our size. That's the business model. Expand fast. Worry about revenue later. Most tech companies haven't even monetized yet when they sell for millions (or billions) of dollars.

But no matter how many times I tell myself this is normal, I feel no better about the state of affairs. We need an investment now.

My previous projections were slightly off. We have two more months left at our current burn rate, but that's it. In sixty-one days, without an outside investment, we are completely out of money. We'll have to close the company, admit failure, give up on our mission to match online daters with people who are truly compatible, and, worst of all, stop working together. I love working with my sister. I love that we're equal partners in this business.

So we need to ace this interview the way I aced AP Calculus. Every single homework assignment on time, a 95-plus percent on every test, and plenty of extra credit.

The doors close. The elevator rises.

Lexi's excitement rises with it. "You know what that means, don't you?" She doesn't wait for me to answer, because she knows I know. "I get five percent soon."

5 percent of nothing is nothing, but I don't say that out loud. I already know Lexi's response to that kind of thing. Bad luck, negative energy, whatever.

She's not the person you push to see reality. Reality isn't a part of her job description. She's all about selling the best possible version of reality.

And I need her now. I need her to sell the fuck out of MeetCute.

This almost six-month relationship with a man she met on MeetCute? That's a top selling point. Even if, for some reason, Lexi can't see that.

I had to wager 5 percent of my share of the company to get her to give the guy a chance, but I'd happily part with *all* my shares to see her successful in life and love. Fortunately, though, she was satisfied with 5 percent, and we'll still be mostly equal partners in this.

"What are you going to spend it on?" I ask, to keep her excitement ramped up.

"A house in Newport to start," she says. "One of those cute three-bedrooms right on the sand. By the Wedge maybe." The famous surf spot in Newport Beach, the place we used to hang as kids, where she'd happily ogle surfer boys. Then flirt with surfer boys. Then go to the Jeeps their parents bought for them to do, uh, activities.

Now, we're adult businesswomen. She still goes to the Wedge once a month, give or take, and she still ogles, but she doesn't go to anyone's Jeep. (Or their Tesla, or Benz, or BMW, or Rav-4, or Lexus.)

She doesn't even invite any damp surfer boys to her flashy sports car.

She has Jake.

Honestly, while I do believe it's happened, like I told her, it's still a surprise. Nearly six months with one person. Lexi in a monogamous relationship. And with the guy who first asked her about how she sees her wedding. That's exactly what Lexi thought she didn't want.

But the app knew.

It always knows.

Is there a better pitch for the success of our app?

Not if you know Lexi Huntington.

The weird thing is, the two of them make perfect sense. Despite his borderline stuffy job as an employment attorney, Jake is as fun-loving as Lexi. They both adore pop music and syrupy sweet alcoholic beverages and lounging on the sand every Sunday. Thus, the giant smile on her face at the moment.

It's not the 5 percent.

It's the text she got from Jake. Their plans to meet later.

"And another house next-door." She wakes from her fantasies of beach homes to check her reflection in the mirrored wall. "For you, of course."

My heart goes a little soft. "You really want me to live next door?"

"Of course!"

I'm flattered, but also skeptical. "Even when you get married?"

Her nose scrunches in distaste. Her eyes glaze over. Her entire body twists into the strangest posture: still beautiful and bubbly but totally disgusted, too.

And there it is: the Lexi I know.

She isn't interested in commitment. Not that I blame her. How can she believe anything lasts when we lost Mom so young? "Why would I get married?" she says.

Not really a question, but I answer her anyway. "That's why people date."

"Oh, really, is that why you're engaged now?" She nods to my extremely bare left hand as if it's proof I'm wrong.

She's right, of course. Even though, in my mind, I want a stable relationship, I spend just as much time single, or in short-term relationships, as she does. My ratio of single to fling is a hundred to one and hers is the opposite, but neither one of us is rushing to walk down the aisle. The results speak for themselves.

"I date," I remind her. "It just hasn't led to marriage yet."

"You ask guys to rate your match on a scale of one to ten." She fixes her long blonde hair and smooths her pink sheath dress. Then she turns to me and starts her work, adjusting my magenta blazer, offering to fix my wine-colored lipstick. "Does that get them all hot and bothered?"

"So bothered that we have sex right there, at the table."

She laughs and it sounds as if she's really saying *this is totally absurd*. "So that's why you stopped going to the place on Main Street."

"And the bar next door," I say drily.

The truth is: I don't take guys anywhere in Huntington Hills. It's the smallest city in Orange County. Basically, a blip between Irvine, Newport Beach, and Laguna Hills.

Okay, blip is underselling it. We've got a population in the tens of thousands and a lot of property with values in the tens of millions (being on a hill overlooking the ocean does that), plus three grocery stores, two dozen restaurants, and way too many shops, med spas, and salons to count.

What we don't have is anywhere even a little bit cool. Even by Orange County standards, Huntington Hills is hopelessly un-hip.

There is one bar and it's constantly filled with moms and dads who want to talk about PTA meetings and HOA dues. And there's that one night a month where older women go to meet younger guys. I accidentally went once, and some guys, who were way too young to legally be in a bar, hit on me, even though I was "actually younger than they liked."

So, when I date, I go as far away as possible. Well, as far as I can go in under two hours. Which means I schedule all my dates on Sundays in Los Angeles. Despite popular belief, Sundays are mostly traffic-free across all of Southern California.

But my love life, or lack thereof, doesn't matter right now.

It's Lexi who is the model of the MeetCute algo's perfection.

"You should try actually dating one of those guys," she says. "You might like them."

"I might."

"But…?" She pulls out the tube of wine-colored lipstick and presses it into my palms.

I focus on my reflection. There are so many buts.

I'm too busy hustling for money. I'm too tired of pretending to like investors. Do I really have to pretend I already like a guy I'm meeting for the first time, too? I'm tired of wearing high heels to meetings *and* dates, even if I mostly wear high-heeled boots. Combat boots are so much more comfortable. And nice, thick eyeliner. Not this tiny line I wear to look professional.

The elevator door opens before I can answer her "but."

Lexi waits for me to finish my lipstick, takes my hand, and leads me into the big, modern lobby.

This is one of the few venture capital firms in our area, and it feels distinctly Orange County. There's a certain bland perfection to the space.

A busy office with a bevy of workers of all races and ages, all in casual yet expensive clothes, all smiling as they work hard. No cubicles. All open offices with windows letting in the California sunlight and bamboo sit-to-stand desks.

Lexi moves through the space with ease. She knows where everything is. She's the one who fits into the big, beautiful world here. Because she's Lexi and she fits in everywhere.

She stops in front of the conference room and whispers in my ear, "We're going to ace this."

"You really think so?"

She nods. "You look like ten million bucks."

"Like a woman who can command a hundred million dollars?"

"Exactly." She takes a deep breath and lets out a steady exhale, then squeezes my hand and leads me into the room.

Willa Wilder is standing at the other end of the long conference table on her own. No assistant. No partners. No man sitting next to her to prove she's a real investor (a time-honored technique many women entrepreneurs use to make sure men take them seriously). But Willa is past that because Willa is the one with the money. Willa is the one who makes things happen.

Okay, maybe Willa is a role model of sorts.

She runs a firm that has forty billion dollars' worth of investments. And she always looks great doing it. Not the way Lexi looks great—in a pink dress, with her long blonde hair and her blue eyes screaming California Girl.

Willa does it in a Boss Babe, *I control this place and I could control the universe, if I wanted* sort of way.

Willa Wilder is exactly who I want to be in twenty years. She radiates power simply by standing tall in her black suit. She dresses without an especially feminine flair—short hair, flat shoes—but still pulls off a skirt-suit with silver earrings.

She's the picture of a successful woman. And she doesn't hide her sex appeal, either. She's all business, yeah, in a *maybe I will have a martini with a twist after this* sort of way.

How does that feel, to have people flock to the power you radiate? Someday I will know that feeling.

Willa smiles as she nods *hello* to us. She's a friend of our father's. We've seen her at his parties, a few times, but we've never met as colleagues. She studies Lexi with an expression of quiet competence, noting the pink dress, the nude pumps, the silver necklace that says *stylish businesswoman*. "You always wear pink."

She moves all the way around the table to offer her hand.

Lexi shakes it. "My power color." She smiles and holds Willa's gaze. "Not all of us can rock neutrals the way you do."

Willa softens. She understands power, and she responds to flattery. Everyone responds to Lexi's flattery.

Outside the frosted glass walls of the conference room, the office buzzes around us. From in here, it's all silhouettes and murmurs of conversation. Are people running numbers on MeetCute? Talking to competitors? Preparing to lowball us?

Deep breath. Utmost confidence. I'm not here to consider anyone else's motivations. I'm here to finalize this deal. "It's nice to see you again, Ms. Wilder."

She smiles. "Please, Deanna, call me Willa."

I swallow hard. I'm tongue-tied. Which is silly. I don't get tongue-tied around people.

But then maybe it's not silly. She has our company's future in her hands.

At this point, it's all decided. That's how these meetings go. I hate not knowing what's already been determined.

Is it a yes or a no?

Do I need to spend the weekend prepping pitches, or can I relax for the first time in two years?

Willa motions for us to sit.

Lexi takes the spot on the right. I take the spot on the left.

Slowly, Willa lowers herself into her leather chair. "The pitch impressed me."

Under the table, Lexi offers her hand.

I squeeze.

"MeetCute is exactly what we need in the dating app space. You're bringing feminine fun into the market. And even better, you're bringing inclusive femme fun," Willa says. "Pink and flowers and champagne and the ability to find someone who appreciates the real you, the you who loves romantic comedies and ice cream."

"Exactly," I say. "The algo matches users who truly relate to each other."

"It's genius," she says. "I've played around with it myself and I love the setup." With the press of a single button, she pulls up our slide deck on the giant TV behind her.

The home screen of the app is a picture of Lexi and me, smiling, with a lot of pink text.

I'm not sure why she's pitching us the app, but I know it's a bad sign. People only talk you up if they're trying to let you down easy.

Still, I nod as she flips to the sample profile. Our system is different. Instead of a picture, users get an answer to a question. They can see three answers to three questions before they swipe left or right—yes or no.

They only get a picture after the initial match. After they're invested in their potential partner's personality.

What do you like to do on a Saturday night? the slide reads, followed by the answer:

I know a lot of people say they're down for anything, but I mean it. A movie at home, a football game, a night of dancing to candy pop. As long as we're laughing together, I'm happy.

That's from Lexi's profile. She had the most popular answer, statistically. Logic agrees: Lexi is irresistible.

"There's only one problem," Willa says.

All of the air leaves the room at once.

Of course, there's a problem. There's always a problem.

"Two problems, actually," Willa says.

Oh God. I swallow hard.

Lexi squeezes my hand. "I'm sure we can work through that."

Willa addresses Lexi. "I love the attempt to match people by personality, but let's face it: people are superficial. They'll be slow to try an app if they think it will attract the unattractive."

Lexi laughs. "I told Dee the same thing when we started. I was sure people would resist an app without fast pictures, but it hasn't been a problem. We're growing quickly. Twice as fast as the next fastest-growing app."

Willa turns off the TV behind her. "Even so. My investment partner isn't sold. That's problem number two."

What partner? Does she really answer to someone, or is this a friendly brush-off?

Willa notices my disbelief. "I'm sold, Deanna. I promise. But I have to bring my partner something really convincing. And that's a big ask. He's freshly divorced. A total non-believer in love. So, unless we see financial returns, we need a poster couple. By next month."

Poster couple. Okay. *What if...*

"Two people. Any gender, any race, as long as they're happy long-term," she says. "Twenty-five to fifty. And attractive. A younger couple and an older couple would be ideal, but I'm sure we'll have time for that later."

Later. Right.

"Now, we need to convince him," Willa says.

"We're still new," Lexi says. "We don't have many long-term relationships."

It's true, we don't. But there is one—

"What about you?" Willa asks.

Lexi blinks in disbelief. "Me?"

"Yes, the two of you. You're successful young women."

Lexi stares out the window, looking for help in the blue sky. I was thinking the same thing Willa is now leading toward, but there's something I know that Willa doesn't—Lexi.

"You're conventionally attractive," Willa says. "And you're the two who created the company. You aren't testing it on yourselves?"

"Oh, yeah." Lexi must have found the answer in a puffy white cloud and then turns to Willa. "Deanna is constantly on dates with guys, asking what they like and didn't like about her. She sends them questionnaires."

"Met anyone worth keeping yet?" Willa asks me.

This isn't supposed to be about me. "Not yet," I say.

"What about you, Lexi?" Willa asks.

Bingo.

Lexi swallows hard. "Me?"

"You do use the app?" she asks.

"Well, not anymore," Lexi says.

"Because she met someone on the app," I explain. "A guy. A very handsome guy."

Willa puts all her attention on Lexi. "How long have you been seeing him?"

"Not long," Lexi says.

"Don't be so modest," I say, keeping my voice light. But inside, I want to kick her. This is our *in*. Is she trying to sabotage us? "They've been together almost six months," I tell Willa. "It's the longest she's ever been with *anyone*."

Willa's eyes light up. "Perfect. We'll have dinner. The two of you and the two of us. Well, the three of you." She nods toward me. "Show up in something a little formal—a cocktail dress and heels—with this guy, and convince my partner you're madly in love."

Uh…

Lexi blinks again.

"Is there a ring?" Willa asks. "It would be great if there's a ring."

My stomach drops. All the way to the earth's core. Our *in* will be an *out*, fast, if Willa pushes her too far.

"A ring?" Lexi goes pale. "No, we, I, uh…"

"Even better," Willa says. "He can propose at the dinner. We can plan for dinner in, say, a month? To give him time to prepare the perfect proposal." She laughs softly, but it's not clear if she's joking, and she doesn't give us time to laugh with her. "I'd love to meet him first, though, as soon as possible. Before we have the dinner to convince my partner. When can I meet Mr. Right?"

Shit, shit, shit.

"What?" Lexi stays frozen in disbelief. Even her smile is still frozen on her face, and it's cold as ice. Fake. Plastic. Not like Lexi at all.

"It's Friday afternoon," Willa says. "The two of you must have weekend plans."

"Don't you have a date tonight?" I ask, fumbling for a way to salvage this.

"What? Yeah. I think so." Lexi's voice is soft and not in the demure, coy way it often is. In the way it is when Dad is pissed. She's scared.

Of course she's scared. Willa is practically eloping her on the spot.

I don't know what to say, how to help. I can't tell Willa to back off—investors hate being told what to do, and we still need her money—so I force a smile and I nod, as if this is all normal pitch stuff.

"At your father's party?" Willa asks.

"Right," I say. "He has a party tonight. We'll all be there."

Wait… *Tonight?*

I try to backpedal, but Willa is already jumping on it.

"I'll see the three of you tonight." She stands and offers her hand. She shakes Lexi's hand. Then mine. "I can't wait."

She *can't wait* to make Lexi Huntington, the girl who has no interest in commitment, the poster girl of love and commitment.

Not a problem. We can handle this.

Totally *not* a problem.

CHAPTER TWO

Deanna

Major problem.

100 percent, colossal, Category 5 hurricane problem.

Lexi says nothing as we take the elevator to the parking garage, get in the car, and drive out.

She says nothing on the twenty-minute ride home.

Even when we turn onto the hill of Huntington Hills, she says nothing. She stares at the radio as it spins competing narratives: ballads professing the beauty of love between girl power anthems and odes to the almighty dollar.

We park right as "She Works Hard for the Money" finishes, as if the universe is trying to tell Lexi to put finances first.

Or maybe that's me. Love songs never move me. They dwell in cliches or lack specificity. Money songs, too, but at least money makes sense.

Money is logical. Money is practical. Money never leaves because you're too detached or too busy with work or too unable to let your guard down. People do.

But Lexi isn't any of those things. And even though she's a bit superficial at times, she's not moved by the digits in her bank account. Our bank account. Lexi wanted to work on MeetCute with me because she wanted to work *with me*, because I promised her that we could make it into something great.

When Mom was dying, she didn't ask me to smile through the pain or pretend she wasn't losing strength. She only asked me for one thing: to take care of Lexi.

For a decade and a half, that's what I've done. I have to do it now, too. I have to make sure my sister gets the best deal possible, creates the best life possible, finds the best partner possible.

"When is Jake arriving?" I ask as I turn into our neighborhood.

Lexi stares out the window, watching apartments fade into two-story houses. Then into massive places like ours. "Later."

"You two can stop by the party to say hi to Willa?" I ask.

"I guess."

"It's a party," I say. "I know Dad has too many and they can all start to feel the same, but this will be fun."

She deflates. She sinks into her seat for the rest of the drive.

After I park, Lexi struggles out of the car. She picks up her pink purse and her laptop bag, and then presses her palm against the door of my silver Tesla. "Six months is a long time."

"You're almost there," I say.

"But that's all I want," she says. "Six months, and I get my five percent. No commitment beyond that. If we stay together, fine. If we don't, fine. I don't want to write any of this in stone."

"You don't have to."

"Don't I? She wants him to *propose*."

"The dinner is four weeks away," I say. "You only need to keep him around for a month."

She rolls her eyes. "Because after we sign, I'm sure they'll forget all about their quest for a poster couple. It'll be totally cool for their pride and joy to break up."

Probably not. But after we sign, we have the money. There's no way they'll write the contract with the provision that Lexi and Jake have to stay together. That's unethical, even by tech billionaire standards. "They can't do anything once we sign."

"But they can, Dee. That's what you don't see. Other people

don't respect the letter of the law the way you do."

"What the hell does that mean?"

"If they see our breakup as a betrayal, they'll screw us over. They'll find a way to do it."

I sigh. I think she's overthinking this. "I'll take care of it," I assure her.

She shakes her head. "I'm going to lie down and enjoy my last afternoon of freedom."

"Come on," I say. "Is it that dire?"

"An engagement?"

"That was just a suggestion, a joke." *I think*.

"It's never just a suggestion," she says.

"You were excited this morning," I say, lightening my tone. "Remember how big you smiled when you got his text? What did it say?"

"He was picturing our honeymoon."

"See." I gesture toward her. "You smiled at a honeymoon."

"There was sex under a waterfall. Who wouldn't smile? But it's a honeymoon that will never actually happen. Or at least I thought." She throws up her arms as if to say *this is impossible* and crosses the sidewalk. Then it's up the winding path to the house.

Okay, mansion. Our house is a mansion. A mansion on a massive lot with an apartment in the back.

We live in the apartment, but we spend plenty of time in the house, too. Dad is lonely by himself and, well, the house is pretty sweet. Big kitchen, bigger living room, big patio next to the big pool.

I follow Lexi up the path. Even though she's wearing stilettos and I'm wearing heeled boots, she beats me inside.

I rush after her. Find her on the plush cream couch, arms crossed, like an adult version of the Lexi who threw tantrums because she didn't have the right outfit for her Barbie.

She's upset. I see that.

But that's all I see. Emotions, people, relationships: none of it is my strong suit.

If I could build an algorithm to explain why Lexi is upset, I could do something. As it is, I have to use the data available to me.

Lexi loves freedom. Lexi hates commitment. Everyone hates losing their autonomy. Mom died right when Lexi was learning to have meaningful relationships with other people.

Of course, she can't imagine a future with Jake. Or anyone.

Of course, she flees from pain at every opportunity. She's had enough for a lifetime.

She rushes to short-term arrangements, and I bury myself in work, but because she's a woman, she's seen as superficial and slutty, and I'm seen as a studious hard worker. It's sexist bullshit. She works hard, too. And I have fun, too. In my own way.

She just needs to remember she likes this guy. She needs to see this as her choice. And it is her choice. I can't force her to do anything.

She doesn't have to stay with him forever, though. Just for a few months. For long enough that everyone can agree they had a great relationship, *and MeetCute made it happen*.

I sit next to her on the couch. "You love his eyes."

"I do." She rests her head against the wall and stares at the high ceiling.

"And he *wears* that suit." The one in the first picture she ever saw of him.

She nods *he does*.

"Do you remember what you said about his tie?"

She smiles as she recalls the bawdy talk. *I'd like to wrap that thing around his wrists and ride his face. Do you think he'd appreciate that?* "That's true."

"Did you do it?" I ask.

She pauses, her whole body going tense. "That's the thing."

"What thing?"

She looks around the living room, checking for possible

eyewitnesses. There's no one. Only leather furniture and framed art. "We haven't."

"You haven't…?"

She checks the space again, taking in the aura of quiet. Which is totally unnecessary. Except for Dad's parties, the place is *always* quiet.

Mom was the one who brought the noise. Who loved music and film and art and light.

Still, Lexi checks the surroundings one more time. "We haven't had sex."

"You…what?" My jaw drops halfway to the floor. If someone gave me a million dollars and a thousand years to come up with a guess for why Lexi is worried about her relationship, I would never have picked that.

Lexi is not a woman who waits. Lexi goes after exactly what she wants, with exactly who she wants, whenever she wants. Before she met Jake, Lexi exclusively dated guys on a fling-to-fling basis.

I can't believe she's gone six months without sex, let alone six months without sleeping with the guy she's dating. The guy she really, really wants.

Is she ill?

"I see it on your face." She hides behind her hands. "I'm a freak."

"No, you aren't. Lots of people wait," I say.

"What the hell am I doing?" She shakes her head, hands and all. "He wanted to take it slow, and I thought he meant a few weeks. I didn't want to be one of those guys, you know?"

"What guys?"

"The guys who dump women because they won't put out."

"You're not a guy," I say.

"The principle applies!" She drops her hands. "Do you think it's all some scheme? To entice me with the promise of sexual chemistry and string me along until I'm desperate to make some sort of commitment?"

"Why would he do that?"

"Women do it."

"What women?" I ask.

"Charlotte did it on *Sex and the City*. And look how that worked out!"

"She left the guy because he was impotent."

Her stare screams *obviously*.

"Are you impotent?"

"Oh my God… Is *he* impotent?" she asks, horrified, as if she'd never considered it until now. "What if it's because he's impotent?"

Hmm…it's a fair point. "There are other options."

"What other options?"

"Medication and sex toys and—" I stop myself mid-sentence. Lexi isn't interested in that. Not for her future husband.

Lexi wants one thing from guys: satisfaction without complication.

Or she did, before Jake. But she's been with him for almost six months. She must want something else besides sex with him, too. Even if she can't see it.

"Did he give you a reason for waiting?" I ask.

"He said he rushed into things with his ex. They didn't get to know each other because they were always screwing like rabbits." She lets out a wistful sigh. "That could have been me. I could be screwing him like a rabbit."

"You still could."

"I can't sleep with him now," she says.

"Why?"

She shoots me a look, like *get real*. "He's obviously expecting something I can't give him."

Is there anything Lexi can't deliver here? "Such as?"

"He wants to make love."

Oh. *That*.

Love.

The one little thing Lexi isn't interested in trying.

Or maybe she is, now, and just doesn't realize it.

"What would you do, Dee?" she asks.

This isn't about me or what I would do. It's about what's best for Lexi. What's best for our company, too. All of it is connected now.

"You like him, don't you?"

She nods.

"Then I'd do it. Stick with him until I knew I wanted to marry him. That's the whole point of dating. To meet someone, craft a partnership, build a life together."

"You make it sound so sexy," she deadpans.

"It's not supposed to be sexy all the time."

She looks at me like I told her the sky is green.

"Life is about more than sex," I press.

This does not compute with Lexi. "That's what people say when they want you to keep having bad sex. Is that what you want, Dee? A lifetime of bad sex? Do you know how many women put up with bad sex from men just because they feel affection for them? Is that what you want for me?"

"No. Of course not." How can I explain this to her? It's not like I'm a bastion of relationship success. That's why I needed to develop an app. To help people like me find matches. And she's not wrong, either. The top two reasons why couples fight are money and sex. A relationship with bad sex is a bad relationship for most people. I need to try a different approach...

"You've had fun, haven't you?" I ask.

"We have," she agrees.

"Maybe you're close enough now to do it," I say. "To give him the intimacy he wants."

"I don't know. Maybe this is a sign. He wants something I can't give him. I've been thinking about ending it for a while. Why drag it out?"

Since when? She hasn't said anything. No, she's just scared and overwhelmed and I can't blame her. All of this pressure from Willa, from the app, from me, to make it work with Jake. More pressure is the last thing she needs. "Just talk to him tonight, and see what he does," I say. "Tell him about what you need. That's all I'm asking."

"It's better to spare everyone the pain of a hard conversation." Lexi shakes her head as if to say *why would I want to tell the guy he's making me wait too long?* Hard conversations are right up there with commitment on the list of things Lexi does not want to do.

Does she really have to end things, though? That's not good for us. That isn't going to convince Willa to invest. But I can't force Lexi to stay with the guy, either. I don't *want* to force her to stay with the guy, really, if she doesn't want to be with him. I need to back off a bit and let her breathe.

"It's your relationship," I concede. "Your choice."

She nods. "And the app?"

"We'll think of something," I say.

She nods *okay* and moves into the kitchen.

I fix tea for both of us. Lexi takes hers to the patio. I bring mine to Dad's study.

For an hour, I disappear into my favorite place: work. Is there anything better than dissolving into what you do?

I don't love pitching the product or negotiating with investors, but I absolutely love programming.

It's the one place everything makes sense.

My flow fades as the noise picks up. Someone is downstairs, setting up the bar. That means it's about three hours until the party starts.

I can see the scene from Dad's window. There's a tall guy in the backyard, talking to Lexi, who's sitting by the pool in one of her pink bikinis—

Wait.

Is that guy wearing a leather jacket?

Caterers don't wear leather jackets. And the men from Dad's company absolutely don't wear leather jackets.

There's no bow tie, either.

The caterers at Dad's parties always wear bow ties.

I look closer—

What? That can't be.

No...

It is.

The tall guy in the leather jacket isn't a helpful stranger.

That's River Beau, the boy next door. The extremely dorky, totally uncool boy next door.

Only he's no longer a dweeb. He's smoking hot.

For a moment, I just stare. Take him in. Process all the changes. His muscular physique, his confident manner, his lack of glasses, his... Is that a tattoo? *Damn*. He's like Clark Kent in his Superman costume. Still River, just different. Better? Maybe. The way a man looks has never been the most important thing to me. He could be a hot asshole now, for all I know. He's been living in New York. That can change a person, and clearly has, at least on the outside.

But even after all these years, he also clearly still wants Lexi. The way he's looking at her is too familiar, reminding me of when we were all teenagers.

And now that he's a hunk, Lexi is staring back. I know that look on her face, too.

Shit.

She's found the perfect antidote for her cold feet. The ideal distraction from her dry spell. I could see her dumping Jake— dumping her future—in a rash, rush need to quench her thirst with River.

Oh, hell no.

It's my job, as her older sister, to stop her from making that mistake. To save her relationship—and the app.

Engagement jokes aside, Willa was clear: the investors need a poster couple, and what better poster couple is there than one of the sisters who created the app and a handsome employment attorney dating steadily for six months?

Lexi and Jake are it.

This is happening.

And the "extreme makeover" edition of the boy-next-door is not fucking it up for us.

CHAPTER THREE

River

After a decade spent living in the world's greatest city, New York, the Huntington house is both smaller and grander than I remember it.

The sheer size defies my imagination.

This place is a castle, with apartments, a pool, and a rose garden. And it's completely lacking the history and taste of an actual castle. Or, say, a brownstone on the Upper East Side. A four-story apartment building in the Village. Even compared to one of those new buildings in the Financial District, the place feels too new. Only it also feels too dated.

As if it's stuck in its strange mix of seventies original construction and nineties McMansion grandeur. Red tile roofs, white paint, wide windows, rectangular pool.

Well, there's no arguing with the pool.

And there's certainly no arguing with the beauty of Lexi Huntington.

Even after ten years and three thousand miles of space between us, as soon as I see her, I fall under her spell immediately. I tried to forget her, and for a while, I thought I had. But now...

She fits perfectly into her surroundings. She's the vision of the ideal California woman—busty, sun-kissed, friendly—in the ideal California setting. A beige patio chair, under an umbrella, soaking in all the shade on a cloudy day.

And the pool. All that azure water casting highlights on her gorgeous face.

She smiles as she removes her round sunglasses. "Hey."

My heart thuds against my chest. *Hey.* That's all it takes.

Ten years without seeing or hearing her and I'm swooning over a friendly hello. I can't help it. There's something to Lexi beyond colors and shapes. Beyond a linear narrative.

This isn't just the dork falling for the popular girl.

It's more.

Kismet. Destiny. Magic.

It has to be—because I'm not nearly as innocent now as I was before, and I still feel it.

"Hey," I say back.

She brushes a hair behind her ear and looks me over carefully, studying the line of my jaw, the cut of my shoulders, the fit of my jeans. I know what that look means.

A million times, I imagined the thrill of Lexi's interest, but the real thing is even more intoxicating.

I don't move. I don't think. I don't even breathe.

She looks me over again, this time stopping at the tattoo on my chest. The one that peeks out from under my V-neck tee.

I didn't believe my ex when she told me it would drive women crazy, but it does.

Of course, at the time, I said, *Why would I care about that, when I have you,* and she laughed. *River, you're such a hopeless romantic.* She must have known then it wasn't going to last. She knew we were fundamentally incompatible. I didn't see it. I saw too much of her light.

The way I do with Lexi.

Only Lexi is a million times more brilliant. Even though I'm older, wiser, more experienced, I'm still a planet in her orbit, powerless to resist her gravity.

"Are you a friend of Ms. Beau's?" she asks.

Why would she ask that? I shake my head.

"Are you subletting a room with her?" Lexi sits up a little straighter. She smiles a little wider.

Wow. Okay, I get it now. She doesn't recognize me.

She just sees me as a sexy stranger. I fight a grin.

Perhaps I should take offense—because I hold that little space in her memory—but I don't. There's something intoxicating about seeing myself through her eyes. I'm not the awkward dork who drew graphic novels instead of attending parties.

I'm a man Lexi Huntington would want.

It's all there, in her blue eyes. That's her gift, really. When she looks at you, you feel like the most important person in the world. How could anyone resist that feeling?

She doesn't notice my lightheadedness. Or my wonder.

Maybe she's used to it, though, having this effect on people. She must be.

The entire world falls at Lexi's feet.

She continues, unmoved. "Staying at the Airbnb across the street?" She cups the side of her mouth with one hand and stage-whispers, "We're not supposed to know, but I won't tell."

"No." I barely get the word out. I'm too in awe.

Lexi is even more beautiful now, as a grown woman.

There's something beyond the symmetry of her features and the curves of her torso. There's a spiritual appeal to Lexi.

"But I've seen you around, haven't I? You seem familiar..." She tilts her head to one side, trying to place me. When she doesn't, she stands up and slips her feet into her pink wedges. "Do you want to come in? Have a drink?"

As if I would turn down a drink with Lexi Huntington. "Sure."

"What's your poison?" She smiles and moves toward the house, happy to have a task, a friend, a chance with her soulmate, too—

Okay, that's probably not it. I'm enamored, not delusional. She doesn't know the way I do, but some part of her sees it, too.

The connection is there.

"Oh! Were you at Dad's birthday?" she asks.

That's one time, back when we were teens. I nod. Though she's got to be thinking of a more recent birthday. Still, this is kind of fun, playing this game of "who am I?" with her.

"You work with him?" She studies my outfit again, likely trying to figure out why a guy who works for her dad's company—the one that owns half the commercial property in the three surrounding cities and makes sure every strip mall wall is exactly the right shade of beige, and every lease goes to exactly the right-for-the-city client—would rock jeans and a T-shirt and a visible tattoo. "He's out right now, but he'll be here tonight for the party."

Party? *Tonight?* "What are you celebrating?"

She plays with her sunglasses. "You're not here to help set up?" she says instead of answering.

"No."

I follow her steps toward the house.

Everything feels strange.

The grass is green, the sky is blue, and Lexi Huntington is intoxicating.

It's familiar and foreign at once.

Lexi turns as the patio door slides open.

I don't mean to stare at her ass, but I can't help myself. My feelings for Lexi are pure. Well...they started pure.

Then Deanna steps into the backyard. *Holy shit.* That's Deanna.

Lexi sighs, a tired sigh. Like she knows exactly why her sister is here and it isn't good.

She looks like the Deanna I know, with the same black boots and wine-stained lips, but she looks different, too. Older, of course. Mature. She's rocking a magenta suit and a sharp bob, and looking more *adult*, too.

I see that side of her.

She's tall, stylish, beautiful in an intense way.

She'd kill in New York.

She must do okay here.

"River." Deanna smiles. "It's good to see you."

Wow, she had no trouble recognizing me at all. I feel myself grin, though I'm not sure why. It's just Deanna. She paid more attention to me back then, she actually talked to me, of course she'd recognize me quicker. That's all this is.

"River?" Lexi turns to me with shock in her eyes. "Really?"

I offer my most effortless shrug.

"How was your flight?" Deanna shifts her weight from one foot to the other, clearly uncomfortable in her heeled boots. But that isn't what catches my attention, really. It's the way her hands are fidgeting.

A sign of weakness. The first sign of weakness I've ever seen in her. Ever. The Deanna I knew was always tough and in control, as if nothing in the world could penetrate her defenses.

"Bumpy," I say.

"Did you miss the sun?" she asks with a smirk.

I nod. She means Lexi. She must have looked at the birthday card I made. "And the warmth. Though it's a bit chilly here today," I say, giving her a pointed look, "with the clouds overhead."

"How's Ida?" Deanna asks, sensibly changing the topic. "I see her all the time, but she only talks about her books."

"When do you ever see her?" Lexi jumps in. "You're never at the pool."

Grandma always loved to join the Huntingtons at their massive pool. I can't believe she still does it.

"At the park," Deanna says. "When I run hills. She walks them. But she hasn't in a while. Is she okay?"

Lexi clears her throat.

Somehow, Deanna catches her meaning, whatever it is, because she says, "Well, tell her I'd love to go on a walk sometime. Or a hike. Not that I can keep up with her."

"She's faster?" Lexi asks.

"No, but she has more endurance," Deanna says, then turns her attention back to me. "Are you two coming to the party? Oh, is Fern here? North?"

My brain takes a moment to process her question. It's still trying to figure out what hidden conversation they're having right in front of me.

"They'll be here next week." My sisters—technically cousins, but they are more like sisters to me—are on their way here for the same reason I came to visit. Grandma's health is declining. Grandma doesn't agree, but it's three versus one. Four, if you count Aunt Briana.

"You can still come in for a drink," Lexi says. "And come to the party later."

"With *Ida*," Deanna emphasizes.

"Yeah, of course with Ida," Lexi adds lightly.

Why are they being weird?

"I'll relay the invite," I say, even though I know Grandma will decline. She's not a fan of the Huntington parties. Not that I blame her. A party a week is a bit much. And Mr. Huntington's circle has no overlap with Grandma's. They're what she'd call *old fuddy-duddies* even though she's Mr. Huntington's senior by at least a decade.

"You're coming in for a drink now?" Deanna asks, her eyes flashing to Lexi.

"Yes..." There's definitely something happening here, and it's about me. *What the hell?*

"Yeah. It's one drink, Dee. The thing we do with colleagues and friends and even Dad's friends." Lexi laughs.

"What about your guest?" she asks.

Guest?

"I have an hour," Lexi says.

"No," Deanna says. "I need your help with my outfit now. Please."

"You two live here?" I ask.

"In the apartments," Lexi says.

So they've moved from their rooms in the mansion upstairs. "Saving money?" I tease.

The joke isn't funny, but Lexi laughs anyway. A full-on belly laugh that sends shock waves through my body.

And I know for sure.

She's flirting.

She wants me.

My entire body flames. I want her desire, her affection, her need, and I want it now. Lexi isn't the reason I'm back here, but that doesn't mean I'm going to ignore her interest.

"No, we're staying close to Dad," Deanna says in answer to my joke. "But we should let you rest. I'm sure you had a long, tiring flight. Thank you for stopping by to say hello."

Deanna shoots her sister a look I can't read. Lexi understands that, too. That's the thing with the Huntington sisters. They understand each other perfectly.

"Sorry, she's right," Lexi says. "We have a lot to do before the party. But I'll see you then, right?"

Lexi wraps her arms around me and pulls me into a hug.

She presses her warm, soft body against mine.

I'm too overwhelmed to really feel it.

An *I can't believe this is happening* blackout.

And then she whispers, "Let's talk tonight, alone."

CHAPTER FOUR

River

Even though I got in last night, I feel like I'm walking into Grandma's house for the first time in ten years. I've been back here before, of course, but only for a quick visit. Never long enough to really absorb the place. This time, I'll be here for a whole month, helping set up a new creative office in LA for the graphic novel publisher I work for in New York. I'm not rushed, forced to focus only on Grandma and not the surroundings. I can take it all in.

The living room looks nearly the same as it did growing up. The black leather couch is in the same place, decorated with the same red pillows. The coffee table is new, sure, but it looks just like the old one. A long glass thing that Grandma swears isn't *nineties California bullshit* even though it is.

The TV is bigger. The bookshelf is more stocked. The DVDs are now in storage or in Grandma's room (the favorites only) because who needs DVDs when you have the Criterion streaming channel, Max, Hulu, Netflix, Paramount+, and Prime?

The backyard is now a succulent garden, no longer a narrow row of grass, and the kitchen is even more pared down, but the rest is the same.

Grandma, too.

Well. Sort of.

She's still tough and in control and unwilling to talk about the situation.

"Is that you, River?" She stands from her spot on the living room couch. "How about some tea?" She meets me in the kitchen with a smile.

She's wearing her usual outfit—a silk blouse and wide-leg trousers—and she's rocking her usual short gray hairstyle. She's even wearing a little makeup, enough to "bring out her natural beauty."

Only she's wearing more than a little now. She's covering the dark circles and adding color to her face. I see it in the difference in her pallor. It's not just the sun. It's her health.

She's thinner than she was the last time I saw her, too. Almost thin enough she looks frail.

"Earl Grey or English Breakfast?" she asks.

"Either." I don't want tea. I don't want a drink. I want to talk about this. So a choice between two black teas is meaningless.

I'd rather have no choice than a fake choice.

But it's also meaningless to try to force her into a conversation about something she's resisting. It has to come up naturally.

"Earl Grey, then," she says.

"How about cookies, too?" I try to make my voice light and teasing, but I don't quite get there. That's the thing about a vivid imagination: it works all the time, not just when you want it to work.

Even the best-case scenario is hard. The loss of her hair, her health, her vitality.

I see the life draining out of her and I hate everything about it.

It hasn't even happened yet and I hate everything about it.

"I'll knit you a sweater while I'm at it." She doesn't give in to my mood. She motions for me to sit. Once I do, she fills a kettle with water and sets it on the stove. The same gestures as always. The same orange kettle. "Overnight, I transformed into a Hallmark Channel grandma."

"Are they horny like you, too?"

"It might not be on screen, but it's there." She laughs.

I grin. "You think that scares me?"

"I'm sure it takes more to scare you, at this point."

That's one of the things about being raised by a grandma who embraces sexual openness. Very little shocks me. Plus, after a decade in New York, I'm shock-proof. "Are you trying?"

"I know you have that idealistic view of sex, River, but it's not always that way."

"What way is it?"

"Sometimes you want someone and that's it," she says.

"Someone in particular?"

"Sometimes. Or sometimes you just want it." She turns on the stove. "There's no one recent worth remembering."

I let out a dry laugh. "I'm sure they're happy to hear that."

"You kids think you invented sex," she says. "How do you think you got here?"

"Mom's court-ordered rehab." That's what landed me here the first time, anyway.

Grandma frowns. "I'm sorry about your mother."

"Your daughter."

"My responsibility."

"She was an adult," I remind her. So much for keeping the mood light. I blame jet lag. And the sudden loss of Lexi's attention. I feel dull without it. Cold. Tired. Even Deanna's presence was energizing, if I'm being honest.

There are too many difficult conversations waiting here. And, somehow, there's also nothing to say. Mom went M.I.A. a long time ago. Case closed.

Grandma is accepting as much help as she deems fit. Case closed.

"I can't help my struggle with finding men." She shifts the conversation back to her favorite topic. "No one is as handsome as your grandfather was. You got it from him, you know."

"I've seen pictures of the two of you. You were very—"

"Don't even think about saying beautiful."

Okay, then. "*Enamored* with each other."

She laughs. "Because we were fucking all the time."

"Well, there are apps for that now. If you're curious."

She presses her lips together, narrows her eyes, then says, "Sweetheart, I know you think I'm tech challenged because I'm older, but I know this world better than you do."

"I don't think that." I'm sure Grandma has far more casual sex than I do. Casual sex has never interested me, but I understand the occasional need for it.

"Why the concern in your voice?" she asks.

"I know men," I say. "Give them an app to hide behind and they're even worse."

She looks at me, considering whether she buys my explanation. She doesn't, but she doesn't press the matter. "The girls next door haven't talked up MeetCute yet? I know you were over there earlier."

"Meet what?"

"A dating app they created."

"Huh." I always imagined they would be entrepreneurs, but a dating app? That doesn't seem like Deanna's style. And Lexi never really dated when I knew her before. But maybe she's changed. Maybe that was just a teenage phase and she's past it now, ready for something long-term. With me? Possibly...

Grandma nods. "Supposedly has the best matching algo in the world. You don't even add a profile pic. It'll find your perfect match based on nothing but cold, hard facts." She holds her hands apart. "Do you believe that?"

"No." If I was on that app, I doubt it would match me with Lexi. On paper, we're too different. But love isn't about what's on paper. There's a magic to it that can't be calculated.

"Me neither," she says.

Grandma is like me in some ways. She believes in magic. Only her idea of magic skews toward sex, not love. She writes erotica. That's her full-time job.

My grandmother, the erotica author.

When I was a kid, she kept the mentions of the subject vague. *Your grandma writes books about relationships for adults.* Then, when I turned thirteen, she explained it to me—along with giving me "the talk."

I already knew a lot from Fern and North, but I still wasn't ready for Grandma to hand me a banana and a condom and say *you're old enough, you need to know how to use these.*

She asked me to come to her if I ever had questions or concerns. She asked about who I was dating, if the relationship was physical, what I wanted.

Some people would find it intrusive or strange. And I suppose it is a little strange, compared to the average American family, but it's normal, too.

We're open about sex.

We don't share lurid details, but we don't shirk the subject, either. People have needs. They fill those needs. Nothing wrong with that, as long as everyone is safe and on the same page. Sure, casual sex isn't my thing. I want an intimate experience. Something closer to making love.

But I don't judge people who see the act another way.

"You're thinking about sex," she says.

I resist the urge to roll my eyes. "You think everyone is always thinking about sex."

"Yes," she agrees. "Because they usually are. If not sex, then what's on your mind? You've got a certain look— Oh." She darts a quick glance in the direction of the house next door. "You're thinking about Lexi."

"I wasn't." At least not right at that moment. "But now that you mention it, yeah, I talked to her earlier. She invited me to her party tonight."

"River." She packs years of intention into my name. "She's seeing someone. The same guy for a while now."

A stone drops in my gut.

No… Lexi is a lot of things, but she's not a cheater. Did I misread her?

I fight to keep my expression neutral. "And?"

"You like her. You've always liked her."

"I'm going to a party, not a private hotel room."

"She looks happy," Grandma says. "The happiest I've ever seen her."

Then why did she invite me to talk, alone?

My thoughts scatter as my heartbeat picks up. Lexi said she wanted to talk—I need to not get ahead of myself. Take this one step at a time. I assumed "talk" meant something else, but maybe I was wrong. Maybe talk just means talk, and she wants to be alone so we can catch up without distractions. Like her sister. There's something going on between them and I don't want to get in the middle of it.

"If she's happy, she's not going to go after anyone else," I say. "And I'd never go after a woman in a relationship."

Grandma returns to her usual firm-yet-loving tone. "Don't be naive, sweetheart. The world isn't that simple."

She carefully pours the tea into two mugs, and I decide to keep my mouth shut. There's nothing more to say—we silently agree to disagree. Grandma knows she can't change my feelings for Lexi just because she's with someone else. Even I can't do that. So she'll just have to trust me on this one. I'm not a cheater. Neither is Lexi.

But I *am* going to the party tonight. And I *am* going to talk to Lexi, alone.

At her Sweet Sixteen, all I wanted was to talk to her. To tell her how I feel. I'm not going to blow this opportunity now that I've got a second chance to do it.

I'll tell Lexi how I feel, and that's it. The next move is hers.

CHAPTER FIVE

Deanna

Thankfully, Jake arrives early. As usual, he and Lexi make a perfect Orange County couple. The flawless blonde in pink and the handsome, tall, dressed-to-kill, but casually of course, Vietnamese man in a suit. They even have matching California accents. (In college, I made great efforts to rid my vocabulary of the word "dude." Lexi went the other way, leaned into her aural resemblance to noted Orange County girl Gwen Stefani).

Dad greets him in the living room. He tries to do it casually, as if he hasn't noticed Lexi has a serious boyfriend, and doesn't care, and just happens to be here, right now.

"Mr. Le—Jake." Dad offers his hand with his usual not-at-all-cool formality. "Lovely to see you again."

"You, too, Mr. Huntington." Jake shakes with the firm confidence of a man who works in corporate law. Then he smiles and his charisma shifts to something equal parts professional and dorky.

"Will you be attending the event this evening?" Dad asks.

Lexi practically runs downstairs. "Daddy." She says it in that Lexi way, like she's a teenager and he's making her look uncool. "We don't have firm plans for the night."

"We don't?" Jake shoots her a curious look, but he catches

onto Lexi's wavelength quickly. I hope Lexi notices that. It's a sign they are highly compatible. "Of course," he says. "There's a theater playing *Alien* in Santa Ana. Lexi's been begging me to go."

Lexi nods *that does sound fun.*

Dad laughs. "You know, that sort of thing used to worry me. Two and a half hours in the dark. Who knows what you kids could get up to."

It takes Jake a second to catch on to the implication. *Making out in a movie theater, the horror.* He nods with his usual deference to Dad.

"You're a good egg, son." Dad rests a hand on Jake's shoulder.

"Ew, Dad, gross. But, yeah, we gotta go, sorry." Lexi gives Dad a kiss goodbye and she drags her boyfriend to the apartment.

She's going to talk to him, find satisfaction, fuck him senseless. Whatever it is she needs.

"They're good together, aren't they?" Dad asks.

"They are." I just hope this physical encounter helps her see it.

She can have it all. Satisfaction. Sex. All that good stuff.

My sister is safe. Her relationship is safe. And our app... Well, that's safe, too.

I enjoy the victory with a blissful forty-five minutes of work. We're always improving the algo, and our latest update, an attempt to tag people's favorite TV shows and use it to improve their match, is struggling. The tags we pulled from various websites aren't working, so we need to hire someone to tag them manually or find a way to tag them with machine learning.

Machine learning is always my preference. Machines lack human frailties. But then they don't understand the strangeness of human emotions, either. And TV is an emotional topic.

I try feeding the AI two dozen of the most popular shows and I leave it running. In theory, it will go through our users' profiles tonight and learn how to tag properly. Or fail to learn. But it will either work or it won't.

When I absolutely can't wait any longer, I retouch my makeup and join the party downstairs.

It's the usual mix of Dad's friends and colleagues. People in their forties, fifties, and sixties in suits or the California equivalent (slacks and button-up shirts or cocktail dresses). Plus a few token "kids our age" in slightly more casual wear. Not that I recognize any of them. Well, maybe the guy in the designer jeans next to the woman in the Reformation dress.

No, I do recognize her. She owns the fashion start-up poised to replace Reformation. Even more sustainable and even more of a *cool babe* aura.

She's an icon. I need to talk to her and learn all her secrets, now.

I cross the busy room to meet her, but someone stops me. A pink-manicured hand around my arm.

Lexi.

"Dee. Kitchen. Now. This is a Cary Grant situation." She doesn't wait for my yes. She doesn't have to. A Cary Grant situation is a code we both know well. It means boyfriend troubles. Well, boy troubles. *Man* troubles. Since the boys in question are rarely boyfriends.

But Lexi does have a boyfriend this time.

It's only been an hour and a half since Jake arrived. Lexi is supposed to be in the apartment, having her way with her boyfriend.

I suppose, after a six-month wait, the guy might not have a lot of stamina. But where's the problem?

She's supposed to be on cloud nine.

She's supposed to be satisfied.

She's certainly *not* supposed to have a Cary Grant situation.

A Humphrey Bogart situation (code for Dad troubles) maybe. Or an Audrey Hepburn (girl troubles). Katherine Hepburn even (it used to mean Mom troubles, but now it means any older woman). There's a whole system of troubles coded with Old Hollywood celebrities.

This is supposed to be a Mae West situation (it's time to leave to get some).

Not this.

What is this?

I follow her into the kitchen. It's not quiet, exactly, but it's not as busy at the party. Only a few caterers plating appetizers and refrigerating champagne.

"Have you seen River?" She finds an empty spot next to the window, one where she can see the party in the backyard, the apartments, the Beau house next door.

Again, she looks to River's room.

The lights are off.

"No," I say. "Haven't seen him."

Wait. The hug. The whisper. The early departure.

The smile.

His smile.

Why would he smile?

Something is happening.

"Why are you looking for him?" I ask.

"Dee." She says my name as if it explains everything.

"Where's Jake?"

"He left."

"Why did he leave?"

"Because we talked." She looks to the fridge and waits for a caterer to finish shelving wine before finding a bottle of vodka.

"What did you talk about?"

"Our relationship. Like you said."

"So you're on the same page?"

"Exactly the same page." She sets the vodka on the counter. Then cranberry juice. Limes. "Do we have Cointreau?" She scans the shelves again. "This is close enough."

"There's a bartender outside."

"Too far." She beams as she uncaps the bottle of vodka.

"Why did Jake leave? Did you break up?" I bite my tongue,

so I don't add *you're supposed to be our poster couple*.

"No."

Thank god.

"We're on a break," she clarifies.

"A what?"

"He totally agrees with me."

That seems highly unlikely. "Agrees with what?"

"We're too young to settle down. We should see what else is out there. See if it's real."

I take a deep breath and let out a slow exhale. I need to think. I need to say the right thing, as a supportive sister, and the smart thing, as the co-owner of MeetCute.

Willa is supposed to be here tonight. She's expecting to meet Jake. *Think*.

Lexi continues, "We're taking two weeks to spend time on our own. See other people. Then we'll come back together. See if the magic is there."

"Even if you sleep with another guy?"

"Of course, Dee. Do you really think I'd take a break that didn't involve sexual freedom?"

"And Jake knows this?" I ask.

"Yes, he knows. How old do you think I am?" She looks at me like she can't believe I don't believe in her. "I know how to communicate."

That's not what she said earlier, but okay, I'll go with that. "What if he sleeps with someone else?"

"When he wanted to wait six months with me? I doubt that."

"But what if he does?" I press.

She shrugs as if she doesn't mind the thought. "That's the agreement."

"Wouldn't you feel jealous?"

"Dee, I'm not thinking about Jake right now. We're seeing other people for a while."

"What about the app?" I ask.

"The meeting is in four weeks," she says. "If the app is as good as you say it is, we'll happily resume our relationship in *two* weeks."

There's a certain logic there, yes. If Jake really is okay with her sleeping with other people, then I don't see the harm. Not to their relationship. But— "Willa is coming tonight."

"So I'll tell her he got sick."

There's logic there, too. That's not the problem. It's more that—

Sex is how Lexi copes. She runs away from any intense feeling to the warm embrace of another body. And this fear of commitment? That's a big, intense feeling.

It's one thing if she soothes herself with a little casual sex and returns to Jake's arms.

It's another if she soothes herself with a little casual sex and returns to her pre-Jake dating pattern: love 'em and leave 'em.

How do I help her with this? How do I keep her on the right path? Lexi *does* care about Jake. She wouldn't want him to leave her.

"What if you're wrong?" I ask. "What if he thinks his way into another woman? Are you sure you want to risk it?"

"Come on." She motions to her pink minidress, as if it explains everything. And it does, really. Every time a guy sees her in pink, he's a goner.

"You're the only beautiful, charming woman on the planet?" I argue.

"In Orange County."

"Hey."

"Charming, Dee." She smiles. "You're the only beautiful, smart, *cool* woman in the county."

The flattery fills me somewhere deep. Not that it's false. Lexi truly believes this. She truly believes I'm the smartest, coolest woman she knows. It's not that she doesn't mean it.

She does. She really sees me that way. Even though I'm

hopelessly out of place here, I still seem like her in-control, intelligent older sister.

But if she's lying to herself…

"Anyway…River." She mentions him casually. Too casually. "Have you seen him?"

"No." And I need to close this Jake thing. "What if you find someone else?"

"Surely, you don't acknowledge that possibility." She smiles at me, certain she's found a flaw in my logic. After all this time in a relationship, she still doesn't believe she's a serious relationship person. "The algo is perfect. Jake is Mr. Right."

Yes, he is a 99 percent match, but Lexi had a lot of high matches. And the algo is assuming people want a serious relationship. It can't control their self-sabotage. "He's the most compatible guy within fifty miles, yes."

We only know the compatibility of people on the app, but we have enough users to make a strong statistical case. There are plenty of very compatible men out there. Lexi is a catch and Southern California is highly populated. But even if we got every single guy in the state onto MeetCute, Lexi and Jake would still be a top match. They'd still be in the 99th percentile.

"Then I'll see other guys, realize they're not as compatible, see the light." She tries to speak my language, but she doesn't quite understand it. She doesn't see relationships the way I do. Few people do.

"If you don't?" I ask.

"Dee, you worry too much." She pats me on the back and returns to fixing her cosmo. "Now, have you seen River? I'm sure he's looking for me." She pulls out her cell phone and sets it next to her cocktail shaker. "Do you want, one too?"

My stomach gnaws at me while I watch her add vodka and ice, close the lid, shake. She pulls two martini glasses from the freezer and strains.

She pushes one to me, even though I didn't say yes. "How

about a toast then?"

"To...?"

"Possibilities."

Okay, that confirms it. She's looking for River for one reason. And I need to stop her, before she makes a mistake.

I have to look out for her.

And the app.

This is our future. Not just mine. *Ours.* But how? I'm not good at solving problems on the fly. I need time to plan and strategize.

So I do the only thing I can think of.

I take my glass, I raise to toast, I tap my glass against hers, and I tilt it forward, so it sprays all over her dress, legs, and shoes. It's not the smartest or most effective delay, but it's something.

"Dee!" Lexi drops her glass as she jumps back. "What the fuck?"

"Sorry. Butterfingers."

She looks at her dress, now stained a darker shade of pink in unusual splotches. "Shit. I better change. But I'm supposed to..." She looks to the house next door again.

"Meet River?"

"I know you don't approve," she says.

"No." I cross my fingers behind my back. "You're right. You should see what else is out there. So that you know for sure Jake is it."

"I should?"

"Yeah. You change. I, uh..."

"You'll stall him," she finishes my sentence. "Are you sure? I don't want you to do something that makes you uncomfortable."

No. That's perfect. "Where are you two going?"

"Why would we be going anywhere? I only invited him to the party."

"Lexi."

She swallows hard. "Okay, fine, you got me. I texted him to

meet me at the park," she says. "You'll really stall him?"

"Of course," I say. "I just need your keys."

"*My* keys?"

"Yeah." Why do I need her keys? That's not a very good claim. "My car is charging. And I can't keep him here. Not where Willa could see the two of you get together."

She nods, somehow following my half-baked logic. Because how the hell would Willa know the difference between River and Jake? This whole situation is running on nonsense.

"I'll take him to a bar," I tell her, "keep him comfortable while he waits. You do need to talk to Willa, anyway. Explain why Jake isn't here."

"Shit."

"Tell her he got food poisoning," I say. "Talk up the app. I can manage an hour or two of friendliness with River."

"Can you?"

"Hey. When we were teens, I talked to him more than you did." That wasn't hard to do, since she had zero conversations with him, but I keep that to myself. "This won't even ping his radar, I promise. Just two old friends catching up." Okay, friends might be stretching it.

Lexi smiles, but she drops it quickly. "Are you sure?"

"A favor for a favor," I say. "You can owe me one."

She looks at me like she doesn't believe me, but she hands me the keys anyway.

CHAPTER SIX

River

After an afternoon of reminiscing about family, Grandma and I spend the evening reminiscing about her favorite topic: work. The rainy spring break trip to the city, the one where we first encountered the independent bookstore without a romance section.

The manager refused to carry a romance or erotica section, even when she offered to send him a box of books. Signed books. Out of print signed books.

He was unmoved by her pictures with Fabio. Can you believe it? (As if I hadn't been there, observing every moment.) Even when she offered to get him on Fabio's Christmas card list. *He's really a sweet guy, you know. I taught him a thing or two back in the day. Writing skills, of course. That was before my husband passed. If I knew him now…*

The snowy Christmas she spent on my couch in New York, trying to coach my hopeless roommate into finishing a single project. Thanks to her many connections, I live in the city rent free. As long as I help her rich friend's son work on his creative projects, I can stay. The guy is never around. He's always partying in Rome or Ibiza, but for some reason, his parents are happy just to have me there as a "good influence."

Then it's the summer we spent in Italy, at another famous writer's vacation home. She refers to his genre (adventure) and skill (middling) as if I didn't meet the guy, and his wife, and hear way too many stories about their middling adventures, sometimes with my grandma.

Then it's stories about Fern and North. Not that either of them spends the summer here anymore. North is married, with two kids of her own. And Fern is busy with her PhD program in chemistry. Grandma always insists she's happy with the alone time, the freedom, but I hear the loneliness in her voice.

It hits me somewhere deep. It overwhelms me. I ran away from home because I needed it. She pushed me into it, she insisted, yes, but that's what she always does. She acts as if she's the strongest, most independent person in the universe.

She stays hands off. She learned that lesson with Mom.

We talk as the sun dips into the sky and the sounds of the Huntington party take over the space.

That's my cue to meet Lexi.

When I suggest she lie down, she doesn't bite. I suggest she read the fantasy romance series I just finished. Even though there aren't dragon shifters, she agrees to give it a chance.

That's a lot for her. She writes erotic romance, yes, but she's not a romantic. And she's not remotely interested in the worlds of fantasy or sci-fi. She tried, when I was young, but now that I've moved on to (mostly) contemporary interests, she rarely stretches.

After she closes her bedroom door, I shower, change into a clean pair of jeans and a fresh T-shirt, and take a moment to collect my thoughts the only way I know how: on paper.

It's strange, sitting in my room, at my desk, after so many years living in New York. Everything feels too big and too small at the same time. Did I really decorate the room with Lichtenstein prints? What an art-school cliche. And the stacks of *Dungeons & Dragons* books. The rows of dice. The character art on the walls.

Why didn't I just write *Super Dork* on my forehead?

The thought fades as I focus on my sketchbook. I don't have time to work, not really, but I need to get some of this out of my head and onto the paper.

That same familiar refrain. *She's the sun and I'm powerless to resist her gravity*.

It doesn't fit into any of my work. Not now. But that isn't the only way to use it. I don't need to lift the phrase whole cloth. I can create another story, one that portrays the idea. Two people, fated to be together, kept apart by forces beyond their control.

A man's need for distance and growth.

A woman's need to sow her wild oats.

A sort of reversal of the usual expectations of romance. More of a Princess Zelda type. A woman who would rather go on adventures than sit on the throne. Who returns home to Prince Charming, only to find the real Prince Charming is the stable boy who was right there, under her nose.

A kind of *The Princess Bride* meets *Zelda* situation. That's the art style too. Fantasy. Only with a modern comic slant. The images form in my mind immediately. I capture one on the page. Then another. Another.

When I break from my trance, the party is humming. Classical music, conversation, laughter.

Shit. What time is it?

Ten to nine.

I check my cell for an update, but there's nothing from Lexi. Only a message from her sister.

Deanna: *When are you coming by the party? I want to introduce you to someone. An artist Dad knows. He works for a company that rhymes with Parvel. Why doesn't anything rhyme with marvel? Not that it's Marvel.*

That's too much.

She's up to something.

Why is she texting me, anyway?

River: *Can't talk now.*

I slip my cell into my pocket and make my way downstairs. Whatever Deanna wants to tell me can wait. I have a more pressing engagement.

Everyone waits for destiny.

Everyone except Deanna Huntington, maybe. She's the only person with the sheer force of will to mold destiny to her own desires.

Maybe that's what the story needs. A complication. A villain. The evil brunette sister is a cliche move. But maybe if I write her with a sympathetic motivation—

My phone buzzes in my pocket again.

Again.

Again.

I give in to my curiosity.

Deanna: *Ah! You're free. It will just take a minute.*

River: *I have plans.*

Deanna: *One minute. That's all. You are coming to the party?*

Not in so many words.

River: *My apologies.*

Deanna: *Should I pass them on to Lexi?*

River: *Sure. Thanks.*

Maybe she's up to something. Maybe she's happy for me. Maybe she has no idea. It doesn't matter. I have a goal. Nothing is getting in my way. And it doesn't matter.

I look out my bedroom window. I survey the party. Just like I used to as a kid. The people milling around the backyard—they look so strange, wearing suits three feet from the swimming pool—the bar, the balloons, the light of the apartments.

There's sound coming from the apartments. A familiar sound. Sade.

Lexi's seduction playlist. It's just loud enough to compete with the waltz music playing at the party.

She has a boyfriend.

Grandma's words echo in my head.

I refuse to believe that. Lexi is a lot of things, but she's not a cheater. If she's interested in me, she's ending things with him. I'll ask her, point blank. If she hasn't ended things, that's it. I'm a strong enough person to resist her charms.

I go downstairs, then outside, and sneak out of the house. I go the other way, around our side yard—away from the party, so Deanna doesn't see me—to the perfect cul-de-sac. Identical to a hundred other perfect cul-de-sacs in the city. Well, except for the sheer size of the Huntington place.

A valet stands at the front of the Huntington place and older people linger by the entrance, smoking (cigars, of course) and sipping bourbon from short glasses.

The rest of the street hums with the sort of Friday night activity I expect in Huntington Hills. Families watching movies on the couch or playing games in the backyard. Moms sipping wine as they chat about their kids. Dads talking football. People who choose to live here do it because they believe in family values. They don't go out of their way to defy gender norms.

I walk toward the neighborhood park down the street. It's a big space, with a soccer field, a handful of eucalyptus trees, a small plastic playground (it was wood when I was a kid), and a parking lot.

There's Lexi's car, the flashy red thing.

And there's a woman standing there, in heels and a short dress.

This is it.

Destiny.

I step into the light, and I see her in all her glory.

Lace-up boots, short dark hair—

Son of a...

That's not Lexi.

That's Deanna.

CHAPTER SEVEN

Deanna

River stares at me with disbelief in his dark eyes.

Does the poor guy really still believe he and Lexi are meant to be? After all this time?

"Deanna." He studies me the way I imagine he studies a landscape he's drawing, noting every detail.

"River," I say, mimicking his tone. Then recall our conversation earlier by the pool. "Ida's not coming?"

"No. Is Lexi all right?" He catches himself and bites his tongue. He's giving it all away. Lexi made plans with him for tonight.

But I already know that. He just didn't know I knew that.

"Lexi is held up with an investor," I say. That's mostly true. "She asked me to keep you entertained in the meantime."

"Why?"

I feign offense. "Am I not entertaining?"

He doesn't say yes, but he wears the *yes* all over his face.

Charm, I tell myself. I have all of Lexi's charm. "An hour or two, max. We'll go to a bar. She'll meet us there later. I'm sure you don't want to wait around here, at a stuffy party."

He stares at me with apprehension.

"Unless you'd rather reschedule? You are on East Coast time."

"I'm fine."

"Great." I pull Lexi's keys from my pocket and tap the fob. The car beeps as it unlocks.

Shit. Am I really doing this?

I fumble with the car door. It takes me three tries to open it.

"Are you all right?" River asks.

No. Of course not. How does anyone keep another person's date entertained enough he doesn't bail? "I'm great."

"You are?"

"A bar." That's what I said. "One in Anaheim."

His lips twitch. "The one bar in Anaheim?"

"It's your kind of place, I promise. And Lexi loves it, too." She loves any place with music and alcohol, especially one with a theme, so she must love the place I have in mind. "Trust me."

He stands there, at the trunk of the car, and studies me again. "Are you trying to get rid of me?"

"What do you mean?"

"Keep me away from Lexi."

"Why would I do that?" I ask innocently.

"I don't know," he says, likely recalling the advice I gave him at Lexi's Sweet Sixteen party, before he left for New York. "Why would you do that?"

"I wouldn't." I motion to the passenger side. "Get in. We'll have fun. A ton of fun."

He raises a brow. "You know how to have fun?"

"With the best of them," I quip.

He stays still. I'm losing him. Or maybe I never had him.

"Do you want to bet on it?" I ask, and I can hear the desperation creeping into my voice.

He chuckles. "You don't have to manipulate me."

"Okay. I'll ask nicely. Will you go to the bar with me, River?"

He smiles, victorious, and slides into the car. "Of course. All you had to do was ask."

River gets in the car, and I do, too. We both buckle up.

No turning back now.

Lexi's favorite slow jams fill the car as I drive away from the park and make my way along the rows of strip malls and walled neighborhoods filled with three- and four-bedroom houses worth a fortune.

River sways along with the music. Maybe because he enjoys the beat. Or because he imagines himself making love to Lexi here. I'm not sure.

He's a romantic, but he's a man, too.

And shit. He's on his phone. Is he texting Lexi?

The music is not helping me keep his mind off her. The fact we're in her car is bad enough. To also have her favorite music playing is not going to win me any battles here.

"How about Fleetwood Mac?" I say the first band that comes to mind. My favorite band. Because they were Mom's favorite. And, hey, that's not a sexy topic, either, but that's okay. As long as I keep him distracted. "Could you stream it for me? My phone is in my purse."

"Sure. What's the password?"

"Lexi's birthday."

He takes my small black bag, finds my cell, unlocks it (of course he has her birthday memorized) and goes to work streaming.

"*Rumours*," I suggest.

He laughs. "Really? You want to listen to *Rumours*?"

"Hey. What does that mean?"

"I've heard you play it a million times." I can hear the smile in his voice as I focus on the road. He's teasing me.

Fine. Good. Whatever keeps him occupied with things not Lexi.

"You hear it all the way across the backyard?" I ask.

"You played it loud enough, back in the day."

"If you have bad taste, we can listen to something else."

Again, he laughs.

"What's so funny?"

"That's a very Deanna Huntington sort of sentence."

Okay… "How's that?"

"If I don't like what you like, I have bad taste."

Ouch. "Not everything I like. But *Rumours*? Why not tell me you hate *Casablanca*?"

"You don't?"

"Who could?" I ask.

"It's not the best showing for women," he says. "Especially not tough women."

Damn. How does he know that I hate how much I love *Casablanca* exactly for those reasons?

It's his grandma's favorite movie—she babysat Lexi and me when we were kids, before River moved in. We spent our fair share of summer nights at his place, with his sister-cousins Fern and North, but we didn't stay close as we got older—

Stop.

What am I doing here?

How is he the one distracting *me* now?

Focus.

"How about that music?" I ask.

Finally, River presses play.

The familiar guitar riff fills the air. Then the layered vocals. The tension in my shoulders eases.

I don't know what I'm doing with him, I have no clue how this night is going to go, but I know how to listen to this. I know how to share its appeal.

He doesn't latch onto the new topic, though. He goes right back to Lexi. "You think less of men who prefer a woman like your sister." He places my cell in the hands-free claw.

"No. Never."

He says nothing, but his *I don't believe you* attitude spreads through the car.

And the silent pressure makes me feel like I should explain.

Defend myself against an accusation he didn't even make.

"I think less of men who see her as some sort of dumb blonde, yes. Or who think she's easy."

I have never judged her for sleeping around. I do wonder why she does it, what she gets out of it, how she could possibly find casual sex with men who don't respect her empowering, but it's not because I think she's wrong. I understand it intellectually. After all, no one asks men who sleep around what they get out of it. We all know sex feels good, physically, and socially, too. She says that's all it is. But I just, well, I can't imagine sex with a stranger feeling that good. How often does *any* sex feel that good?

"I don't think that about her," he says. "I've never thought that about her."

"I know." I don't want to talk about Lexi. Why do all the men in my life want to talk about her?

Really, I love my sister, I do. I just wish I could have a relationship with a man, any relationship, any man, that didn't end up involving her somehow. But that's impossible, because Lexi is such a big part of my life. And I wouldn't want her *out* of my life. I just want the men in my life to see me as an individual, not as one half of a pair.

"This was my mom's favorite." I focus on the music, for his sake and mine. We both need a distraction from Lexi.

"I know it was." Compassion slips into his voice. Or maybe it's pity. I can never tell with people.

Thankfully, he doesn't say *I'm sorry you lost her* or something way more horrible like *everything happens for a reason.*

He doesn't say anything.

He listens to the song, in silence, until the next one starts. "What did she love about it?"

"The seventies were her thing." I smile. "The bareness of the music, the confessional lyrics. That was her favorite part. Stevie Nicks turning her heartbreak to gold."

"She was romantic about it?" he asks.

"It's not romantic," I say. "It's bullshit. Why does a woman have to bare her soul to find success?"

"Maybe she wants to bare her soul."

He would think that.

"Maybe that's the only way she can understand her pain," he adds.

He would think that, too.

But it's also what Mom thought, and I hate that I want to hug him for saying it. I hate it as much as I hate how much I love *Casablanca*. But it's different, because *Casablanca* is a great movie (gender issues aside) and River is another guy who thinks Lexi will save him. "You sound like Mom."

"Do I?" He seems pleased by that. "What was she like?"

He moved in about a year after she died. But he was around a few times before that. His mom visited his grandma, and River was with her. "You never met?"

"Once, I think," he says. "When I was really young."

"Do you remember anything?"

"Only her smile."

She did have a great smile. My stomach feels light. I want to talk about it. I'm desperate to talk about her, at any time, in any situation. But with him?

I guess with him.

I need to keep the conversation alive somehow. "She was passionate." Stormy, sometimes, but there's no sense in focusing on the bad. "She did everything at a hundred percent. Lexi takes after her that way."

I glance at him for a moment. His dark eyes study me. There's no sexual intent in his gaze, but my cheeks flush anyway. There's something about his stare. An intensity. An honesty. A desire for more honesty.

Right now, he's not thinking about Lexi.

Right now, he's listening to my story. I need to say more if I want to keep his attention.

I swallow hard, put my focus back on the road, and push the words from my lips. Honesty, intensity, truth. All that artistic bullshit. That's what holds his attention.

"She was like you," I say. "An artist. A musician. That's how she met my father. He saw her singing and fell in love."

He laughs. "Really?"

"That's the story they told us a million times, but it's hard to imagine Dad at the dive where she used to play."

"Well. Opposites attract."

Interesting. "You believe that?"

"To a point. Does your app disagree?"

"How do you know about my app?" *Oh*— "Are you a member?"

"No." He laughs. "Grandma told me about it."

My shoulders drop. "The app isn't about attraction."

"What *is* it about?" he asks.

"Compatibility."

"Right." I see him nodding in my side vision. "Grandma mentioned that. But your parents were married for a long time, too," he counters. "Until death."

"Because they wanted the same things," I say. "That's part of being compatible."

"Even as opposites?"

He makes a fair point. I understand what he's saying, and it's true. My parents didn't always get along perfectly well—they had disagreements like any other couple. So yes, there had to be attraction in the equation that kept them together during the times when compatibility wasn't quite enough. But that doesn't mean attraction trumps everything, which is the side of his point I do *not* agree with.

"Yes," I say instead, because it's not a lie. "Even as opposites."

He's silent for a moment, a moment that stretches too long, and just as I'm sure he's about to hit me with another good point— one I might not be able to shrug off so easily—he alters course.

"What happened at the bar, when they met?" he asks. "Did

your dad show up in his three-piece suit and ask the bartender to list their scotch selection?"

"Probably," I say. "Probably lectured the poor guy on the differences between scotch, whiskey, bourbon, and rye." I drop my voice to the tone Lexi and I used to use to imitate Dad. "A bartender should know liquor. Scotch and bourbon are types of whiskey. Scotch is made from barley and aged. Bourbon is a mix of grains, mostly corn."

I catch him smiling.

"Oh," I say. "You didn't actually want to know."

"You couldn't stop yourself from telling me," he accuses with a laugh.

Maybe. Probably. "Did you know?"

He doesn't answer. "Would you throw the drink in the bartender's face if he used the wrong type of whiskey?"

"If I asked for a perfect Manhattan and he didn't use rye?"

He laughs again. "Can you imagine the horror?"

Damn. That was a trap and I fell for it. "I've never thrown a drink."

He smiles big now, amused, playing me like a fiddle.

Why is everyone so much better at charming people than I am? I'm supposed to be charming him here, not the other way around.

"What's the rest of the story?" he asks. "With your parents?"

"Why? Do you want to see how I compare to my father?"

"I know how you compare to your father," he says. "I'm curious about your mother."

Huh. No one suggests I'm anything like my mother. The lightness fills me in other places. All the places. "He was there, at the dive bar," I continue, "drinking inferior scotch. And, to add insult to injury, the bartender served the drink on the rocks. Scotch, on the rocks! The incompetent fool!"

River laughs, and it warms me inside. Because my distraction is working, of course. That's all it is.

"He's not about to throw the drink in the guy's face," I say, "but he's ready to leave. His friend is there for the babes, and there are babes, definitely, but they're not Dad's type."

"Dare I ask?"

"He was looking for a proper wife," I say. "A woman from a nice family who wanted to have kids, stay home, support him. That was the only way he'd accomplish great things, the way his father expected him to. And he knew that kind of woman wasn't at Tom's Bar and Grill."

"No, of course not. Tom's has fast women and bad liquor."

This time, I laugh. Has River always been this funny? Charming? Sexy?

No. I'm taking this distraction thing too far, feeling an attraction I shouldn't. I need to snap out of it. I need to focus on the road, not his dark eyes or his snug jeans or the lines of ink on his right arm.

Is that *all* comic-art style, or just what I can see?

Nope. I'm driving, not gawking. I continue, "So Dad is at Tom's and he's about to tell his friend he'll wait in the car. Then he hears it. The most beautiful voice in the world. This woman, singing about her heartbreak, about how deeply she hurt after a relationship fell apart, and how much she wants someone to put her back together. And he looks at her—and that's it. He falls in love right there. Or so that's how the story goes."

River nods. "Love at first sight."

"You really believe that?" I ask.

"You don't?"

"Of course not. She was beautiful. He was horny. That's what initially got them together. Then the falling in love happened later, once they got to know each other. Compatibility took over. Compatibility is what *kept* them together." I've seen plenty of pictures of Mom in her youth. She was gorgeous, with long blonde hair and green eyes and full lips. She wore a leather jacket over her sundress, showing off innocence and experience, the same way Lexi does. Dad was totally attracted to her with just one look. But that isn't love.

"You don't allow *any* possibility of love at first sight?" River asks.

"No," I say. "Why would I?"

"Because it happens."

"To who?"

He shrugs. "To anyone. It's not something you can plan or calculate." He doesn't say *with an app*, but I hear it loud and clear. "It just happens, and you don't know it's happened until it's already done. Plenty of people can vouch for that."

Except he isn't talking about "plenty of people." He means Lexi—he means how *he* feels about Lexi. He has to. Who else would he mean? He's had it bad for her since "first sight." I've known this for as long as I've known *him*.

So much for this distraction, it isn't working. Time for a Plan B. Yes, most people are more likely to get frisky after a few drinks, but not someone as romantic as River. He wants a perfect first date with Lexi. Which means clear-eyed sobriety. So...getting him drunk is not a long-term solution, but it works for tonight.

CHAPTER EIGHT

Deanna

Outside, Depressed Mode looks like any other bar. Another unassuming strip mall. The sort of small, slightly run-down collection of stores that covers the east side of the county. All the more charming for its lack of perfection. A reminder that the county's west side is perfectly planned and curated within an inch of its total lack of life.

A local pizza place, a tattoo parlor, and the county's only Goth bar.

Inside, Depressed Mode is all purple light and ornate black frames. The place is small—about the size of Dad's living room—and it wears its theme in every corner. Posters of Cthulhu-inspired monsters. Framed photos of coffins. A pink-on-black menu printed above the bar. All themed drinks named after popular Goth or Goth-adjacent bands.

Even though it's prime party hour (past it in Orange County, really), the place is quiet. Two singles chatting at the long bar against the wall. A couple in one of the booths on the left. Another, in matching black catsuits and dog collars, swaying to the EDM beat on the right.

I guess that's the dance floor. It's much smaller than the massive ballrooms where I learned to waltz and foxtrot, but I know how to work it all the same. Mom made sure we learned how to dance to anything, at any time, at any place.

She would have loved this bar. The loud music, the over-the-top lights, the energy. Even though it's a slow night, the place buzzes with the mix of sadness and, well, horniness I associate with Goth kids.

"Is this my scene?" River laughs as he follows me inside. He's distracted, momentarily at least.

"Is it not?" I only know the place by reputation, but it exceeds every expectation. It's perfect for him.

"Shit." His face fills with recognition as he looks at the bar. At the bartender, specifically.

A short woman in a tight black dress and thick makeup studies us intensely.

Do I look as out of place as I feel? My outfit screams *spoiled rich girl*, not *I love Robert Smith*. And that's fair because I don't really like Robert Smith. I don't hate The Cure—who could—but I don't buy into the sentimentality, either.

Crying over pictures of someone?

Realizing you're in love because it's Friday—

What is that song even saying?

It's probably about drugs. Most of the best "love songs" are. Mom taught me that. Along with her preference for seventies singer-songwriters over eighties soft boys.

"That's my ex," River says as he stares at the bartender.

"But this isn't your scene?" I ask.

"Do me a favor?" He takes my hand and leads me toward the bar. "Don't take the bait."

"What bait?"

"Whatever she throws out there."

Okay. "A favor for a favor."

He nods *whatever* and slips his hand around my waist.

My stomach flutters. Which is silly. I'm only here to keep the guy busy. Sure, he's obscenely hot now, but—

"Alice." He greets the bartender with a smile. "This is a nice surprise."

She offers a scowl in response. "I thought you were in New York." She packs a *why didn't you stay in New York, as far away from me as possible* into the sentence.

"I was," he says. "I am. I'm visiting."

"It's been a while," she says.

"It has."

Alice studies me the way other women study Lexi, with a glint in her eyes that tells me I'm competition.

I'm used to the feeling in academic and professional settings, but here? My cheeks flush. My chest swells. A strange mix of pride and self-consciousness fills my body. "It's nice to meet you, Alice. I'm Deanna." My manners kick in and I offer my hand. First, an introduction. Then a compliment. "I love your dress."

"Thanks." She shakes with a firm grip. "You, too. On both counts." She looks to River. "It's a slow night. Plenty of dance floor to ignore."

"River doesn't dance?" I ask.

"He asked me to senior prom," she says. "Then he stood there, on the sidelines, the whole time. But maybe he's learned."

Oh. She definitely thinks I'm his girlfriend. And that I dance, I guess. Which I do, but how would she know that by looking at me?

"I dance," he says.

Alice scoffs and moves on to more pressing matters. "Still drinking cosmos?"

"They're pink," he says, as if that explains anything to anyone other than me.

They're Lexi's drink. That's the reason.

Alice looks to me. "Cosmo for you, too, princess?"

"With your best vodka. And no triple sec. Cointreau or bust."

She grins. "You know your cocktails."

"I dabble," I say.

"Have you bartended?" she asks.

I nod. "For a semester in college."

"Now?"

"I'm a programmer," I say.

"A nerd," she says to River. "That is your speed." She addresses me again. "We have fresh lime, but our cranberry is a mix."

"I'll live."

She smiles warmly at me, then turns to River and goes straight to ice. "Have you ever asked him about his art?"

"What specifically?" I ask.

"The project with the blonde," she says.

I'm sure there are a lot of projects with a blonde. The same blonde, in different settings. Especially back when he was in high school. Those were his peak Lexi years.

"We were going to work on a project together," she says. "A fantasy musical."

"Ambitious," I say.

"That's high school. He had this whole role cast. A beautiful blonde princess," she says.

Okay, I see where this is going.

River shoots Alice a *don't* look.

She ignores it. "The sketches were beautiful. And specific. I thought maybe she was based on someone. An Old Hollywood celebrity. Or maybe his mother. Have you ever seen a picture of his mother?"

"Yes." I've seen the pictures in his grandma's house, and I saw her once or twice when she came to visit. She looks more like River. Dark hair, dark eyes, intense stare.

"Then you know," Alice says. "Not a blue-eyed blonde with fuck-me tits."

"That's a rude way to describe another woman's body." Even if Lexi uses it herself, as a compliment-slash-question to mean *is this outfit sexy enough*.

"Not the woman. The drawing. She was pure male fantasy."

She fills a cocktail shaker with vodka, fresh lime, orange liqueur, cranberry. "The woman was pretty, too. Not quite so exaggerated."

That's my sister she's talking about. I bite my tongue. "She can't help having great tits."

"Is she okay?" Alice asks River.

River laughs. Amused by me, again. "Absolutely not."

"You're right, though. I shouldn't judge other women. Especially given my outfit." She points to her own ample, well-displayed chest. "And my own taste in women," she adds. "But I'm not the better person."

Is that an apology? I can't tell.

"I still hate River," she says. "But I'm not mad anymore. I'm just glad I got out. Do you know how awful it feels to love someone who's in love with someone else?"

"I do," I say.

River raises a questioning brow at me, and I want to kick myself for letting that slip.

"Then you know." She slams the shaker on the bar with a soft *thud*, then strains the drinks into two martini glasses. "Here. On the house. Consider it a consolation prize." She looks to me. "Good luck, princess. Lord knows you'll need it."

River doesn't object or press her. He nods a goodbye, takes one glass, and motions for me to take another.

I move away from her glare, find a booth on the left, and sit down.

There's something strange about the space. It's cozy—we're close together—but it's exposed, too. Everyone here can see us. Anyone can watch us.

"Do you really drink cosmos?" I ask. "Or is that to mess with me?"

"Could be one. Or the other. Or both." He brings the drink to his lips. His eyes flutter closed as he takes a sip. He holds it, enjoys it, swallows, sighs like he's tasting heaven.

Or maybe like he's imagining the taste of Lexi's lips.

"That might be laced with arsenic," I say.

"It might." He takes another sip.

Well, I'm not about to let the dorky boy next door out-drink me. I bring the glass to my lips and take a tiny taste. The cocktail is good. Great, actually. The perfect mix of tart and sweet, with only the faint taste of alcohol. "The blue-eyed blonde... That was Grace Kelly?"

"Am I supposed to blush?"

"Lauren Bacall maybe?" I offer.

He doesn't take the bait.

Of course it was Lexi. Who else would it be?

"How long have you been drawing her?" I ask.

"What does it matter to you?"

"She's my sister," I say.

He doesn't reply. He takes a long sip. He swallows hard. He sighs.

I copy the gesture, but I don't have the patience to hold a staring contest. And, really, there's something about his dark eyes. They're intense. The eyes of a tortured artist.

Plus, the dark hair, the strong shoulders, the tattoo peeking out from the V-neck collar of his T-shirt.

As if he's reading my semi-dirty thoughts, he slides off his leather jacket and drapes it on the bench next to him.

Tattoos. A full sleeve on his left arm. The right arm bare. Why is that so sexy? Something about the commitment. Or the asymmetry. As if he's too beautiful to need symmetry.

"Why were you drawing Lexi?" I ask.

"What do you mean?"

"With Alice. You were dating someone else, but you were still drawing Lexi. Isn't that as good as cheating?"

"Cheating is an action."

"Oh, so it's only cheating if you touch someone else?"

"Yes," he says.

"Really?"

"Really." He nods.

"It's just…that's such a stereotypical male take."

His laugh diffuses 5 percent of the tension in the air. "That's what surprises you?"

"Maybe it shouldn't. Maybe your grandma has the same take."

"I know what you're doing," he says.

I take a long sip. Let the mix of cranberry, citrus, and vodka dissolve my inhibitions. I don't want to crush the poor guy, but maybe that's what I need to do. "What am I doing?"

"Trying to distract me."

"From?"

He sighs. "Lexi isn't coming, is she?"

"What are you talking about?"

"Don't play dumb, Deanna. You're too smart to pull it off."

My chest flares with the strangest mix of flattery and indignation.

"You don't approve of me," he says, "so you're trying to keep me away from her."

What? "Why wouldn't I approve of you?"

He hesitates, like he's unsure if he should admit to something. Then he says, "Because I'm not in the same class."

"Oh, please," I scoff. "Your house is worth three million dollars."

"My grandma's house," he clarifies. "And she bought it for less."

Fair point.

"What's the guy do?"

I blink at him, confused by the topic change. "What guy?"

"The one Lexi met in the app."

"How do you know about that?"

"Again, Grandma," he says. "She knows everything."

Right. "He's an employment lawyer."

"Not an artist."

"Get over yourself." I wave him off. "Lots of people are artists. Rich people, especially. It's a rich kid job."

He sits back, his expression hurt.

Ha. Got him.

Except I don't feel good about the dig. I feel like an asshole, actually.

"It's not because you're not good enough for her," I say. "It's not about you at all, really. It's about her." And didn't we already have this conversation ten years ago? Has he forgotten? He was supposed to forget Lexi, not forget what I said to him about her.

"Flattering."

I raise a brow. "Is that sarcasm?"

"I'd think you'd recognize it," he says with a smirk. "I'm trying to speak your language."

This is getting too personal. "Why did you draw Lexi?" I ask again.

He stares at me, hard. "Why do you care?"

"I told you why. Just answer the question."

He sits back and blows out a breath, his eyes going distant for a moment, then says, "It was a project for AP Studio Art. We had to pick a subject we didn't understand. Break it into lines, shapes, colors. To view it through different lenses."

"So you'd understand?"

He nods.

"So you, what, you break her into cubes, all Picasso like, and you suddenly get it?"

"That was the idea."

Interesting. "Did it work?"

"It offered a million insights. The symmetry of her face. The golden ratio in her figure. The way the light bounced off her hair." He looks to Alice again. "But it didn't help me understand why I want to be with her."

"Do you understand now?"

"That was high school. I'm an adult now."

It's not an answer. It's not an acknowledgment he still wants her—or a denial. But there's no need for him to deny it. It's obvious. "She's not interested in you," I say, tired of dancing around the obvious. "Not the way you're interested in her."

"And what way is that?"

"You think you love her," I say. "But you don't. You have a crush. And they call it a crush for a reason." Sometimes you have to be cruel to be kind. Or to be effective. So here goes. "Because when you realize the other person doesn't return your feelings, you're crushed."

He gives me a look I don't quite know how to interpret. "And you know her feelings?"

"She's my sister," I say.

"I suppose you know everything."

"Most things," I say.

"What do you know about love?" He finishes his drink.

"It's not love. It's a crush. And it's not love on her side, either. It's attraction. She loves her boyfriend."

"They're still together?"

Did Lexi tell him she was breaking up with Jake? Is that what they were whispering about before?

They're just on a break, though. They'll be together again soon.

He notices my lack of an answer. Takes it as a *yes*.

"She might have feelings for you. They're not love." My eyes dip to his broad shoulders. "Don't pretend you didn't do the whole muscle makeover thing on purpose."

He lets out a dry laugh. "I don't pretend."

"So you understand—"

"I have a conventional appeal now, yes," he says.

"That's what Lexi wants, what she's always wanted."

"And you know what she needs?" he asks in a tone that screams *it's a trap*.

I say, "Yes," anyway.

He stares at me, victory in his dark eyes. "Do you believe in love?"

"What?" What the hell does that have to do with anything?

"It's a yes or no question."

"Love is a chemical reaction in your brain. Dopamine and serotonin and oxytocin and vasopressin. There's nothing to believe in or not believe in." Seriously, why do people even debate things like this? There's science to explain it.

"But what about true love? Soulmates? The Sting and the Police song. 'Every Little Thing She Does is Magic.'"

"That isn't love," I say. "That's infatuation."

He raises a brow.

"There's no such thing as magic. Or soulmates." Seriously, get real. I know he's an artist, but how could anyone look at the data and think, of all the billions of people in the world, only one can complete me?

"What if I convince you otherwise?" he says.

Why would he do that? I take a sip, to try to find some thread of logic. But there's nothing. It's nowhere.

"Will you back off then?" he asks.

"If you convince me of the *magic* of love, I step out of the way of your, what, *destiny* to be with Lexi?"

"Call it that if you want. But yes."

"And what do I get if I win? If you don't convince me love is, what, more magic than science?" I ask.

"Or equal parts magic and science," he says. "However you want to see it." He takes a long sip, debating what to offer me. "You want her with this app guy, right?" he asks.

"It's what's best for her." *And the company*, but I don't add that.

"If I can't convince you, I'll help you keep them together," he says.

Wait...what? "You will?"

"Absolutely.

Score. "And what do you get if you win?" I ask.

"You back off. Give me a chance to be with Lexi," he says.

"So if I win, you leave Lexi alone. If you win, I leave the two of you to destiny?"

"Exactly," he says.

"But how are you going to prove love is real or not real? That's so ambiguous."

"Fair. Let's set a definition now, then," he says. "If you don't agree in, say, three weeks, I'll concede."

"You trust me that much?"

He nods.

This is a good deal. A great deal. And it will keep him busy. I nod. "So... What's our definition of love?"

"An attachment to someone that gives you warm, fuzzy feelings and butterflies."

"Too vague. By that definition every puppy I see on Instagram is my soulmate."

He nods, thinking for a moment, trying to come up with a more scientific response. "How about this? When you love someone enough, you act against your own self-interest. You put them first. Would you agree to that?"

"It's not specific to romantic love."

"But it exists in romantic love."

"If you love someone, set them free?" I ask.

He nods. As if that means I need to leave my sister free to be with him, in whatever way she wants, because I love her.

And I nod back. If he does love her, then he should let her go, to be with a person who actually suits her.

It's a good deal, though. If it gets him to keep his distance from Lexi.

Because Lexi said her boyfriend break is for *two* weeks, and I'm sure she'll be back with Jake at the end of it. Our dinner with Willa and her partner is in *four* weeks. So whatever happens with River in the next *three* weeks? Is just more data I can use to support the app. It's win-win-win.

"Okay. Three weeks." I offer my hand. "Do we have a deal?"

CHAPTER NINE

Deanna

ove is a concept with a million definitions. There's really no way to prove any one idea fits the bill.

But I know him enough to know his image of love:

The pure, true love we see in songs, movies, books.

The selfless love that causes someone to put another person first. Not the familiar version—of course I believe in that—but one that also marries sexual attraction. One that extends beyond infatuation.

Over another round of drinks, I outline the concept.

River signs his own losing ticket. He insists he can trust me to be honest. That I'll know when I feel it.

Then we set the terms.

Three weeks. Until the week before our investor dinner.

Of course, at any point, either one of us can admit defeat: admit love is magic or not magic.

And just for fun—and maybe because of the drinks—we throw in another term. If I lose, I have to get a tattoo of his choice. Somewhere visible. Somewhere that will mark me as a rebel, not a professional woman. He has full right to my left arm.

And I have full right to his currently un-inked arm.

Even with the buzz, I know it's silly, but I love the idea of seeing *Love Sux* on his arm.

Once I'm satisfied with the terms, we shake on it.

"It's your funeral," I say.

"This is the place for it." He releases my hand, finishes his drink, stands with a million-dollar smile. It's similar to his *I'm getting some from Lexi* smile, but it's different. too. Sure. Smart. Sexy.

It melts me in places that are usually ice cold.

Which is ridiculous. That smile is for Lexi, not me, but the logic fails to penetrate.

"Another round?" he asks. "Or would you rather admit Lexi isn't coming?"

"I'm not in charge of what Lexi does."

"Did you tell her we're here?"

"She knows." Well, she knows I'm keeping him busy at a bar. Just not which bar.

"Of course." He glances at my purse without comment. "To celebrate our wager then."

Right. Our deal. He fails to convince me, admits defeat, helps Lexi stay with Jake. Win/win for me, lose/lose for him. "You're going to face her hate?" I nod toward Wednesday Addams at the bar.

"She's not as scary as she looks." Despite Alice's intense glare, River approaches the bar with the necessary mix of confidence and compassion. He offers her some sort of apology and places two bills on the bar.

She fixes the drinks and accepts the cash, but she keeps the glare.

Does he deserve it? Should she move on?

People are puzzling. As with any puzzle, there's a certain thrill to putting the pieces together, but when the pieces refuse to fit—

Computers are easier. Logic. Rules. If A means B, and B means C, A always means C.

If Deanna is too cold for her ex-boyfriend, and her ex-boyfriend claims he wants a high-achieving woman, then Deanna is too cold for most men.

But I already knew that. I just didn't want to believe it.

Lexi: *All done. Great talk with Willa. She bought Jake's absence no problem. Are you keeping River warm for me?*

She sends a truly unholy combination of emojis.

Right. Willa bought Jake's absence—for one night. But she expects to see him, to see them as the poster couple, soon.

Deanna: *What do you mean warm?*

Another unholy row of emojis. I understand eggplant and water drop (way too visual), but what the hell do the dancer and the chili pepper mean?

Is she making up dirty texts?

Lexi: *I think it's different this time. I really felt something when I saw him. A need all the way to my core.*

That's not different. That's normal for her. I've heard this speech a million times.

Lexi: *You won't get it, I know, but I felt that magic. Like the Sting song. There's no other way to explain it.*

When did people start talking about Sting again?

Deanna: *What about Jake's magic?*

Lexi: *It's not shiny anymore.*

Of course it's not! That's not how relationships work. They aren't magic and they aren't shiny, but I'm not going to talk her into the theory today.

Lexi: *Where are you two? I'll come.*

Deanna: *Oh no. I forgot to leave my keys.*

Lexi: *I'll grab the spare.*

Dammit. There's a spare in my room and another in Dad's office. I keep backups of backups and now it's biting me in the ass.

Deanna: *Phone is about to die. I'll keep him warm for you and bring him home early. Should I start with a lap dance or some light flashing?*

Lexi: *I would pay to see that.*
Deanna: *Love you.*
Lexi: *Don't do anything I wouldn't do.*
Deanna: *Does that leave anything out?*
Lexi: *No.*
Lexi: *Where are you?*
Deanna: *I'll send a pin.*

I turn my phone on airplane mode and shove it in my purse right as River returns to the booth. He sets the drinks on the table and slides into the booth opposite mine.

"Any poison?" I curl my fingers around the stem of my glass.

"Likely."

"She doesn't forgive you?"

"She does." He tests the drink. "She might do it anyway."

"To hurt you?"

"Spare you." He takes another sip. "Her words. 'I hope that girl knows you'll never love her.'"

"Tell her I do know."

He looks at me funny, like he wants to object, but he doesn't. "I guess I already know you don't offend easily."

"You don't, either."

He smirks. "I don't remember you glaring at books as a kid."

"What?"

"Were you always this cynical?"

I bring the drink to my lips, swallow a hearty mouthful of cosmo. Fuck, Alice is a great mixologist. Is that pomegranate? What a perfect addition. It's not even pink anymore. It's wine-red. The color of my favorite lipstick.

"That story about your parents?" River asks.

"What about them?"

"You don't believe it," he says.

I take another sip and let out a soft sigh. "Did you ask her to add the pomegranate?"

"She said you'd appreciate it."

"Why's that?"

"Because I'm the kind of asshole who worships Hades and Persephone."

A laugh spills from my lips.

"Exact quote."

"She's literary."

"A musician with fuck-me tits can't be literary?"

"Did you just say fuck-me tits?" I ask.

"Her words," he says.

"You can't say it. You're a guy. It's different." I take another sip. "Do you worship Hades and Persephone?"

"Did you really not play Hades?" He refers to a Roguelike game that swept the scene a few years ago.

"My ex did." And, yeah, I played with him. It's a great game. Bright and fun and hard, with a million ways to customize, but I hate it now, because I think of him. "I don't play games often." Not anymore. I don't have time.

"Why did you stop?"

"Why did you stop carrying Spider-Man comics everywhere?"

"It's easier to read them on a tablet."

"I'm too busy to play anymore," I say.

"Was he the guy?" he asks.

"Who?"

"This ex. Is he the guy who turned you into a cynic?" River asks.

"I'm a realist," I say. "And no. A guy didn't turn me into anything. This is how I am."

He doesn't react to my accusation of assumption. "Did you love him?"

"Why? If I say yes, do you win our bet already?"

"Not necessarily." He takes a sip and lets out a low, deep sigh. "Fuck. That is good. Did you love him?" he asks again.

"I thought so," I say. "Now, I don't know."

He raises a brow.

"I don't know if I really knew who he was."

"What did you like about him?"

"Everything," I say. "We made perfect sense on paper. Two programmers with similar interests and goals. We both loved puzzles and watching old movies and lying on the beach after a long day."

"What about him, specifically?"

"I don't want to think about him."

"Why not?" he asks.

"Because he's my ex. Because that phase of my life is over."

He shakes his head. "Our agreement only works if I get full access."

"Full access?"

"To anything I want to know."

"If I say no?" I ask.

"I'll call Lexi right now," he says. "She'll come here. Or we'll meet at your place."

"She'll lose interest the second you two have sex."

"According to you." He pulls his cell from his pocket. "Let's find out if you're right."

No. We won't find out. We'll never find out. "I liked his glasses."

"His glasses?"

"He had these big, round, wire-framed glasses. Harry Potter glasses. They made him look smart in this sexy yet earnest way. I liked that."

"How did you get together?"

The mix of lime and vodka dissolves a tiny hint of my inhibitions. "We were in the same data science study group, back in college. He'd always walk me home and we'd talk about teachers and what we wanted to do with our futures. And then, one night, when he walked me to the door—I lived on campus at UCI, during the school year—he said, 'I'd like to kiss you' and I said, 'I'd like that, too,' and he did."

"He asked?"

"What? Are you going to say consent's not sexy?"

"No." He takes a long sip. "I'm surprised he's the one who asked."

"Why?"

"You seem like the type who steers."

"Are you going to say I wear the pants, too?" I ask.

He laughs. "I'm not that stereotypical." He studies me the same way he did earlier, like I'm a landscape he wants to understand. "Did you like it, him asking to kiss you?"

"He didn't ask. He said he wanted to kiss me. That's different."

"It is."

"It was sexy," I say. "A little shy, sure, but I liked that about him. I like shy guys."

"Guys like me?"

Why would he say that? My cheeks flame. "You're not shy anymore."

His cheeks redden, too.

"No." I swallow a sip to buy myself time to think, but I don't come up with anything. "I don't like shy guys anymore. But I did then."

"Was he shy every step of the way?"

He's a romantic. Why is he going straight to sex? "In a way. But he always let me know he wanted me. And that felt good. Which is stereotypical of me. Women want to feel desired. It's a stereotype, but the data shows it's common."

"Men are the ones messaging women?"

I nod. "And liking profiles. And sending compliments."

"You know all that?" he asks. "Isn't that an invasion of privacy?"

"Users only supply as much data as they'd like to supply." Most opt-in completely. Most of us gave up on Internet privacy a long time ago. Or they're willing to sacrifice it for love. After all, the more access we have to users, the better we understand what they truly want, which means we can match them with someone they truly want. "We don't look at the info for kicks. We use it to help people find the perfect match."

"What does that mean?"

"Someone compatible."

"Someone they'll love?" he asks.

"Someone with the same goals. Someone who's statistically likely to match well."

He doesn't address the issue of compatibility. "Were you happy with him?"

"At first."

"What happened after the kiss?"

"He pursued me," I say. "He'd ask me on dates, buy me flowers, take me to the beach to watch the stars. After a few weeks, we did more than kiss, and then we got official. Back then, I wanted to be around him all the time, in his space, near his scent. At first, I thought that was love."

"What was it?"

"Infatuation. Chemicals in my brain, trying to keep me close for long enough to propagate the species. My body doesn't understand the concept of birth control. It only feels that drive to fuck."

"That's all sex is?" he asks.

"All? No. But that's a lot of it."

"Did you feel a drive to fuck him?" he asks.

"At first."

"And then?"

"Then I didn't."

"Why not?" he asks.

"We didn't want the same things there," I say.

"What did he want?" he asks.

"No." I shake my head. "This was plenty of access. You're going to have to buy me another drink for that one." I look to the dance floor. Sure enough, the kids in matching collars are still there. This is the perfect place to discuss Stephan. It really is.

"Give me a clue."

"No. If you want to know, you can buy me a drink, or you can take me to the dance floor. Your call."

CHAPTER TEN

River

Even after two drinks, Deanna moves with effortless grace. Every gesture is smooth and subtle. Refined in a way I can't begin to articulate.

She lifts her glass to her lips and takes a dainty sip. Her wine-stained lipstick stays perfect. Her attention stays on me.

There's an intensity to her stare, but it no longer feels disarming. She's not trying to pick me apart. She's trying to dive deeper, to flip through my pages, read every line.

Why does that sound so fucking dirty?

The vodka is going to my head. Not to mention the jet lag and the wine-red lips.

Deanna Huntington is a beautiful woman. I'm still a man. I still notice.

That's all it is. A physical, biological reaction. It doesn't mean I want her.

It means it's been too long, and I need a solo session when I get home.

I swallow my sip and collect her empty glass.

"One more," she says. "Then we talk."

"Who will drive home?" I ask.

"Uber," she says. "But who's going to collect Lexi's car

tomorrow?"

"Lexi."

Deanna laughs. "Sure. She deserves that."

I raise a brow.

This time, her laugh is big enough to light her entire face. Unlike Lexi, she doesn't shine like the sun. But she glows in her own way.

The moon. This soft, silver symbol of feminine beauty.

"That's the first sign of sibling rivalry I've heard from you," I say. "Ever."

"Nice try, River, but it's time to pay your bill." She offers her hand as if she's asking for cash.

I pick up the glasses.

The light fades as I turn away from her, but it's different than it is with other people. Some of the glow lingers. Because I still have her attention? Or because that's what Deanna does?

I'm not sure.

I face Alice with a smile. "Another, please."

She shoots me that same *are you really wasting that girl's time* look, shakes her head, and fixes two drinks. "Let her down easy, okay?"

She writes *I mean it, River* on the receipt. I don't argue. I slip the paper into my back pocket, carry the drinks to the table, and sit across from Deanna.

"All right, Mr. Beau." She wraps her long, narrow fingers around the stem and pulls the glass to her. "What exactly do you want to know?"

"Everything."

"Greedy," she says.

She's teasing, but I feel it. I feel greedy in a way I haven't in a long time. I want to know what happened with this guy. I want to understand why she's cold and distant.

What sort of person devotes themselves to love—creates a dating app designed for forever relationships—when they don't believe in it?

"What was it you didn't like?" I ask.

"I guess there's no coy way to say it." She brings the drink to her lips, sips, and lets out a sigh of pleasure.

It's a sound I've never heard from her. A sound I never expected to hear.

Deanna Huntington wants things. Deanna Huntington groans over a perfect cocktail. And a perfect experience with the first half of the word, no doubt.

"He wanted a Domme," she says.

"And you?"

"What do you think?"

"I can see you in thigh-high boots, cracking a whip." In only thigh-high boots. I see it far too vividly, actually.

"I look hot as hell in thigh-high boots," she says.

"Do you have pictures?" Where the hell did that come from?

"They're only for people I'm fucking."

"There are other people?"

"Not part of the deal." She mimes zipping her lips.

"So, what? Thigh-high boots and whips and telling him what a bad boy he was?"

"And orgasm denial."

Fuck.

"That was his main thing."

"Complete denial?"

"Teasing until he couldn't take it anymore."

"Did you like it?"

"On occasion. But it got old. I started to crave vanilla stuff. Missionary. Eye contact."

"Freak," I say.

She blushes as she laughs. "I know. I should be more creative. But that's not my strong suit."

"Maybe you need help."

Her eyes go to my chest.

"Someone who can create what you like, not what he likes."

"Are you offering?"

Yeah, let's go to the bathroom right now.

What the hell is wrong with me? Deanna is beautiful and sexy in that smart, sarcastic way, but we're only friends. We're not even friends.

"And you?" she asks. "Are you another vanilla-loving freak?"

"This is about you."

"It's only fair," she says. "I said something. You say something."

"There's not much to say."

"No, I suppose you're in New York, going to orgies. No. One of those masquerade parties. Masks and nothing else."

"Sounds like a story."

"One of your grandma's."

"At least five," I say. "Should we ask her for recs tomorrow?"

"Of course." Deanna laughs. "She writes the best stuff. I can't get into anyone else. They never write their heroines hard enough."

It figures Deanna would love Grandma's tough women.

"She gave me this series she called the HBICs. *The Billionaire's Millionaire.* All these high-achieving women paired with slightly richer men. Because the publisher didn't believe readers would fall for a poorer guy, even if the poorer guy was worth two billion."

"I know that one."

"And *The Billionaire and the Maven.* I love that one. The whole series."

The one set around high-achieving women.

She has a book type.

"And you?" she asks. "Any Dommes in your past? Or were you the one holding a whip?"

My head goes to all sorts of places it shouldn't. Dangerous places. But cursing the mental images only brightens them.

Deanna Huntington, in only her boots, utterly in control as she slides onto me.

Not going there. "Do you see anything as romantic?"

"No. I want a sex story."

"It's not that interesting."

"Neither was mine."

It came with some powerful visuals. But, sure, I can move through this. "Faith."

"Was it a relationship or just sex?" She doesn't add *I know you're too into Lexi for another relationship*, but it fills the air anyway.

I wasn't, then. At least, I didn't think I was. I thought I was over her. "We were friends with benefits. We both agreed to a course of experimentation. Dirty talk, pictures, bondage."

"You tying her up or the reverse?"

"Are you looking for your next sub?" I mean the words as a joke, but they send my blood rushing south anyway. This is too much talk about sex. I need to discuss something else.

She takes a long sip, looks around to check the coast is clear. The bar is still empty. The four people on the dance floor are still swaying. She leans in and whispers, "Are you asking?"

I ban the mental image from my mind. "We did it both ways. We tried a lot. And it went well. For a while."

"The suspense," she teases.

"She wanted to have a threesome with another woman. Her request. And what guy turns that down, right?"

"It's a common male fantasy. I've seen the data."

Does her app really collect data on sexual fantasies? She must know a lot of secrets. "I helped pick the woman, I organized the meeting, I went out for drinks. But even after three margaritas, I felt stiff."

She raises a brow.

Right. "Tense. Awkward. I tried to get into it. I kissed the other woman. I watched them kiss. But when it was time to touch her, I couldn't do it. No matter how much Faith insisted it was fine. More than fine. Sexy. I felt sick. I stopped things and we got into a fight and that was it. We made up a few days later, but we never really got past it."

"And that was it, the end?"

"I was leaving anyway."

"To come here?"

I nod.

"Why did you leave?" she asks. "You have a job in New York."

"I can work remote."

"Still. You don't have a reason to be in California."

"I have meetings in Los Angeles. We're opening a new office."

"Then why aren't you staying in LA with your sister? Why are you staying here, in Orange County? And don't say it's because you're fated to be with Lexi, because we both know that isn't it."

She's right. I didn't come here for Lexi. I didn't expect to see Lexi, much less feel my high school crush rushing back to me when I did.

I came here for another woman.

Grandma.

Her cancer is back.

Of course, Ida Beau isn't interested in anyone's opinion on how she should pursue treatment.

I'm sworn to silence.

Maybe it is fate. That's what I would have said, in any other situation.

With Grandma being sick?

If that's fate, I don't accept it.

I won't.

• • •

We trade stories about exes. Funny stories, too. But they don't have the gravity to pull my thoughts to the moment.

There's too much in my head.

Deanna is gorgeous here, under the strange purple lights, the steady electronic beat punctuating her sentences.

The story about an ex who planned a romantic picnic at the beach, only to stare at a babe on a surfboard the entire time.

The other ex who attempted a romantic weekend at Big Bear, as a surprise. Without the warning to take extra motion sickness medicine, Deanna spent the entire drive ill and threw up on his expensive seats.

The time Stephan's parents called right as she slipped into her leather catsuit.

I'm not proud that the mental image of Deanna in skintight leather is what finally grabs my attention, but I am a man. I feel the same base impulses as other men. And this one is strong enough I want to savor it. To enjoy a million hours of imagination. A thousand of the real thing.

Deanna Huntington, in some fancy hotel room, unzipping her catsuit, climbing onto the bed, riding someone like a stallion.

She notices the light in my eyes, tilts her head to one side, studies me carefully.

This time, she's not looking through me. She's looking at me like she's imagining what she wants to do with me.

"What's that look?" She swallows the last drop of liquor. "You're thinking something."

Too many things. "I'm always thinking something. The same as you."

"Not the same as me."

"No?"

"You think sweet, romantic things."

Not always.

"I think of devious things," she says.

"Catsuits and whips?"

She smiles. "Algorithms and spreadsheets."

"Really? You're thinking about spreadsheets right now?"

"Yes. Which is why we need to dance. Well, I have to dance." She slides out of the booth and offers her hand. "A promise I made to my mom. You can join or not."

Who the hell could resist a promise to a dead mother? She's too good at this. I follow her, take her hand, join her on the dance floor.

The club is a little more crowded now. A dozen singles dancing alone. A hot and heavy couple in schoolgirl outfits, grinding like they're, well, still in high school. A man and woman in all black, making out like there's no tomorrow.

And the two of us.

Deanna shifts into dance position immediately.

I fall into it, too. Grandma wanted me to belong in this world. She sent me to lessons. Just in case.

"Or maybe like this. Close position." She places her hands on my waist. At first, her grip is soft. Tentative. Then she sinks into it.

She looks through me.

I need the intensity. It's the only thing that pushes the storm clouds from my head.

She curls her fingers into the cotton fabric of my T-shirt.

I bring my hands to her hips and pull her body into mine. Her chest against my chest, her hips against my hips, her legs around mine.

She's offset. That's the dance description. A proper position. One where we can't align the parts desperate to align.

For all her sharpness, Deanna is soft against me. The slim curves of her body, the slick fabric of her dress, and something deeper, some way of sinking into me.

She feels good.

When was the last time someone felt this good?

My hands dig into her hips.

We shift in time with the music, pressed together, so close to where we're supposed to be, but so far, too.

One song flows into the next. Then the next. With the electric beat, it's hard to tell.

She breaks our touch and turns around, so she's pressed *all* the way against me, her back against my chest, her ass against my pelvis.

My hands go to her hips reflexively.

Blood rushes south.

Conscious thought flees my brain.

My body takes over. And my body isn't concerned with ideas of love and commitment and destiny. My body wants release, any release.

And closeness. Any closeness.

Even with the wrong person. Even with the worst person.

How can she be the worst person when she feels so right here?

I stop fighting my desire. I stop thinking of the blonde princess, the center of my fantasies.

I move with Deanna, in reality and in tune with her, with myself, with every beautiful thing in the universe.

She gasps as my hard-on presses against her ass, but she doesn't stop. She keeps the same perfect, torturous rhythm, grinding against me again and again, until I'm not sure if I want to beg for mercy or more.

We stay there for a few songs, then she releases me, brings her lips to my ear. "Bathroom. Be right back."

I feel the loss of contact immediately. My body wants hers. It needs hers.

It's not happening.

It doesn't matter.

Sure, I watch her walk away, but that doesn't mean anything, either. Only that the teal fabric of her dress hugs her hips just so.

I'm a man.

And an artist.

I notice shapes. Lines. Colors.

The pink flush on her cheeks. The color of wine on her lips. The patent black of her boots. Say, as the heels dig into my back.

Fuck.

I rush to the men's room and splash cold water on my face. It doesn't work.

A million memories hit me at once:

Deanna, diving into the pool in a simple black swimsuit.

Sweat dripping from her skimpy jogging outfit.

The sparkle of her eyes as she listens to Carole King in the backyard, sure no one is watching.

Yes, she's gorgeous. So what?

After one more splash of cold water, I gather my jacket and meet her on the dance floor.

I don't have to ask what she wants. It's written all over her face: the fun is over.

"Lexi is on her way," she whispers in my ear. "She hasn't been drinking, so she's good to drive. She'll be here any minute." She takes my hand and leads me outside and I can't help but wonder if she texted Lexi so nothing more could happen.

The air is cool. The temperature drops so quickly here. I forgot how that feels. The loss of the day's warmth.

Deanna's Tesla is already here. And there's Lexi, wearing a pink dress and a smile, waving for us to come inside.

"I guess this is it?" Deanna asks. "Destiny. Right?"

Right.

This is what I want.

Everything I want.

Exactly what I want.

Deanna is the one who doesn't belong in this picture.

Not Lexi.

And not me.

CHAPTER ELEVEN

River

Deanna tries to insist on sitting shotgun, but Lexi insists harder. After they debate, I take the seat, and the two of them talk outside the car.

It's strange to watch the most willful woman I know (besides Grandma) bend.

Is this a common occurrence? Does she bend for Lexi all the time?

For some reason, it's easy to imagine. It's easy for me to imagine most things. But not things where Deanna Huntington is a reasonable, caring, compassionate person.

Reasonable? Absolutely. Certain she knows what's best for her sister? Obviously. But loving?

From a certain definition, maybe. A sort of fifties father, sitting in his study drinking scotch (neat, of course), calling her kids (sister) in to explain what they're going to do. Not what they should do. What they will do.

In a menswear-inspired pinstripe suit.

A sexy version, with nothing under it.

Suddenly, the image comes to life in my head. Only there's no kid. Instead, Deanna climbs onto the desk, undoes the button of her pinstriped jacket, motions for me to *come here*.

And then she's on the desk and I'm on top of her and I'm tasting her lipstick—

No.

What the hell is wrong with me? This is Grandma's influence. She's only willing to watch sci-fi or fantasy films if they include an enemies-to-lovers trope.

We watched the original *Star Wars* trilogy about a million times.

And then Grandma and Fern and North argued about whether Harrison Ford was sexier as Han Solo or Indiana Jones and—

Fuck, Deanna would make a sexy Han Solo, wouldn't she? Or an Indy. I can see her in nothing but a vest, pointing a blaster at an enemy. Or in that open-shirt, fedora, whip-wielding pose of Indy's.

The whip. That's why so many people prefer Indy.

And it suits her.

"Find My Phone was your idea!" Lexi's loud voice pulls me into the moment. She slides into the car and smooths her suit jacket. Then her pink dress. "You did step into your role, Dee. Drinking too much to drive home."

Deanna slides into the back seat and slams the door. "Uh-huh."

Lexi ignores her attitude as she turns the car on and pulls out of the parking lot. "And I'm taking your role. Only one drink. All the responsibility." Lexi turns to me with a wide smile. "I hope you didn't miss me too much."

The attention warms me. She's still the sun, her intensity still overwhelming. Only now, between streetlights and neon signs, its brightness feels wrong. Out of place.

"When did Willa leave?" Deanna sits up straight. She looks to the rearview mirror, pulls her lipstick from her purse, applies another coat of deep red.

There. The second she smooths her dress, she's picture perfect. If I didn't know better, I'd think she was on her way to a party. She doesn't show a single sign of intoxication.

She's the other Deanna again, the one who never admits weakness.

"She only stayed long enough to rub a few elbows," Lexi says.

"And she approved of your plan to—"

Lexi turns on the radio just in time to cut Deanna off. One of the slow-jams satellite stations. "Sorry. Should I put on something a little more sisterly?" She switches to a pop channel.

A girl-power anthem fills the space. Something popular when we were in high school.

"Let's not bore River with shop talk, huh?" Through the rearview mirror, Lexi makes eye contact with her sister. "I already kept him waiting long enough."

Deanna opens her mouth to speak but she stops herself. "Sure. I won't bore you with the details of our wager, either."

"You two have a wager?" Lexi asks. "Anything juicy?"

"No," she says. "But he knows the terms. What he isn't going to do."

"Is this a riddle?" Lexi shakes her head. "Or is it the scotch talking?"

"You drink scotch?" I ask.

"No. She's teasing," Deanna says. "We had cosmos in your honor."

Lexi lets out a sigh of pure flattery. "How sweet." She stops at a red light and looks to me.

Again, the warmth of her attention overwhelms me.

"Did you miss me?" she asks.

I can't find any words.

She smiles. "I'll take that as a yes." She looks to the street as the light turns green. "Did you really need to go to Anaheim? There's a perfectly good bar on Main Street."

"This seemed more like River's vibe," Deanna says.

She laughs. "I haven't ever seen him wearing eyeliner."

She's been paying enough attention to know?

"Really, it's more your vibe," Lexi says. "Remember that guy you dated in high school?"

"Which one?" Deanna asks.

"The one who wore black nail polish," Lexi says. "Who got you hooked on combat boots?"

"Mom bought my first pair of combat boots," Deanna says.

"Who actually convinced you to listen to Joy Division," Lexi says.

"They're not terrible," Deanna says.

"That's a high compliment from her," Lexi says. "Whatever happened to that guy?"

"I don't know. We broke up after a few months."

Lexi laughs. "Bored with him?"

"No." Deanna stares out the window. "He wanted a different kind of girl."

"One who wore even more black?"

"No. A curvy blonde," she says. "A California girl."

Lexi's nose wrinkles in confusion. She isn't putting the pieces together.

But they're obvious. The guy wanted Lexi.

Is that Deanna's experience with men? Even the Goth guy goes for the bubbly blonde? The contrast is appealing. I see that.

It must hurt her, though, to always be in the shadow of the sun.

No wonder she doesn't believe in love. No one's offered it to her.

"Is Depressed Mode still fun?" Lexi asks. "I haven't been since high school."

"It's twenty-one plus," Deanna says.

"I have my ways."

"A fake ID or a fling with a bartender?" Deanna asks.

"Dee, I know you don't approve of rule breaking. But you'd get it if you got it," she says. "Bartenders are hot."

"River knows something about that," Deanna says.

Lexi's blue eyes go wide. "A dirty story? Do tell."

Dirty.

Lexi.

Me.

All the thoughts leave my brain at once.

She doesn't wait for me to find a thought. "Aw, I bet you broke her heart." She presses her hand to her chest with utmost sympathy. "The poor girl probably had no idea what she was in for."

Deanna actually laughs out loud. "Really?"

"Yeah, really." Lexi turns to the back seat. "Do you have a problem?"

"No." Deanna mimes zipping her lips.

Lexi holds her sister's gaze for a moment, then she settles into her seat. "Did you break her heart?"

"I—"

"They dated in high school," Deanna says, cutting me off.

"And?" Lexi asks. "No one broke your heart in high school?"

"You're right," Deanna says. "She was pissed to see him, even after all these years."

"Wait a second." Lexi cups her ear with one hand. "Did I hear that right?"

"Don't rub it in," Deanna says.

"I was right?" Lexi asks.

"Yeah. You were right. Take the win," Deanna says.

Lexi turns to me with an even more radiant smile. "She's never said this before."

"I guess you two can bond there," Deanna says. "Breaking hearts."

I can't get a word in between these two.

"I've never broken a heart," Lexi says.

"Are you kidding?" Deanna asks. "A million guys cried to me over you."

"They did not." Lexi turns to me for a brief moment. "What happened with your bartender?"

There's a beat of silence before I realize she asked me a question. "I apologized," I say.

"That's big of you," Lexi says. "I don't know if I've ever apologized to an ex. I tell them what I want straight up. Fun. No strings. I can't help it if they develop feelings. Or if they refuse to believe I enjoy casual sex because I'm a woman."

From her spot in the back seat, Deanna clears her throat. She mutters something that sounds a lot like *I told you so.*

But maybe that's my imagination.

"Were you the one who broke up with her?" Lexi asks.

"Alice," Deanna offers. "That's her name." She mutters something else, but I don't catch it.

Again, Lexi ignores her. Again, she takes my non-response as a yes. "Did you want to hurt her when you ended things?"

"No." I find the words to respond. Barely. "But I knew I would."

The light turns green. Lexi presses the accelerator and whizzes along the quiet street.

"It wouldn't be fair to pretend otherwise," I say.

Lexi nods. "That's true."

"Did you tell her the truth?" Deanna asks.

"People don't want the truth," Lexi cuts in. "They think they want it, but they don't. Do you really think that guy I dated last year, Greg What's-His-Face, would be better off if I told him, 'the truth is, you're a bad lay. I'm bored out of bed. I'm bored in bed. I'm bored. On that note, you should really try to mix it up a little more in the bedroom. Would it kill you to spend more than two minutes on cunnilingus?'"

Jesus.

"His next girlfriend would have been better off," Deanna says.

Lexi's laugh softens the tension in the car. "Well, I can't argue with that last part."

"Did you realize it at the time?" Deanna asks.

"No, I thought he was eager to move things along at first," Lexi says.

"The boredom," Deanna says.

"Oh. Right." Lexi laughs again. "Yeah, of course. But I was trying to make it work." Lexi looks to me. "Sorry. We're being totally rude. You know how it is when you're with your sister."

"I'm just so easy to talk to," Deanna teases.

Lightness fills the space and I can't help but let out a laugh.

Deanna's funny. She's way too funny. It's putting me on her side.

But then we don't have to be adversarial. She might see things that way, but I don't. We can work together, even if she believes I'm only here because I want Lexi.

"Is she a babe?" Lexi asks. "Alice?"

"She's a smoke show," Deanna says.

"Heartbreaker," Lexi teases. "Tell me the story."

"Deanna heard it," I say.

"It's fine," Deanna says. "Start in the car. Finish at home. I'm going to go to bed, anyway."

Lexi frowns at the mention of bed, but she continues anyway. "Yeah, River, tell me everything. And don't skip the good parts."

. . .

I try to tell the story, but, again, I can't find the words. Lexi's attention is too overwhelming. I start and stop half a dozen times.

Then Deanna takes pity on me, puts me out of my misery, and relays what I told her, minus Alice's anger over my high school obsession with Lexi.

Despite the lack of dramatic turns, Lexi hangs on every word. She nods *uh-huh* and gasps *really* and stares at me as if she can't believe the deep truths I'm revealing via her sister.

When we arrive at the Huntington place, Lexi parks on the street. Deanna steps out of the car, but she doesn't go home. She stands there.

"Are you going to wait for me?" Lexi asks her sister.

"Yeah," Deanna says.

"I'm fine," Lexi says. "Why don't you head home. Shower. Give me a minute or two alone, huh?"

Deanna studies the two of us. She shoots me a cutting look. I'm not sure what she means beyond *don't touch her*, but I know she means that.

Lexi watches, impatiently, as Deanna walks around the house, through the backyard, into their apartments.

Then she turns to me with that big, beautiful smile.

And I can't find a single word.

This is exactly what I imagined a million times. Okay, not exactly. But close to what I imagined. Privacy in a car with Lexi.

The two of us, listening to Sade, kissing over the center console, whispering sweet nothings.

Only we're in Deanna's Tesla, on the street, without a single note of music.

"Did you have fun?" Lexi asks.

I manage a nod.

"Really?" She tilts her head to one side. "I was worried she wouldn't keep you entertained."

Again, I nod.

"She teased she'd keep you warm for me. With a lap dance. I don't suppose she made good on that?" Lexi laughs at the mental image.

I...do other things. Go other places. Deanna, in only those combat boots, sliding backward into my lap, whispering dirty promises in my ears.

When did she get so fucking sexy?

When did my body stop listening to my heart?

I need to go home, get my head on straight.

I try to find something to say, some *I've wanted this for so long, too long, I can't think now.* Instead, I say, "How long have you lived back here?"

"Three years," she says. "Since Dee's ex broke her heart." She looks to the apartment. "It really hurt her. She thought they'd be together forever. They were together for ages."

"She loved him?"

"I don't know," Lexi says. "I'm not sure she thinks about things in those terms. And if she did, I wouldn't understand them anyway." She turns a little more toward me. "Hey, what do you say we go for a drive?"

Energy surges through my body, but it's a fast surge. It underlines my exhaustion. "Soon."

"Tomorrow?" she offers.

"Fern and North are coming tomorrow."

"A family reunion?" she asks. "Perfect. Let's go out. All four of us. Five of us. If Deanna wants. But she never wants."

I nod.

She smiles. "How about I walk you home?"

"It's a long way."

She laughs hard, even though it's really not that funny, gets out of the car, and helps me out.

I take her hand and follow her onto the sidewalk, up the stone path to Grandma's house.

We stand there, under the porch light, exactly where I pictured us a million times.

This is where we whisper, *I had a great time,* and kiss.

"I'll see you tomorrow." Lexi squeezes my hand. She looks up at me with affection and need in those big, blue eyes.

It's what I imagined, but doesn't feel the way I imagined. It's not perfect. I'm not finally whole. "Tomorrow."

"Until then." She moves closer, rises to her tiptoes, and brings her lips to mine.

A soft hint of a kiss.

I expect cranberry, pomegranate, vodka—

The taste on Deanna's lips—

But there's nothing. Only Lexi.

It's everything I imagined.

It's nothing like what I imagined.

CHAPTER TWELVE

River

At home, I hang my coat on the rack, next to Grandma's silk trench (as she says, "It may not rain in California, sweetheart, but it does rain men. I need to look my best.").

"You're out late. Did you finally sleep with the girl next door?" Grandma asks from her spot on the couch. "Or do we need to go over mechanics again?" She smiles. "Should I grab a condom and a zucchini?"

"Please don't."

"A banana?"

"Yes, the fruit in question is the problem."

She laughs. "How was the party?"

"Fine."

"Only fine?" She checks the time on her slim silver watch. "Past midnight?"

"I didn't stay long," I say.

"Oh? Finally take that drive to make-out point?" she teases. "How many virginities do you think she's taken there?"

"Why? Are you competing?" I don't feel my usual need to rebuff the question. Sure, Lexi sleeps around. So what? I never cared about that. But I don't typically enjoy the thought of her with another man.

Only right now, I don't care.

I can't see us there.

I can't see any of it.

Grandma's laugh pulls me back to the scene. "Sweetheart, do you really want the answer to that?"

"You were married for thirty years," I say.

"I wasn't married for a long time before and after that."

"Meet a lot of seventy-year-old virgins?" I ask.

Grandma shoots me one of her signature *don't be naive, darling* looks. "A lot of men enjoy an older woman."

"You're right. I don't want to know this." Really. I love Grandma. She's basically my mom at this point. But I don't need to picture her with a younger man. Or any man. "Did you finish the bottle?"

"Wine after midnight?"

"I'm living dangerously."

"No," she says. "Two glasses left."

"You drank all that on your own?" I ask.

"Mr. Huntington stopped by for a glass."

I raise a brow. "Don't tell me."

"Of course not. He's not a virgin." She starts to push up, but she doesn't have the strength.

I pretend I don't notice. I take the glass to the kitchen, fill hers, pour another for me, recycle the bottle, and take a moment to compose myself.

She's not well.

She needs help.

And she's crystal clear on what she wants from me.

Company. Only company.

No debates, no opinions on her treatment plans, no carrying her up the stairs or bringing home her groceries or cooking.

She's taking care of herself, as much as she can, as long as she can.

I can live with that, or I can leave.

By the time I step into the living room, I present a serene expression.

I place the glasses on the coffee table and sit next to her. "What are we watching?"

"*Damages.*"

"The one with the evil lawyer?"

"Everyone thinks a woman with power is evil."

"Doesn't she have people killed?" I ask.

"Okay, she's a little evil," Grandma says. "But that's what it takes to succeed."

"How'd you do so well then?"

She laughs. "I've made my share of compromises."

"Anything you regret?"

She pretends not to notice the *thoughts of a dying woman* tone to the question. "There's a lot I'd do differently, but I don't regret anything. How could I when I have you?"

This isn't like her. She's pragmatic. She moves forward. She doesn't look backward. "When did you get sentimental?"

"When I had your mother. And your aunt."

"Kids? That's what does it?"

"Yes. But it makes you painfully pragmatic, too. There's no one who fights harder to survive than a mom."

"You sure about that?" *Shit.* I'm supposed to stay away from heavy things. Not dive headfirst.

"Oh, sweetheart." She pats my shoulder. "Your mom is fighting. It's just a different battle for her."

"She *was* fighting." The first time she went to rehab. The second, too. All these years since her last slip? Not so much.

"I won't tell you she'll get there, because I don't know. But I know she loves you."

"Grandma." I don't want to get into this. I won't get into this.

"Okay," she says. "Are you going to tell me about the date?"

"It wasn't a date."

"But you were with Lexi?"

"No. Deanna."

"Deanna Huntington?" she asks.

"Do you know another?"

"The brunette who lives next door?" She can't help but be incredulous.

"It wasn't a date," I say.

"You spent the night with her, but it wasn't a date?"

"A few hours is not spending the night. But it's a long story." And I'm way too tired for this conversation. Maybe still buzzed a little, too.

"You like her," she says.

"Based on what?"

"The way you said her name."

"No." I shake my head. "I know you don't approve of my feelings for Lexi. You never have."

"They're not feelings. They're—"

"I'm not having this conversation." Not again. "I'm not here for Lexi or Deanna. I'm here for you."

Her expression gets stern. "You promised." There are a million implications. *You promised not to put your life on hold. You promised not to linger in this pain. You promised to stay away from here until you grew into a man who was over his teenage crush.*

She's right.

I'm not ready to be here. But now that I am? I'm not leaving for anything, either.

CHAPTER THIRTEEN

Deanna

The warm water of the shower washes away the remnants of the day. I let memories of negotiations and sisters who suddenly covet the boy next door drift to the back of my mind.

Kinda.

I try, okay? I'm not great at the whole *not obsessing* thing. More *doing everything I can to reach my goals*. But sleep is an important part of goals. And I won't sleep well if my mind is racing.

My skincare routine and silk pajamas help me slip into rest mode. Then I step into the living room and see Lexi sitting at the kitchen table, and I lose my tiny hint of calm.

"Deanna." She taps her heel against the hardwood floor. She's still in her party outfit (a new pink dress and one of Jake's blazers, which really doesn't say *I want to break up with you*). Even though it doesn't fit our fluorescent kitchen, she looks completely where she belongs. She always does.

"Alexandria." I copy her tone. "Is there an urgent matter to discuss?"

"How much did you drink?"

I hold up three fingers.

"Are you drunk?"

"Am I not allowed?"

"No." She sits back with a smile. "I'm surprised. Impressed, actually. I didn't think you'd let loose during pitch season."

We're always in pitch season, but then I never let loose, so she has a point.

"Do you want the play-by-play on Willa?" she asks.

"Right. Of course." Quickly, my inebriation and attempts at relaxation disappear. There's work to do. What else matters?

Lexi gives a quick explanation. She talked up our latest app tweaks, explained Jake's absence as a client emergency, and promised to show up at the investor dinner in four weeks as the picture of commitment.

"What about Jake?" I ask.

"What about him?" she asks. "He knows where we stand. And we're set to meet to talk next week. No problem."

"Wait. You're going to see him during your break?" I ask. "I thought you were taking time apart."

"Maybe we should finish this conversation in the morning," she says. "When you're sober." She lets out a hearty laugh. "I always wanted to say that to you."

"How does it feel?"

"Fantastic. No wonder you revel in it." She stands and cops a triumphant pose. "I, Alexandria Huntington, am the most sober sister in the room. For the first time in my entire life."

"Great work."

"Thank you." She smiles. "River is sweet, huh?"

"Very."

She looks at me carefully.

"He isn't like you," I say.

"Like me how?"

"He's romantic," I say.

"Dee, everyone is romantic compared to me."

"But he likes you," I say. "He really likes you. In a serious kind of way. Not a one-night-in-the-back-seat kind of way."

"I'll make sure we're on the same page," she says.

I doubt that. It's more likely she'll break his heart. Or, somehow, he'll spread the word of love and convince her relationships are great. If he's desperate to convince me, he's probably desperate to convince her, too. "What did you say to Jake anyway?" I ask. "Did you tell him you put things on pause because you wanted more physical action?"

The confidence drains from her face. "How?"

"What do you mean how?"

"How do you say that to a guy?"

Lexi doesn't know how to broach a topic? Wait. "Isn't this your expertise?"

"Relationship conversations?"

"Seduction?"

She looks to the floor. "What am I supposed to do? Put on my Horizontal Lambada playlist, pull out a bottle of wine, and tell him I want to slip into something more comfortable?"

"Is that what you normally do?"

"It's different," she says.

"How?"

"I like him."

"Then why did you break up with him?"

"Because I can't be with someone I like, who I haven't fucked," she says. "You know that."

And all at once, reality clicks into place. She's afraid of intimacy, and she uses sex to hide it.

She's afraid of getting too close to Jake. She's basically admitting it.

I feel a surge of validation. I *am* doing the right thing for her. So what if it's a little manipulative and happens to be the right thing for the app, too?

"Because I need a man who satisfies and, well, I can't risk finding out he doesn't right before we get fake engaged, can I?"

"No one is asking you to get fake engaged."

"Doesn't mean they won't," Lexi counters.

True. And her point about Jake is actually pretty logical. "Wait a few weeks and then broach the topic."

She laughs. "Oh, Dee, you'd get it if you got it. I just need some D. That's the truth of things. I need it and I can't wait, and I won't cheat, so—" She shrugs as if saying *this is what makes the most sense.*

And that's the weird thing.

It does. In a Lexi sort of way.

"How about we go out tomorrow?" she asks. "Well, I already invited River out. Fern and North are coming in. We'll go dancing. Meet some guys. I mean, with four women, how could we not? I'll even play your wing woman."

"Guys are never interested in me when you're around." No. She's distracting me. I won't be distracted. I will keep her and River apart, and I guess I have to go to do that.

"Please," she says. "Tons of guys are hot for you. They love mean brunettes."

"Hey."

"Smart brunettes."

I guess I'll take it. "Okay. Tomorrow." After I figure out all of this. Or some of it. I'm starting to lose track of her logic.

She crosses the space to hug me good night. "Sweet dreams, Dee. Dreams of D more like it. Or maybe that's me." She squeezes me one more time and releases me.

Once she leaves, I check my cell for texts from River. Nothing about the night, my sister, whether or not he's still in love with her.

But then why would he talk to me?

We're barely friends.

And we're at odds.

He wants her. I want him away from her.

Until he sees the light and realizes it's never going to happen, we're playing this game.

And he's going to lose.

Even if it kills me.

• • •

I wake with a mild headache and a moderate sense of concern. There are too many potential problems. I need to keep Lexi away from River and figure out a million technical issues with the app.

Plus, the actual dinner with investors.

A large glass of water and a six-mile run help. The shower and the enormous mug of English Breakfast seal the deal.

It's Saturday, the perfect day to disappear into the one place that makes sense: work.

I can only spare a few hours—Lexi and River are keeping me on my toes—but I need them. There's nothing better than a long, uninterrupted day of work. And the weekend is the best time for it.

There's no one at the office to interrupt.

Only me and the code and the endless supply of tea.

I slip into my pre-begging for money coding attire of combat boots and a stretchy black dress; pack my laptop bag with my computer, Kindle, water bottle, lipstick, sandwich lunch, and noise-canceling headphones; and head out.

The record playing in my head (Cheap Trick, "Surrender") scratches the second I step into the backyard.

Lexi is sitting on the patio table in shorts and a crop top, sipping coffee and talking to River.

Okay, it's not just River. It's Fern and North, too. And they're doing most of the talking.

But still.

She's smiling, and he's staring.

My stomach plummets.

It's not even eleven on a Saturday! She's usually asleep at this time. And she usually goes straight from bed to her noon Pilates class.

"Hey." Lexi waves me over with a smile. "Working hard, as always."

"Uh-huh." I approach.

"How's the hangover?" Lexi laughs. "Wow. That feels good to say. Amazing actually."

Fern, the second oldest Beau grandchild, laughs. She has the same hearty laugh Ida does. And the same effortless elegance. She's wearing a linen dress and wedge sandals, her dark hair cut short, her square face framed by her square sunglasses. "Hey, Deanna. It's been forever."

"I saw you running earlier—you looked hot in your jogging outfit," North says. She's a few years younger than Fern, in her late twenties, and she's every bit as elegant as her sister. Only in that casual, *I barely try to be this cool* way. She's in high-waisted shorts, a loose white tee, and seafoam Converse. "Do you really run every day?"

"Most days," I say.

"She swims at the gym the other days," Lexi says. "She makes me look like a slacker."

"I throw myself a parade if I walk up the hill," North says.

"Please. You go dancing for three hours straight, three times a week," Fern says. "Did she tell you she's competing now?"

"Only for fun," North says.

"Fun makes it sound like she's not talented, but she's as good as one of the dancers on that show with the celebrities," Fern says.

"Only in bachata," North says.

"And tango," Fern says. "What's the other one? The new one?"

"Are you two going to let Deanna get a word in?" River asks.

They trade a very sisterly look.

As much as I want to stop and appreciate the bonding, I can't. I have work.

"Are you heading out?" Fern asks. "That's too bad. Grandma and I are going to the beach."

"You, too?" I ask North.

"No. I'm exhausted," she says. "I got up early to beat the traffic."

"It's Saturday," Fern says.

"And I live in Los Angeles," North says. "Where there's traffic at all times."

Fern nods sympathetically. "I don't know how you stay here, Dee. This city is hopelessly uncool."

"Not living next to Ida," I say.

Lexi nods in agreement. "River and I are going, too." She smiles at me. *Look how well this is working.* "Too bad you can't join. Since you're working."

"No," I blurt out.

Everyone looks at me like I'm nuts.

It is nuts, choosing anything over work, but this is work, too.

I need to stop this, keep Lexi and River as far apart as possible. Now.

"I could use a swim." I shrug as if I don't even like working. "I can get to this later."

"You sure?" Lexi tilts her head to one side. "You look busy."

"Positive," I say.

"We're leaving in twenty minutes," River says.

"Why don't Lexi and I meet you there?" I suggest.

Lexi pouts. She was hoping to ride with him, I guess. Getting guys alone in her car is her MO.

But she nods anyway. "Sure, Dee. Let's pick out outfits." She blows River a kiss. "Until then." She leans in to whisper something in his ear.

I don't hear her, but I know what she's saying. I know because other guys have relayed the story.

She's inviting him to a make-out spot.

One where she can have her way with him.

River said he won't make a move. But he didn't promise he'd turn her down if she threw herself at him. (And even if he did, is he really strong enough to resist her?) No. I can't count on his self-control. I need to help him stick to the terms of our agreement. I need to keep him away from Lexi.

CHAPTER FOURTEEN

Deanna

Thankfully, Lexi wants to take her car. That means a detour to Depressed Mode, where we swap my car for hers (and kill almost an hour, round trip), and she agrees to my suggestion to buy snacks. And look for new bikinis at the place on Main Street in Newport.

Sure, I suffer through a dozen wardrobe changes, and I spend a few hundred dollars on a new teal bikini and a black cover-up, but I kill another hour. And, well, I look hot.

Really hot.

The sharp lines of the triangle top and the string bottom suit me.

Lexi showers me with compliments, the way she always does, then she marches back to the car, drives the rest of the way to the beach, and parks in an expensive lot.

I don't argue, even though there's a ton of street parking a mere three-quarters of a mile away. Three-quarters of a mile might as well be a million in Orange County. And, well, it's not like we can't afford it. I use the time to send Jake a *can we talk* text.

Lexi is afraid to broach the topic of sex with him, but I'm not. If I tell him she needs to see some action, he can deliver.

I've seen the man at karaoke. He has the energy to keep up with Lexi anywhere.

Even though it's a Saturday in June, the beach is still quiet. We're far enough away from both the mega surf spot, the Wedge, and the Newport Pier. The beach is mostly surfers and people watching surfers, sunning themselves, reading under umbrellas.

The families prefer to stay closer to the pier. It's mostly adults and teens here.

The Beau family is already set up near a lifeguard stand, with a blanket, an umbrella, four mesh chairs, and a cooler full of snacks and soda.

Fern spots us and waves hello.

River stands, turns, watches Lexi and me approach.

Only, instead of staring at her, he studies me. He even smiles. Not an *I want you* smile. A *game on* smile.

In his dreams.

The second we arrive at the family, Lexi strips out of her white sundress to show off her bright pink bikini.

She looks great, of course. Tan, curvy, totally comfortable in her skin. Even though she's wearing one of those cheeky bottoms with about an inch more fabric than a thong.

She bends to grab the sunscreen, offering a view of her assets to all the guys on the sand. "Could you help with my back?" She peels herself up slowly and shoots River a serene smile.

"Oh, I've got it." Fern volunteers before River has a chance to say a word. "Do you need help, too, Dee?" She motions to her brother. "River. Help Dee with her sunscreen. If she needs it."

Is she trying to push us together? Or is she simply on the same keep-River-away-from-Lexi mission?

Fern gets to work on Lexi's back. After a brief pout, Lexi sinks into their conversation. She and Fern laugh about one of the guys who used to live on our block, the one who always did push-ups in the park.

River dressed the part of the gentleman in a button-up linen shirt and European-style swim shorts. (They're *short* in the best, most deliciously thigh-baring way. Thighs. Who knew?)

He tries to play the gentleman, too, by not staring at Lexi's ass, but he doesn't quite get there.

Until he looks at me.

Then, all at once, his attention is strictly on me.

He doesn't stare the way he stares at Lexi, but I feel an intensity to his gaze all the same. A heat.

Or maybe that's the bright sun.

Why is he staring like that?

Right. Sunscreen. I pull an extra bottle from the beach bag and hold it up.

"Here?" he asks.

I lead him a few feet away. Far enough that we're out of earshot of Lexi and Fern and Ida.

"You'll have to take this off." His fingers skim the back line of my black cover-up.

It's strange. The fabric is sheer, almost transparent, but I don't want to remove it. I want to keep it as a shield.

Why do I need a shield from him?

He only has eyes for Lexi.

Only he's looking at me.

I take a deep breath and let out a steady exhale. This is good. If he wants me, even if it's strictly physical, he might realize his feelings for Lexi aren't the love he sees them as.

Maybe he'll want me enough to get caught up in the moment.

That's another way to keep him away from Lexi.

To keep him busy, with me.

I can take one for the team. Really, it's not an altogether unpleasant mental image. What would his tattooed arm look like on my hips anyway?

Or between my legs?

On my throat?

Ahem.

I blink and focus on my surroundings. The warm sand, the spray of salt water, the crash of waves, the blue-green ocean bleeding into the bright yet cloudy sky.

It all feels more intense as I pull my cover-up over my head.

He looks me over slowly. He doesn't try to hide it. Not the gaze and not the attraction.

My skin flushes. My chest and stomach and cheeks, too. I turn, so he can't see, so he gets my back.

He takes the sunscreen from my hand, squeezes a dab on his palm, and brings his fingers to my shoulder.

Slowly, he rubs the cream into my upper shoulder. The feeling of his touch is so strange. Familiar—he is my next-door neighbor—but charged with something totally unfamiliar.

An attraction.

A desire.

Is it coming from him or me?

Am I falling for the guy obsessed with my sister?

Maybe he's right about destiny, and this is mine. Forever fated to fall for the guy who loves Lexi.

I close my eyes and push the thoughts away. No. This is a normal neighbor-slash-friend thing. Sunscreen. We all need it. And he's helping.

It doesn't mean anything.

The flutter in my stomach is out of place. The goose bumps on my skin, too.

And the sheer thrill as he rubs sunscreen into my upper back—

That's nothing.

He works slowly and carefully, down my back, then he goes to my shoulders, and he says something.

I don't hear it. "Huh?"

He leans close enough to whisper. "Should I get the front, too?"

I see it immediately—his hands on my chest, my bikini top on the floor. "No. I've got it. Thanks."

He hands over the sunscreen. "Good luck."

With what? He leaves before I can ask. I watch him join Fern and Lexi's conversation as I slather lotion across my chest, stomach, legs.

After I'm fully covered, I drop the bottle in our beach bag, and I join Ida at the chairs.

We're only ten feet from the rest of the gang, but we're too far away to hear anything.

Still, I don't want to stare. I need to look at something else. The beautiful blue sky, maybe. Or the miles and miles of sand. The twenty-something guy in red board shorts and thick sunglasses, sitting at the lifeguard tower, surveying the scene.

He sits there and watches all afternoon.

A tedious job but an important one. Sure, he mostly sits there, staring at the expanses of blue. But if there's someone drowning, he needs to jump into action.

He needs to be ready at any moment.

"Are you going to watch them talk the entire morning?" Ida asks, pulling me out of my head.

"It's almost afternoon," I say.

She laughs the way River does, with the perfect mix of enthusiasm and distance. "The entire afternoon then?"

"I have a book." And the ability to put my attention elsewhere. Say, on Ms. Ida Beau. She's an amazing woman. She's even totally on trend, somehow making the Coastal Grandma white linen outfit into something sexy. And sexy in a mature way. In a way that says *I have all this knowledge and experience to impart.*

"Anything good?" She raises a brow.

"Not by your standards." I pull my Kindle from behind me and place it in her palms.

She wakes the device and scans the home screen. "None of this is dirty." She points to an especially dry business book. "Well. Maybe this."

"I told River the same thing."

"Oh?" She raises a brow.

"Spreadsheets are sexy."

This time, her laugh is soft. "We feel sexy in our element. We feel sexy when we feel competent."

Is that it?

"Usually, we think of men that way. They want to feel useful. Sometimes, to an unhealthy degree. But it's true for women, too."

"Maybe that's you," I say. "Writing about sex."

"It is me." She nods. "And it's you."

My eyes go to Lexi and Fern and River. Even with Fern right there, Lexi wraps her hand around River's arm.

She laughs as if he's the funniest guy she's ever met.

She's flirting.

She's going to keep flirting.

I need to stop her, but I'm already too tired of this.

"You're not in your element here," Ida says.

I force myself to look away, but Ms. Beau's gaze isn't any easier to take. "What are you talking about?"

"Your sister. Is she serious with that boy, Jake?"

"She was," I say. "She…"

"Has cold feet?" Ida offers.

Yeah. That's it exactly. I nod.

"I had them, too," she says. "Even though I loved Benjamin. I loved everything about him. But I wasn't sure if I wanted to be a wife. It wasn't a great time to be a wife, but that was only part of it." She looks at her grandson as he smiles back at Lexi. "There was another part, too. The same fears about forever."

That's hard to believe. "You look so happy in pictures."

"We were. I was over the moon. But the second he mentioned marriage, I felt that fear. And your sister is like me."

"Obsessed with sex?"

She laughs. "She values her freedom, but she loves him."

"She does."

"You want them together, too, don't you?"

I nod.

"So why are you sitting here?" she asks. "Keep my grandson busy for a while."

What?

She lets out an easy laugh. "I guess you need a little help." She waves to her grandkids.

Immediately, Fern and River turn to her. They drop the smiles and adopt serious, almost concerned, expressions.

Weird.

Really weird.

"River, sweetie, could you do me a favor?" she asks.

He practically runs to us.

"Don't fuss, sweetheart." She pulls her sunglasses from her bag and slides them on. "I only want a little quiet."

"Quiet?" he asks.

"Yes, you kids are too loud. Can you grab me an iced tea?" she asks. "Take Deanna with you."

He looks at me as if he's going to ask why, but he doesn't.

"And Fern, why don't you show Lexi that cute lifeguard we were talking about?" Ida suggests.

Fern laughs.

Lexi, too. "A cute lifeguard? Okay. I'm willing to bite."

Ida turns to me. "Why are you still standing there? You look like you need caffeine as much as I do."

Why is she on my side?

I don't know, but, for once, I don't question the good fortune. I jump on the chance.

I take River's arm and lead him away from the beach.

To somewhere else. Anywhere else.

As long as I keep him distracted.

CHAPTER FIFTEEN

River

Newport Beach is nothing like its name. Well, it's new money the way the name Newport suggests, but it's not quaint or cute and homey.

The residents disagree. Especially along this stretch of the beach.

This coffee shop sure is determined to call itself quaint. Hardwood floors, wicker chairs, *Surf's Up* and *Life's Better by the Beach* posters on the wall.

It's small and cute and completely full of shit. The same as the beach-going patrons sipping lattes from ceramic mugs. The same as all the coastal cities in the county.

Sure, the cities are less stuck-up closer to Los Angeles (and San Diego), but they're all expensive places, filled with wealthy people who are determined to hold onto their surfer roots. Or artistic roots, in the case of Laguna Beach.

When I first got to Huntington Hills, I stared at the wide streets and clean sidewalks with wonder. Could a place really be this beautiful, charming, peaceful?

It looked a lot like the Riverside suburb where Mom lived, but it was so much more picturesque. Not to mention cooler. It's probably ninety-five degrees in Riverside today. With the beach breeze, the seventy-something weather isn't just comfortable. It's perfect.

And, here, in this small coffee shop, with all the windows open, we're basically in paradise. If paradise is a Mediterranean climate and a bunch of suburbanites who think they're slumming it because they bought a three-year-old car.

As a kid, I marveled at the money everywhere. I'd seen it at my grandma's place, sure, but I was never there long enough to notice the Ray-Bans or wander the outdoor mall with the koi pond.

At thirteen, I loved and hated it in equal measure.

For a long time, I wanted to fit into the big, beautiful world. Lexi Huntington was my role model. She wore designer clothes, but she never called attention to them. She kept her hair and makeup perfect, but she never looked like she cared about them. She charmed guys *and* aced classes.

Deanna was too much like me. Sure, she always looked perfect, and she never showed effort, but she always stuck out like a sore thumb. She was the only girl in glasses at the beach. The only girl in black at the park. The only girl reading at the pool party.

She read *Star Wars* novels, too. She loved video games, too. She sat on the sidelines, too.

Then, she got older, and she learned how to fake it—or maybe how to remove herself from the situations where she didn't belong—and I stopped noticing.

No, I stopped looking.

The signs of her oddball nature are obvious. She's wearing a black cover-up in a room full of white and turquoise, and she stands with confidence and poise completely out of place in the pretend laid-back atmosphere.

Maybe that's it. She doesn't look like she belongs here, but she doesn't look like she gives a shit, either.

More like she's ready to make the world belong to her.

She looks fucking gorgeous.

No. Not just gorgeous.

Sexy.

Is that sheer black thing designed to drive me insane or is it a lucky side effect?

The thin fabric flows over her chest, stomach, hips, ends mid-thigh. It's just sheer enough I see the outline of her bikini, the shape of her chest, waist, hips.

Thankfully, the barista saves me from my dirty thoughts. From Deanna's, too, it looks like.

She finally manages to pull her eyes from my tattooed arm to order an English Breakfast for herself and an iced tea for Grandma. Then she goes right back to staring.

She's obsessed.

It should annoy me. It does sometimes, with other women. I'm the same person I was before the makeover. Why am I suddenly interesting, now that I wear snug jeans and rock an arm of art?

When I put the art on paper, no one cared.

Now that it's on a bicep, it's fascinating.

Not that I can fault her. The work is beautiful. A mix of classic tattoo scenes—an octopus wrapped around a ship, a sparrow surrounding a heart, a rose wrapped in thorns—only with a pop art style instead of a traditional one.

And, well, I love her stare. I love the intensity of her green eyes, the focus in her posture.

She wants me.

And I want her to want me.

The realization is strange, absurd, but I can't deny the desire thrumming in my veins.

"Sir?" The barista clears her throat and taps her seafoam apron. "Did you want anything else?"

"An English Breakfast," I say.

Deanna laughs as I pay. "What a copycat."

No. I want to taste what's on your lips.

What is wrong with me? I'm not here to flirt. I'm here to get her to admit love is real.

"You invented English Breakfast?" I ask.

"I perfected it." Her raspberry lips press into a coy smile. Her eyes brighten. Tough-as-nails, soft-as-silk Deanna Huntington.

Silk isn't soft. Silk is slick. Silk is sexy.

Don't pretend it's about softness when it's about something else entirely.

Deanna is sexy.

I'm not denying that.

And I'm not giving in to it.

This isn't fate or destiny or anything big and beautiful.

It's the two of us, settling our wager.

I wait for the drinks and join Deanna at her seat, in the corner.

"Shouldn't we get back?" I ask.

"After we fix the tea." She looks out the big wide window and watches a teenage couple stroll down the street. They're exactly the stereotype of a California couple.

Two tan, toned blondes in board shorts and Hurley tank tops. They're even wearing matching blue checkered Vans. (Started in Anaheim. Fern is obsessed with their new HQ and the checkered lining painting around the top of the building.)

"Five minutes to brew it. Then we add milk." She surveys the table. "Almond milk work for you?"

"Sure."

"Are you always easygoing?" Her intense eyes find mine.

"I want to see your idea of perfection."

"So, under normal circumstances, you'd throw the almond milk in the barista's face and say, 'I told you oat milk, dammit.'"

"Damn. And I thought I suppressed that TikTok," I say.

Her laugh is easy, comfortable. Like she's here because she wants to be here, not because she's trying to keep me from Lexi. "I can't imagine that."

"Me neither."

"Do you think Ida will mind waiting a few extra minutes? If I tell her it's for this." Deanna smiles, reaches into her bag, and pulls out a chocolate bar. "She got me into it."

Dark chocolate and tea. Grandma's favorite afternoon snack. A wave of nostalgia hits me all at once.

This is home.

The drink, the place, the people.

I hate that it's home, but it's home nonetheless.

"Aren't you worried it will melt at the beach?" I ask.

"No. I've tested the process extensively." She smiles. "With the sun, it will melt on the sand. I keep it in the cooler. Out of the sun, chocolate melts just below body temperature." She undoes the paper wrapper. Then the foil. "That's why it melts on your tongue."

Deanna Huntington melting on my tongue. The vision forms in my head immediately. Deanna, in only those boots, again, splayed over my bed, legs wrapped around my cheeks as I lick her to orgasm.

Where the hell did that come from?

I don't even see Lexi this vividly. No. Those images are soft and sweet.

Sex isn't always romantic. Grandma and I agree there.

But it should be.

And I've never felt that connection I'm supposed to have, the one that comes from pure, deep love. From finding your other half.

Deanna isn't my other half.

I don't care how much I want to touch her or taste her.

She stands to get the milk, and my thoughts go right to disarray.

She walks with confident, purposeful steps. Her long, sheer dress sways as she moves, brushing against one hip, then the other.

Brushing her long legs.

Begging for my hands.

She turns to me, smiling as she holds up a pitcher of cream. She notices immediately.

I'm staring.

I want her.

I *need* her.

The knowledge spreads over her face slowly. A confidence in her eyes. A curl of her lips. A blush on her cheeks.

She's nervous and sure at once.

And it's way too sexy.

Uh-uh. No way. Thoughts in line. Now.

Deanna moves back to the table and sits without a word about my stare. She pours a splash of tea into her cup, tastes, approves.

Then a little milk in each cup.

The rest of the tea.

She holds up her cup to toast. "To a perfect ritual."

I tap my glass with hers, bring the porcelain to my lips, and take a sip.

The drink is better than I expect for a coffee shop. Robust and creamy, with that hint of honey and malt. An excellent English Breakfast.

"Perfect?" she asks.

My eyes flit to the lipstick marking her cup. This time, it isn't just right. It's human. "Not quite."

She breaks off two squares of chocolate and hands one to me. "Now?"

I let the treat melt on my tongue. It's good chocolate. Rich and fruity, with just enough sugar to cut the bitterness.

Perfect for her, really.

"Now," I agree.

She smiles with pride and satisfaction.

Is that how she smiles when her partner comes? When *she* comes?

Now that's a mental image.

Deanna, in my lap, in that sheer black cover-up, with nothing under it, head thrown back, eyes closed, lips parting with a low, deep groan.

She lets out a low, deep groan as she tastes the chocolate.

I pinch myself to make sure I'm awake. I am. She's here, across from me, gorgeous in the sunlight.

And she's actually groaning like she's about to come. All right, her groan is reasonable for a woman in need. Too reasonable.

It's my head, my desire to watch her experience every kind of pleasure, to give her every kind of pleasure.

No.

She's here for a reason, but I have a cause, too. If she can work me, I can work her.

"Why did you start your company?" I ask.

"Shouldn't we head back?" she asks. "Your grandma needs her tea, too."

Probably. "You'll still have to answer."

"Okay."

"After I use the bathroom."

She nods.

I stand and move to the back of the shop. The door is locked. And my thoughts are way too eager to return to her groan.

I pull out my cell for a distraction. The comic I'm reading maybe.

Only there are two sets of texts waiting for me. One from my sisters and one from Grandma.

I look at my sisters' first.

North: *We don't have official family meetings, River. We use chat, like normal people.*

Fern: *We're glad you're here, but we have a system in place. You know Grandma. She hates that any of us know. She won't accept help.*

North: *She's even more stubborn than you.*

Fern: *Me or him?*

North: *Who would be more stubborn than you, Fern?*

Fern: *Um, rude. But, yes, we do have a system, alternating weeks. Me, North, Mom, Dad, and a few of Grandma's friends. We're glad you're here but we don't need to rework the system.*

North: *As long as you're here, you can pick up my weeks. I can't always make it from LA with everything happening at home.*

They don't expect me to stay. They don't trust me with it. Maybe it's normal older sibling stuff, but it's bullshit. I bought a ticket the second I knew.

I reply with an *I've got it* and look at my messages from Grandma.

Grandma: *Change of plans, sweetheart. I don't need the iced tea anymore. I'm heading to another spot with Lexi and Fern. We took Lexi's car. You can use mine. But I don't want to hear from you until six. Unless it's really an emergency.*

River: *If I need something at home?*

Grandma: *You have a change of clothes in the car. Love you, sweetheart. Have fun.*

And that's it.

Subject over.

Am I really fussing too much or is this some strange attempt to matchmake me and Deanna?

That's not Grandma's style, but this isn't, either.

What the hell is she doing?

The bathroom opens. The previous occupant leaves. I step inside the small space and put my phone away.

This is some kind of setup, yes, but I can use it to my advantage.

CHAPTER SIXTEEN

River

The coffee shop is the same as it was a moment ago, but it all feels different. The windows still let in the sunlight and the beach breeze and the hum of traffic and conversation. Deanna is still sitting at the corner table, poised and powerful, sipping tea as she stares at the quiet street.

She's still beautiful in ways I can explain as an artist.

Only she's also appealing in a way I can't explain. The way Lexi was. *Is*.

She doesn't glow to the same extent her sister does. She's not the sun. She's the moon. Even in the daylight. She's soft and shimmering and mysterious.

She breaks a square of chocolate, places it on her tongue, lets out a soft sigh. An *I need this* sigh. An *I need you* sigh.

It's been too long.

I'm not usually a slave to my body's demands. I don't ignore my physical needs to the extent Deanna clearly does, but I tame them to focus on what matters.

Right now, they're leading.

My body wants hers and that's the only thing that matters.

I roll my shoulders as I approach the table. We're here, for the afternoon.

I can enjoy that.

I will enjoy it.

Maybe she's as correct as I am. Right now, I don't feel a pull to Lexi. Right now, I want to be here. With Deanna.

She stirs as I slide into the seat across from her.

"Grandma ditched us," I say.

She laughs. "Did she find someone to take home?"

"Something like that."

She takes a long sip of her tea. Lets out another sigh of pure, deep pleasure.

My body whines in response. It's out of patience. It's ready to be inside her.

Not happening.

I need to focus on something else. Anything else. Say, my mission here. "Do you want to believe in love?"

"So we're starting with softballs?"

My laugh is easy on my tongue, but it does nothing to erase the sexual tension in the air.

It hits a whole other nerve.

"You don't like small talk," I say.

She nods. "It would make my life easier. I wouldn't have to give investors a speech about my parents' perfect marriage and my drive to help other people find the same."

"It isn't true?"

"Nothing is perfect."

"Besides the tea," I say.

"Even that." She takes a long sip. "But the imperfections make it more perfect."

I get that. "It's the same in art. The imperfections are what make something beautiful. Like this." I brush a hair behind her ear.

She turns her head to one side, soaking up the gesture.

"The way your hair is always falling to your cheek, defying your attempt to keep it in a neat line."

"That's beautiful?" she asks.

Sexy as fuck. "Very."

"I'm not sure most people would call that an imperfection."

"Most people don't know someone as put together as Deanna Huntington."

She holds my gaze. "Is that a compliment or an insult?"

"An observation."

"I'm not as tough as I look." She takes another sip of tea. "It fools people. It fools Lexi and Dad. And it fooled my ex-boyfriend, too."

"Stephan?"

She nods. "He wanted someone softer. Someone with vulnerability. It was there. It was always there. He just didn't see it."

"Maybe you didn't let him."

She doesn't respond to the accusation. "That's why I made the app." She laughs. "It sounds pathetic, that way. I made the app because I got dumped."

"Like Stevie Nicks."

She raises a brow.

"Turning your pain into success."

"I guess so." Her smile is sad. "I wish I could tell Mom that. 'Look, I'm doing a Fleetwood Mac. I'm taking my heartbreak and spinning it into gold.' You don't spin gold. Silk. Something. I don't know." She looks out the window, watching the world outside.

"You miss her?"

"Every day. People think money buys happiness. And money is great. You know that. You didn't always have this life. Before you moved in with Ida…"

I nod. I grew up with a very different life. Even though we were only fifty miles away, we were on another planet. One with small apartments and overdue bills and store-brand mac n' cheese for dinner.

"I know your grandma isn't rich the way my dad is rich. She

bought the house a long time ago, before it was worth millions. And it's one lot. Not three." She laughs. "Did Dad ever tell you that? How the city was willing to build a property over two lots, but not three?"

"When would he tell me that?"

She nods as if to say *right*. "He's used to getting what he wants. And he was that way with Mom, but he was different, too. He wanted what she wanted. And she wanted what he wanted."

"They never clashed?"

"They clashed, sure, but they never let it get to them. Or maybe I was too young to see it. Maybe they hid it well. I don't know." She breaks off another square of chocolate. "What the hell was I just saying?"

"Your dad didn't hand you the keys to the kingdom."

"Right. Yeah. He didn't offer us a job at his business."

I didn't know that. "Isn't that what old money families do?"

"We're only old money by West Coast standards."

She really believes that she didn't inherit the world.

"You think I'm a spoiled rich girl," she says.

"I didn't say that."

"Well, I am spoiled. I complain about my sixty-thousand-dollar car all the time. I send Lexi texts when I buy something that breaks too soon. I try to buy from other start-ups, women-owned start-ups, whether they price high or low. Some have great products. Some don't."

"Saving the world through wardrobe upgrades."

"Women do more than make clothes," she says.

"Sorry. Am I a sexist asshole?"

"A little." She lets out a soft laugh. "Beauty and clothing are big markets. And it's easier for women to succeed there. They're not taken seriously, but investors don't take the categories seriously either, so." She shrugs.

"You don't get an advantage as Deanna *Huntington*?"

She pauses, then says, "I'm sure I do. But it's not like in the movies. Dad didn't ask me to take over the company. He made it clear I was not welcome to take over the company. I'm sure he would have found a spot, if I really needed one, and he did introduce me to a lot of people. I'm sure some of them helped because of my last name. But a lot of them ignored me because of my gender, too."

"I can't imagine that."

"Because you're not a woman," she says.

"I can't imagine anyone not seeing the sheer strength of your will," I clarify.

Her cheeks flush. "Apparently, it's easy to miss."

That's not possible. She radiates strength, power, grace.

"When I was younger, people assumed I was another trust fund baby. They thought I was killing time until I inherited a fortune."

"Did he help with the company?" I ask.

"No," she says. "He said we needed to try doing something on our own. Maybe he'd bail us out if we really needed it. I don't think so. I think he'd want us to learn from our failure."

"I can't see that."

"You don't know him," she says. "He's got a hard-knock-life side."

"No ponies?" I joke.

"Where would I ride a pony?" She laughs. "Do you see me as that much of a cliché?"

"I thought you lived a charmed life, sure, but I knew you worked at it, too." I ignored it sometimes because it reminded me of how hard I worked at everything. Because she made the work look effortless, and I felt like I was trying all the time. "I can't imagine you killing time. Dominating time, maybe."

She blushes.

My cock stirs. It's sexy, yes, but more than that, it's adorable. Tough as nails, always in control Deanna, blushing at my words.

She's beautiful. I didn't expect that to move me as much as

it does. I didn't expect to find her as sexy as I do.

But I really didn't expect to feel this pull toward her. To want to hear her laugh again and again. To crave the sight of her smile. To adore the flush of her cheeks.

I want to make her blush again and again.

For hours.

For days.

I want to be the one who can knock this strong, confident woman off balance. I want to see her find her center again. I want to watch her grow.

"I didn't mean that." Sort of.

"Dirty mind."

"Really?"

"You've never noticed?" she asks.

"Not until recently."

"Telling a guy you tied up your ex tends to do that."

"Has it come up with other men?" I ask.

"On dates, yeah," she says. "I go out all the time for the app."

My stomach churns. I don't like the mental image of her with some guy in a suit, leaning in to whisper, *I can do a lot with that tie. You want to go to my place and find out?*

It's a ridiculous image. It's not her at all. But I can't rid myself of the picture.

Deanna, with some tech billionaire, making out in the elevator to his penthouse, lying in bed after athletic sex, bonding over the difficulties of running a company.

She notices my distaste. "I don't throw it out there on the first date. 'By the way, my ex was kinky.' But it comes up sometimes on the second or third date."

"You're going on second and third dates?"

"A few times," she says.

"Do you sleep with those guys?"

"Softballs, huh?"

"The balls maybe."

She laughs. "You sound like Lexi." At the mention of her sister, she loses all the brightness in her expression. It's like she suddenly remembers why we're here, that I'm meant to be with Lexi.

It doesn't feel as obvious as it normally does.

I tell myself this is a physical reaction, that's all, but I don't quite believe it. And I don't know how to feel about that.

"I'm not going to judge you for it," I say.

"I know. You wouldn't adore Lexi if you judged women for sleeping around." She swallows a sip of tea. "No. I haven't slept with any of them. Not because I'm following some sort of rule."

"People still do the three-date rule?"

"I don't know. I don't think anyone ever did it. The average is a lot higher."

I smile.

"What?"

"You're always using data to explain your decisions."

She gives me a look. "What else would I do?"

"What feels right."

"Using data feels right," she says. "Rules feel right. They keep you safe. They keep you from doing something stupid."

"But you didn't have a rule."

"Nothing on the first date," she says. "That was my only rule. Not that I ever wanted to break it. I've never felt like I could trust a guy I just met. Even if we've been talking for a bit."

"That's smart."

She sighs. "I don't know how people do it," she says. "Casual sex. Even once I get past the whole *this guy might be an axe murderer* stage, I don't feel safe enough to really trust someone with my body. My needs."

"You haven't slept with any of the guys?"

"One of them," she admits.

"How was it?"

"Guess."

"So good you wanted another date?" I grin.

She shakes her head.

"What was bad about it?"

"Nothing was bad. It just wasn't good." She looks to the window and my gaze follows for a moment. There's a young couple stopped at a streetlight, staring into each other's eyes. "It's never been that good for me," she says, pulling her attention back to me. "Not the way it is in your grandma's books."

"It's hard to compete with fiction."

"It's not that…" She shakes her head. "I don't go in expecting a fantasy. Just the sort of respect for power and strength the men claim to have."

"And what happens?"

"Guys feel emasculated by my success," she says. "Or they think it makes me less sexy somehow."

Clearly she's been dating the wrong men. "Maybe they're not man enough to handle you."

She scoffs. "Now you sound like one of those guys…what are they called? The assholes with the faux psychology term?"

"Alphahole."

"Exactly."

I smile. "Describes me to a T."

Her eyes go to the tattoo on my arm. Then her fingers. A soft brush of my wrist.

My entire body roars to attention.

She catches herself touching me, but she doesn't stop. She traces the line. "Sometimes, they're guys in a suit. Sometimes they're bad boys. With tattoos."

"That is the perfect way to describe me," I joke.

"A tattooed bad boy. Watch out, Orange County."

"Is that all it takes? Tattoos?"

"I think so, yeah." She traces the line up my arm. "Here, anyway. There isn't a single tattoo shop in Irvine, Newport, or Huntington Hills. The Irvine company would never allow it. And the Huntington company isn't about to let the Irvine company outclass them."

She continues tracing the line up to my bicep.

I squeeze my hand to keep myself from letting out an audible reaction to her touch, then turn my arm over to give her a better view.

"What do you call this style?" Her fingers are on the sparrow woven into the sleeve.

"The artist called it pop-classic."

"Of course." She laughs. "The future head of Marvel Studios needs comic-inspired ink."

Marvel. *Right.* "I don't dream that big."

"You do, too. It's just different. You want to run your own small press. Publish cult classic comics."

"I do." How the hell did she guess that? No one guesses that. Even though it feels obvious to me. It's not the most original goal for a graphic novelist. Especially not one who works for a large press. There's a lot I love about my job. I still work with artists and writers. I still bring their stories to life. But I rarely bring a fresh, exciting idea to the world. Mostly, we publish long-running franchises and big-budget cash-ins. There are good graphic novelizations. There are good TV shows and movies turned into comics. But we end up putting out a lot of books of fan service. Nothing new, unique, challenging.

"You'd be good at it, I think," she says. "Working with artists, developing stories. Why don't you do it? Your grandma must have the money. She's always talking about her nest egg and how she wants to live rich, die broke."

All at once, the air leaves the room.

Grandma's death.

Grandma's health.

My whole body tenses.

Deanna must notice—she's still got her hand on my arm—but she doesn't say anything about it.

I jump onto the opposite topic. Life. Our wager. "Have you ever felt passionate about someone?"

Her eyes go wide, and she retracts her hand. Her lips curl. "Why?"

"Maybe that's why you don't see love as something romantic and magical."

She looks at me funny, like she's not sure why I'm changing the topic, but again, she doesn't press. "Maybe. But I don't see how you're going to fix it."

I do. I see, in vivid Technicolor, a thousand scenarios. Deanna and I in the back seat of her Tesla, her teal minidress pushed to her waist, her arms wrapped around me. Deanna laughing as we hurry back home.

Deanna splayed over her bed in some fancy silk chemise.

Deanna in *my* room, in *my* bed, in nothing but her boots.

The room here, at Grandma's house.

Then the one in New York.

I see her there. All over the apartment. On the leather couch, reading a book. Sitting on the windowsill, staring at the city as she brainstorms. Taking a business call in the kitchen.

Naked in the shower.

Naked in every inch of the place.

"Unless you're going to hire someone," she says. "A professional."

"When was it the best?" I shouldn't ask. I shouldn't dive into these waters, but I can't linger on the other topic, either. "With who?"

"No. I'm not telling you that one."

"That's not our deal."

"Our deal is love, not sex. But if you want info, you have to give info. Your best. Ever."

That's the thing.

I don't have a best, either. Most of my sex is good. Very good. But it never feels like the movies, like an erotic romance, like a love song.

Physically, it satisfies.

Emotionally, not so much.

Because I've never been in love. Because my heart has always been devoted to Lexi.

Only, right now, my body argues for me.

It would feel different with Deanna.

It would feel fucking fantastic.

She leans closer.

My heartbeat picks up.

My blood rushes south.

My brain knows she's not about to whisper *let's dive into the ocean, take off our swimsuits, and fuck right there on the beach,* but my body is far too tuned in to the proximity.

She smells good, like oranges and sunshine. No. Not sunshine. Sunscreen. All this time in New York, and I'm still a California boy, deep down. Still turned on by the scents of sunscreen and chlorine.

"Do we need to talk somewhere more private?" She nods to a mom reading a paperback while her young daughter plays on an iPad.

"The waves are loud." The words barely form on my tongue. I don't want to move. I want to stay close to her. And I want to drag her to the car and dive between her legs.

"Too many people," I say.

"The secret beach." Lexi's secret beach. Where she invited me, earlier today.

Already, the scene feels fuzzy. I can't imagine the bubbly blonde. I can't see the two of us together.

"It's not that secret," Deanna says.

"We'll have to swim until no one can hear."

She lets out a loud laugh. "Are you daring me?"

"Do you see everything as a dare? Or a bet?"

"You already know the answer to that."

Instantly, my head finishes the sentence. *I dare you to strip naked and run into the waves with me. I dare you to take me home and have your way with me. I dare you to kiss me.*

That feels more intimate than any other mental image.

And, for the first time in a long time, I want it in a way I haven't wanted anything. Not even Lexi.

There's something wrong with me.

Really wrong with me.

And, right now, I'm ready to run straight to it.

CHAPTER SEVENTEEN

River

Deanna laughs as a candy-coated pop song spills from the stereo. We're in Grandma's car, melting from the heat of the sun, with a twenty-minute drive on our hands.

Twenty minutes until the cold water of the Pacific.

I need it now. I need something to keep my senses.

I pull out of the parking lot and onto PCH. It's a straight shot for most of the way, only there's traffic. Not July or August traffic, but enough to notice the rows of two-story houses lining the road.

Deanna doesn't look out the window. She doesn't notice the bright blue sky, the puffy clouds, the signs for the massive outdoor mall Fashion Island.

She stays here, with me. "Is this music your choice? Or Ida's?"

"Grandma's."

"I'm not sure which seems less likely: you or Ida loving girly pop."

"Her," I say.

Deanna nods. "She's tough."

"Tough people have soft sides."

She blushes, and my entire body buzzes.

The air conditioning isn't working fast enough. I turn it up, and it whirs so loudly it blocks out the music, but it doesn't help.

Deanna's blush is far too sexy. "You know I live and die by seventies folk-rock. But I don't know what sort of music you like."

She doesn't. No one does, really. I don't blast jams. I don't even listen to my favorites. Not often.

Not because I don't love them—I do.

I just hate the places my head goes.

"Let me guess. Video game soundtracks." She laughs at herself. "Or John Williams. The *Star Wars* score, of course. And *Jurassic Park*."

"No."

"Oh, I know." She laughs again and her eyes light up. Suddenly, she notices the brightness filling the car and finds her sunglasses in her purse. "Those guys with guitars who sing about their broken hearts."

"All music by men?" I ask.

"No. The ones who are sensitive," she says. "Like, uh, what's his name...Ed Sheeran."

Now I'm the one laughing. "You think I'm that obvious?"

"We're all obvious sometimes."

That's true. But it's also not true. Sure, I might guess Deanna loves fancy dark chocolate. I might even guess she loves the beach—she is from California after all. But I'd never guess her love of Fleetwood Mac or her need to prove herself worthy of her dad's power and influence or her softness. "Is that it?" I reach for something to steady me. "You had a crush on Ed Sheeran?"

"Not him. But a few guys with guitars. I think it's the law. All teenage girls fall for at least one guy with a guitar."

"I can play guitar." Where did that come from?

"I remember," she says. "You used to play 'Wonderwall.'"

"It's a good song."

"It's kind of a sensitive guy cliche."

"And I suppose you're too sophisticated to enjoy the song?"

"No," she admits. "It's a good song. And you sang it well, too."

Oh, *hell*.

She heard me singing.

I feel cracked wide open. On display. Naked—only I'd feel a hundred times less exposed without my clothes.

"Is that the kind of music you like?" she asks. "The soft nineties rock."

I swallow hard. I force my eyes to the street. The traffic is moving fast now. The ride is easy. "Do you like it?"

"No," she admits. "It's too sincere. I like witty lyrics. The guys who have sharp tongues."

"Sounds painful."

"The Lexi-isms don't suit you," she says bluntly. "I don't believe your head is going straight to sex."

It is. Thank fuck it isn't showing.

"Why are you dodging?" she asks.

I'm not. She's dodging. Okay, maybe I'm dodging, but she is, too. "You prefer the guys who pretend they don't have pain."

"You could say it that way."

"Because you connect more with them than the people who run to their pain."

"Who does that?" she asks. "It defies human nature."

"What about Fleetwood Mac?" I counter.

"It's different that way," she says. "She's working through it, not reveling in it. Or maybe it's the same. I don't know. Maybe I love it because my mom loved it and it's not more complicated than that."

Maybe. I could see that. "And you love these guys because you relate to them."

"Yeah." Her eyes fill with surprise. She doesn't understand how I see her.

I don't, either, to be honest.

"I wanted a few guys when I was really young," she says. "Then I moved on fast. To preferring a vision of us as peers."

A laugh spills from my lips. "And how did a programmer relate to a musician?"

"Music is all math," she says. "Patterns. Musicians understand that intuitively, not analytically, but they understand it all the same."

"And the cheeky lyrics?"

"Well…" Again, she blushes.

And again, my body begs me to pull the car over and have her right here, in the parking lot of the small chain market, in broad daylight, with enough onlookers we're sure to face arrest.

"I thought I liked witty guys," she says. "But I tried them. I manually adjusted the algorithm to test it. To see if I did like witty guys."

"How do you measure wit?"

"A combination of message text, interests, and questions. We tag people's favorite movies, TV, songs. Well, we've got songs okay, but we're struggling with movies and TV. With humor especially. It's subjective."

"So, if guys like these witty artists, they get points in witty?"

"That's the simple explanation," she says. "There's an element of machine learning, too, where the AI learns from what is working and uses that. But I overrode all that. I added a filter so I'd only match with witty guys."

Wow. "And?"

"I liked some of them, on the first date," she says. "But by the third, I was tired of them. They were so determined to prove they were smarter than I was, funnier. You know there's this saying that when women say a man has a good sense of humor, they mean 'he makes me laugh,' but when men say it, they mean 'she laughs at my jokes.'"

I believe that.

"And I like someone who makes me laugh, but I don't want it to be a competition."

"I don't believe that."

"Really."

"No." I shake my head. "You can't turn your competitiveness off."

"I can, too."

"I won't make a bet, because it would only prove my point."

She smiles. "It would, I guess." She settles into her seat, easy, happy, in tune with the music and the sunshine. And me. "What kind of music do you like?"

No. Not yet. "Do you think those guys are romantic, deep down? The lyricists? Maybe that's why they're so cheeky and guarded?"

"No, but I can see why you'd say that." She turns the stereo down and looks to me. "And you probably don't see it, and I don't know why I'm admitting it, but I started to hate those guys because I saw the worst of myself in them."

This is good. Useful for my mission.

Only I don't really care about my mission at the moment.

"I always want to feel like the smartest person in the room. It's not a great trait. Maybe it has benefits, but it's got a lot of drawbacks. Especially in my world. Rich men want to feel like the smartest person in the room. I really had to learn to bite my tongue."

"That's hard to imagine."

"It was hard to do," she admits. "A lot of my exes hated it… that I was so concerned with intelligence, so logical. I don't know. I love my brain, but I get tired sometimes. I want to turn it off. I'm sure they get annoyed, too."

It's not annoying. It's fucking beautiful.

No. I don't want to say that. Maybe it's annoying, but it's beautiful anyway. That's what a real relationship is: seeing all the parts of someone, not just the easy ones.

I never notice women's flaws. Not when we first start dating. I only see the pretty parts. Then I fall, fast, and I hit the ground and notice all the issues. The tendency to stay out late, the lack of interest in art, the inability to clean up after themselves. There's always something. A lot of things.

No one ever compares to the vision of perfect love in my head.

And Deanna doesn't, either.

But right now, I can't form that vision. Only a fractured, messy, imperfect one with a fractured, messy, imperfect person.

Which makes me want to tell her something I've never told anyone. "I like my mom's music, too."

She notices the change in the mood. My mom isn't exactly a frequent or fun topic.

I want to know all of her, especially the parts she hides, the things she deems too ugly for public consumption.

"Nineties rock," I say. "Nirvana, Soundgarden, Hole, Bikini Kill. Smaller bands no one remembers." The odes to heroin that pass as love songs. They're salt on the wound, and I'm addicted to punishing myself with them.

She waits for me to continue.

I don't.

For a few minutes, we let Grandma's pop song fill the car. It fades to the next, to something softer, a ballad.

I take the twisty streets, park a few blocks from the secret beach, on a hill filled with houses just like the ones on our block. Big, symmetrical mansions in shades of blue and white and beige and sand.

Deanna waits until we step out of the car. Until we walk along the clean sidewalk, through the hidden path, to the small beach.

She looks at the kids in the dark water, the families on the sand, the teenagers listening to music on a shared pair of headphones.

This is a small beach. More of a cove or a bay, really. The size of the Huntingtons' house. Less crowded than the long expanse on the other side of Newport Harbor—from the wedge all the way to Seal Beach.

This is tiny. Cliffs on both sides. A minimal view of the rest of the coast.

A space for us.

Ours.

It belongs to all these other people, too, but it feels like it's ours, all the same.

"Do you think about her a lot?" She steps onto the sand and finds a spot for her bag. "Your mom?"

"Sometimes."

"Are you in touch?"

"Sometimes."

She looks at the ocean, watching the sun glimmer off the waves. "Is that too personal?"

"We're supposed to talk about sex. That's why we came all the way out here, where no one will hear us."

She doesn't call me on dodging the question. "We will. But we have to do this first." She motions to the water. "Swim."

I can't help a grin. "After you."

CHAPTER EIGHTEEN

River

Deanna shatters my previous image of her in one moment. She takes my hand, races to the waves, and squeals as she jumps into the cold water.

She releases her grip, wades to her waist, dives under a wave.

She emerges with a come-hither expression that sends my blood racing south. The Pacific Ocean is no match for the appeal of Deanna Huntington.

Maybe in January.

But on a warm June day, it doesn't stand a chance.

She looks way too good in that teal bikini. All long, lean curves, short wet hair sticking to her cheeks, water dripping off her chin and chest.

Even though her makeup stays perfect, she shows a tiny sign of vulnerability. It's not her clothes, her grooming, her posture even.

It's the way she looks at me like she'll die if I don't join her.

She wants me.

There's no way she's faking that enthusiasm.

She offers her hand again. "Are you going to stand there? Or have fun?"

"This is fun." Too fun. There's something primal about

watching her in the water. In the big, beautiful ocean, the source of life and danger for half the planet. The two most powerful forces in the world: the Pacific and Deanna Huntington.

My body wants both.

I want to feel her against me, slick and soft and pliable.

Get a grip.

She blushes as she catches me staring, but she doesn't call me on it. She smiles and dives under the water, graceful and gorgeous and utterly in her element.

She loses herself in the motions. The way she loses herself during sex.

No. The way she *should* lose herself during sex. The way someone needs to help her lose herself during sex.

I need it, too.

It's been too long. And it's never been what I wanted. It could with her. For some reason, I believe that. But this is complicated. Too complicated.

The thought dissolves as Deanna emerges from the water and motions *come here* with her first two fingers.

That's what I need. Everything I need.

I follow her deeper, wading into the waves.

Deeper.

Everyone who grows up in this neighborhood learns to swim well.

Mom made sure I had lessons, but she didn't send me to summer practices or take me to the beach. I didn't spend much time in the water until I moved in with Grandma, and by then, I was too old to learn it in my bones.

I lack Deanna's grace, but I still feel in my element. It's a rare feeling for me, especially in California, especially at the beach.

This isn't my place.

It's not the cool water or the warm sun or the murmur of family fun.

It's her.

I wade to her, then I kick off the sand and I swim.

She watches me approach with interest in her eyes.

"We're somewhere private." I reach her. "Time to spill."

She smiles and places her hand on my shoulder. "Can you reach the bottom?"

"I'm only an inch taller than you." Not that I mind. There's something about being the same height. We align in just the right way.

She towers over me in her higher heels, but I don't mind that, either.

She's beautiful and powerful. She should show it.

If she wants to wear heels to drink or dance, I'm not going to deny her.

Get a grip. Now.

The water is cold, but it's not cold enough, not even up to my neck.

The brush of her hand pulls me back to the moment.

Deanna slips her arm around my neck. "Comfortable?"

"You're the stronger swimmer."

She grins. "What happened to the chivalry?"

"I don't remember offering chivalry."

"You used to draw all those knights and princesses and dragons."

"Used to," I say.

"You wanted to do the art on Magic cards."

I did. "You noticed?"

She nods and smiles. "Why did you stop?"

"My tastes changed." Intent drops into the words. My tastes changed. In art. In food. In alcohol. In *her*.

"I can carry you." She moves closer. Her thigh brushes my hip. Her feet brush my back. "If you need the help."

Slowly, she hooks her legs around my waist.

She keeps a few inches of water between us.

I hate those inches.

I need those inches.

I bring my hand to her lower back and pull her closer.

Two inches between us.

One.

One half.

Bit by bit, her body sinks into mine. Her pelvis, her stomach, her chest.

In the water, we're both slippery. I have to work to hold onto her.

I want to work to hold onto her.

Here.

Everywhere.

I don't remember why we're here anymore. I don't remember our wager or my ulterior motives. Or hers.

None of that matters.

The interest in her eyes, the softness of her skin, the need in her expression—

That's the only thing that matters.

This is the Deanna no one else knows. The woman who misses her mom, who wants to understand love, who never shows anyone else where she hurts.

I want to see.

I want to see everything.

I don't know how to say it, so I pull her closer. The water fights me, tries to pull us out to sea, to crash us into the shore.

Again and again, I pull her closer.

"It's easier if you don't fight the current." She releases me enough to sway with the water.

I sway back toward her. Then away. Back and forth. Always coming closer. Never touching. "Deanna Huntington is giving me a lesson in surrender?"

"It's not a metaphor," she says. "It's a technique."

It is, though. It explains everything. "You're dodging the topic."

"Why do you care what I think of love anyway?" she asks. "Do you really believe in this mission? Do you really see that future? Can you picture it?"

"What future?" I ask.

"Lexi."

The word feels wrong. It steals the warmth from the air.

Yesterday, the answer was obvious. Now, it's murky. Strange.

"How would I picture her?" I ask.

"What do you picture, when you think about your life?" She looks into my eyes, all softness and curiosity. "Art on the walls of the MoMA? A graphic novel series? A penthouse downtown?"

"Straight to material things?"

She shakes her head, still soft. "A home. Decorated with art, probably. That guy who does the comic-inspired stuff."

"I have four Lichtenstein prints in my room at Grandma's."

She smiles and digs her fingers into my shoulders. "Do you see that?"

Right now? I dream about Grandma getting better, sticking around for a long time. "What do you imagine, Deanna?"

"Why?"

"I need an example," I say.

"I'm not a dreamer."

"Then as close as you get."

She nods and sways along with the water.

For a long moment, we stay there, in the cold water and the warm sun, comfortable with the silence between us, the strange mix of tension and closeness.

There is something here, something I don't understand.

"Sometimes, I visualize," she says. "I didn't believe in it at first, but my therapist, the one I saw after Mom died, talked me into trying it. I always feel silly when I do it, but it helps with nerves."

It's not hard to imagine her nervous. Not right now.

I can see Deanna in her car before a date, fixing her lipstick again and again, wondering if the guy is going to make her laugh.

In some big modern office before a meeting, rallying all her confidence, trying to figure out how she can convince a man who doesn't take her seriously to consider her company.

"Before our last investor meeting, before I met Lexi to drive to her office, well, while I was still in my room, at home. I sat there in my magenta suit, trying to imagine it going well. The meeting in the conference room at first. A lot of interest from Willa. She's a woman in her fifties, a VC, venture capitalist, with all sorts of power. I imagined her taking us out for drinks to celebrate. Then I started looking bigger. Millions of users. Tens of millions in monthly payments. Features in famous papers, appearances on morning news shows, a billboard in Times Square."

"I can picture you there."

"Overwhelmed by people?"

"And pride," I say.

"And Lexi, right there, next to me, loving every second of it."

Lexi again. She still feels wrong, here. Too much light, too much sun. Like putting a hat on a hat.

The mental images of a future with Lexi are far away. Clouded by the vivid images of Deanna. In that magenta suit, on a midtown street, holding an old-school briefcase and telling off the guy on the other end of the phone.

"You'd look good there," I say.

"In a magenta suit."

There's something intimate about sharing a mental image. Like sharing a bed. "And an 'I Heart New York' T-shirt."

"Never." She pushes off me.

My body feels cold immediately. I want her closer. I want all this.

"Your turn." She treads water a few feet away, waiting. She swims back to me. This time, she wraps herself around me quickly. "I can say please."

"Can you?"

"Please, River. Tell me a dream."

I laugh. "Was it hard to say that sincerely?"

"It's a little cheesy for me, yeah." She curls her fingers into my back again. "But I want to know."

She does.

She's interested in me. My needs, my wants, my future.

It's not the romantic or sexual interest I expect. I'm not sure what it is. Only how much I love it.

"I dream about Grandma walking me down the aisle," I say. "Sometimes, I see the woman I'm dating." There were times it was Lexi. A lot, even. She was the princess in the fairy tale. It was easy to imagine her in a giant wedding dress. In an elegant ballroom. The sort of place a Huntington belongs.

For a moment, I see it. The tiara in her blond hair, the seamed bodice, the huge skirt.

Then the image shifts, and I see Deanna in a modern silk dress. A sheath with a deep V-neck and a low back. All long and elegant and understated and powerful.

A ballroom at first. Then a rooftop bar. Some place in midtown. On a day like today.

Well, the New York version. Humid and hot—too hot for a suit and a silk gown—but perfect nonetheless.

Sunset, twinkling lights, champagne toasts.

Grandma, beaming with pride as I dance with my wife.

"Other times?" she asks.

"Sometimes, it's no one in particular. A vision of a life I'm supposed to have." The image is too vivid. Way too vivid. I look at her. At the scene. Deanna, up to her neck in water, in the Pacific.

Only that fits, too. I can see the two of us on the beach. The same outfits. Or something breezier. A chiffon dress and a linen suit. New York elegance in California.

She belongs here, yes, but she'd belong there more.

A few weeks ago, I would have said Deanna fits anywhere. But she doesn't. She just doesn't care as much as other people do.

"You want to get married?" she asks.

"I do."

"Kids?"

"I don't know." My relationship with my parental figures is complicated. I love Grandma, but I don't want to be anything like my mom or my dad. Not as a parent. Addiction has genetic influences. I'm careful around alcohol. I never dabble in drugs.

I don't want to give that to a kid.

"Do you?" I push the question back to her.

"I thought I did, when I was younger," she says. "Now, I'm not sure. Work is always first, and I like things that way. I like waking up, knowing I can go into the office if I want, or stare at code all night. I don't want to do that to a kid. I know what it's like to grow up with a parent who doesn't put you first, no matter how much they might want to."

"It's hard," I say.

She nods. "Describe it to me. The wedding you're dreaming about."

"It's different, at different times."

"The last time, then."

When I heard the news about Grandma. It was about six months ago now. "It was sunset at the beach."

"Really?"

"I was homesick. It was too cold in New York. I wanted sun and ocean and the lack of pretension you find here."

"A lack of pretension?"

"A different kind," I say. "Everything felt like bullshit. I wanted to picture something real." I bring my eyes to hers, expecting disbelief, but I don't find any. "I imagine you see weddings as bullshit."

"No." She swims back to me, brings her hand to my shoulder. "But I don't find them romantic the way other people do." Her other hand, to my other shoulder. "What do you like about the image of yours?"

Everything. My family all in one place. My grandma,

celebrating. The feeling of love in the air. "When I go to a wedding, I watch the couple. They're in the middle of this strange tradition where they promise their lives to each other in front of friends, family, strangers, and they're not thinking about what it means. Or who's watching. Or what they'll eat for dinner. They're completely lost in each other."

"That is romantic," she says.

"Not what you see, though?"

She shakes her head. "But I can almost picture that."

Me, too. I see the two of us, right here, staring into each other's eyes. I see the two of us in an airy hotel room, Deanna stripping out of her white lingerie and climbing into bed with me.

An entire honeymoon's worth of sex.

I need that, now.

How can I need that now? Last week, I was sure I was meant to be with Lexi.

Grandma would say something sarcastic. It's been too long. I want to fuck someone. As soon as I do, I'll realize there's no such thing as destiny. Only dick-stiny. Something ridiculous like that.

Maybe she has a point. Maybe I need to take the edge off. See if I feel the same way with more blood in my brain.

I can do that. Later.

For now, I need to stay on task. To focus on how she feels, not how I feel.

I release her and suck a breath through my teeth. I need air. I need sense. "You hate them?"

"No. I just don't love them. I don't feel what people are supposed to feel. Stephan always gave me attitude about it. Even though he was a realist, too."

A cynic, but this time, I don't argue. Maybe she's right. Maybe she's the realistic one, and I'm the one who isn't in line with reality.

"It was small things. He asked me to skip underwear when we went out for drinks, and I told him I'd have to wash my dress too soon."

Deanna Huntington, naked under her dress. *Fuck.*

"It's not that I was against the idea. There is something sexy about it. But he didn't ask. He told. And I wanted him to ask. Or at least *offer* more to me."

"Promise you'd come on his hand at the bar?" The words are too easy on my tongue. The vision is too vivid.

She raises a brow. "Is that your move?"

How about we try it right now? "I don't have moves. I do what feels right."

"What feels right, right now?"

Touching her. Kissing her. Taking her back to the car to fuck her.

But I don't say any of that. I dive under the water, and when I surface, I say, "Swimming."

CHAPTER NINETEEN

Deanna

When I was a kid, I loved the ocean. I loved racing through the surf, wading into the water, diving under the waves.

Dad never loved the beach. Mom was the one who loved the Pacific, who came to California to be near the ocean (and the entertainment industry).

She loved spending weekends at the beach. Sometimes, Dad joined. He sat under his umbrella, reading books in rash guards, breaking to adore Mom or us.

Sometimes, she brought her guitar, and the two of them took turns singing as Lexi and I raced through the waves.

Sometimes, she brought a book and read with him.

Other times, she braved the waves with us. She wasn't like most adults. She dove under the water, embraced every cold drop.

Then she died, and we didn't go to the ocean anymore.

I didn't remember my love of it until I was in high school, until my friends started using the beach as a spot to hang. It was more of a make-out point than anything, and I wasn't cool enough to hang at most of those parties (or inclined to swap studying for socializing), but I found my love all the same.

The roar of the crashing waves, the deep blue-green hue of the water, the blue sky bleeding into the ocean. An obvious contrast during the day. A subtle one at night.

I feel like that now. Like the sky above the ocean at night. Like I could dissolve into the water, stay one with it forever.

For the first time, in a long time, I'm exactly where I'm supposed to be.

And then I find River, and I wrap my hand around his wrist, and, somehow, I'm even closer to where I'm supposed to be.

He pulls my body into his, pushes off the sand, wraps himself around me. "Your turn."

I laugh as I carry him toward the sand. "You're too heavy."

He releases me and dives under a wave.

Even though I dive just in time to feel the perfect pull of the current—a light sway, toward the depth, then toward the sand, just enough to keep me exactly where I am—I feel a different sort of pull.

Toward *him*.

I like him.

That complicates things.

Or maybe it simplifies things.

Maybe this is what we both need. A little fun that cures him of his feelings for Lexi and ends my long dry spell.

I want him.

I feel it everywhere. And the more I watch him swim, those feelings expand. Even though he's awkward in the water. *Because* he's awkward in the water but loves it anyway.

That's what I need in a partner, someone who knows how to have fun, even when things aren't perfect.

Because I can't do that. I need someone else to lead.

So, when we finish swimming and he asks if I want to go home, I say no. I insist on lunch at my favorite nearby restaurant, and I spend the drive lost in images of the two of us together.

• • •

River tears into his carne asada tacos with gusto. "I forgot good Mexican food existed."

He looks out of place here, on the pristine patio, at the fast casual place just off PCH. Not the sort of Mexican place you find in San Diego or even Anaheim. A very Newport Beach sort of place.

Stone tables, bright pillows on the bench seats, big orange umbrellas. And all the customers in classic California-cool attire.

A dad and his teenage sons, all in shorts, rainbow sandals, and T-shirts for the high school in Irvine, the one where the SNL actor shows up to do announcements a few times a year (annoying the students every time). A couple around our age in athleisure, and two older women in breezy, floral print kaftans.

Everyone else fits into the bright surroundings. Well, everyone except the two college girls in the corner. They look sorta like me and Lexi. The woman with short hair and black nail polish laughs as her friend swipes left and right.

A dating app, probably.

Are they using MeetCute?

For once, I don't care enough to watch them. I don't want to think about work. I want to be here, at the little square table, surrounded by succulents and sunshine and Mexican love songs.

It's not that I need to focus on my mission here. I am here for a reason. To keep River away from Lexi.

But somehow, that doesn't feel necessary the same way it did yesterday. I want to stay close because I want to be close. Because this feels good. Easy.

We've never shared a meal together. Not the two of us.

This is what people do on a date. They go to dinner, they go for drinks, they go home.

But we can't go home. That's far too complicated.

Maybe the car. The back seat.

Or the office. No one is there on a Saturday.

No. Home is okay as long as Lexi is out. And Lexi is always

out on Saturdays. With friends. With Jake.

Only Jake isn't in the picture, right now. And I need to make sure he's in the picture. How the hell do I keep him in the picture? Beyond playing cockblocker.

At the moment, I feel other motives more strongly. A desire to climb over this table and mount River, for example.

He catches me staring. "Do I have something on my face?"

"A little. Here." I motion to the left side of my lips.

He wipes salsa from his mouth. A totally normal, not at all seductive gesture that feels sensual as hell.

It's the sun, the salt in the air, the T-shirt sticking to his chest.

He's still in his board shorts. I'm wearing my cover-up over my swimsuit.

We're barely dressed. We're in full-on California teen summer sex mode. I'm not a teen anymore, but I still have all those feelings, those cravings.

A bonfire by the beach. A make-out session on the sand. A little light touching in the back seat of a car, parked in some distant spot, hoping the cops wouldn't show up, because it's still Orange County, wherever you go, until you get to Long Beach (north) or Riverside (east) or San Diego (south). Though there's really nothing between south Orange County and San Diego. Coastline and Camp Pendleton.

Not that the details matter.

Only I can't stop picturing details.

Right now, I see it: the two of us in the back of my car. Then in my bedroom, the one in the house, that's still filled with *Star Wars* paperbacks and eyeliner stains. I'm in my twin bed, peeling off my bikini top, pushing my bottoms off my hips.

And River is standing there, watching, taking me in like the artist he is.

"Still?" His voice pulls me back to the moment.

I'm totally gone. I need to get laid. Or at least touch myself. Or mount him right now.

No. Not that one. The middle one.

He wipes his lips again. The way I imagine he'd wipe them after—

Ahem. "You're good." I dive into my pollo verde tacos. They taste familiar, like lime and tomatillo and home, but they don't sate my craving. They don't fill me where I'm hungry.

I finish one and lick the salsa from my fingers.

River laughs. "You make everything graceful."

"This is graceful?" I hold up my salsa-streaked hand.

"The way you do it, yes."

I shake my head.

He nods.

The compliment hits me somewhere deep. It's honest. Real. How he actually sees me.

It makes me warm everywhere. Too warm.

I turn my focus to my food. Lime. Tomatillos. Soft chicken. Homemade corn tortillas. Is anything better than a homemade corn tortilla? The freshness and flavor are in a whole other league compared to the store-bought ones.

A groan falls from my lips.

His pupils dilate.

This isn't working. I'm only thinking of sex. The two of us, naked, right here on the table.

Thankfully, he shifts the topic. "I've never imagined you eating tacos."

I laugh a little. "Why wouldn't I?"

"It's not an artisanal jam and hazelnut butter sandwich. Or lobster mac n' cheese."

"Is that what we ate?"

"What did you eat?"

"Normal mac 'n cheese," I say.

"What do you consider normal?"

"Something less fancy than what your grandma makes," I say.

His laugh is soft. Easy. "She loves cheese, yeah."

"Cheddar and peas. Not, what, gouda and caramelized onions?"

"Name-brand boxes," he says. "That's what my mom made. Then what I made. Even when I got here."

"What does Ida cook?"

"Basic stuff. Sandwiches, meatloaf, roasts," he says. "But she doesn't do it often. She works a lot, too."

She's like me that way, yeah. She loves what she does. She loses herself in it. "Was that lonely?"

"Sometimes." He doesn't take the bait. He turns the topic back to me. "Did your mom cook a lot?"

"Before she got sick, yeah." I swallow hard. I don't usually talk about this, with anyone, but I want it off my chest. And it's incredibly unsexy. It'll keep my thoughts in line. "At first, friends dropped off casseroles. Then Dad started buying ready meals. We had a freezer full of them."

"What was that like?"

"Mushy," I say. "Frozen food always tastes mushy."

His eyes bore into mine. "What was it like, losing her?"

I don't know what to say, how to explain it. There's no way to understand without going through it. Not really. "Horrible."

"I'm sorry," he says. "I never thought about how hard it must have been."

I swallow a sip of my water. "Which part?"

"All of it."

There isn't anything to say. I don't have a logical response and I don't do emotional responses well. I never react the way people want. With tears of sorrow or *no, I'm sorry that this is awkward for you.*

"You don't have to talk about it," he says.

I finish the glass, but it doesn't cool me off. The heat isn't the flush of desire. It's something else. A sense of vulnerability. As if I'm not wearing anything under my sheer black cover-up. "I didn't really understand what was going on at the time. I knew about death. I knew about dying. But only as philosophical concepts and biological realities. The way it felt was different. Watching her fade, actually seeing her life force slip away one day at a time… She didn't ask me to be strong for her, but I tried anyway."

He studies me carefully.

As if I'm not wearing a cover-up, either.

But it's not the stare of desire. It's like he's looking at my naked brain. My naked heart.

It feels strange, too much and just right at the same time.

"I didn't want her to have to comfort me. I hate when that happens. When something hurts me, and it makes someone else uncomfortable. They expect me to say something to ease their awkwardness, but I can't. I won't."

"You don't have to say anything to me."

"I know."

"I am sorry," he says. "About all of it. Watching her fade. Losing her. Having to grow up on your own."

"I had my dad."

"It's not the same," he says.

Right. His dad isn't even in the picture. And his mom has been out of it for a long time. "You know what it's like to grow up on your own."

"I have Grandma."

"Still." My heart rate slows. My skin cools. It's easier, throwing this back to him, but I'm not throwing it exactly. I'm passing the ball. I'm sharing. No. We're sharing. "Was it hard, losing your mom? I know she's alive, but she's not around, right?" I don't know the details, really. Only that Ida curses her daughter.

"It was a relief," he says. "And an agonizing loss." His eyes go to the sky. He stares at the expanse of blue, looking for something among the big, puffy clouds.

Because he's uncomfortable with the subject of grief? Or because he doesn't want to talk about his mom?

I don't know. I always hate when I don't know, but it's

different here. Not an intellectual frustration. An emotional one.

He brings his attention back to me. "I'd rather talk about something else."

"Okay." I want to stay on this, and I want to run a million miles away.

"You still owe me an answer."

"Straight from death to mommy issues to sex?" I ask.

The joke eases the tension in the air. It sends a smile to his lips. "Of course." He takes a long sip of his water. "It's your turn to share. What was it you liked? What was it that worked for you?"

CHAPTER TWENTY

Deanna

Why don't you want to talk about your mom?

It's ridiculous to accuse him of deflecting with a deflection of my own, but the question bounces around my brain all the same.

I rarely share details about my pain. Any pain. But when it comes to my mom, I keep those feelings locked up tight. People don't want to hear the truth. People don't want to hear *my mom died when I was thirteen and it was horrible watching her fade. I hated every minute of it. I miss her every day.*

They want to hear something nice, something pleasant, something that tactfully informs without bringing down the mood.

But Death isn't well-mannered. And all the polite terms for it are bullshit. Mom didn't pass on. She faded and died, and I had to be strong for her and Lexi and Dad. Because she was scared, and I couldn't put my fear on her.

And the appropriate reaction to *how are your parents* isn't *my mom is dead, actually.*

But then I guess *my mom dumped me with my grandma* isn't the appropriate answer, either.

River is not the hopeless romantic artist he sees himself as.

Sure, he's a romantic, and he's artistic, but he's not jumping to pour his emotions onto the table. He's not diving straight into big, messy, ugly things because they're honest and real and whatever else people use to describe art.

And I'm not holding everything back, even though I'm an analytical programmer who struggles with feelings. I'm not as cold as ice, even if I am a merciless businesswoman.

We fit into our roles in certain ways.

He struggles with his as much as I struggle with mine. He isn't all butterflies and storm clouds. He's logic and reason, too.

Maybe that means he can move past old hang-ups. Old obsessions.

Into someone else, someone different.

"Deanna?" River leans a little closer. He keeps his voice soft, caring. "Are you okay?"

"Tired."

"We can get more tea or some coffee."

"Soon." I want to move away from the subject of death, too. Even if it's to the equally dangerous topic of sex. But I need to keep it abstract, not personal. "I'm trying a version of the app with sexual compatibility."

His pupils dilate. Again.

"It's a secret," I say. "Because it always overwhelms things. Sex."

"It tends to do that."

"People don't know how to combine sexual and romantic compatibility. Especially when it comes to apps. Either you're looking for marriage, and sex is a secondary or tertiary concern, or you're looking to hook up, and the rest is irrelevant."

"Is it that simple?" he asks.

"Maybe not, in people's heads, but from a marketing point of view, yes. The second you mention sex, that's the focus of the app."

"You're not answering my question," he says.

"What question?"

Epiphany fills his eyes. "Who was the last person who blew your mind? What did you like about it?"

"I'm getting there."

He raises a brow, but he doesn't object.

"That night, after the meeting, one of the guys on the marketing team emailed me about sex. The concept. How we'd add it to the app. He had good questions, so I met him at the hotel bar."

His eyes flit to my lips, my shoulders, my chest.

I feel naked, but it's in the best possible way. "I showed up in my suit. He was in his, too. Back then, I wore black, not pink, which only made me look more—"

"Like a Domme."

I hesitate. "Is it obvious where this goes?"

"You have a type." His smile is wicked. "Not that I blame the guy."

My cheeks flush. Because he sees me. Because he wants me. "He started talking about how much he loves a powerful, in-control woman. It took me five minutes to realize what he meant. I had to call Lexi to bail me out."

"How'd she do it?"

"She came downstairs and distracted him."

"How?" he asks.

"She flirted."

"Was he more interested in her?"

He wasn't. At the time, I thought he was. I thought he was moved by her blonde hair and her sweet smile. But he wasn't. "No. That's the first time that's ever happened."

"I doubt that."

"Forgive me, but I can't take your word for it." *Because you have a crush on her. Because you want her. Because you believe she's your everything.*

"Sure, I had a crush on your sister," he says. "I'm still a man."

He *had* a crush. Not *has* a crush. Since when?

"A man," I muse. "That means you're moved by boobs?"

"That means I know an appealing woman when I see one," he counters.

"As long as you want a Domme."

"And you want someone who's willing to take control." It's a statement, not a question.

He sees that. He sees what I want. How I want. "Sometimes."

"Boss in the boardroom, sub in the bedroom?"

"Not always. Only sometimes."

"Have you asked anyone?"

"What?" My throat is dry. I need water. All the water. But my glass is empty.

"Have you asked a guy if he's interested?" River asks. "Put it in your profile? Tested out a competing app? Gone back to Depressed Mode in a sub collar?"

"Once," I admit. "Not the collar or that bar, but the rest of it."

"What happened?"

"I didn't trust him enough." There was something sexy about it, but the danger felt too real. "I couldn't relax into it."

"Do you want to try it?"

"Are you offering?" The words fill the air. The city. The state. The planet.

"Are you asking?"

Yes. Let's go to my place—assuming Lexi is out—and we can use one of your ties. Do you have ties? Fuck it. I have ties. And rope. And those black leather handcuffs with fuzzy insides, so they're comfortable without looking over-the-top.

River doesn't push forward or fall back. He looks me over slowly, noting my bare lips, my long neck, the sheer black fabric covering my chest and torso. "Is that why you tested sex in the app?"

"Huh?"

"To use logic and science to see if you attracted a certain kind of guy?"

"Yes." My chest flames. My stomach and cheeks, too. I'm obvious. Too obvious.

"I'm sure you do," he says. "You radiate power and competence. People who want that everywhere see it in you."

"Are you going to say it's destiny?"

"No. Other people will see it and want to claim it. To control the most powerful woman in the world. Anyone who enjoys control would get a thrill out of that."

"Would you?" I bite my tongue, but it's too late. The words are out there. I'm asking him, again. There's no denying that.

He doesn't answer. "I'm going to use the bathroom."

"Then we should go home."

"Sure."

I refill my water. I chug the glass. I use our phone-finding app to check Lexi's location. Perfect. She's at the Pilates studio her friend owns.

And there's a picture of them on her Instagram. She tags the studio and mentions tea and dinner plans for after.

Really, she should be more careful with her social media. Anyone could find her. Stalkers, ex-boyfriends, current boyfriends, crushes, sisters.

I use the bathroom, too.

When I'm done, River is standing outside the restaurant, out of place in the Orange County strip mall. He doesn't belong here. It's not the tattoos or the European swimsuit. It's something about him. Something I feel, too. Something I want.

He experimented with his girlfriend.

He knows how to do this.

I want to do this with him.

But I don't say anything about it. I follow him to the car, I climb in, I babble about the artist on the stereo. Anything and everything I know about music, which isn't much. The principles, the mathematical parts, the progressions. The emotion, the lyrics, the magic?

None of it means anything to me.

And I feel everything. Even with the cheesy pop song. Even though its inane lyrics describe a teenager's idea of sex.

I feel it everywhere.

We park in front of his house. He opens the door for me and walks me along the sidewalk. The street is booming with backyard barbecues and front yard games. All quiet parties and kids laughing and dad jokes and wine moms.

We listen to the sounds of the neighborhood all the way to my house, around the side yard, to the front door of the apartment.

I unlock the door.

He stands behind me. "Did he kiss you?"

"What?"

"The guy who tied you up. Or was it something else?"

"He held me down." My cheeks flush at the memory. Then the vision shifts, and River is the guy on top of me and I'm on fire. "Yes. I think so. I don't remember."

"Have you ever felt a kiss everywhere? In your bones?"

"I don't know. How does that feel?" I push the door open.

He places his hand on the knob. "Should we talk inside?"

I open it wider and walk in.

He follows and presses the door closed.

And then we're alone in my apartment. In the apartment I share with my sister, in the big, beautiful living room.

"Do you trust me?" River moves closer, but he stays behind me.

I should say no. I should stop whatever this is. But I can't. I won't. "Yes."

"Do you want to feel it? The magic you don't believe exists?"

"Desire isn't magic."

"You don't think a kiss is romantic?"

"It's sexual, too."

"It feels different. When you care about someone."

Is he saying he cares about me? That I care about him? I'm

not sure. I don't have time to figure it out.

"Do you want to feel it or not?" His fingers brush my hair. My neck. The place where my cover-up meets my skin.

"As an experiment," I say. "For the sake of science only."

"If that's what you want."

It's not, but it's the only reasonable thing to do. It's the last reasonable thing I can do. "Okay. One kiss. As an experiment."

"A kiss like we mean it."

"Let's call it a make-out session." I mean to say it with humor, but I stumble over the words. I'm awkward around him. When it comes to this. Maybe he's right. Maybe there's more than sex here. Because I know enough about sex. I don't stumble with sex. Romance on the other hand…

"Do you want a safe word?"

"The word 'no' is fine."

He nods, running his thumb over my cover-up. "How do I take this off?"

"Is that part of it?"

"Yes."

"Like this." I break our touch enough to pull the cover-up over my head.

"Are you sure about this, Deanna?"

My entire body buzzes. "No. But I want to try anyway."

CHAPTER TWENTY-ONE

Deanna

River runs his fingers along my neck. Then down my spine. A long, slow line to the strap of my bikini top, then over it, down my lower back, to the tops of my bikini bottoms.

He traces the line up again, only this time, he stops at the bikini top, and he undoes the strap.

He's undressing me.

I should say *wait* or *no* or maybe *this is a bad idea.* Anything reasonable. But I'm out of reason.

And I don't want to say no.

I want to feel every minute of this. All of it.

He pushes the straps off my shoulders.

The fabric falls at my feet.

"When's the last time you were completely in your body?" He moves a little closer, until he's only a foot away, and he traces a line down my lower back.

"The ocean."

"Have you ever been there with someone else?"

"I don't know." Maybe. Not in a long time.

"Now?"

"Now what?"

"Are you thinking anything?"

"Everything," I say.

His chuckle breaks the sexual tension in the air. "I love that about you." Then he traces the waist of my bikini bottoms, and all the sexual tension is back. "I love your brain."

"That's the sexiest thing I've ever heard."

"You're the sexiest woman I've ever seen."

No. That's not possible. We're here, in the place I share with Lexi. Next to the house where he fell for her again and again. But I don't want to say that. I don't want to say anything.

Of course it's not possible. It's not real. It's part of this experiment. This game we're playing.

I think.

It's hard to concentrate with his hands on my skin.

He draws a line up my back again. Then down, all the way to the Lycra, along to my hips.

He pushes the bottoms over my ass and lowers himself to pull them to my feet.

He lifts one foot, pushes the bottoms off that, then the other, then rises and shifts, so he's right behind me.

Then against me.

He doesn't touch me. Not yet. He keeps his body against mine, the now-dry fabric of his T-shirt against my back, the rough material of his shorts against my ass. And the hardness beneath them.

It feels too good. Way too good.

I'm ready to drag him to my bed. But that's not what we're doing. We're not here to have sex. We're experimenting. Of course, we didn't set any limits. We could have sex. If I want.

I do want.

I really, really want.

Slowly, he brings his hands to my hips, his mouth to my neck. He places a soft kiss on my skin, at the place where my neck meets my shoulders.

Then he moves higher. The brush of his lips on my skin.

Enough my entire body buzzes. Enough the room spins.

Higher.

To the line of my jaw.

My cheek.

I'm naked, and he's in his beach clothes, and we're in the middle of my sunny California apartment, but I feel someplace else. Like we're in one of those books where the billionaire seduces the virgin.

He's just as powerful as a rich guy in a suit.

And I'm just as desperate for his touch.

River presses another kiss to my jaw. He keeps one hand on my hip. Brings the other to my breast.

He cups me softly.

Desire races through my veins. I want his touch. I want his hands everywhere, all the time, always.

He drags his lips down my neck again, along my shoulder, then back up, to my jaw.

Then he moves to my other shoulder and presses his lips to it. His other hand finds my breast.

Then it's his thumbs against my nipples. Slow, soft movements as he kisses me with an impossible amount of patience.

Up my shoulders and neck.

Then down again.

Up and down.

I reach back for him, but he grabs my wrist to stop me. His touch is hard, rough, but it's gentle, too. Enough to show force without hurting.

He is stronger than I am. Bigger, if barely taller. He could hurt me. But he won't.

I trust him in a way I didn't trust my previous partner here. In a way I didn't trust any of my partners. In a way I've never trusted any man, ever.

He kisses a line up my neck and stops at my ear. "Turn around." He releases me.

I turn so I'm eye to eye with him. No, in my shoes, I'm taller than he is. It's funny. For once, I don't feel tall. Not compared to him. I feel just right, like we align perfectly.

I step out of my shoes.

He steps out of his and brings both hands to my hips. Again, his lips find my ear. A soft brush. The heat of his breath. "Promise you'll tell me if you want to stop?"

"I promise."

He presses his lips to my ear. Then my cheek.

He pulls back enough to look into my eyes, to stare at me with those gorgeous, dark eyes.

Then his lids flutter downward, and his lips find mine.

A soft brush. The taste of mint ChapStick and lime.

Then harder.

Hard enough I feel heat everywhere.

My lips part.

His tongue slides into my mouth.

He uses the same slow, steady movements. There's a certainty to his kiss, like he knows this is exactly what he wants.

For the first time in ages, the world feels simple and beautiful. He wants me. I want him. We both want to try sex this way.

There's no need to make it complicated.

He backs me into the wall next to the door and he sinks into me. His body against mine, the weight of him keeping me pinned.

Between a rock and a hard place. That's how they say it. A wall and a hard place, I guess.

What a place.

I need the place.

Again, he kisses me slowly, with patience.

Again, he brings one hand to my chest. Again, my lips part to make way for his tongue.

He kisses me as he toys with me.

Again, and again.

Until I'm shaking.

And then, he wraps his hand around my wrist and lifts it above my head.

One.

Then the other.

He keeps my arms pinned there as he sinks into me again. As he kisses me.

This time, there's less softness. All hardness and need and passion.

His tongue slips into my mouth and dances with mine.

With his other hand, he toys with my breast. Slowly circles. Then harder ones. Back and forth. Left and right.

Perfect, horrible torture.

I arch my back, rocking into him, trying to feel more of him, all of him. His board shorts are rough against me, but I don't care. I can feel his cock, hard, under them, and I need that.

No. I need them gone.

I try to reach for him, but he keeps my arms pinned to the wall.

Desire floods my body. He's actually doing this. Actually leading. No. More than leading. Not quite what Stephan expected of me, but something a lot more than leading.

It's perfect.

It's everything.

I kiss him back as I rock my hips into his. Again and again, until he's groaning against my lips.

Finally, he brings one hand to my hips. My stomach. The top of my pelvis.

And right as he's going to touch me properly, the doorbell rings.

What the hell?

It rings again.

"Lexi?" A familiar male voice calls. "Can we talk?"

Jake. *Shit*.

That's Lexi's boyfriend. Or kind of ex-boyfriend. Whatever

she wants to call him. He came here, instead of replying to my texts. Or maybe I've been too distracted by lust. Maybe I've forgotten my goal. That's what River said about love. You act against your self-interest.

But it's not the only reason we act against our self-interest.

My number-one goal is this app. And here I am, letting a man get in the way.

Shit, shit, shit.

River releases me. Disappointment streaks his eyes, but he still takes a step backward.

"I should go," he says.

"But—" I don't want him to go. Even though that's foolish. Even though talking to Jake is the important thing.

I shake my head, then nod. Yes. He should go.

I need to talk to Jake. I need to figure this out. I need to not sleep with the guy who wanted to sleep with my sister two days ago.

Even if I don't care who he wanted two days ago.

I just want him.

Now.

"Which room is yours?" He takes another step backward.

I try to bring my eyes to his face, but I just can't look anywhere except the hard-on straining against his board shorts. "On the right."

"I'll grab you something to wear."

"Okay."

"Deanna?" Jake asks, from outside. "Is that you?"

"Yeah," I call. "I just got out of the shower. Give me a minute." I swallow hard. "Lexi isn't here."

"Okay," he says. "We can talk, too."

Yes, we should. I should say…something logical and smart and effective. Whatever that is. "I…uh… Make it two minutes." I move to my room.

River emerges, holding a black silk robe. "I guess I'll leave you to it."

"Thanks." I take the robe and move into the bedroom.

"Is there a back door?"

"Yeah. That way." I motion to the side door on the other side of the living room. "You can stay."

"Rain check."

Don't look at his cock. Don't look at his cock. Don't look at his cock.

Bam.

My eyes go straight to his crotch.

I'm not sure how the board shorts remain in one piece. He's really straining the fabric.

He laughs. "I'll take them off next time."

"Another experiment?"

His posture shifts to something harder. "If that's what you want."

No. I want everything, but I say yes, anyway.

He leaves.

I throw on a dress. I can't greet my future brother-in-law in lingerie.

I try to push thoughts of sex aside as I answer the door, invite Jake inside, try to figure out how the hell I'm going to get him and Lexi back together.

CHAPTER TWENTY-TWO

Deanna

"Do you want something to drink?" I say to Jake and motion to the kitchen, but I barely see the shiny white counter, the coffeemaker, the tea kettle. Instead, I see River backing me into the tile, turning me around, taking me from behind.

It's not too late to tell Jake to leave.

To call River back.

No. It is. Yes, my body is still buzzing, but the moment is gone. I'm in a loose black dress. He's somewhere else. The magic is gone.

No. There's no such thing as magic.

This is dopamine and oxytocin and whatever other hormones send blood racing south. I'm not a biologist or a neuroscientist. Right now, I'm barely a logical programmer. Right now, I'm a woman who desperately needs to ride the boy next door.

Ahem.

"Whatever you're having," Jake says.

"English Breakfast, okay?" I offer.

"Yeah. Sure."

I motion for him to sit. He takes a seat at the dining table and stares at the wall.

I fix the tea for both of us, bring the mugs to the table, and sit opposite him.

His eyes stay on the wall.

He looks off, by Jake standards. In a slightly wrinkled polo shirt, jeans that fit a little too big, and sneakers with scuffed soles.

Usually, he's picture perfect. Today, he's, well, human.

He doesn't make small talk or pretend he's fascinated by his tea. He does the last thing I expect.

He reaches for my hand and squeezes hard. "You're a great sister to her."

Uh… "Thanks."

"Lexi adores you. You know that, don't you?"

Of course I know my sister loves me. But it's not that simple. Lexi sees me as a badass because I'm so tough and take no prisoners, because I'm able to deny my physical needs in a way she isn't. She relies on that. We both rely on that. "She likes you, too."

He wraps his hands around his mug and stares at the milky English Breakfast. "I like you, Dee." He calls me by my nickname. Almost everyone does.

Everyone except River, really.

"When Lexi described you, I didn't believe her. A straight shooter without a single weakness. How is that possible? But she was right."

I guess it's normal for little sisters to see their big sisters without flaws, but I wish, just once, someone would notice how hard I work to hold everything together.

"I want to ask you something," he says. "And I hope you'll be honest, even if it hurts."

"Okay."

"Okay." He pauses a moment, then says, "Is there someone else?"

"Huh?"

He takes a long sip of his tea and swallows slowly. "Thanks

for the drink."

"Sure." I swallow a sip to buy myself time to think. There is someone else, but not the way he means. Or maybe I don't know what he means. "She hasn't been seeing anyone since you've been together."

"So, she meant it? She needed to think?"

"In her way."

His eyes fill with curiosity. He doesn't know what that means. Or he doesn't want to know. "So it wasn't an excuse?"

"Huh?" I ask.

"Because she's in love with someone else?"

I laugh.

His lips curl into a frown. "Is that funny?"

Yes, but not to him. "It's just…not Lexi. No. She's not in love with someone else. I can promise you that."

"Then why did she want to pause things?"

That's harder to explain. "Did she tell you about the meeting?" I ask.

"Which one?"

"With Willa Wilder," I say. "She wants the two of you to show up at an investor dinner with a ring. As the poster couple."

For a moment, his entire face brightens, then he remembers something—probably the situation they're in now, the break—and it falls.

"Is that what you want?" I ask. "A future with her?"

"Of course."

"But you know her well enough at this point."

"She's not a commitment kind of girl," he says.

See. He gets her. They do belong together. The algo was right. It's just the two of them getting in their own way.

"And you want that?" he asks. "To see us together for the company?"

"Of course," I say. "But I like you together, too." Mostly. No. All the way. He's good for her. And she's been happy with him, as happy as I've ever seen her.

"Is she sleeping with other guys?"

"I don't know," I answer honestly. "Maybe. Wasn't that your agreement?"

"Yes." He swallows hard.

"She's a very sexual person."

"I know."

"And you two haven't—?"

"She told you that?"

"She tells me a lot," I say. "Not details." She offers, sometimes, but I decline. "Is there a reason?"

"Why we haven't had sex?"

I nod.

"Of course."

I know what Lexi says. But what's his story? "A good reason?"

"A great reason."

Okay. I try to hold his gaze, but it's too much. It's strange, talking about my sister and her boyfriend this way.

He takes a deep breath and lets out a steady exhale. Slowly, he works up to his confession, as if he's a witness about to implicate a co-conspirator. "I'm too good."

"What?"

"I'm too good in bed," he says. "It's ruined all my relationships."

"Your skill ruined your relationships?"

"Yes." He stands and paces the length of the table. "I meet women. And they think I'm a sort of sweet, dorky guy. Because—" He motions to his polo shirt and his boat shoes.

"Even here?"

"Everywhere."

"Women expect something different with me," he says. "Someone less—"

"Horny?"

He chuckles. "You are a straight shooter. She was right."

"What is it exactly?"

"The size. The skill. The imagination. Everything."

Holy shit, he *is* Lexi's perfect man. "You haven't told Lexi this?"

"Only that I wanted to wait because my ex...all my exes. It's always the same thing. They have one taste and it's all they want to do. We don't eat, we don't sleep, we don't go to movies or museums or meet my parents. We fuck. All day, all night, until the flush of a new relationship wears off, and they're too chaffed to keep it up."

"You're that good?"

"See. Six months ago, I would have said, *I'll show you, baby*, and that would be it. We'd be horizontal in twenty minutes. Or vertical. I can do a lot vertical."

Uh...

"But I'm not that guy anymore. I want love. Someone who loves me for my heart, not my dick."

"And you don't have that now?" I ask.

"Do I?"

My head spins. This is...ridiculous and completely right for Lexi. "Lexi cares about you. And she needs D. Her words. That's what I know." I know more, too. "And this waiting, I think it's been good for her, too. Because she's usually more love 'em and leave 'em. And she's actually had time to get to know you."

He nods, like *see, it's working*.

"But she's waited long enough."

"I should find her right now? Take her back to my place?"

"That's what I would do."

He nods, turning over the words. "Is it really that simple? We have sex and she asks me to play her fake fiancé and we're happily ever after?"

"Maybe. If you two both agree to that." If they have sex, she'll probably lose interest in River. Assuming he's even still interested in her. Since this is all an experiment. Not a normal thing. "Probably. But...can I give you some advice?"

He nods.

"Don't ask her what happened," I say. "During this break. If there was someone else, it doesn't matter. It's not personal. It's just Lexi trying to meet her needs."

He nods, taking in the information. "There is one other concern."

"Oh?"

"Yeah… What if it's not good?"

It's a rare man who acknowledges that possibility.

"What if we're too nervous? I… I've never waited six months before."

That is a lot of pressure. "That's what round two is for."

He nods. "I should take her somewhere for the weekend. That way we have time for rounds two and three and four."

Yeah. That's…exactly right. Jake might just be the man to tame my sister. "Perfect."

"Or should I back off?" he asks. "Give her the time she needs to think about things? We agreed on two weeks. It hasn't even been two days."

Right. He shouldn't come on too strong. Or maybe if he's coming on too strong because he wants her to come, that's fine. "How about I feel her out?"

"How so?"

"Mention the idea. Say you asked me what I thought. Text her."

He nods okay.

I pull out my cell, check my messages (nothing urgent: nothing from River, which I try not to care about), and text Lexi.

Deanna: *Hey! Jake just asked me about you. He wants to take you away for the weekend. But he doesn't want to get in the way of your "thinking time."*

I don't expect her to text back right away—she is with a friend—but she does.

Lexi: *A surprise trip? Where?*

Deanna: *I'm thinking hiking and then a campsite. Peeing* *outside turns you on, right?*

Lexi: *Not funny.*

Deanna: *Don't worry. I warned him to bring extra TP. Men always underestimate how much women need.*

Lexi: *OMG Dee! I would kill you.*

Deanna: *If you survived a weekend in the mountains.*

Lexi: *I'd survive long enough to kill you.*

Deanna: *I'm going to suggest Palm Springs. Or maybe Catalina?*

Lexi: *Wine country.*

Deanna: *I'll tell him.*

Lexi: *No. Too many bnbs in wine country. I want a nice hotel. Modern. With a view and absolutely no entertainment besides each other. Wait. Was he clear about what the weekend entailed?*

Deanna: *Very. Though I'm not sure what he plans to do with the other 47 hours and 58 minutes.*

Lexi: *I go a lot longer than that.*

Deanna: *But will he, after six months?*

Lexi: *Aw, that's sweet. I'll be flattered. I swear.*

Deanna: *You should tell him that.*

Lexi: *I will.*

Oh god, she will. That's sweet in a disturbing way. No. It's good she's open. And it's good she's back on Team Jake.

So why don't I feel more relieved?

If Lexi and Jake are happy, then I don't have to worry about River's crush. Or if he has a crush. I don't need to spend time with him. Or prove anything to him.

Only, River adored Lexi through dozens of her conquests. He's never been bothered by her relationship with another man. Will this really shake off his crush? He says he's over her, but how could a romantic like him get over his supposed soul mate so quickly?

Deanna: *I'll pass the news on.*

Lexi: *Thanks, Dee. You're the best. Let's find you some D tonight. Too bad River canceled on us.*

He did?

Wait. Does she mean it's too bad because I could have sex with River? Or because we could enjoy his company?

It's Lexi.

Of course she means sex.

But then again, it's Lexi. That doesn't mean she's over the idea of having him herself. She'd happily step aside for me. But if I'm not interested, anything goes.

The ball is in my court.

Deanna: *Oh?*

Lexi: *Yeah. A work deadline or something. But I'm still gonna take out the ladies. Find you someone.*

Honestly, I'm not worried about her running off with someone. I'm not. But it never hurts to be careful.

Deanna: *You're ridiculous.*

Lexi: *No, babe, I'm re-dick-u-lous. And this time tomorrow, you will be too. Gotta go. Love you. Don't forget I like a California King. No feathers. Big pool. Tell Jake.*

Deanna: *All the important stuff, yes. Love you too.*

After I put the phone away, I convince Jake to make reservations. Which means I only have to keep my eye on Lexi until she's snuggled up with Jake at some adorable hotel.

I can do that.

Even if I'm way more interested in figuring out where River is going tonight.

CHAPTER TWENTY-THREE

River

All afternoon, my thoughts whirl. I drive to a park I used to love, the one everyone calls Castle Park, even though that's not the real name. When I was a kid, the jungle gym resembled an actual castle. Stone walls, sand, wooden bridges.

Now, it's all brightly colored plastic.

The same soccer and baseball fields behind the play place. The same community center. The next generation of excited children and tired parents.

I look up from my spot under one of the overgrown trees. I need to get out of my head. Which means I need to draw what I see.

No imagination, no editorializing, no exaggeration.

The lines, exactly as they are.

It's an exercise for young artists, so they learn to see what's there, not what they believe is there. The world doesn't break into lines and curves the way we imagine in our heads. Neither do colors.

It's different.

And it takes practice, to see what's really there.

I draw a teenager reading under a tree.

A dad kicking a soccer ball with his two daughters.

A young couple watching their kids the way Mr. Huntington watches Deanna and Lexi—with that mix of pride and expectation.

Do the poor kids feel it already? The weight of the expectations. The pressure.

For all of Mom's faults, she never put that on me. She never expected anything of me. When things were good, that was good. I got to be a kid. Then things weren't good, and—

She didn't expect me to take care of her, or fix my own dinner, or get myself to school, but she left the responsibility in my hands.

When I first moved in next door to the Huntingtons, I cursed Lexi and Deanna's luck. A father who loved them enough to give them everything in the world, to expect the world. From far away, it looked like a gift.

Now?

It's obvious it's a curse.

I'm not supposed to be here, thinking of Deanna, but I am. I can't think of anything else. I can't feel anything else.

Only need. Desire. Affection.

A need so deep and pure I can barely breathe.

She asked for magic.

I promised magic.

Only I'm the one feeling it. I'm the one overwhelmed by my desire to drag her to my bed, my home, my life.

I watch the sunset. I leave the park. I sit in the driver's seat of my car and turn over my texts from Deanna.

Deanna: *Are you really skipping drinks tonight?*

Deanna: *The outfit Lexi picked for me is beyond extra. Do people still say extra? Probably not. But it's the best way to describe this. It's a lot.*

Deanna: *You should come to the bar, after dinner. Since we were interrupted before we could finish.*

In any other circumstance, I'd assume she means sex. The thought is tempting—so tempting it heats the car by twenty degrees. I see it already: the two of us in the too-cramped back seat, struggling into a position, laughing at the awkwardness, then falling into it.

Her lips on my neck.

My hands on her thighs.

Her groan in my ears.

I need that groan. Here. There. Everywhere.

Deanna: *We'll be there at eight.*

I need to say something honest. But Grandma swore me to secrecy. The four people who absolutely, positively cannot know about her condition are the Huntingtons and Mom. She doesn't want anyone close to her, physically or because of blood ties, to know.

She didn't want to tell me, or Fern, or North, or Aunt Briana. If she had the choice, she wouldn't have told me. I don't like it, but I understand it.

I hate the looks of pity I get when I mention my situation with my mother. I never tell anyone. Not friends or girlfriends or teachers.

Like grandmother, like grandson.

River: *Show me the outfit.*

Using sex as a distraction. Grandma would be proud. Or maybe disappointed.

It's not smart. For once, I need to think about what I'm doing with a woman. I need to follow logic, not my heart.

This is complicated.

Only I don't care. I want her too much to care.

I'm outgrowing my naive ideals.

Or I'm regressing to a horny teenager.

Both maybe.

Deanna: *You have to earn that.*

River: *How?*

Deanna: *You show up here.*

River: *Not a picture?*

Deanna: *Aren't you more the behind the camera type?*

River: *I do self-portraits too.*
Deanna: *Is that an offer?*
River: *I take requests.*
Deanna: *Okay. I want something really freaky.*
River: *I'm listening.*
Deanna: *The tattooed arm.*
River: *Are you drinking already?*
Deanna: *You really think I need to be tipsy to admit I find you sexy?*

A part of me does. A part of me is the awkward kid in my room at Grandma's house, drawing blonde princesses because that's as close as I can get to the object of my affection.

A part of me is still attached to her, will always be attached to her.

But the other part is ready to let go.

It doesn't want a blonde princess.

It doesn't want to hold onto anything.

I don't want to stay on the sidelines and observe.

I want this. Her. Tonight.

It's terrifying. How can I trust my own desires if they change so quickly? But then again, maybe they haven't. Maybe it's just that one part of me, the one that will always adore Lexi, holding onto the only familiar thing he has.

I could stay in tonight, draw until it makes sense. But, for once, I don't want to examine my feelings. I want to act. I need something warm and vibrant and real.

I lay my arm over the dash and snap a photo. It's not the most artistic shot, and it's not the most well lit. A million better versions enter my mind.

My arm around her waist. Her chest. Her neck.

Between her legs.

But then she's not here. I'm here. In a public place for fuck's sake.

I need to do this with subtlety.

A tease for a tease.

I place my hand on the button of my jeans and snap a photo. The angle is a little awkward, but it's more interesting than my arm on the dash.

I send.

Woosh.

Deanna: *Tease.*

River: *Always.*

Deanna: *Don't say you didn't ask for this.*

A minute later, she sends a photo, from her nose to her chest. Sparkly pink fabric covers her pale skin. Thin straps. A low neckline.

Not at all Deanna, but sexy all the same.

River: *Do you like it?*

Deanna: *You're supposed to say something about how desperately you want me.*

River: *I want you desperately.*

Deanna: *Better.*

River: *Leave now. Meet me somewhere.*

Deanna: *I promised Lexi I'd go out with her.*

River: *Can I convince you?*

Deanna: *Can you?*

She leaves the offer hanging in the air.

There are things I can say, promises I can make, promises I'm tempted to make. *Let's drive to that make-out spot and fuck in the back seat. Let's go to your room and test drive your bed.*

Let's skinny dip in your pool.

I don't care, as long as I can feel you.

But I can't promise to let go, put her first, disappear into the moment. Not right now. Reality occupies too much of my mind.

Not just the bigger situation with Grandma, not just her sickness, but the discussion I need to have with her.

She isn't going to like it, and I have to get over that. Maybe then I can give Deanna the attention she deserves.

River: *I'll see you at ten.*
Deanna: *Until then.*
She texts the address of the bar.
And I head home, to face a conversation I don't want to have.

· · ·

I use the backyard entrance, shower, change into jeans and a T-shirt. The second I step into the main room, I feel like a little boy. Underdressed, under-informed, under-equipped to deal with the reality of this summer.

"Going out tonight?" Grandma asks as if she doesn't know the answer. She's sitting on the couch, sipping red wine, snacking on a homemade charcuterie plate.

It's just us. Fern and North are already out. "In a while."

"Anywhere interesting?" She pretends she doesn't know my plans—as if Fern and North didn't tell her everything—as she spreads fig jam over a cracker. "Or anyone?"

"What are you doing?"

"Sharing." She adds white cheddar and offers the snack to me. "Your favorite."

"What are you doing with the neighbors?"

"Plotting against you, of course," she deadpans.

"Grandma."

She sets the cracker on a small plate and pushes it to the other side of the coffee table. "Fern wanted to have a girls' day. That's all."

"And you didn't invite Deanna for some reason?"

"Yes. Some reason." She shrugs as if she doesn't know what I mean.

Which is bullshit. "Don't."

"Don't what?"

"Interfere."

"The world doesn't revolve around you, sweetheart." She fixes herself a jam and a white cheddar cracker. "Did you eat dinner?"

"No."

"Then come. Bring the bottle and the rest of the block."

I bring the cheese but not the wine.

Grandma frowns as I take the seat next to her, but she doesn't ask for alcohol again.

"You have a bad strategy, you know." I take a bite of the cracker. Let the mix of rich fig, creamy cheese, and crunchy flour dissolve on my tongue.

"I do?"

"What do you think will happen if I fall for Deanna?"

She looks at me carefully. "I think she'll break your heart."

"Me, too."

Surprise streaks her expression.

"Is that what you're doing?" I ask.

"Orchestrating heartbreak?"

"Giving me a reason to go back to New York early."

"Sweetheart, I'm not that conniving."

"It won't work," I say.

"You won't fall for her?"

"I won't leave if you're not doing well."

The mood in the room changes immediately. No playfulness. No teasing. No fun.

We're all business now.

Grandma is against this. I know she is. She's clear about a few things in life: her love of work, her appreciation of sexual freedom, and her kids and grandkids flying out of the nest.

She doesn't want this, but I need it. I need to help, right now. I didn't help enough last time. I was too young to know how to help. I was too caught up in my own head, my feelings, my fear.

"Even if she breaks my heart," I say. "Even if she never wants to speak to me again. If Lexi says the same. If Mr. Huntington comes over here with a shotgun—"

"A shotgun, really?"

"A vintage pistol."

She nods. *That is more realistic.*

"If he challenges me to a duel. Says he'll shoot if he sees the man who broke his daughter's heart again."

"Are you planning to break her heart?" Grandma asks.

It's a good play. I almost latch onto the question. Of course not. Of course, I don't want to hurt Deanna. And I won't. Not intentionally.

I want to argue.

But this is all a distraction.

Grandma isn't worried about Deanna or Mr. Huntington. She wants to keep me from making sacrifices for her.

It won't work. "I want to tell you now," I say. "So you know."

"About you and Deanna?"

"I said I'd stay a month, but I'm not going back until September."

"River."

"No, Grandma. We agreed."

"This isn't what we agreed," she says.

"I'm not fussing," I say.

"You have a life there."

"It's only three months. And I have a job I can do anywhere." Sure, I need to fly in for meetings every so often, but everything else is doable with email, chat, call.

"What about that promotion you mentioned?" she asks. "The one that will let you shape new artists? You'd need to be in the city to find people."

Yes, and I'd love the opportunity, but I know what matters to me. This matters to me. "I'm not like you, Grandma. I don't live for work the way you do."

"You love the city."

"I love you, too." I'll be back in the city eventually. That's the part neither of us want to say. If she's that unwell, she won't be here long. I won't stay long.

"River." She packs a million pounds of intention into the word. Most of all: this isn't our deal. But we didn't agree to those terms, either. Grandma said one month, no fussing, take it or leave it.

Now, I'm proposing the entire summer, and fussing. But I'm working on the fussing.

Grandma swallows another sip of wine from her nearly empty glass. She speaks slowly. Carefully. "You need to think about your future."

"This is my future." I reach out and take her hand. "I don't want to look back and think about what could have been."

"But you will if you keep putting me first."

"I'm going out tonight, aren't I?"

"Are you there, River?" she asks. "Or will I get a call from Deanna in a few weeks, asking why you're never present? Why you're always stuck in your head? What it is you can't stop thinking about?"

"Why would she call instead of coming over?"

"Will I?" she repeats.

"I can't control her actions."

"You know what I mean."

I do. She wants me to promise I won't get lost in thought. She wants me to promise I won't let her illness get in the way of my romantic life. But I can't promise that. This is a big deal. And Grandma is, will always be, my first priority.

"She likes you."

"She likes me enough."

"Sweetheart, what are you talking about? She was looking at you like she wants to have her way with you."

"She was not."

"She was. And when you went to her house today—"

"You saw that?"

"I live here, don't I?" she asks. "What did you two do there?"

"My sex life is none of your business."

She smiles. "Do we need to have the talk again?"

"Fuck off."

Her smile widens. "Okay. Let's make a deal—"

"We already have a deal. You don't have any bargaining power."

"You'd deny a sick woman?" A playful tone drops into her voice. It's a joke. Only it's not a joke, too. It's the truth.

And it works like a charm. "Are you going to use that every time you don't get your way?" I ask.

"Of course."

My laugh breaks the tension in my shoulders. Grandma has always had a cutting sense of humor. Difficult situations only sharpen it.

"You can stay—"

"I can already stay—"

"No, sweetheart, this is my house," she says. "You can only stay in it if I allow you to stay in it."

"You'll kick me out of your house?"

"You know I'm good for it." She refers to my mother. She kicked her out of the house when she refused to get clean. Cutting her off seemed like the only way to help her.

Grandma didn't know she was pregnant.

How would she have bargained if she knew? Would she have offered Mom money to leave me with her?

Why is that such an obvious solution?

No. Grandma's illness is enough trauma for one summer. I don't need to dive into my mommy issues, too.

She's bluffing, though. That's the thing she doesn't realize. I know she's bluffing. She kicked my mother out because it was the only solution she saw, the only way she could help with Mom's drug addiction.

Grandma acts tough, but deep down, she wants us here as much as we want to be here.

"You promise to give this thing with Deanna your all, and I

won't object to you staying here as long as you want," she says.

"What if she ends things tonight?"

"You talk her out of it."

I raise a brow.

"Did you have sex?" she asks.

"Grandma."

"She's not going to end things before then. Or after. She's not her sister. She's a woman who wants a real relationship."

"Hypothetically," I say.

"Wouldn't you want to talk her out of ending things?"

Yes. The desire overwhelms me. I need the spark I have with Deanna. The brightness of it.

Not the too-harsh light of the sun, but the soft shimmer of the moon.

Fuck logic.

She's logical enough for the both of us.

"If she ended things, I'd respect her choice," I say. "Whether I liked it or not."

"As long as you give it your all."

"You have to stay out of it."

"Of course," she says.

"I mean it."

"Me, too." She offers her hand.

I shake, even though I don't believe her.

"Now...where is it you're going tonight? And who are you going to do there?"

"If I say I need the room, will you clear the house?" I ask.

She cuts another slice of cheese and plops it in her mouth. "You know the answer to that."

Of course she will. Fern and North, too, probably. "I won't."

"I can leave anyway."

"No. I want to wait," I say.

"You want to torture the poor girl?"

Of course she sees this as some sort of slow-burn torture.

"I've been home two days."

"Exactly, torture," she says.

"Or I make it to three."

It's a good goal. Three days.

I'm not sure I'm going to accomplish it.

But it's a good goal, nonetheless.

CHAPTER TWENTY-FOUR

River

Sips Don't Lie is the hippest place in the city to our south. Of course, we're still in Orange County, so that isn't saying much.

The decor screams of suburban kids trying to stake their claim as independent artists. Dark paint, framed records, bare light bulbs hanging from the ceiling. The kind that went out of style a few years ago.

The people fit into the place, too. Twentysomethings in a mix of designer gear and modern basics. The crowd is young, the dance floor is full, the vibe is a strange mix of Lexi and Deanna.

Pretty and popular and offbeat and thoughtful, all at once. Plus, the jazz-inspired pop music.

The bright pink fabric of Deanna's dress catches my eye right away. She's standing around a table in the back, chatting with a tall, dark-haired guy in slacks and a tie.

Lexi and my sisters are there, too. North stands out the way I do. The way Deanna does. She's too cool for a place like this, and it shows in her stylish mix of high-top sneakers and a dress from an independent designer. Fern fits in better. She's in a black dress and heels. A normal "going out" outfit.

And, of course, Lexi is in a soft shade of pink, blonde hair in long waves, makeup soft and feminine.

She's beautiful. As beautiful as she always is. And she's bright, too.

But I don't want her light right now.

I want Deanna.

It feels real. More real than anything.

But it's happening so fast. It's hard to trust.

I hear her laugh from across the room. Or maybe I feel it in the air. The magenta fabric. The long line of her back. The curve on her lips.

I want that laugh. The smile. All of it.

Jealousy fills my veins. It's rare I care enough to feel jealous. Right now, I want to deck the guy flirting with her. It's not a strong enough urge to overpower me, but it's there, and it's new and strange.

There's a reason I've never felt this before, but I lose interest in the logic the second his hand goes to her lower back.

No.

I want to be the one touching her.

Now.

The guy moves closer, close enough to whisper.

She tenses as his hand dips.

I want to say I move because she's uncomfortable, and it's true. But I also move because I don't like him touching her.

I cut through the space as casually as I can. I'm not afraid of a fight, but I'm not eager to court one, and I'd rather stay out of sight of my sisters.

I cut between a group of chatting friends and come to Deanna and the guy.

She looks up at me with surprise in her eyes.

I copy her MO—something smart and strategic—and mix it with mine—something fun and surprising. "Baby, how could you." I wrap my fingers around her wrist and pull her toward me. "With him?"

The guy looks at the two of us with confusion in his eyes.

"I specifically said a redhead," I say.

"A redhead?" she asks, and I can practically see the gears turning in her head.

"Yes, baby. I only had two rules. Any guy you want, as long as he's a redhead and as long as I can watch," I say.

She meets my gaze and raises a brow.

I mouth, "You trust me?"

She nods and looks to the guy. "He's got freckles."

"Freckles?" I scoff. "You think freckles are enough?"

"Isn't that your thing?" She feigns a look of confusion, as if she can't believe I'm not satisfied by someone who freckles instead of tans.

"No. Of course not." I turn to the guy. "It's not personal."

He stares at me in horror, struggling to catch up. Then he does and his light eyes go wide.

Deanna continues the game. "Make an exception. Please."

"It's only two rules," I say. "I know you love rules."

She struggles to hold in her laugh. "What if we get a wig? Will that work?" She turns to the guy. "What do you think? Are you open to that?"

"No way!" I answer before he can. "The curtains have to match the drapes."

"You know? I've got an early morning and I have to get out of here." He practically runs through the crowd to get away from us.

Deanna bursts into a fit of laughter.

I wrap my arms around her and pull her closer.

She sinks into me, her chest against my chest, her head in the crook of my neck, her joy filling every inch of my body.

She feels good. This feels good.

Nothing else matters. Only this.

"The curtains have to match the drapes." She wraps her arm around my neck. "You really said that."

"You don't know about my kink?" I ask.

"That's why you couldn't make things work with Alice," she says. "But not good for me." She pulls back and motions to her dark hair.

It's messy. I never see it messy.

There's something unbearably sexy about it.

I bring my lips to her ear. "Do you want to get out of here before the peanut gallery notices us?"

"I thought you'd never ask."

• • •

"Do you trust me?" Deanna asks as she slides into the passenger seat of my rental car.

"Why?" I start the engine.

She buckles her seat belt and reaches for me. For my thigh. "Your phone." She laughs. "Unlock it for me."

"Are you going to check my texts?"

"Your folder of nudes."

"I can send those to you."

Her smile is wicked. "The music. You're streaming it."

I pull my cell from my pocket and use Face ID to unlock it.

Her hand brushes mine as she takes it. She taps the screen a few times and a sultry jazz song fills the car. Something familiar. An old standard that fits Deanna like a glove.

"This isn't real jazz," she says. "Real jazz skips around. It requires focus. Or it steals it. I can't listen to it in the background. My brain keeps going back to the music, trying to find the pattern. But this kind of thing—a jazz-inspired slow jam—it gives the same feel without taking all the attention." She leans into the back seat with a sigh of pleasure. "And it's still sexy."

Very. The thought fills my head as I pull out of the parking lot and turn onto the street. We're twenty minutes from the house. Fifteen maybe, if we get all green lights. I don't want to wait. I want to be alone with her. I don't care about anything else.

"I trust you," she says. "About some things. Not everything."

"You don't know me that well."

"Do you really believe that?"

In some ways. Not in others.

"I think we know each other pretty well. You've seen me naked after all."

"Is that the definition?"

"One of them." Her eyes pass over me slowly, with that Deanna-like mix of curiosity, interest, need. "But I don't really want to talk right now." She turns her attention to the road, studying it, figuring something out there. "Turn right at the light."

That isn't the way home. That's the way to the toll road, to the 405, to Irvine, to the 55 even. We're on the other side of the freeway. We're far from all of that.

"Trust me, okay? I know where we're going."

I do trust her. That's the strange thing. Even though we've only been together for a few days, I trust her.

She directs me through the hills then onto a strange side street. Up the hill there, and all the way to the empty power plant—or an observatory of some kind—at the top of the hill.

This is it. The make-out spot all the kids coveted. Top of the World.

The same place her sister took guys. At least, that was the rumor. At the moment, I don't care. Lexi is a faraway memory. A strange echo of the person I was, the way pop music from middle school is.

Of course, I loved it at the time. Now, with all the distance and taste adulthood brings, I see it as a reminder of a different time, a younger version of myself.

Right now, I don't want anyone or anything else.

Only Deanna.

"Where do we park?" She laughs as she studies the gates of the plant slash observatory slash whatever the fuck it is. "I've never been here."

"Me neither."

"I think I saw something down the hill."

I turn the car around in a very awkward K-turn and find the spot she meant. A dirt overlook.

I park on it.

Silence falls as I turn the car off. A strange sensation fills the cabin. The sexual tension of the two of us together. And something else, something from a long time ago.

My desire to come here with Lexi, once upon a time. Deanna's observation of her sister. The rumors about the place. It was supposed to be magical. Sexy and romantic. A place that cemented your relationship as everything or nothing—

Either it was just sex, or it was love and you'd know, based on what you did here.

Or maybe I invented that. I don't know anymore. So much of our view of the world is inventions of our mind.

The assumption a face breaks into certain dimensions. Only it doesn't. The eyes are halfway down the face. Lower than most people expect.

We all see through a faulty lens.

And mine—

I don't know what the fuck I'm doing with it anymore.

"This is her move, you know," Deanna says. "Slow jams, fast cars—"

"My Prius is a fast car?"

She laughs. "Slow jams, slow cars—"

"Hey—"

"And a scenic overlook." She looks at the city, all spread out beneath us, quiet and twinkling with possibility. "Should we get out of the car and marvel?"

"Is that why you invited me here?"

"I don't know. What do you think she does?"

"I don't care what she does."

She turns to me and swallows hard. "I'm not good at this."

"You are."

"No." She shakes her head. "I don't know how to let go. That's why it was so easy for me with Stephan. He gave me rules. I followed them. I relaxed into that."

"We can make up rules."

"Like what?"

"You tell me if anything is too much."

She nods.

"Or if you want anything. Whatever comes to mind, you can say it. You won't upset me."

"Nothing will?"

"I'll get over it."

She doesn't seem to believe me, but she doesn't argue. "It's that easy?"

"And you let me lead."

"Let you Dom?"

A laugh spills from my lips. "Eventually, maybe. But we start here."

"I want to feel like me." She pushes the straps of the dress off her shoulders. She rolls the garment down her stomach, lifts her hips to roll it over her ass, kicks it off her feet.

Fuck.

"Much better." She lifts again, this time to push her black panties off her hips, and then she settles into my lap, naked except for her boots. "How does this go?"

Sex in a car isn't my expertise, but I can make it work. "Put the seat all the way back."

She does.

She shifts onto her side, leaving me just enough room to slide onto my side, on the passenger seat.

Deanna repositions us, so I'm on my back, and she's on top of me. "I have a condom in my purse," she says.

"I have one, too."

"Oh. Good." She settles into my lap. "I don't know how to do this."

"You fooled me." I bring my hand to her cheek.

She looks down at me, vulnerability and desire in her eyes. "I fool everyone. They think I'm this perfect, put-together person, but I'm not. I have problems, weaknesses, the same as everyone."

"I know."

"Do you?"

I think so.

"No. I don't want to talk anymore. I… Let you lead. Okay. I can do that. But first—" She leans down and brings her lips to mine. A soft brush. Then a harder one.

I pull back with a sigh. "Deanna."

She digs her fingers into my hair. "I love the way you say my name." She looks into my eyes again. "Like it feels good on your tongue." She shifts her hips, rolling her pelvis against me.

Her softness against my hardness. Only the rough fabric of my jeans and the thin cotton of my boxers in the way.

It's too much. Far too much.

But it gives me the hint of restraint I need to do this right.

I pull the rubber from my back pocket and place it on the dash.

She looks down at me as I look up at her. There's an intensity to the eye contact. To the desire in her green eyes.

She's beautiful, yes, but that's not why I want her. And she's sexy as sin, but that's only a part of it.

There's something inside her that fits something inside me.

The emotional. And the physical.

Every ounce of the physical.

Desire rolls through my body as I pull her into a kiss. It takes everything I have to stay soft and slow, to stay patient.

This is what I want, to ease her into it, to tease her until she can't take it anymore.

But, well—

I might have to cop one of her moves, make a strategic choice to do things faster. Since I didn't make the strategic choice to rub one out before this.

It's been so long since I've wanted someone this much, since I've needed this kind of restraint.

No. I've never wanted someone this much. And I've never felt this unrestrained.

She tastes so good, like Deanna and lime and possibility. The hesitation in her posture dissolves as she kisses me. Abandon takes over.

That's the only word that explains it. She kisses me like she's trying to take something from me and give something to me. Like she'll die if she doesn't find what she needs, like I'm the only thing she needs.

She's intense and purposeful, the way she is everywhere.

Firm and yielding.

Determined and playful.

The Deanna I adore everywhere is the woman I want here. And I do adore her everywhere. The feeling spreads through my body, competing with desire, then mingling with it, forming something deeper and purer and stronger.

I need her lips, her hips, her sex, her orgasm, her affection.

Everything she has.

All of it.

She pulls back with a sigh. "Take this off." She undoes the top button of my shirt. "Please."

"Can you let someone else lead?"

"I said please."

I smile.

She laughs.

For a moment, the car fills with the sort of awkward energy I imagined at the park. The strange situation, the difficult posture, the limited space.

Then she curls her hand around my neck and all that

awkwardness dissolves into need.

I need her. Here. Everywhere.

I don't take off my shirt. I bring my hand to her hip and pull her body into mine.

She kisses me hard, her tongue circling mine, her need mingling with mine.

My fingers brush her pelvis. Then lower. Lower.

There.

The soft flesh I need.

She gasps as I draw a circle against her clit. She places her hand over mine, guiding me to the right pressure, the right speed.

She groans against my lips as we hit it. "River." She pulls back with a gasp. She digs her nails into my shoulder.

Then it's the button of my shirt. The first two. Enough that she can press her palm against my chest.

Her hand feels good against my skin. Like it belongs there.

We belong here.

Right now, I only need one thing and that's Deanna Huntington coming on my hand. And then on my cock.

I bring my lips to hers and work her with those slow, steady circles.

This time, she dissolves into me, sinks into me.

I lead and she follows. We stay together in that perfect rhythm, with just the right pattern. We move together, again and again, as her nails sink into my skin and her moans dissolve on my lips.

She's almost there.

Right where I need her.

I work her exactly how she needs me.

Her nails sharpen in my skin.

Her groans vibrate down my throat.

"Fuck." She pulls back with a sigh. "River." She knots her hand in my hair. "Fuck."

Her eyes flutter closed. Her head falls to one side. Her brow furrows. Her lips part.

Then every part of her expression releases into a waterfall of bliss.

She's beautiful here.

She's everything.

She tugs at my hair as she pulses on my hand.

I work her through her orgasm, watching every perfect moment. She's a fucking work of art. She's poetry.

No, she's a million times better.

She's real.

Her eyes flutter open as she catches her breath. She looks down at me, hazy with bliss, but determined all the same.

She scoots back on my legs, undoes the button of my jeans.

I lift my hips to move the jeans, and my boxers, away.

She watches me with wide eyes, studying me with the intensity only Deanna can bring. As if she wants to memorize every line, every curve, every inch.

If I didn't know better, I'd feel like a specimen, an animal at the zoo. But I know better. I know this is how she shows appreciation. I know this is her version of a work of art.

Pleasure floods my senses as she wraps her hand around me. She starts softly. Then harder. As hard as I need.

A groan falls from my lips.

Then she kisses me, and she works me with that same pressure and my body takes over. No thinking. Only the sensation of being in the moment, with her, exactly where I'm supposed to be.

After her next stroke, I wrap my hand around her wrist.

She gasps as I grab her, so I make my grip harder.

Her pupils dilate. Her chest heaves. She likes it this way. Not quite forceful, but close.

And it's as thrilling as I imagined, leading the most powerful woman in the world.

"Condom." I release her wrist.

She takes another heavy breath and reaches for the packet. She keeps her eyes on me as she tears it with her teeth and rolls it over me.

My hands go to her hips. She follows my motions as I lift her and position her body over mine.

I bring her lower and lower.

Until she brushes against me.

My body begs me to relent, to take all of her, all at once. She already feels so good. Too good.

But I need to take it slow. She's trusting me, here, and that means more than anything.

I lift her and tease her again.

And again.

Until her eyes flutter closed, and her hands find my chest, my neck.

Then, when I'm sure she's as desperate as I am, I pull her over me, one perfect inch at a time.

She envelops me with her soft flesh, stretching to take me, arching her back just enough to pull me deeper.

She's good at this. I don't know how she can see it any other way.

Her fingers curl into my neck. "You feel good."

"You feel like heaven."

She arches her hips again. She has that itch, the urge to lead.

I can work with that. "Show me, Dee." I curl my fingers into her hips. "Show me how fast you like it."

Deanna brings her hands to my shoulders and uses them for leverage, lifting higher, then taking me again.

Slowly, to start.

Then a little faster.

A little harder.

I try to watch her work, but it's too intense. I have to close my eyes to contain the sensation.

There's too much bliss in the car. It's overwhelming.

"No." She brings one hand to my chin and runs her fingers over my jawline. "Watch."

My eyes blink open.

She runs her fingers down my neck with a soft, slow touch. "I love the way you watch."

I do, too.

I study her expression as she drives onto me again. The need in her eyes. The softness in her brow. The curl of her lips.

The dark hair, falling back and forth.

The sharp collarbones.

The bounce of her breasts. They're small, maybe, but they're just the right size for my palm.

I cup her with both hands. I watch as I toy with her perfect pink nipples.

She groans and my attention goes to her lips, her eyes, her neck.

There's too much of her to see. I want all of it.

A mirror. Next time, I need a mirror. A camera. To record this forever.

If she's game.

Now, I need this, all of it.

I pull her closer.

She groans as I take her nipple into my mouth. I wrap my lips around her and test different speeds and pressure. A sharp flick of my tongue. Then a soft one. A corkscrew. A counterclockwise one.

She digs her nails into my skin as she drives over me again and again.

For the first time in a long time, I feel it: the sense we're one. Not just because our bodies are joined. Because we're working together. Because we're in tune with each other.

She's not a vision in my head. She's another fucked-up person with flaws and needs and inconsistencies. And we're in a too-small car, on a too-warm night.

The imperfection makes it perfect.

My thoughts dissolve as she brings her lips to mine. She rocks her hips against mine, pulsing around me as she comes, pulling me closer and deeper with every contraction of her body.

The intensity of it overwhelms me.

She works through her orgasm, then she slows and catches her breath. "Use me."

Use Deanna Huntington.

"Use me to come. However you need it." She looks down at me. "Please."

The *please* almost undoes me. It's rare on her lips. It's mine. A tone she doesn't use with anyone else.

I bring my hands to her hips and tilt her a little closer, then I guide her over me.

Again and again.

Exactly how I need.

And then she breaks, rolling her hips in a perfect figure eight, and I come right there.

She draws the shape again and again, working me through my orgasm, groaning as I fill her.

She waits until I spill every drop, then she pulls back, untangles our bodies, finds her dress.

I wrap the condom in a tissue, stuff it in the now-used box, help her into her dress.

She fixes my boxers, jeans, shirt buttons. All but the top two.

I move into the driver's seat.

She stays in the passenger.

The car still feels electric, but it's not charged the same way. The energy is different. Softer and harder all at once.

Because I had her and she had me and I really want to do it again.

"How does the rest of this go?" she asks.

"We go home," I say. "Do it again."

I expect her to object, to tell me it was a one-time thing, a chance at magic. But she doesn't. She nods and boots up the stereo.

CHAPTER TWENTY-FIVE

Deanna

Halfway back to the house, it occurs to me:
I live with my sister. Yes, I have my own room, but I don't have privacy in my apartment. Not the kind I need for this.

And with River staying with his grandmother all summer, I'm ready to guide him to a hotel.

"I share a place with Lexi." I don't want to bring her up. It dissolves the magic. And there is magic, as much as I can't explain it.

"I have an idea." He pulls onto the freeway. "Fern. She wants this to happen. I didn't see it earlier, but I do now. Text her as me. Ask her to keep Lexi busy."

"Really?" I ask.

He nods *really*.

I find the texts on his cell, the thread with his sister, and I text as him.

River: *Do me a favor. Keep Lexi busy tonight. Ask her to sleep over.*

Fern: *Called it. I knew you wanted to bop D. She's totally your type. North owes me $20. You're all good on the Huntington Apartment front. Lexi already went home with someone. To his place.*

She always goes to their place. Or somewhere else, in her car. That's part of her MO.

Does she miss Jake enough she's seeing *him* or is this someone else? Fern wouldn't know the difference.

No. It's not my problem. Jake knows they're on a break. He knows they're free to see other people. I advised him to forgive her if she sees someone else.

If he can't do that—

Well, that's his responsibility. Not mine.

I really hope he can. Because they are strangely perfect for each other. They're both super freaks.

River: *Who?*

Fern: *Don't tell me you care, Mr. Romance. I know you're not enough of a cad to go after two women at the same time. Or are you? I'll come home and cockblock you right now.*

River: *No. Of course not.*

Of course he isn't.

This is our night.

And if Lexi is with another guy, well—

It's her life. And I am comfortable with that. Whatever it means for the company.

Right now, though, I actually don't care about the company, or her relationship with Jake, or her habit of finding a new guy every two weeks, or anything except fucking River again.

I'm not used to this feeling of work not mattering.

It's scary and thrilling and I don't care about that, either.

Because I really need to fuck him again.

• • •

Despite every intention of having my way with River, I fade the second I step inside the apartment. By the time I get to my room, remove my heels, and do away with my dress, I'm exhausted.

He notices. "Go to bed."

I shake my head. "This first."

"In the morning. When I get all your energy."

My cheeks flush. Dirty talk is one thing. The sort of sweet yet sexy things he says are another.

How can anyone make sex sound so sweet and caring? The more kink, the sweeter, really. He's a freak. That's the only explanation.

Not that I mind.

I brush my teeth, wash my face, climb into my short pajamas then into bed.

He goes to take his turn, but I fall asleep before he gets back. I sleep soundly and wake with all the warmth and ease people associate with Sunday mornings.

The scents of tea and ham waft into the room.

The tea is normal, but ham? When did we buy ham?

I soak in the feeling of the cool sheets, the warm blanket, the heat from the other side of the bed.

When I was dating Stephan, I tossed and turned all night. He cursed my insomnia. Some nights, he gave up and slept on the couch. Or I slept on the couch to keep from disturbing him.

It didn't bother me. I never understood the romance of sleeping next to someone. It's not as if I absorb the closeness while unconscious.

Right now, feeling the warmth River left, inhaling the faint scent of his shampoo—

There is something about it, something intimate about the sheer domesticity.

After I sneak to the ensuite bathroom and move through my morning routine, I slip into my silk button-up shirt and shorts and meet River in the main room.

He smiles the second he sees me. Then he notices my attire and his smile shifts from *I'm happy to see you* to *damn, I really see you*.

He does. Which is strange.

I've been on two dozen dates with "great matches" and none of them see me. He does. Why? Is it the algorithm or me or some other factor?

The question dissolves as his eyes pass over me. Desire pushes all my thoughts aside. Then I notice the rest of him—he's only wearing boxers—and my brain shifts into full want mode.

Must have River now.

It feels so good, to release my thoughts, to not live in my head, even if it's for a minute.

"Good morning." He says it with ease, like he's said it to me a million times.

"Morning." The words are more awkward on my tongue. I don't remember the last time I invited someone to sleep with me. Even with Stephan, I rarely stuck around for long enough to see him in the mornings. I had to run, or finish work, or study.

He motions to the ceramic pot on the counter. "Tea?"

"Are you going to offer crumpets, too?"

"Eggs Benedict."

"And I'm the fancy one?"

"It's easier than you'd think." He motions to the table. "Sit. I'll bring it when it's done."

I don't follow his instructions. I meet him at the counter and wrap my arms around him. He's warm and hard and safe. I don't remember the last time someone felt this safe.

"You keep distracting me and I'll burn breakfast."

"We could skip breakfast."

"Do I need to tie you to the bed to make you behave?" His voice drops to something low and breathy.

"Yes."

"Later."

It's appealing. Very appealing. But it's scary, too. Trusting anyone that much. How much I want to trust him everywhere.

Despite my desire to test his claim, I go easy on River. I fix a mug of tea and slide onto the kitchen island, watching him work from the table. I'm close enough to see the muscles in his back, but not so close I absolutely have to touch him.

He melts butter and blends eggs with the comfort and ease of someone who's done it a thousand times.

"Do you normally cook like this?" I ask.

"On weekdays, I keep it simple. Eggs and toast."

"That's simple?"

"Compared to what your personal chef makes."

"I don't have a personal chef." My cheeks flush. "Or any chef. I microwave my oatmeal myself."

"You eat oatmeal?"

"What's wrong with oatmeal?"

"It's plain for you," he says.

"I add raisins and cinnamon."

He laughs.

"Am I that funny?"

"Yeah." He slips English muffins into the toaster. "You're determined not to be the person people think you are. But you're not sure who that is, so you change tracks all the time."

"I do not."

"And if I said you seem like a girl who loves a simple breakfast?"

It's true. I shouldn't care what other people think of me, but I do. I hate when people assume I've never worked hard, or done anything for myself, because of my last name. I didn't ask for it. I understand I grew up with privileges other people never experienced: great schools, a beautiful, safe neighborhood, access to anything I want to do. But I don't like when people erase my effort. My loss. It's not like it hurt less, losing Mom, because we had plenty of money. I spent more than half my life without her. "I'd say you're right. I've fixed my own oatmeal since I was thirteen."

"Do you cook anything else?"

"Do sandwiches count?" I ask.

"If you heat them."

"Grilled cheese?"

He laughs. "The Huntington family sitting down to grilled cheese. I don't see it."

"Why do you think we're so different than you? We live next door."

"You're right." He nods as he flips the ham. "I was in awe the first time I saw my grandma's house. I didn't want to fit in there. I didn't want to be a part of this world. My mom and I lived in an apartment in Riverside. We didn't have any of Grandma's money. She'd— How much do you know about my family?"

"Only what you and Ida have told me," I say.

"What does she say about my mom?" he asks.

"She's not in the picture."

"Anything else?"

I shake my head.

"Really? No." He nods with understanding. "Grandma never answers a question she doesn't want to answer. She's good at turning things around."

"What do you mean?"

"Ask me something inappropriate," he says.

"Uh…" I say the first thing that comes to mind. "Have you ever put anything in your ass?"

He laughs. "That's your first question?"

"Are you doing it now? Or is that a legitimate response?" It's a good strategy, actually. Smart. But it's not his style, really. He's not a strategic communicator. He's earnest and in the moment, trying to tap into real emotions.

"It is what Grandma would say." He laughs. "I guess I take after her."

"No. She'd say something like, *sweetheart, if you have the desire, you have to take the plunge. If not, don't,*" I say. "But I know what you mean."

"She would."

"Oh yeah, that's a direct quote."

He turns to me and raises a brow.

"Lexi asked her once," I say. "She wasn't about to ask Dad for sex tips."

"Grandma gave her sex tips? No. Don't tell me."

"You don't want to picture that?"

He shakes his head.

My stomach flutters and churns at the same time. There she is again. Lexi.

Sure, this is our apartment. She's my sister and my business partner. It's normal that she takes up space in my thoughts.

But here?

I don't want her here, right now. I don't want to wonder if he thinks of her. Or if he wants someone more like her.

I just want to be. For once, I just want to be.

I close my eyes, take a deep breath, and focus on the moment. The savory scent of ham, the robust taste of tea, the warm sun streaming through the windows.

River, standing at the stove, in only his boxers.

The man looks just as nice from behind. Strong shoulders and back, tight ass, muscular thighs. Not that I'm objectifying him. Well, maybe a little.

Where were we?

Right. Moms. Big, emotional topics. Not the time to trace the tattoo curling over his shoulder.

Really, who needs big, emotional topics when we can touch? Breakfast first, maybe. Then touching. Sex. Nonverbal communication. Way better than verbal communication.

That's science.

He doesn't bring it back to moms or push away. "Can you set the table? No. You'll argue with a direct order."

"Here."

"There, too." His eyes flit to the bedroom door. "Not that

I'm complaining."

My chest flushes. "I have manners."

He motions *go ahead and show me*. Which, yes, does make me want to prove him wrong. But only for a second. Only because, for so long, he's seen me as a spoiled rich girl.

Even if he doesn't now, he did. And I hated that he didn't see me. Even if I was too scared to let anyone in.

Letting my Huntington training kick in, I set the table. Plates, mugs, silverware, napkins. Everything in place. Everything just so.

River meets me at the table with breakfast. Two perfectly arranged English muffins topped with ham, poached eggs, and hollandaise. Eggs Benedict. A fancy dish. What he thinks of me. Or maybe how he thinks he fits into this world.

No, we're still Californians. Our idea of a fancy breakfast always includes avocado. This is his life in New York showing.

He can't help but show flashes. That's how much he belongs there.

"Have you cooked for your grandma, since you've been home?" I ask.

"A little," he says. "She's stubborn. She wants to prove she can take care of herself."

"Maybe she wants to take care of you."

"I'm twenty-six."

"You're still her grandson."

"You let your dad take care of you?"

"Now, yeah," I say. "In college, I tried to make it on my own." He raises a brow.

"Okay. I wasn't totally on my own. He paid my tuition, but I tried to pay for the rest. I got a job at a lab. When that wasn't enough, I worked nights at a bar."

"That's where you learned about cocktails?"

I nod. "They're a formula. They make sense."

"And you like things that make sense."

"Doesn't everyone?" I already know the answer. No. He doesn't. He likes magic. And magic can't make sense, or it wouldn't be magic.

He doesn't answer.

I don't ask him to. "I worked hard. I bought store-brand bread and Lipton tea."

"How long did you last?" he asks.

"A semester," I admit. "It's too hard to work while going to school. I don't know how anyone does it."

"People do what they have to do to survive."

"Why do you have a chip on your shoulder?" I don't mean it as harshly as it sounds, but he doesn't shrink from them. "About money?"

"Ida isn't as rich as Mr. Huntington."

"Sure, she bought the house a long time ago, when it was worth less. But she's a successful writer. She makes a lot of money. Especially after that one TV adaptation." One of the streaming networks made a series from her books. "I've seen her royalty checks."

After my first business class, I asked Ida how money worked for her. We'd covered various arts but not from the perspective of an artist. I was curious to know averages. Though her numbers are far from the mean.

"It's nowhere near the Huntington ballpark."

"And she invested her husband's life insurance money, I know. She tells that story a lot. She always jokes about how he was useful for two things."

"Sex and money?"

I nod. "Do you think she means that?"

"I don't know. He died before I was born. I never saw them together. It could be her way of coping with grief. It could be her way of making light of poor treatment."

"It's hard to know with her."

He nods.

"That is one thing I love about my dad," I say. "He's used to getting his way and everyone caring what he thinks."

"So you take after him?"

I flip him off.

He laughs and cuts a slice of Eggs Benedict.

"I do," I say. "You're right. He always treated me and Lexi that way, too, like our opinions were valid, even though we were young. Even though we were women."

"He's a good dad."

"Is it about your grandma?" I ask. "The money thing?"

"Not exactly."

"Then what?"

"My mom," he says.

"Do you want to talk about it?"

"That depends," he says. "On what we're doing here."

"We're eating breakfast."

"No. This. Us."

Oh.

"What do you want, Deanna? Is this one night of magic or is it more?"

CHAPTER TWENTY-SIX

Deanna

Is this one night of magic or is it more?

My mouth goes sticky. I don't know how to answer the question. I don't know the plan.

This is all off script.

I threw away the script sometime yesterday. Probably when I accepted his offer to kiss me. And let him strip me naked in the living room.

That happened ten feet away from where we are now, but it feels like it happened ten thousand miles away, six years ago.

This is moving fast. Too fast.

But then—

"Aren't you leaving next month?" I ask. "Don't you have a job in New York?"

"Can you keep a secret?" he asks.

"No," I say. "I'm not a good liar." *Usually.*

He studies my expression, deciding if he trusts me. He must, because he leans in close, and he lowers his voice. "I'm not leaving until September."

"You're here all summer?"

He nods.

"And after that?"

"I have business in New York, but I don't know if I'll stay."

"You don't know if you'll stay or come back here?"

He nods.

"How am I supposed to predict a future like that?" I ask. "If you might go back to New York, at some time, between, what, six months and sixty years?"

"You're right," he says. "It's not a fair question. I'm not sure I can answer."

He's not sure if this is one night of magic or something more.

Oh.

Well.

That's the plan. He's proving his point about love. So, if that's all he's doing here, that's fine. It shouldn't bother me since he's following the plan. But then I said that, didn't I?

"It's not you, Dee," he says.

My cheeks flush at the sound of my nickname. It's different on his lips. It just is.

"It's me. No. I don't mean it like that, the cliche."

I want to jump in and object, but I stop myself.

"There's something happening in my life," he says. "Something that takes a lot of my attention. I don't know how much I have to give."

"Okay."

"Okay?"

"Have you met me?"

He laughs. "Deanna Huntington, the workaholic?"

"It's true."

"You've barely talked about work all weekend."

"I have, too." And I started this whole thing to keep him away from Lexi. But that's a distant memory. It's irrelevant. "And I don't know what this is. I'm not like you, River. I don't run to my feelings. I have to think about them for a while, understand them, imagine a future."

"Make a plan?"

"What's wrong with a plan?"

"Nothing." He takes a long sip of his tea. "Would you really be okay, seeing where this goes?"

"No." That's the truth. I'm not good at being in the moment. Or living without a plan. Or going off script. "But I'd rather do that than end it now."

"It might get messy."

"It's already messy," I say. "But we are friends, aren't we? No matter what, we're friends."

He nods.

"I want things to stay that way. If you ever feel like something is threatening that, tell me. If you're tired of being with someone so logical, tell me."

His brow furrows with confusion. He doesn't understand what I mean. Not yet.

Every other guy does, eventually. I don't know if he will. For once, I don't want to assume he will. "Or if you realize this isn't what you want. If either one of us decides this is better as a fling, we say that, and we end as friends. No questions asked. No hard feelings."

"So now you have a plan?"

"A plan to not have a plan, yeah."

He smiles.

"I know. It's funny. I'm so Deanna."

"You are."

"I would prefer steps and concrete information," I say.

"An algo that tells you if we're a good match?"

The thought makes my stomach twist. Why? Isn't this what I'm doing? I'm trying to use logic to help the world find love. I think of all the matches on the app that went nowhere. They weren't perfect, but some were good. Good enough I could expect a short relationship. So where the hell is my logic? "No."

"Really?"

"Yeah."

"Should I check for a fever?"

"No," I say. "Maybe. But I...I don't know. I don't want to think. Is that okay?" I can't believe how true it feels. I don't want to think. Of all the people in the world, I'm the last one who can stop thinking. But I don't care. I feel it.

He sees me in a way other people don't, and I love it. I feel myself with him in a way I don't with other people.

Even if I don't understand that, either.

"I don't want to think, either." He cuts another slice of Eggs Benedict. "But I have to feed you before I do anything else."

"You don't have to."

"I do," he says. "I like taking care of you."

Which is scary. I don't let anyone take care of me. Because what if they leave and I don't know how to take care of myself anymore? Not practically and not emotionally.

"You don't let your guard down easily."

"You, either."

He raises a brow.

"You're like your grandma. You're good at making a no sound like a yes." I take a bite. Let the rich, creamy sauce dissolve on my tongue. "Asking me a personal question to keep me from following up on yours."

"I am, aren't I?"

He is, but I understand that. I understand how hard it is to talk about these things. "You don't have to talk about your mom," I say.

"I know." He takes another bite. He fixes his tea. He sips.

For a few minutes, we stay there, focusing on breakfast, enjoying the warmth of the morning, the company.

Then he starts. "She's a drug addict. There are nicer ways to say it, but they all get at the same thing. She chooses heroin over everything else."

For a moment, his expression steels. He breathes through it, takes another sip, eats another bite.

Then he continues, "Grandma kicked her out when she was nineteen. It was her third warning. 'If you bring that into my house again, you're not welcome here.' That was it. Mom came to her for money a few times, but she was too proud to ask for other help. Even when she got clean."

"Where were you in all that?" I ask.

"She was pregnant when she left." He relays the information the way I would: as facts. *This is the timeline. This is what everyone claimed happened.* No editorializing. No feelings of his own. "She swore to Grandma she wasn't using, that she was only holding for her boyfriend, but Grandma didn't believe her."

"Do you?" It's not like me to pry this way, but I want to know. Not for the sake of holding onto the information. Because I want to know where he hurts and help him guard the wounds.

"I don't know. I think she tried. I think she wanted to be a good mom. There's no history of withdrawal in my medical records. That happens, sometimes, when the mother is using opiates during her pregnancy. The fetus develops a dependence." His voice softens. His eyes get hazy, the way they do when he's working on a drawing, like he's off somewhere else in his head. "That doesn't happen to everyone. And I don't remember when she first started using. Or maybe she always was."

That's hard. That's impossibly hard. I want to say something, comfort him, but I don't know how. I'm not good at this.

"No. I remember. One day, I came home from school, third grade, I think, and something was different. She was different. I didn't know why but I knew she was off," he says. "She got hazy. She stopped caring about things like making dinner or getting places on time or paying bills. She had a boyfriend who helped her with money. He'd hand me the checks and say, 'Thanks for taking care of your mama, little guy.'"

"How old were you?"

"Eight or nine."

"Damn."

He laughs. "Yeah. Damn." He takes a long sip of tea and drifts back to that hazy, faraway place. "He was decent to her. He wasn't decent to his family—he was married with kids—but he was decent to her."

"You knew he was married?"

"He didn't take off his ring. He took her on dates sometimes. Or he took her to the bedroom. I wasn't old enough to realize the nature of their arrangement."

"Sex for money?"

"A sugar daddy kind of thing. He was a wealthy guy. He kept us in a decent place. Until he ended things, we lived a pretty good life."

"How did you know he had a family?"

"He didn't hide it," he says. "He showed me pictures of his kids. When I got older and moved in with Grandma, I saw him with his family once, at a soccer game. He lived here. He grew up here, with my mom."

"That close?" I ask.

He nods.

I give him a chance to catch his breath. I try to find something wise to say in my tea. There's nothing, so I offer what I have. "I'm sorry."

"Don't be. I've spent half my life with my favorite person in the world."

"Still. I know how it feels to lose your mom."

"It's not the same," he says. "She's still alive."

"But you had her and you lost her. It's hard."

He looks at me funny, like he's just putting something together.

"What?"

"I'm an asshole."

Sometimes, sure, but not at this particular moment. "Why?"

"I thought you lived a charmed life," he says. "'Cause you grew up in this big house, with all this love and attention."

"I did."

"You watched your mom die," he says. "I have no idea how hard that is. How hard that must have been, as a kid."

"It's not a competition."

"I wasn't fair to you," he says.

"You didn't know me."

"I judged you," he says.

"Everyone judges everyone."

"I told myself I was better than that." He takes a long sip. "I'm sorry."

"You don't have to apologize. I judged you, too."

"I'm sorry anyway," he says.

"I'm not."

His smile breaks up the pain on his face. "Good. You wouldn't be you if you were."

"Is that a compliment or an insult?"

"You know it's a compliment."

I do. That's the weird thing. I know he really, truly likes me the way I am. "Thanks then." I take another sip of my tea, even though it's too cold. "How did you end up here, with your grandma?"

"The guy ended things because he wanted to recommit to his wife. Mom never found a better way to cover the rest of the rent. We got evicted and Mom was running out of money, so she came to Grandma. After that…I know her story and Mom's, but I don't know the truth."

"What's her story?" I ask.

"Grandma says Mom came by, asking for money, and she made a deal: six figures for her parental rights. Mom could go off and do whatever she wanted with the money, but she had to make Grandma my legal guardian."

"Do you believe that?"

"It makes sense, doesn't it?"

Yes, but it's not really my place to say. "Your mom's story?"

"Grandma was vindictive. Angry. She threatened Mom. She'd call CPS. She'd call the police, with evidence of neglect, of drug use. She had friends on the force, power she wasn't afraid to use."

"If your mom didn't leave you with her?"

He nods.

"Do you believe that?"

"Grandma has good intentions, but she's driven."

"And driven people will do anything for what they want sometimes." I know that better than most.

"It's probably somewhere between those two things," he says.

"I, uh, thanks."

"Thanks?"

"For telling me that. People don't really share with me."

His eyes pass over me slowly. There's a heat to it, but it's subtle. More affection and curiosity than anything. "You're intimidating."

"Still?"

"Even more, the better I know you."

I fight my blush with my tea, but it doesn't help cool me. "I'm trying to be sentimental here."

"I know."

"It's not my strong suit," I say.

"I know. It's sexy."

"But this is—"

"Serious, yeah. So what. Do you want to keep talking?"

"Are you trying to distract me?"

"Yeah," he says. "Does it matter?"

CHAPTER TWENTY-SEVEN

Deanna

Seduction is easier in the moonlight. Or the city light. Or the candlelight.

Here, under the fluorescent bulbs of the kitchen, with the morning sunlight streaming through the sheer curtains, in the middle of the big, open room?

The dining table isn't sexy. The counters, either. The couch, maybe.

But then he stripped me here yesterday and I didn't really notice the lighting. And I am wearing silk pajamas. Silk is sexy. In theory anyway.

No. I'm not Lexi. I don't need slow jams and fast cars. I need something all mine.

What would the most confident version of Deanna do?

That's the better question.

I push my breakfast plate aside. "Is it a bad sign we're dodging important conversations?"

"Or a sign we're too sexy to resist?"

"Did you just say that?"

"How would you say that?" He stands and offers his hand. "Cause I know how to explain my side."

I stand, too.

He moves around the table. "I wanted to strip you the second you stepped out here."

"Yeah?" I meet him at the head of the table.

He looks down at me, his dark eyes on fire with need. "This." He runs his thumb over the hem of my shirt. "This is Deanna Huntington."

Maybe, but it's a lot of people. "This is a really popular brand of pajamas," I say. "A start-up run by a woman who couldn't find any affordable luxury sleepwear."

"You know her personally?"

What does that matter? "Do you need an introduction?"

"You do know her." He smiles and brings his lips to mine.

I murmur through the kiss. "Why is that funny?"

"You're different in private." He runs his thumb over my shirt again. "More modest about your success, your ambition, your connections."

"We met briefly at a summit for women entrepreneurs. It's not a big deal."

"See."

"No, it's not that." I hook my arms around his neck. "Wait. Why are we talking?"

"You're sexy when you blush."

We're still in the main room. We should move to the bedroom in case Lexi comes home soon. But then Lexi never gets home early from overnights. And I'm too on fire to move. "No, no, no. If you don't have to talk, I don't have to talk."

"You don't have to talk." He undoes the bottom button of my blouse. "And I don't have to do this." He slips his hand under my shirt and drags his fingertips up my skin.

The soft brush of his touch ignites a fire inside me. It's been less than twelve hours since we drove to the top of that hill, but it feels like it's been a million years.

I need him to touch me here. Everywhere.

I need it in a way I've never needed anything.

He teases me with soft brushes of his hands. Higher and higher and higher and—

There.

His index finger brushes my nipple. Then the middle finger. The ring finger.

He moves to soft, slow circles.

I try to find some way to spur him on. "River—"

"Yeah?" He barely gets the words out. He wants this, too. Wants me, too.

"Are you really stooping to blackmail?"

"Blackmail?" He draws a circle around my nipple. "No. This is a negotiation."

"You're an artist."

"And?"

"Why do you only speak in deals?"

He laughs. "People think artists are sensitive. Softhearted." He looks at me, the picture of calm negotiation, as he draws circles around my tender skin, again and again.

My eyes flutter closed.

My fingers curl into his stomach.

"But the arts are the most cutthroat place in the world," he says. "You wouldn't last a day."

"Uh-huh."

He draws another circle around me. "Keep talking."

"We're talking?"

He presses his lips to my neck. "Why are you shy about your connections?"

"I'm not. The meeting was bullshit. A photo op so some tech guy could tell the world he supported women. He didn't do anything to help us. He didn't even rent the ballroom for the rest of the afternoon."

"He didn't respect you?"

"No more talking."

"Keep talking." He toys with me again.

My body hums with desire. I don't want to talk, but I don't want him to stop, either. As long as he doesn't stop, I can talk about anything. But what the hell are we talking about anyway?

Some meeting.

The fake women's summit. "Yes, he didn't respect me." I let my forehead fall onto his chest. "He didn't respect any of us. I see it all the time. These men who think it's cute two women in their twenties made a company. As if we're their daughters or granddaughters, and we're asking them to buy supplies for our lemonade stand."

"Bastards."

"Bastards who rule the world," I say.

"Older men?"

"Younger ones, too. They're a little less obvious about talking down to us, but they still put us in a category. Women inventors. Women's projects. Women's problems. As if dating is something only women do. As if men don't need clothes or clean houses or childcare."

"You hate them?"

"Sometimes." I find enough sense to blink my eyes open. Look up at him.

His eyes are filled with desire, too.

And he's way too sexy like this, all power and control and need and dark eyes and dark hair and nimble, artist's fingers.

"You're sexy when you're angry," he purrs.

"You're a freak." And that is one of the hottest things anyone has ever said to me. He leans down and presses his lips to mine. A hard, fast kiss. Then another, just as hard, but slower.

His hands go to my hips, and he pulls my pelvis against his. I feel his hardness against me, and it feels so good.

Why does that feel so fucking good?

"Keep talking." He places a kiss on my neck.

"Do I need to hit a certain word count?"

He presses his lips to my neck a little slower, a little softer.

My body hums.

Another kiss. "You could admit it."

"Admit what?" Seriously, why are we talking?

He holds steady, speaks with confidence and clarity. "You downplay your accomplishments."

"Having a vagina isn't an accomplishment."

In response, he rocks his pelvis against mine again.

I'm not sure if that means *hell yeah, it is* or *I like yours* or *keep talking or I stop*.

But then I don't care.

As long as he keeps doing that.

Wait.

I don't have to play by his rules. I don't have to play by anyone's rules but my own.

I press my palm into his stomach. "The app is amazing, and I designed it. The base of it, I built alone. My ideas. My code. My insights. From there, other people helped. We have a small team, but they're amazing. I'm not shy about saying I started this. I know I did. I know I kicked ass with it."

"You did."

"You have no idea if I did or not. Don't pretend."

"No, I do," he says. "I signed up last night."

"You did?" River opened up the app. He signed up. That's not his thing. That's an odd choice. Is it for me, or him, or some other reason?

"After you fell asleep on me."

A million things flit through my head at once.

"Do you need to get your phone out and check?"

"No."

"You sure?"

No.

"I used a fake name."

"I can check your IP address. My IP address. You used my Internet." It's easy to back solve these things. Even if people

know how to hide what they're doing, it's pretty easy to figure it
out when you have access to all the available data.

"Will you?"

"Only if you want me to."

"No," he says.

"Okay."

"Really?"

"Why wouldn't it be?"

"Because you can check the algo," he says. "See if we make
sense as a match."

Oh. Right. A match.

He's not saying we are. And he's not saying we aren't.

There's a reason for that, but my thoughts are fuzzy. There's
not enough blood in my brain. It's sweet, I think, him checking
this for me. Or at least giving me the opportunity to check.

That's a good sign.

Of course we're a match. Why wouldn't we be a match? We
have shared interests and similar goals. We're even from the
same place.

Those are all factors in matching. Well, the place isn't a factor,
but it tends to correlate.

But I'm not here to work.

I'm here to fuck him. "Sex. Now." I bring my hand to his ass
and pull his body into mine. "Pants off."

"They are off."

"Underpants."

"Did you just say underpants?" he asks.

"Less talking. More removing clothes."

He smiles as he wraps his arms around me and lifts me.

"What the fuck?" I don't look heavy, but I'm tall. Men
underestimate my weight. They try to carry me when they can't.

River does it with ease. "I've got you." He does.

I feel it. I really do. I wrap my legs around his waist.

He carries me across the room with steady steps. He pushes

my bedroom door all the way open, moves into the room, lays me on the bed.

I look up at him with hazy eyes. "Can you close that? Please."

His pupils dilate. He likes the *please*. Because he sees me as well-mannered yet bossy. Because it fits the idea he had of me and the one he has now. Because he wants to control the most powerful woman in the world.

He really meant that.

He closes the door.

I grab the condoms from the bedside table, tear one from the line, and toss it on the sheets.

"You can't rush me," he says.

"You want to bet?"

His laugh should break the sexual tension, but it doesn't. "You have a problem."

"Is that a no?"

"Sure. Let's bet." He meets me at the bed. "I win, you come on my face." He places himself between my legs and drops to his knees.

"If I win?"

"You come on my face." His fingers curl into my thighs. "But a little sooner."

His touch feels so good. My thoughts start to dissolve again. "How do I win?"

"You win no matter what." He presses his lips to the inside of my knee. Then he draws a line up my leg, planting soft kisses all the way to the hem of my shorts.

He pushes himself up and climbs onto the bed, on top of me.

I sink into the mattress and into him at the same time.

River brings his lips to mine. He kisses me softly, slowly. The brush of his lips. The taste of tea.

Then, my lips part, and his tongue slips into my mouth.

He kisses me with the same steady tenderness, and he brings his hand to my shirt, to the top button.

He undoes it slowly, traces a line to the second, undoes that, too.

The same with the third.

The fourth.

The last.

My silk top spills open, revealing my chest, my stomach. I'm exposed and I'm freer for it and I love all of it.

He circles his tongue with mine, then pulls back, and presses his lips to my neck. He drags his mouth over me slowly, placing kisses on my collarbones, my chest.

He wraps his lips around my nipple and sucks softly. Then it's the flick of his tongue. Those slow counterclockwise motions, again and again.

He teases me as he pushes my shorts off my hips.

It's too much. It's not enough. I need more of it. I need all of it.

I don't wait for his action. I rub myself over my silk panties. The fabric is the perfect amount of friction. Soft but rough. This layer I need gone that drives me out of my mind.

"Bad girl." He grabs my wrist hard.

Need floods my body. I love the way he does that. I love it way too much.

"You're playing dirty."

"I always play dirty."

He pins my arm to the bed.

Again, my entire body shudders. "Don't stop."

"No, Dee." He releases me and shifts enough to pull me to the edge of the bed. "If you want to come on your hand, don't stop on my account." He looks up at me, this perfect mix of need and defiance in his eyes.

My body begs me to relent. To stroke myself to satisfaction. Or do away with my panties and invite his touch. Whatever it takes to find release with him.

There is something about the intensity of his stare—

The way he's watching—

It sets me on fire.

I hold his gaze as I push my panties aside and bring my ring finger to my clit.

I'm too revved up. The light pressure almost sends me over the edge. The teasing, the control, the intensity of his stare—

It's all too fucking sexy.

But I want this to last. So I use slow motions, to start.

Only they're not slow enough. I'm close already.

My eyelids flutter closed.

My breath hitches.

My toes curl.

I push myself closer and closer with every stroke.

He stays there, hands wrapped around my thighs, attention on me. His breath fills the space. His fingers brush my skin. His eyes stay on me.

Even though I'm not looking, I can feel it.

But I need to see it, too. I blink my eyes open and look at him.

The intensity in his dark eyes undoes me.

With the next stroke of my finger, I go over the edge. My sex pulses as I come. It's all fast, too fast, but I don't want to stop, either. Pleasure spills through my pelvis, down my thighs, all the way to my toes.

My body shudders with release.

I collapse with aftershocks.

Then, he's there, his lips against my inner thigh. Then higher and higher.

The soft brush of his mouth.

Again.

Again.

Then his flat, wet tongue.

Too much and not enough.

He doesn't tease me here. He works me with steady strokes, pinning my legs into the bed as he tastes me.

The pressure inside me winds quickly. Tighter and tighter,

until it's too much to take. Then he scrapes his nails against my thigh, and he pushes me into the bed, just a little harder, and I come from the force of it.

My sex pulses against his mouth as I buck my hips, taking more, taking every bit of him I can get.

He works me through my orgasm, then he pulls back, wipes his mouth with the back of his hand.

There's something sexy about the gesture. Impossibly sexy.

River stands.

I sit up enough to push his boxers off his hips. He looks so good here, in the light of day, in my room.

Naked in my room.

And completely rapt.

All of his attention is on me. And all of mine is on him.

I'm not sure which of us is in control anymore and, for once, I don't care. I don't want to stop and examine the situation. I want to feel him come.

I wrap my hand around him. I pump him with steady strokes, then I scoot back to the edge of the bed, and I lower myself onto the ground, onto my knees.

He groans as I take him into my mouth. Slowly, at first, so I can taste every inch of him.

Then I pull back and take him again. It's almost too much. I'm out of practice. And, really, I've never understood the fuss. With most guys, it's too much work, and it's thankless, too.

But right now, I understand all of it. I feel every ounce of it. I need to take him, drive him out of his mind, consume him the way he consumed me.

It overwhelms me.

It pushes everything else aside.

I press my tongue flat against him, and I take him again.

He presses one hand to the back of my head and guides me over him. He brings his other hand to my breast, teasing my nipple as I take him again and again.

The two of us, a perfect circle of pleasure. I feel that. I want to give this to him because I need him. Because I like him. Because he makes my entire body shake with desire.

His thighs shudder as he gets closer.

His posture changes. He rocks into me, pushing deeper, almost too deep, but I want to take that, too. All of it.

Then he says my name like it's his favorite thing in the world and all my other thoughts fade away.

I bring my hand to his ass, and I take him deeper.

With the thrust of his pelvis, he comes. He groans my name as he rocks into me. And I do everything I can to hold on as he spills into my mouth.

I wait until he's finished, then I pull back and swallow hard.

He looks at me like I'm heaven sent, and I feel something more familiar: the gratitude I've seen in past relationships. The wall that falls after a man comes. The lack of defenses.

But that feels different, too. Because I know him. Who he is, what he wants, what he likes about me.

I know him in a way I never knew Stephan.

And I want him to know me in another way. I want him to know all of me. Not just the version who uses her sister for seduction inspiration. Or the version who puts on a bold face for investors. Or the version who plays tough to keep everyone away.

No. That's not a game.

I am tough.

But I'm soft, too.

I want to show him all of that.

And that's really fucking scary.

. . .

The afternoon is perfect. We sneak out of the house for lunch at another spot by the beach. We come home, kiss goodbye in the car, head to our separate living spaces (both of us have family dinner tonight).

Lexi is in a good mood, but she doesn't mention where she went or what's happening with Jake, and I don't ask. She doesn't ask me what I've been up to, either. I savor the feelings. I text River from my room. Silly things. Serious things. Naughty things.

All week, it's the same.

We work all day, we kiss after dinner, we send good-night messages. Sometimes, it's just a kiss and a few pictures. Other times, he comes to the apartment, and we have sex in my bed.

I play my favorite Carole King record. I dance to "I Feel the Earth Move." I sing in the shower and don my favorite sundress and sit by the pool with a book.

A perfect week. Even with work deadlines and late nights and the uncertainty of Lexi's plans with Jake.

For once, I don't worry about her. Not until she comes into my office Thursday night, right in the middle of my attempt to make plans with River.

She locks the door behind her, and she looks right into my eyes and says, "Dee, I need your help."

CHAPTER TWENTY-EIGHT

Deanna

"Willa just texted." Lexi holds up her cell phone. "She's going to Palm Springs this weekend."

"It's a big place," I say. "I'm sure you can avoid her."

"No. Her boyfriend owns the Palme d'Or."

"He named the hotel after the famous audience award at Cannes?"

"It's got palm in the title." She throws her arms in the air, like *how should I know?* "All the good palm names were taken, I guess."

"And…"

"And she's going to be there," Lexi says. "At the hotel. Ready to watch us by the pool. Ready to watch us at the bar. She'll probably want to grill Jake at dinner."

"Aren't you back together?"

"No." She brushes a blonde hair behind her ear. "We're still on a break."

"You're taking a weekend away together while you're on a break?"

"I need to see what's out there." She folds her arms over her chest. "Didn't we agree on that?"

Right. We did. And— "It's your relationship."

"And she's going to be there, judging it, assessing it as good or bad. How am I supposed to get in the mood when I'm being watched? And don't say 'that's what she said.' Even though, it's obviously what she said." She throws herself onto the office couch and kicks off her black pumps. "I can't do this."

Is Lexi right? Is Willa really here to check the status of our relationships? Maybe she wants to check in. Or chat. Or have her own vacation. Why is it so hard to figure out people's motivations? I trust Lexi's judgment, usually, but she's a little…anxious when it comes to her future with Jake. I don't want this to ruin their reunion. "We can cancel," I say.

"That will look suspicious."

"But didn't you say she's a businesswoman and she won't care if you and Jake are really in love, as long as you look good?"

Lexi scoffs as if she can't believe anyone would say such a thing. "She's going to think I'm sure. And I'm not sure. And I can't ask him to play my perfect boyfriend if I'm not sure, can I?"

Honestly, I don't know.

"He loves me," she says. "I know he loves me. I'm not stupid."

"Do you love him?"

"How am I supposed to know?" She pushes herself to a seated position. Her blue eyes focus on me. Her lips curl into a frown. "You loved Stephan, didn't you?"

"I thought so."

"But not anymore?"

"No." I sit up on my desk and place my palms against the edge. "I did love him. I'm not confused about the love part. It's the…*him* part I don't understand."

Her face screws in confusion. "Is this a riddle?"

"No."

"Love or love not. There is no try?" She attempts the Yoda quote.

"I think it's the opposite," I say. "Love is trying."

"Isn't it easy?"

"Infatuation is easy."

"What's the difference?"

"Lexi, you know infatuation." I sit on my desk. I try to find my best sister-advice posture. But I don't know what I'm doing here. Not anymore. "You fall for a different guy every two weeks."

"Every week, thank you," she says. "And I've been with Jake for six months."

"Last weekend?"

"What about it?" she asks.

"Didn't you go home with someone?"

"With Jake, obviously," she says.

Obviously. She thinks everyone can see she'd rather go home with him than anyone else. That isn't the Lexi from six months ago. That's a Lexi who believes in commitment.

"But I couldn't do it." She shakes her head again. "It was too much pressure."

"The sex?"

"No. The words. He said it, then. He said he loves me, and he respects what I want, even if I want to be on my own. But before that, he really wants to try being with me. Physically."

She turned down sex?

"And I can't do that... I can't sleep with a guy who loves me when I don't know if I love him. That's a whole different thing!"

"You stopped because it was wrong?"

"Well, it wasn't because I wasn't in the mood. I was wet enough to drench the Sahara."

"That is more information than I need."

"Are you kidding, Dee? I'm horny twenty-four seven now!" She hides her face in her hands. "And I want him so much. I do. I don't think I've ever wanted anyone this much."

"So have him."

Her voice softens. "What if there's nothing there?" She looks at me, all concern and sincerity. "What if the only reason I keep showing up is because I want to jump his bones?"

"You've been dating for six months."

"And it's been exciting," she says. "And different than with other guys. What if that's all it is?"

"No one knows how they're going to feel in the future."

"You do," she says. "You always know where you're going."

I shake my head. A few months ago, I would have agreed with her. A few months ago, I had a plan. Now? Not so much.

She comes to me because I'm wise, and I'm wise in certain places, but not here. Not when it comes to love. "What do you want?"

"I want you to come with us to Palm Springs."

What? "I meant with him."

"Keep Willa busy for me," she says, undeterred. "I can show up for one dinner, as the perfect girlfriend, but I can't do any more than that."

"It's not necessary," I say. "Willa loves you."

She lets out another scoff loud enough to wake the people in Riverside. "Willa thinks I'm an idiot. Haven't you noticed her comments?"

No. Never. Lexi is charming. Everyone sees her that way.

"Every time we see her, she asks why I'm wearing pink. She might as well say, *why are you here, Malibu Barbie. Why isn't there a smart person in charge of marketing at MeetCute?*"

No... There's no way I missed all that.

"She likes people like you," Lexi says. "Serious people. She laughs at me."

"At your jokes."

"At *me*." She pins me with a stare. "Please, Dee, you know I never ask you for anything like this."

She doesn't, that's true.

"And you can bring River."

"Huh?"

Lexi's laugh softens the tension in her brow. "Come on. Everyone knows you're sleeping together. You two weren't exactly quiet last night."

Oh. My cheeks flush. My chest, too. A million things go through my head at once. Everyone knows I'm sleeping with River. They *heard* us. "You don't care?"

"Oh? Because of those comments from earlier?" She waves her hand, like *get real.* "Yeah, he's hot now. So what? Hot guys are a dime a dozen in southern California."

"What about the tattoos?"

She shrugs.

Which is not like her. She's always liked a guy with tattoos and a leather jacket.

"I wouldn't have gone for him at all if I knew you liked him. You should have just told me. You two are cute together. Really." She says it without a hint of jealousy or betrayal. With pure, sisterly pride.

Did she ever like him?

Does *he* still like *her*?

I'm in my late twenties. Why am I worried if the guy I'm screwing liked my sister?

Because she's Lexi. Because I've heard it from every guy I've ever dated.

Isn't that what Stephan said when he left?

Why can't you be more like your sister?

Sometimes, they even use those words.

Beautiful, charming, easygoing, fun-loving Lexi and intimidating, intelligent, difficult Deanna.

"Dee?" She scoots over and pats the spot next to her. "Are you okay? Do you not want to bring him?"

No. I want to be there with him. I can see the two of us in the pool, swimming around each other, or hiking to a spot to watch the stars, or fucking on the big hotel bed. "Not if I have to keep Willa busy. You know I can't do two things at once."

"Combine them. Double date."

"He might be busy," I say.

"He's not. I asked Ida."

"She knows his schedule?"

"Yeah. They share a Google Calendar."

Of course they do. "Okay. I can come."

"Good. Now, can you explain this to me? If what I have with Jake is love?"

"Maybe. Tell me what happened on Saturday." I slide off the desk and sit next to her on the couch. "Maybe that will help."

She looks around the office. She checks her cell—three texts from Willa, two from Jake—then places the device face down on the couch. "The second we got to Jake's place I could feel it. This was going to be the night. He lit candles. He played Sade. He asked if I wanted a drink. A cosmo. He'd bought everything to make one. He'd been practicing."

He does love her.

"It was overwhelming. I had to excuse myself to use the bathroom, the one in the bedroom with more privacy. And I saw it there. Rose petals on the bed. Actual rose petals. And there was a gift-wrapped box and a card, too. It said, 'I love you, Lexi.' That's all it said. And I just couldn't do it. Because what if we weren't good? What if he was too fast or too slow? Or I forget how to do things?"

"Then you try again," I say.

"Is this love, though? Feeling sick because you're worried about disappointing someone? Or them disappointing you?"

"It might be."

"Oh god." Her face goes pale. "I love a man I haven't fucked."

"Is that a bad thing?"

"What if we don't fit there?" She shakes her head. "How am I supposed to live with that?"

"You don't have to."

"But the app… What if this is a deal-breaker for Willa?" she asks. "She already hates me. She's looking for a reason to write me off. To not work with us. I know it."

"Even if it means the end of the app," I say. "You don't have to."

She throws herself against the couch again. "Really? That's okay? You'll forgive me?"

Does she think I wouldn't? "Of course."

"But…it's not theoretical, Dee. The guy Willa is bringing to the resort. He's the guy who co-owns the firm. This is our real test. The dinner in a few weeks won't matter if we fuck this up. She's going to believe it's real now. Or we're never going to convince her."

CHAPTER TWENTY-NINE

Deanna

Lexi looks at me with expectation in her blue eyes. I'm the wise sister, the honest one, the loyal one.

Only I'm none of those things. Not right now.

"I know it's a lot of pressure," I say. "I can't help with that. I can't control what Willa will do. But I'm on your side, whatever you want."

"Even if we lose funding and close shop?"

"Even if."

Lexi frowns. "I don't know if I'll forgive myself."

"We'll figure it out, Lexi. Whatever happens. I promise."

"I don't know if I can," she says. "I don't know if I can figure out what I want with all this outside influence. How am I supposed to have a sexy weekend with an investor judging my relationship?"

"How about you leave early," I say. "Get a day alone with him."

"Maybe."

"Let's picture it." I squeeze her hand. "Pretend Willa isn't there. Pretend no one knows you two matched on the app. Or that it's a faraway concern. Right now, it's just the two of you, in the presidential suite, all weekend."

"I don't know," she says. "I can't see it."

Okay, let me try another tactic. "What did you do on Saturday? After you shut him down?"

"I said I had a headache. Like a woman in a nineties movie." She groans as if saying, *what a terrible lie.*

"Then?"

"He made me peppermint tea," she says. "And he offered to rub my back. And he lay with me while I closed my eyes."

"And?"

"It was nice."

"Really nice?"

"Yeah. I didn't know it was possible to feel good just holding someone."

"Welcome to relationships," I say.

"Do they always feel this awful?"

"Only sometimes," I say.

"I hate it."

"Because it's new and scary."

"Ugh." She rests her head on my shoulder.

I hug her sideways, the way I did when we were kids. "You're not one to back down from a challenge."

"I do like him," she says. "And I want to try. But I won't pretend to be someone I'm not. I won't pretend I'm Ms. Commitment."

"Okay." I take a deep breath and exhale thoughts *of New Yorker* profiles and *Forbes 30 Under 30* lists. "Follow your heart."

"Are you sure?"

No, but I know this is the right thing. "Yes."

"What if she doesn't think we're a couple the right way?"

"I'll tell her to fuck off."

"Really?"

"Really." This is more important. Sisterhood is always more important.

Even if it means we lose everything.

But it won't come to that. I know exactly how to play this.

CHAPTER THIRTY

Deanna

Trip preparation moves quickly. We arrange hotel rooms, carpools, rough plans to keep Willa busy.

River's sisters drive out with him, early, to spend the day at some sort of fancy spa. I stay for a work meeting, a video call with a machine learning expert, someone who understands artificial intelligence a million times better than I do.

It's strange, to consider ceding control, to consider bringing in outside opinions. But it's time. I can't run this on my own. Not if we secure this funding and kick up our advertising enough to take the crown from Tinder, Hinge, OKCupid, Bumble, or Coffee Meets Bagel.

After the call, I go home, pack, and drive to Palm Springs on my own. The big houses blend into smaller ones, neighborhoods of matching homes and perfectly square four-unit apartment buildings. Then the strip malls and gas stations. Everything spreads out as I move east, through Riverside County. When River was a kid, the county had a reputation as a home of meth houses and crime. It was an inflated one, no doubt—we also called Anaheim Anacrime because it was less safe than Irvine and Tustin—but one with some truth.

Riverside is still expensive, by most people's standards,

but it pales in comparison to our neighborhood. To the entire California coast. The crime might be minimal, but the heat isn't. And unlike Palm Springs, a cozy resort community, Riverside isn't all strip malls and concrete. Or maybe everyone has a pool in the backyard.

Did he grow up in an apartment complex with a pool? A little peanut-shaped one, maybe. I can see him there, sketching palm trees instead of swimming, the dorky kid with a scrawny frame and too much interest in his eyes.

He didn't fit in there.

He doesn't fit in here.

That doesn't make sense. Our future. There can't be a future if he belongs in New York, and I belong here. And I belong wherever Lexi is.

Or maybe I need to take one of those quizzes, to find out the truth. There must be one with a decent algo, but none of them can quantify the love I have for my sister. She's more important than sunny days, mild winters, beach access, cool bars, great restaurants, low crime.

Maybe that's the problem with this.

Maybe there is a magic we can't explain.

But that's sacrilege, isn't it?

. . .

When I get to the hotel, the sky is dark and the space is quiet. River is in our room, on the phone with Ida. I kiss him hello, unpack enough to change into my swimsuit, and head straight to the pool in the courtyard.

It fits perfectly in the quaint hotel. A big, rectangular pool with clear water, surrounded by off-white lounge chairs, palm trees, and the cream hotel rooms behind that.

There's a strange mix of seventies nostalgia and modern

shapes, as if the hotel is trying to marry its history and its future. It doesn't quite work. Some things don't go together. Orange County and New York. Love and logic. Starlight and city light.

Even here, with the glow of the pool and the soft streetlights of the quiet town, the stars shine bright. Brighter than they do at our house anyway.

I slip into the empty pool, float on my back, watch the stars move through the sky. Though I guess it's mostly the Earth moving around them. Everything in the universe is moving, changing position all the time, but it feels so constant. The same way the water in the pool rocks back and forth, with its own mini current.

I move, but I stay in the same place.

It means something, but metaphors aren't my forte. That's River's department.

The cool water envelops me as I dive under the surface. Bit by bit, the day melts away. Then the week. The year.

All those questions running through my mind dissolve, until one thought occupies my brain.

I need to touch him again.

It feels like ages pass as I dive under the water, then surface. Again and again, the cool, safe feeling overwhelms me. It allows my concerns to fade away.

Finally, I surface, and I see him, dropping towels on a lounge chair, turning to watch me.

He's in that same pair of board shorts, and his strong thighs are easier to ogle from here. He is too hot. It isn't fair. But then life never is. And I'm not in the mood to curse or question it. I'm in the mood, period.

I move toward the edge of the pool and motion *come here*.

He walks toward me.

I push off the edge and motion *come here* again.

He smiles, all ease and interest, and slips into the pool with me. The shock of the water registers on his face for a moment, then he dives under, swims to me, surfaces with another big smile.

"Hey." He cups my cheek with his palm. "Are you okay?"

Do all the questions in the back of my mind really show? No. It doesn't matter. I don't want to think about them. Only about this. "Better now."

He traces the line of my jaw.

"Is your grandma okay?" It's not like her to check in, but then maybe he's the one checking in. That's his style.

"She's probably cursing Fern and North for keeping her busy."

"She needs time for her gentleman callers?" That's what she always said, when we were kids.

"Probably." Under the water, he brings his hands to my waist and pulls my body into his. "Do you want to talk?"

"Absolutely not." My pelvis melts into his. Then my stomach, my chest, my lips.

He kisses me softly, with care and attention.

The rest of the world slips away. Who needs the rest of the world? Why do I care about it anyway?

What could ever feel better than this?

I dig my fingers into his upper back. "I've never had sex in a pool."

He motions to the women in the jacuzzi behind me. Two of them, older, around Dad's age, or maybe Ida's, with that same mix of enthusiasm and grace Ida has. "Is it the audience?"

"And the security cameras." I motion to the cameras in the lights. One to our right. One to our left.

"You noticed that?"

"You notice everything, too."

"Different things." He pulls me closer. "You sure you don't want to talk?"

"Do you?"

"No," he says. "I want to swim."

"That's not the s-word I was hoping for."

"How about soon?" he offers.

I can live with soon.

CHAPTER THIRTY-ONE

River

Deanna is at home in the water. For all her non-California girl qualities, she's exactly where she's supposed to be in an empty pool, at a fancy hotel in the desert.

She grew up with that massive pool in the backyard, but I rarely saw her there. Bits and pieces of memories form in my mind:

Deanna in a black one-piece, diving into the water.

Deanna dipping her feet in her running outfit, laughing about something with her sister.

Deanna, diving into the water, naked, with a guy. Some guy with glasses and a deep affection for her.

I'm not sure if it happened or if I formed the image in my mind. All those fantasies blurring together. One I had of Lexi, maybe.

But this isn't a fantasy. It feels like a dream, sometimes, but never a fantasy. It feels impossibly real.

Because unlike in a picture-perfect image, I'm not graceful in the water. I don't belong here. I love watching her, yes, but I don't have a fraction of her talent.

She dives and surfaces over and over. Because she wants closeness. Or because she wants distance. I'm not sure.

But then, it doesn't matter. I've offered my best. That's all anyone can do. If it's not enough for her—

I understand that. For once, I understand that.

See, Grandma is wrong. I am growing. I don't need to stay away from California to spread my wings. I can learn plenty here.

Sure, Fern and North spent all day convincing me to move back to New York. They insisted they have it covered. Fern is ready to move in with Grandma—she's between places anyway—and Grandma has plenty of money for a nurse, if it comes to that.

Independence is the Beau family tradition. Grandma doesn't want to rely on me, or Fern, or North. And she'd much rather send me away, to spread my wings and fly, than have me here with her, even if she needs me.

But that's the thing she doesn't get. I've already spread my wings. I built a life in New York. I have a career. And, yes, I won't do as well if I work remotely for a while, but I'll survive.

Grandma won't stop me from staying. No one will force me to move. But everyone will remind me to return to my own life. Everyone will underline the importance of living your own life.

Only, for once, family doesn't take precedence in my mind. For once, my head doesn't go straight to the clouds. It stays here. With her.

The next time I dive, I stay under for long enough to watch Deanna submerge. But without goggles my vision is blurry.

The chlorine stings.

I have to surface to see straight.

It means something, but right now, I don't care. I don't want to consider anything else. Only this moment. Right now.

Maybe that's going backward, falling too hard, too fast, without concerns for practical things. Maybe I shouldn't trust her to be the practical one, but I do.

This time, when Deanna surfaces, I meet her in the middle of the pool and guide her to the shallow end.

She checks the coast is clear—no guests, no guards, even if

we are in the view of the security camera—and she brings her lips to mine.

She tastes like chlorine and mint and Deanna. There's a visceral, physical satisfaction to it. My body knows hers. My body needs hers.

Under the water, I bring my hands to her hips. I find the strap of her bikini and trace the line of nylon.

She slips her tongue into my mouth as she rocks her hips against mine.

She feels good here, in the pool, soft and smooth and slick.

Vulnerable.

Open.

I want this side of her to be mine. Even if I leave and it's not forever. Even if it's not for long.

She groans as my hard-on brushes her stomach.

Her fingers dig into my shoulder. "Do you have a condom?"

"Upstairs."

"Me, neither." She kisses me again, with the same mix of hunger and need. "I mean me, too."

It's far. Too far. But I don't have to wait to have her. Not completely.

I kiss her again.

She kisses back with the same mix of need and hunger. A physical hunger and an emotional one.

It fills me everywhere.

It turns the cold water warm. Sends blood rushing south. Sends my thoughts to faraway places.

I bring my hand to her chest, push her bikini top aside, exposing her breast.

For me. Only for me. My body blocks the camera.

And I love seeing her, halfway out of her swimsuit, for me. Only for me. Like the entire world exists for us. Only for us.

She sinks into my touch immediately, groaning as I toy with her nipple. Her head falls into the crook of my neck. Her lips brush my ear. "Don't stop."

Never. "I love seeing you here." I draw another circle around her. "I love having you at my mercy."

"You mean that?"

"Why wouldn't I?"

"I don't know." Under the water, she hooks her arm around my waist. "I didn't believe it, that anyone would want to—"

"Take charge of the most take-charge woman in the world?"

"Yeah. Or maybe. No offense, but it's not really your personality."

"Not anywhere else, maybe." I don't lead the way she does, but I lead myself. I follow my instincts. "But here, it's perfect."

She runs her fingers over my shoulder, dipping her hand below the water. "Touch me."

"I am touching you."

"Fuck me."

"Not here."

A whine falls from her lips, but she doesn't say please this time. Instead, she kisses me hard, slipping her tongue into my mouth, exploring me the way I explore her.

I tease her with slow circles then I move to her other breast, expose her, toy with her again and again.

Then, when I can't take it anymore, I slip my hand between her legs.

She guides my fingers under her bikini bottoms.

She feels different under the water. Softer and slicker. The friction isn't the same. I have to test different speeds, pressures, to find what she needs.

A little harder than normal. A little smoother.

Then she tugs at my board shorts, and I know I have it.

I kiss her back as I work her. She groans against my mouth, bucking against my hand, taking everything she can from me.

She's greedy and hungry and eager and I love everything about it.

With my next stroke, I push her to the edge. I go slow, drag it out, until she's digging her nails into my skin.

Then, finally, I give her what she needs.

She groans against my lips as she pulses against my hand. Her body tenses in my arms, then she unfurls, every part of her relaxed and soft and easy.

After she catches her breath, she looks up at me with hazy eyes. "I think security knows what we're doing."

"And?"

She smiles. "If we get kicked out of the place tonight, you're driving home."

I shake my head.

"No?" She offers her hand. When I take it, she leads me to the steps.

"No." I follow her onto the concrete. "I'll find another hotel."

"Should I take this off then?" She motions to the strap of her bikini top.

I nod.

She checks our surroundings again, then does it.

She undoes the hook of her bikini top and lets the fabric fall to the ground.

I scoop to gather it.

Deanna covers herself in a towel, grabs the room key, and rushes me to the elevator.

Thankfully, the small space is empty.

After I push the button, I back her into the wall, kiss her hard.

Four flights aren't enough. I want to spend eternity in here, teasing her, feeling all of her against all of me.

But when the doors ding, and she leads me into the hallway, I don't care where we are, as long as I'm with her.

She slides the key into the lock and groans as it flashes red.

"Too fast," I say.

"How are you so steady?" Her voice is all frustration and need.

It's sexy as hell. "Practice."

She does it again, a little slower. No go.

A laugh spills from my lips.

"I'll start right here," she says.

"Do it."

For a second, she considers the dare. Her eyes light up. Her teeth sink into her lips. Her chest heaves with her inhale. She's willing to risk a public indecency charge. Or the thrill of exhibition moves her. Or both.

She doesn't mount me.

She tries the lock again. This time, it works. The button flashes green.

Relief floods her body as she steps inside.

This is where we both want to be. The large, rectangular room. It's the same place I checked into yesterday, with the same sheer white curtains over the balcony door (and the thick beige blackout curtain pulled back), the same pastel palm tree paintings on the walls, the same king bed, the same white sheets and cream comforter.

Only I don't see it as a hotel room that's trying way too hard to look elegant. I see it as the place where I join with her. The place where we melt together.

And that makes all of it beautiful. Even the hideous corporate art.

Well, maybe not beautiful, but special all the same.

She takes in the room for a split second, then drops her towel and her bikini bottoms and goes right to the bedside table. Condom. Lube. There.

The water washes the natural lubrication away.

She doesn't say it and I don't ask. I'm old enough to know better. To know it's not personal. There are a million reasons why someone might need a little extra wetness.

Medication, moods, marathon sessions. Maybe that's tonight. I can have her again and again.

Since this is our night. Plans with other people start tomorrow. Tonight?

It's all ours.

And I know exactly what I want to do.

"I brought something," I say.

"Oh?" She climbs onto the bed and looks up at me with enthusiasm in her eyes.

"Bondage rope."

Her pupils dilate.

"If you're ready to try it."

"Yes."

"Are you sure?"

She hesitates. "No." She looks up at me, need and affection and trust in her green eyes. "But I can say when anytime."

"We can wait until tomorrow."

"No." She shakes her head. "Now. Well. With a wardrobe change."

"The board shorts don't do it for you?"

"There's not enough to remove."

That's true. There isn't enough to tease her. "Five minutes to change."

"Should I shower?"

She's so practical, even here. A month ago, I would have found it annoying. Now, it feels like her. And that's sexier than anything. "Don't. I like the taste of chlorine on your skin."

"Me, too." She pushes herself up on her arms. "Just easy on the shoulders. They're inflexible from all the time on the computer."

"Okay."

She looks up at me again, holding my gaze, looking for something inside me. Then she slides off the bed, jumps to her feet, and rushes to me.

She kisses me softly, tenderly.

"Thanks, River. Really." She runs her thumb over my chin.

"I wouldn't have tried this without you."

The compliment undoes me. I'm teaching Deanna Huntington something. Maybe I won't win our wager. Maybe these aren't the lessons in love I imagined, but this is just as pure and bright and magical.

She shifts into the bed.

I grab jeans and boxers and slip into the bathroom to prepare.

I'm going to dominate the most powerful woman in the world.

What a task.

What a thrill.

CHAPTER THIRTY-TWO

River

Despite my excitement, or because of it, nerves threaten to overwhelm me as I prep in the bathroom. I wash my hands and face. I dry enough to dress in boxers and jeans. I run through visions in my head. Not plans—I don't plan the way she does—but possibilities.

Deanna, spread over those white sheets on her back, groaning as I hold her arms over her head.

Deanna, on her stomach, arms bound behind her back, hips bucking as she reaches for me.

Deanna, groaning with a perfect mix of bliss and agony as I lick her to orgasm again and again.

There's no way I can last through all those scenarios. I need to move fast but steadily. I need to give her what she wants.

And she wants to let go. I want her to let go.

It's that simple.

I take another deep breath and I step out of the bathroom.

The main room is the same. White walls, pastel paintings, sheer curtains, the hum of air conditioning.

And Deanna Huntington, sitting on the white sheets in a sheer black bra and panty set.

Fuck, she looks good in black mesh. Edgy and sexy and

completely where she belongs.

"Did you wear that for me?" I let my voice drop to something low and seductive.

She looks up at me, the perfect mix of defiance and need in her green eyes. "No. For me."

That's exactly right. That's what I love about her. She's not the vision of an ideal woman, the one I saw in my head. She wears sheer black mesh for her. She asks for what she wants, and when she doesn't get it, she finds a way to take it.

Desire courses through my body. I'm humming, I'm buzzing, I'm every metaphor in the history of the world and I'm none of them. Because this isn't art. This is real. The two of us together, in messy, beautiful reality.

I want all the messy, imperfect parts of her.

"Do you wear it to work?" I take another step toward the bed.

"No."

"On dates?"

She looks up at me. "Will you get jealous if I say yes?"

Yes. "Did you picture someone taking it off?"

She nods.

"Stand up."

She rises with grace.

"Turn around. Let me see all of you."

She locks eyes with me for a moment, then she breaks contact to turn and show off her firm ass, her long legs, the elegant line of her back and neck.

"You're beautiful."

"I know."

My balls tighten. She's too sexy for words. It's painful, in the best possible way.

I close the distance between us. One foot. Six inches. The rough mesh against my jeans. My hands against her hips.

I trace a line over her panties, and up her spine, to the hook of her bra. Gently, I undo the hook and push the straps off her shoulders.

She groans as I cup her breasts. "River." She melts into me, her back against my chest, her ass against my cock.

When she's barefoot, we're aligned just right.

I press my lips to her neck as I run my thumbs over her nipples. She groans from the contact, lost in that hazy place of bliss and anticipation.

I love watching her here. I want to watch her all night.

But I don't have the stamina. Not this time.

So I tease her until I'm ready to burst out of my jeans, then I trace a line down her back and push her panties off her hips.

Deanna groans as she kicks them aside.

I hold her close with one hand. Slide the other between her legs. She's wet, but not enough for this. Not yet.

I shift her forward. "Hands on the bed."

She does as she's told, leaning forward, presenting her ass for me.

I push her onto the bed, firmly enough that she feels it, but not so hard she hurts.

She looks good there, too, gorgeous and ready and pliable.

She gasps as I pull her arms behind her back.

"Keep them there." I hold her wrists with one arm. Reach for the cuffs in the bedside drawer with the other. The position is awkward, too much stretch, but it's better for it.

Because this isn't a vision.

This isn't champagne and rose petals. Or leather and chains.

It's the two of us, melting together.

I slip the cuffs over her wrists. Tighten the right. Then the left.

She groans as she tests them, trying and failing to pull her arms apart.

I test her with more hardness. I grab her thighs.

She melts into that, too, so I pull her back, to the edge of the bed, and nudge her legs apart.

"Stay there." My voice drops to something I barely recognize. A deeper, firmer tone. One that exists solely for her.

She notices it, too. She doesn't say anything or move, even, but I feel it in the air. The energy changes.

We're both slipping into our roles.

We're both entranced.

I grab the lube and the condom and place both beside her. Then I spread the slick gel over my fingers and bring them to her sex.

She groans as I test her entrance, pushing her apart as gently as possible. Then, in one swift motion, I slip two fingers inside her.

This time her groan fills the entire room. The entire state, maybe. I feel it that deeply. I feel it everywhere.

I stretch her again. Then once more for good measure. Then I pull back, undo the button of my jeans, let the denim fall off my hips.

Then the boxers.

She turns her head to try to get a glance. Finds the mirror to our right.

It's not in the best spot, but it's enough for her eyes to go hazy. She watches as I roll the condom over my cock and align our bodies.

I push inside her, one sweet inch at a time.

The sight of our bodies joining nearly takes me over the edge. This is too good. Too much.

But that's why there's a round two. For more. For better. For practice.

I bring my hands to her hips, then I pull back, and drive into her again.

"River." She tries to reach for the sheets, groans as her arms hit the restraints.

"Say that again."

This time, my name rolls off her tongue like it's her favorite word, like I'm the only thing she's ever needed.

I drive into her again.

She watches as my cock disappears inside her.

As I dig my fingers into her skin.

As I pull her body into mine.

Again and again.

The rest of the world fades away. It's the two of us, this moment, the utter perfection of it.

She feels good. Too good. And the way she groans as she watches the action—

It's too much.

I have to pull back to catch my breath.

She sighs with need, like she can't bear another moment without our bodies joined.

It's the same for me. I need her here. I need this.

Deanna arches her back. "Please." The word hovers in the air, uncertainly, unsure if she wants to stay there forever or flee right away.

It's so rare on her lips and so right at the same time.

She doesn't offer it to anyone else. Only me.

I bring my hands to her hips, position our bodies, slide into her with one swift motion.

This time, I slip my hand under her pelvis. I bring my thumb to her clit and rub her with slow circles as I drive into her.

My eyes flutter closed.

My body takes over.

I move in time with her, guiding her, feeling her, embracing every inch of her softness.

She comes first, groaning my name, pulsing around me, pulling me closer and deeper.

Her body trying to take mine.

All of her grasping for all of me.

The intensity of it undoes me. Pleasure spreads through my body as I spill inside her. All that soft sweetness. All the sweat and groans and need.

After I spill every drop, I pull back, take care of the condom, undo the chain holding the sides of the cuffs together.

Deanna rolls onto her back and looks up at me with hazy eyes. "Fuck."

"Did I leave you speechless?"

"Fuck is speech."

My lips curl into a smile. "Deanna Huntington, the most capable woman in the world, is totally at my mercy."

"*Was* totally at your mercy." She smiles back, all defiance and challenge, the Deanna I know everywhere else. "Maybe she will be if you do it again. But right now?" She positions her arms in a shrug. *Who knows?*

"Is that a dare, Dee?"

"I remember this guy telling me I don't need to make everything a dare or a challenge or a bet. I can just ask for something. Get it."

"Are you asking?"

"Oh no. It's a dare. He was right. I can ask for something and trust someone to give it to me. But a dare is more fun. Don't you think?"

CHAPTER THIRTY-THREE

River

After we catch our breath and take turns in the shower, we watch an old Katharine Hepburn movie. Deanna spends the entire film calling out every instance in which Katharine Hepburn behaves unlike her.

When we finish, she shakes her head. "How could you think we're similar? We're not similar at all. Sure, we're both tall and elegant, and we have strong faces and look fantastic in suits. But that's where it ends."

"What about the grace and power?"

"Okay, that, too. But, come on, I would never take back my ex. I don't care if he's Cary Grant. He's mean to her. Why does she take that? Probably 'cause all the writers were men."

"Are you asking me to argue with you?"

"No." She smiles and presses her lips to mine. "You'll know if I'm trying to start an argument."

I kiss her back and I take her again. No ropes or teasing or claims. Just the two of us joining together, melting into each other, enjoying the night, falling asleep in the messy sheets.

. . .

This time, I wake to breakfast. The scent of tea and eggs and hot sauce. Deanna in her silk pajama shorts set, pulling the silver cover off the room service tray, sitting at the table as she fixes her tea.

"My version of cooking." She rolls a napkin, places it in her lap. "Eggs Benedict via credit card."

"I could teach you when we get back." It's strange, mentioning the future. After last night, it feels inevitable, but it's not. Life here is complicated. And if Grandma and my sisters get their way, I won't be here long. I'll be on the other side of the country. "If you want."

I rise slowly. A lazy stretch. A long yawn. The firm ground beneath my feet.

She gives me a long, slow once-over, studying my bare shoulders, chest, abs, thighs. "Were we talking about something?"

I tease her, "Aren't you objectifying me?"

"You're an artist." She pulls her eyes away for long enough to pour tea into her mug. "You should be used to it."

"Objectifying myself?"

"Yeah. All those self-portraits."

It's not a bad point, actually. "Sometimes. Mostly, I work on other people's projects."

"What do you actually do at the company?" she asks.

"The art in adaptations and other contract stuff," I say. "I got the idea from Grandma. She used to buy me graphic novel adaptations of classics. I brought it to my boss. He asked me to spearhead the project."

"I can see you there, in some New York office building, guiding artists to find their vision." She looks me in the eyes. "Is it anything like that?"

"Mostly phone calls and Zoom meetings, but otherwise, yeah."

"Do you miss it yet?" she asks. "The city?"

"Sometimes."

"When do you think you'll go back?" There's hesitation in

her voice. Worry.

She's thinking about it, too. What this means. What we mean. "I don't know. Grandma doesn't want me to stay. North and Fern don't, either."

"But you want to stay for her?" she asks.

"For a few reasons."

She smiles, but there's a sadness to it, like she knows my reasons are semi-tragic. "Go. Brush your teeth so I can kiss you."

"Yes, ma'am."

"Don't call me ma'am. I'm not that old."

"Yes, mistress."

"Don't even." She tosses her napkin at me.

I catch it and press it to my heart, as if it's a token of her love. Maybe it is. This is how Deanna expresses herself.

With those beautiful sharp edges.

After I go through my morning routine, I move into the main room. I take in the sight.

As an artist—

The diagonal line of the high ceiling, the light flowing through the wide windows, the angular woman, navy blue against the sand decor.

As a man—

This beautiful, powerful, tough as nails woman in her silk pajamas, inviting me into her life.

"Are you going to stare all morning?" she asks.

"I might."

"I might start stripping."

"Don't stop on my account."

She shakes her head.

For a moment, I hold steady, then I copy her *come here* motion.

She laughs as she rises, meets me in the middle of the room, wraps her arms around my neck.

She kisses me softly.

Tenderly.

She pulls back with a sigh. "Sit. Eat. The food will get cold."

There's so much to say, maybe too much. I sit across from her, fill a mug with tea, pick up my Eggs Benedict.

"Thanks," I say.

"I owed you breakfast," she says.

"For the entire weekend. I appreciate it."

"Thank you." She brings her mug to her lips and takes a long sip. "For last night."

Why are her manners so sexy?

"But, uh, before you go gushing about the weekend, I have to ask you something. And I want you to promise you'll tell me the truth."

"About what?" I ask.

"Promise."

"I'll be as honest as I can."

She nods, accepting the answer, but not necessarily liking it. She starts to talk, stops herself, starts again. "Do you still have feelings for Lexi?"

CHAPTER THIRTY-FOUR

River

Do I have feelings for Lexi? The question belongs to another world, another universe, another version of myself.

The air in the room feels different. Stiller and colder.

I need to explain this with the honesty she requested, but I need to start somewhere, too. "Not the way you mean." I cut my English muffin in half. "I don't want her. Not as a girlfriend or a partner or a fling."

"You don't want her at all?"

"She's a beautiful woman, yes. I notice that."

"You did more than notice," she says. "For a long time."

"But not anymore."

She presses her lips together. "Never?"

When does never start and end? Deanna and I have been dating—or whatever we're calling this—for a week and a half. But we've known each other for years. "Not since I kissed you."

"It happens with every guy, you know. All of my exes. Stephan. Mark. Raj. Yosuke. Ben. Alan." She slices her Eggs Benedict in half. "The guys from high school and college, too. Even the ones who said they liked smart women. Who said my glasses were sexy. Who claimed to love my mind. The second Lexi came to visit, they wanted her."

"How do you know?"

"They were obvious about it. Sometimes, they tried to be subtle, but they never managed. And, really, I don't blame them for looking. She's beautiful."

"You're beautiful, too."

"Not in the same way." She takes a bite and thinks through her swallow. "She's basically the picture of the ideal woman."

"*A* picture of the ideal woman."

"You agree?"

"She's curvy and blonde and bubbly, sure." We both grew up here. We both know the vision of a California girl.

"Guys say they like smart women, but they always end up going after the bubbly blonde."

This isn't about me, not really. It's about her. But I don't push her there. I offer her space to expand. "What happened?"

"It depends on the guy. Sometimes, she didn't know I was interested and…it's not her fault. She asked. I always lied and said I didn't want them. And I'd end up sitting there, on my couch, consoling this guy I liked because my sister threw him away. Asking myself if I was a pathetic loser or a good friend."

Hurt spreads over her face. And something I never see on her: regret.

Deanna takes another bite and swallows hard. "It wasn't always that bad. Sometimes, it was small things. They managed to compliment her while making it clear they preferred a woman like me. At first. Then, their affection for her would seep into our conversations. They'd ask why I couldn't be more friendly or easygoing or charming. Why I didn't do my hair or dress the way Lexi did. They didn't always mention her specifically, but I knew they were thinking of her."

"What if they weren't?" I ask.

"What else would they be thinking?"

"Maybe they were frustrated," I say. "And they didn't know how to say it."

Her brow furrows. "Because I'm too difficult?"

"Because they don't know how to accept an equal," I say.

She shakes her head *no, that's not right*. "But Lexi is as smart and capable as I am."

"Is she as easygoing as she seems?"

"No," she admits.

"There's probably a reason why she sticks with casual relationships."

She nods. "That's why we're here, actually."

What is she talking about?

"She's freaking out because this thing with Jake is getting serious and she doesn't know how to do it, and I just…I just can't do any of this if you still like her."

"Not the way you mean," I say it again.

She presses her palms together, all vulnerability. "What do *you* mean?"

This is a rare side of her, but I can't exactly stop and treasure it. "Was there a guy you liked when you were a teenager?"

"A few."

"Someone you never expected to date? A member of One Direction," I say. "Or an actor."

"Do I look like a One Direction fan?" she asks.

"Was there someone like that?"

"Sure," she says. "Ryan Gosling was dreamy."

"Do you ever think about him now?"

"If I see a headline with him," she says.

"How do you feel?"

"Young," she says.

That's it. But it's not all of it. There's so much and I barely understand it myself.

There are too many layers around it. And those layers are a mess. Thorns and barbed wire.

For years, I avoided facing it. I used my crush on Lexi as a way to not face it.

She's always been a fantasy. And I won't lie: my desire to escape into a fantasy is still there. Only it's different. It's smarter, now. It wants to latch onto someone else, to find a vision of them that's all wedding bells and happily ever afters.

"It was like that," I say. "She was out of reach, the way a celebrity was. And it was different, too. I wasn't happy to move in with Grandma. Mom was never going to win Parent of the Year, but she was my mom. I loved her. I wanted to protect her. I wanted to stay with her. I hated this new, shiny place. I had no idea how anyone felt at home here. Then I saw Lexi."

Apprehension fills Deanna's face.

"It was like something out of a movie," I say. "This beautiful blonde, about my age, sitting at the pool in a pink bikini. All bright and brilliant and interested in me."

"She makes me feel like that, too," she says. "It's different, because she's my sister, but—"

"She is bright and charming."

"She is." Deanna nods. She waits. She gives me space to explain.

I do my best. "For the first time, in years, I felt wanted. I saw the beauty and possibility in the world. She became that for me. A fantasy of a life I could have."

"You fantasized about being with her?"

"Sometimes," I say. "But it wasn't about sex or love or companionship even. It was about feeling that energy, the glow, being near the center of attention, being able to charm and smile and fit in any place I go."

"She does that."

"And I never felt that. Not here."

"But you do in New York?" Something else fills her eyes, but I can't place it.

"Mostly," I say.

"I guess I can't argue," she says. "I love to be around my sister. Because she's my sister. And because she's bright and vibrant."

"You're a good sister."

"Sometimes," she says. "Do you still feel that? The desire to be with someone like her?"

"No, but she's attached to these ideas. Visions of a different life, the life I could have had if I'd grown up with Grandma. If I was a different person. If I wanted different things. But I'm not. I don't want different things. I want to be with you," I say. "Not anyone else. You. I meant it. I'd be heartbroken if this ended."

"Unless you break mine first," she says.

"I wouldn't forgive myself." I don't know what to say, so I reach for her. My fingers brush hers.

She stirs, but she doesn't move.

"Do you ever fantasize like that?" I ask. "A different version of you?"

"Sometimes," she says. "I would make a great Dr. Ian Malcolm. You know, Jeff Goldblum's character in *Jurassic Park*? I'd rock the leather jacket and the sex symbol status. And chaos theory—I love the idea of it, even though it scares me. Because it scares me."

"Do you want that life?"

"No. There are a little too many T. rexes in that one."

I snort out a laugh, and it eases the tension in the air. "A T. rex–free vision?"

"I would make a great sex symbol." A teasing tone returns to her voice.

She's okay.

We're okay.

For now, at least.

"Sometimes, I wonder how my life would be different if I'd gone to a different school," she says. "Started a different company."

"Does that mean you don't want the life you have?"

"No," she admits. "And you never want that life, that fantasy?"

"Not often."

She looks me over carefully. "Well…if you mean it, if you

really are over her, then I could use your help."

Huh?

"Lexi could, actually. She loves this guy. At least, I'm pretty sure she does, but she doesn't have a vision of romance the way you do. And she needs that. She needs the veils blowing in the wind and whatever else romance is for her. But I understand... if you don't want to do it."

"No. I do."

"You want to help my sister see her future with another guy?" she asks.

"See the future that's right for her. It might not be this guy, though."

"Okay," she says. "I trust you."

"You do?"

"Yeah. I do." She holds out her hand. "As long as you promise you'll do what's best for her. Not for me. Not for you. Not for Jake. For her."

I start to shake.

"No. Like this." She holds up her pinkie. "Me and Lexi always pinkie-swear. It feels right."

We pinkie-swear,

And then, she explains everything.

Jake and Lexi meeting, via the app. Lexi coming home, the first night, already over the moon. The second night, shocked he didn't invite her home. The third, aghast he turned her down.

And when he asked her to wait—

Lexi saw it as a challenge, even if she didn't admit it to herself.

They were doing well. Lexi didn't even notice how long they'd been together, until Willa brought up the suggestion for a poster couple. As soon as Lexi felt that outside pressure, she panicked. She lost interest. She ran.

But she loves him. She does.

That's what Deanna believes, anyway.

"I promised myself I'd stay out of it this weekend," she says.

"And I meant that. I want to give her time and space to figure it out for herself."

"But?"

"But Willa and her boyfriend are here," she says. "And they'll be watching. She won't have time or space. She needs someone on her side. Someone who believes in love and romance and happily ever after." She looks me in the eyes. "She needs you."

Lexi needs me.

Damn.

My high school dreams come true.

In the strangest possible way.

CHAPTER THIRTY-FIVE

River

After breakfast and another cup of tea, we meet Lexi and Jake at the hotel restaurant.

The two of them are sitting on the outside patio, in matching shades of pink, laughing at a shared joke.

They don't look like two people on edge, yet to consummate their union. Or two people concerned about their sexual compatibility.

They look just-fucked.

Sure, they cleaned up well enough—neat hair, clean clothes—but they're both wearing a post-orgasmic glow.

It might be the desert sun, or the rising temperature, or the hotel coffee.

But I doubt it.

For a moment, I imagine a different scenario. What would have happened if Lexi had met me at her car the first night I was here, instead of Deanna, driven me to the county's favorite make-out spot, turned up the slow jams as she turned off the engine.

It's hard to imagine. Even though I pictured the scenario a million times. Even though, a few weeks ago, I wanted it as much as I wanted anything.

That guy is a completely different person. One who doesn't

understand the world the way I do. One who barely understands himself.

There's no jealousy in my stomach. No romantic notion of what could have been.

I'm glad I spent that night with Deanna. Not just because I adore her. Or because I don't want to be the other man. Or because I feel so good, right here, next to the smartest woman I've ever met—

Because she shattered all the illusions in my way.

Next to her, everything is clear.

"Can we go back to the room?" Deanna adjusts her square sunglasses and squeezes my hand. "Have sex again?"

"Why not there—?" I motion to the hotel lobby beyond the big glass doors. The white couch next to the bar.

"In front of everyone?" she asks.

"Public sex is too much?"

"Semi-public." She leans in and presses her lips to my neck.

Right at that moment, Lexi notices us. She stands, squeals, holds up a napkin reading *6.0*. "Adorable."

Deanna's blush deepens as she explains the reference. "A perfect ice skating score."

I can imagine her on the ice, twirling in a skirted one-piece, nailing every jump and turn. I can imagine her in a million places.

Lexi practically runs to us. "Is there a reason I haven't seen you all day?" She laughs. "No. I know the reason."

Deanna blushes and hugs her sister. "No."

"Sure."

"Really." She whispers something.

Lexi laughs and releases her. "I'll let you go then. How much time do you need? Is twenty minutes enough? Or do you prefer the agony of teasing?"

"Do I prefer that?" Deanna winks.

Lexi actually blushes. "Be honest, River. Is my sister an evil tease?"

"No," I say. "I am."

Lexi and Deanna share a look, then Lexi greets me with a handshake. "Do you want to have some tea before lunch with Willa?"

Deanna nods. "I booked a spa session for after, so we have an out. But first, I want to talk to Jake for a minute." Deanna nods unconvincingly. "To plan a surprise for your birthday."

Lexi's brows rise. She doesn't totally buy it, but she still nods and leads us to the table.

Jake is a tall guy with an aura of Orange County wealth. Maybe he didn't grow up with money, but he has it now, and he's not afraid to show off his designer watch and his expensive shoes.

He stands and shakes my hand. "Nice to meet a friend of Deanna's."

"You, too." I return his firm grip, sit, go through a short introduction. After a few rounds of *getting to know you* questions (he's an employment lawyer, he grew up in Irvine, he loves to surf, he adores Lexi), Deanna and Jake say goodbye and head toward the pool.

Here I am, with a mission to help Lexi follow her heart. Only I'm not needed. Not really. Lexi is smitten. It's written all over her face.

And there's something else in her blue eyes, something I usually see on Deanna. *What do you think you're doing with my sister?*

"Are you taking care of her?" Lexi turns and hails the waiter.

"Trying," I say.

"She makes it hard." She smiles at the waiter as he approaches. "Another coffee and a—" She motions for me to finish.

"English Breakfast," I say.

She waves goodbye to the server, waits for him to leave, and turns to me with concern in her eyes. Immediately, her voice drops to a tone I've never heard on her. Something firm and serious. "She likes you."

"I like her."

"She's funny, don't you think?" She watches Deanna and Jake sit at the edge of the pool, remove their shoes, dip their feet.

Deanna looks right there, in her short teal dress, her eyes on the crystal-blue water.

She looks gorgeous, actually.

"Hilarious," I say.

"Is that what you like about her?"

"One of the things," I say.

"What else?"

I shoot her a curious look. "Is this a quiz?"

"A test."

"How do I pass?"

"You went to art school, right?"

"I have an MFA." I nod.

"It's like that. There's a rubric. A mix of technical elements and style."

"That doesn't sound like you."

"It's not." She takes a long sip of her coffee. "I'm trying to learn from her."

I don't know what to say. I care about Deanna deeply, but I don't know how to prove it. How does anyone prove their feelings? Why would they?

And if this is the sort of talk I used to have with my sister's boyfriends (not that any of the guys ever listened), I don't have the answers she wants.

I don't know what our future holds.

If she belongs here, and I belong somewhere else—

There's really no way to fix that. I may not be practical, but I see that.

"It's hard, though," Lexi says. "I'm not like her. You aren't, either, I think. We both know something she doesn't: certain things don't follow logic. Sex, for example. Or love."

This isn't the Lexi I know, but then I never really knew her.

I'm only getting to know the person under the sunglasses and the pink. "You're not as agreeable as you seem."

"I know." She smiles, and for a moment, I see that usual Lexi charm. Bright and brilliant. Only it's too bright, too brilliant. She's playing it up. Forcing a fake expression.

The pretense fades as she studies me. Her lips straighten, her eyes focus, her jaw softens.

I see her. The actual Lexi. The girl who loves her sister more than anything.

"I've always admired her drive," Lexi says.

"Me, too."

"How do you think it feels, to want something as badly as Dee wants to take over the world?" she asks.

"I don't know." I want my time with Grandma, here. I want her to accept my help. I want Mom to get sober. But that's different. None of that is within my control.

"Me neither. I never want anything the way she wants success for the company. Especially not with school and work. Those things never felt important to me. Not the way they're important to her."

I know what she means.

"But then I do want it, the company, because I want her to do well. I want to finally pay her back, for all the times she came to my rescue."

"You do all that work for her?" I ask.

The server interrupts with our drinks.

For a moment, silence falls. He puts a carafe of coffee and a fresh cup and saucer in front of her. A steel pot of water, a basket of English Breakfast bags, a cream pitcher, a tiny jar of honey, a lemon, and the same cup and saucer in front of me.

The same setup in every nice enough hotel. When Grandma was healthier, we used to travel, to see the country, the continent, the world.

Was our trip to Seattle our last trip?

Will we ever go anywhere again?

I push the thought away as I fix my tea.

Lexi stirs her coffee carefully. "I work hard but not half as hard as Dee. And I'm not even a quarter as brilliant as she is. I'm a good marketer. I enjoy the work. There's something fun, about figuring out how to present something to the world."

That sounds exactly like the Lexi I imagined. And the one I'm getting to know, too.

"And with MeetCute, I get to embrace pink and sex and love. Mostly love, sure, but that's fun for me, too. Different."

"I've seen the app."

"It's fun, and I have fun with it, but I don't love work the way Dee does. I don't want to go into the office on Saturday or stay up late to perfect a pitch or put success ahead of my other priorities."

"Most people don't."

"Maybe." She takes a long sip of her coffee.

I stir cream into my tea. The English Breakfast is a little weak—the water isn't hot enough—but it still soothes my stomach.

Lexi is getting at something. I don't know what it is, but I can tell it's important, so I pause, give her room to expand.

After another sip, she continues. "Dad always asked why I wasn't more like Deanna. Serious, studious, committed. All the things a good Huntington should be. All my teachers were the same. Even the ones who didn't know Dee, who had never taught her, who worked at a different school. They found a way to compare us."

"Do you resent her?"

"Not anymore," she says.

She's good at hiding things.

The second I meet her gaze, she shifts, back to that typical Lexi smile. Only this time, she realizes it right away. "Have you told her?"

"Told her what?" I ask.

"About your grandma."

"What?"

"Her condition."

Time stops. The world around me freezes. The blue sky, the palm trees, the bright concrete. Even the people around us, the older couple mid-conversation, the executives in summer wool sipping iced tea, the family in the pool.

Everyone stops.

Lexi studies my expression carefully. She lowers her voice to something sympathetic. "She didn't tell me."

She wouldn't.

"I was at the hospital, for my yearly. And I saw her. She's easy to recognize with that silk trench coat. Who wears a trench coat in southern California?"

"She says it's raining men."

"She's a riot." Lexi's laugh dissolves in the air. The lightness fades. Even with the bright sun and the white concrete, the world dims in response to the reality of the situation. "I was going to say hi, but then I saw where she was going. Oncology. That's where my mom…where we sat, as kids, watching her chemo treatment. I didn't really understand what it was then, only that what the doctors gave her was supposed to make her better, but it made her sicker. And then she died anyway, and…she was sick before, wasn't she? Your grandma?"

"More than ten years ago."

"And this was more than a normal follow-up?"

"Yes."

This time, she freezes, and everything around her moves. The breeze ruffles the white table linen. The palm trees sway. The sun shines. "Shit." She moves with a tiny motion of her hand, a half an inch toward mine. "I'm sorry."

"Thanks."

"Is she going to be okay or…?"

"It's too soon to say." I don't know how to explain it, so I fall back to the words she repeated a million times. "The doctor insists her odds are good. And she says she's fine, that she's only worried about losing her hair, and about me sticking around for too long, but it's hard to believe that."

Lexi's eyes fill with sympathy. "I know what you mean. Is she trying to stay strong for you, or..." She looks to her sister, watches as Deanna laughs at one of Jake's bad jokes. "I know I should give you more grace, with the situation, but I overheard your sisters at the house once."

"Do you eavesdrop on everyone?"

"They were yelling," she says.

They do yell.

"And they said you're supposed to leave soon, go back to New York, but you're arguing about it."

"That's what Grandma wants," I say.

"But you want something else?"

"I want to be here for her," I say.

She studies me carefully. "And leave, when she doesn't need you here anymore?"

Right. I see what she's trying to say. "Deanna knows I don't plan on staying here forever."

"She could help, you know. Be here for you."

"I know," I say.

"But you won't tell her?"

"I promised Grandma I wouldn't say anything."

"She's falling in love with you," she says.

How did I become the focus of this conversation? "I'm supposed to talk to you about Jake."

"What about him?"

"Talk you into love," I say. "But you already understand it. The way you sacrifice for her, put her first."

Lexi shakes her head. "She's such a hypocrite."

Probably.

"She denies any help. Pushes it away with a ten-foot pole. Then she insists on inserting herself into my love life,"

"You don't want her there?"

"I asked for her help this weekend, sure." She sips her coffee. "With Willa. So I wouldn't feel so under the microscope. That's not sexy, you know? It's not romantic, either. Who can possibly feel like they're in love with someone they're expected to love?"

"You want autonomy."

"Doesn't everyone?"

I nod. "Deanna explained, the thing with the app. You're a perfect match?"

"Near perfect." She nods. "But I hate that, too. I hate the app telling me what to do. Even without the investors and the need for a poster couple...I just want to prove it wrong."

"You want freedom?" I ask.

She nods.

"But you're not free, if you reject something because everyone expects it of you. It's no different than doing something because everyone expects it of you."

She sits back, thinking it over. "That's actually really smart."

"Actually?"

"Let's face it. Neither of us is known for our brains."

A laugh spills from my lips. "Only for our beauty?"

She nods *obviously*. For a moment, lightness fills the table, the air, the resort. Then she shifts back to the matter at hand. "Is that why you want to stay here? Because your grandma wants you to go?"

That's probably a part of it.

"What will you do," she says, "if you leave? Are you going to end things with Dee or ask her to come with you?"

CHAPTER THIRTY-SIX

Deanna

Jake distracts me with the sort of expertise he could have only learned from Lexi. He asks a technical question about the app. Then he asks another. And another. And another.

I don't even notice when Lexi comes to pull me away for meeting prep. She helps her boyfriend up, then she pulls him into a deep, slow kiss. A kiss that screams *I'm going to have my way with you later.* Or maybe *I already had my way with you today.*

They seem different, somehow. I can't explain it. I don't know the logic. Really, I rarely understand the logic when it comes to Lexi.

But they're here, and they're happy, and they're right. And, when she says goodbye to him and leads me back to her room to prep, I find all the signs.

The messy sheets. The open lingerie drawer. The Bluetooth speaker. The empty bottle of champagne sitting in the ice bucket, next to two dirty glasses.

"You had sex?" I ask.

She giggles in that Lexi-like way. "Dee!"

"Since when is that an inappropriate question?"

"We're supposed to prep for lunch with Willa."

Screw prep. No, get through prep ASAP. I toss her the first

question on the list. "What's MeetCute's motto?"

"We know you better than you know yourself."

"And how are we sure?"

She quotes the relevant statistics about our match rates. "And I, Lexi Huntington, am the picture of a woman who couldn't find Mr. Right. Really, I dated a lot of guys, but it wasn't until the algo worked its magic that I found a serious relationship."

There's no magic, but it feels like magic. That's my motto. Only it doesn't sound right anymore.

"That's as far as I'll go." Lexi stands firm. "Maybe we'll get engaged or married. Maybe we'll break up in a month. Either way, I found a serious relationship, and that's a first for me."

"I love it." I throw my arms around her, relieved and proud all at once. My sister is happy, and we have our poster couple, all in one. "It's perfect."

"You're supposed to object." She shakes her head and moves into the bathroom.

"Why?" I ask. From my spot in the main room, I watch her fix her makeup, my curiosity piqued.

"So I can throw your meddling in your face," she says. "And counter you with some meddling of my own."

"Why would you do that?" I ask.

"Because you're totally in love with River," she says.

No. Maybe. I'm not sure what it means to love someone, not anymore. I care about him, I want the best for him, I feel an ache when he's away. Maybe that's love.

I need a rubric. A score sheet.

There must be one, somewhere.

"And he…" She finishes with her brow liner and motions for me to come over. "Let me do your makeup. Some neutrals Willa will like so she respects one of us." She rolls her eyes in that Lexi-like way I recognize.

She hates when people assume she's dumb because she loves pink, but she really hates when women do it. Because that's just internalized misogyny.

I don't see the disrespect she gets from Willa, but I don't argue with her. If she feels out of place, she feels out of place. I understand that feeling. Even if I can barely imagine Lexi out of place anywhere.

I meet my sister in the bathroom and take the spot on the marble counter. It feels familiar. Something we did as kids a million times.

She swipes shadow over my eyes, then the brows, the bronzer, the mascara. The same familiar steps.

When she finishes with my lipstick, I ask, "Was it good?"

She smiles wider than I've ever seen her. "Amazing. It's true what people say. It feels different when you love someone. And after six months, I was so fucking horny. I came like a waterfall."

There's my sister.

"And you and River are so cute," she says. "But there's something we have to talk about there."

"I know he isn't staying forever," I say. "I know he's going back to New York eventually."

"No." She pauses, steps back, takes a big, deep breath. "It's not that."

That's the elephant in the room. Or the, uh, I don't know… something in the something. That's the issue between us.

"It's the app."

"What about it?"

"He signed up," she says. "With a fake name, yeah, but it's clear it's him. And Willa might notice, if she's been looking at the backend stuff, looking at our matches."

People who get access to the code always want to see the matches of people they know. But— "What's that matter?"

Sadness fills her eyes. "Listen, Dee, I know you believe in the algo. I know you think it's magic—"

"It's not magic."

"*Like* magic, whatever, but maybe it's not perfect. Maybe it needs more help."

What is she talking about?

She leaves the bathroom, finds her phone in her purse, returns.

And I figure it out the second she unlocks her screen. But it's different, seeing it on the screenshot.

The perfect algo, the one that helped Lexi find love for the first time in her life, has spoken.

And it can say, with 100 percent confidence:

River and I are not a match.

We have less than a 30 percent chance of success.

That's the *worst* match I've seen on my profile.

We're doomed.

CHAPTER THIRTY-SEVEN

Deanna

The image stays burned into my brain.

The picture of River, slipping his hand into the pocket of his jeans, the familiar lines of ink on his wrist. The comic-inspired flower.

And the fake name on the screen. *Ocean Ty*. A play on River Beau. A stupid play. Because what's funny about any of this?

Lexi offers strategic possibilities, but I barely register any of them. It doesn't make sense. The algo is good. It's working for her. It's working for everyone.

There's something wrong with me.

I'm the problem.

I'm the one who isn't fit for love or connection or forever.

The rest of the app proves it. He has plenty of high matches. I have none.

He belongs with women in New York. Statistically speaking.

He knows where he's supposed to be.

And I know where I need to be. Here. Yes, I'm statistically unlikely to find love here, but I need to be near my sister, my company, my house. I need to be someplace where the world makes sense.

Really, there's no sense in drawing this out. There's no sense in enduring the agony of falling further in love, breaking up, losing each other.

No. The algo has spoken.

Love isn't in the cards for me.

I need to do the right thing and release him. So he can be where he's supposed to be. So he can live the life he's supposed to live. Focus on whatever it is that's occupying him.

I say yes to Lexi's third suggestion, the one about deactivating his profile so Willa won't notice it. But there's really no need for her tips on hiding our relationship or creating a fake profile. Or going through the algo again, or my answers, or his, to see where we went wrong.

There must be something else, his grandma's searches messing up the compatibility. Or one of us not being honest with ourselves.

It's only a quick chat. A check-in before our real meeting tomorrow. The entire time, I stay in my head. I barely nod yes or no. I barely catch any of Willa's words. Something about Xavier. The guy here with her. The guy joining us for dinner tomorrow.

He's also her business partner.

He loves the app. He loves our pairing. He's sold on Jake and Lexi, though she doesn't explain why or how.

We have everything we want.

The funding we need.

The future.

Happiness for my sister.

Success. All the success I ever wanted.

And it feels completely empty.

CHAPTER THIRTY-EIGHT

Deanna

In the hotel room, River is stretched out over the bed, sketching the scene at the pool. The tall palm trees, the square hotel buildings, the sun shining off the bright blue water.

He looks good in shorts and a T-shirt. He almost looks like he belongs here, in Southern California, in my bed, in my life.

But we both know that isn't true.

"Hey." I barely force the words from my tongue. They're too hard. Everything is too hard.

"Hey." He turns to me with a smile. And then he sees my face and the smile disappears. His dark eyes fill with concern. His brow furrows. "You okay?"

I swallow hard. I haven't had to do this much. Usually, guys end things when they get tired of me. Or when I end things, they're happy for the excuse. Because they already know they'd rather be with someone else. Someone softer.

Lexi is a better match with him, of course. Not a fantastic match, only 75 percent, but better than I am.

But that isn't what bothers me. No. None of it bothers me. There's no reason to feel misery. There's no need to fight reality.

He belongs with someone else. He belongs somewhere else.

It doesn't matter how I feel.

"You should go back to New York." I force the words from my tongue. "Maybe not today. Maybe not tomorrow. But soon."

"And for the rest of my life?" He tries to ease the mood with the *Casablanca* quote. Or maybe he tries to prove a point.

I don't know anymore.

"I decide what I do," he says seriously.

"We don't belong together." I don't believe the words, even though I know they're true, even though I have proof. "And I'm not going to be an albatross around your neck. You belong somewhere else. And I belong here. We should end this now, before it gets too complicated."

"Even if that's true—"

"It is true," I say.

"What if *you* belong in New York?"

I shake my head. "I need to be here with the company, with my sister." As much as I don't fit into Huntington Hills, I mean every word. I can't imagine a life three thousand miles from my Lexi. "And you need to be there. It doesn't matter anyway. We're not a good fit. You saw it, too."

It takes a couple seconds, but an epiphany fills his eyes when he realizes. "Because we're not a match on the app?"

"Why didn't you tell me?"

"Because you didn't ask," he says. "Because I didn't think it mattered."

"I do."

"I love you. That's what matters."

"No, it's not." I shake my head, not even letting myself process his words. "This is real life. Other things matter."

"Do you love me?"

I don't know. How can anyone know? I care about him, yes, and that's why I have to do this. Because it's what's right for both of us. "I'm sorry."

"Dee."

"It just doesn't make sense, and it's just...it's too much fun. I need to end things, before I get more invested, before we both get more invested in something destined to fail. We owe that to ourselves."

"Is that all it is? Logic?" he asks.

"What else is there?"

His eyes fix on mine. His posture firms. He's sure. He's strong. He's proud. "What about the magic?"

"What magic?"

"Tell me you don't feel anything and I'll walk away, now," he says. "Tell me you aren't drawn to me. Tell me you don't feel sparks when we're together. Tell me you don't picture a future. Tell me that, any of it, and I'll leave. No questions. No argument."

I can't tell him that.

There is something here. I am drawn to him. I do want him to stay. I want it so badly, but it doesn't make sense.

"I'm sorry, River," I say.

"Tell me you don't feel anything," he repeats. "Then I'll leave."

"I feel something." That's true. But this is true, too. "An infatuation. A crush. Good sex." It takes all my strength to say the words. "We're caught up in that." That's the only thing that makes sense. We're having fun. Because how could it be more? No. My feelings are misfiring. Everything is off. This is the only thing that makes sense. "I'm sorry, but it's not enough."

He shakes his head, but he accepts it.

I offer him the room.

And he packs and leaves.

And I don't feel any better. I feel empty and miserable.

Maybe that's love. Letting someone go, even though it hurts, even though you'd rather hold on.

• • •

After a few hours of crying, I do what I always do at times like these.

I go to the place where the world makes sense. Only it doesn't, not anymore.

Work is supposed to be the one place I'm in control. Instead, I don't have a clue what any of it means.

For hours, I go through the code. I look at recent matches. I read testimonials. People love the app. Sure, there are users who don't manage to find someone, but they're few and far between. They're people like me.

Too picky, too difficult, too cold.

They just aren't cut out for love.

We're the problem, not the app.

I stare all afternoon. Into the evening. Until my cell buzzes with an alarm. Fifteen minutes until dinner.

Right.

I dress and do my makeup as quickly as possible. My teal sheath is a little too formal for the resort, a little too wrinkled to look professional, and without my usual hair dryer, my bob isn't in straight-line shape. But I have wine-colored lipstick and dark eyeliner, and are there any problems that can't be solved by thick eyeliner and lace-up boots?

Well, anything besides the one-hundred-degree afternoon temperatures.

Despite the heat, I don the boots. I even grab a leather jacket. I'm staying in the air-conditioned hotel anyway.

Around the corner, down the elevator, to the lobby bar where Willa and Mr. Perfect, Willa's boyfriend, are waiting.

Willa greets me with an extremely professional handshake. She introduces her boyfriend with the same business-like demeanor. This is Xavier, he's a great deal. Let's start the bidding at a hundred thousand dollars.

He is handsome. I'll give her that much. He's the kind of guy I normally date. He's tall, with dark hair and dark eyes, and smart-hot glasses that fit Willa's nerdy energy. Unlike the guys I normally date, he's wearing his suit. A subtle navy with a beautiful, vibrant magenta tie.

To match our app.

Because, according to Willa, he's a match.

A perfect match.

For me. My *only* perfect match.

Xavier isn't her boyfriend. We were wrong about that.

He's her brother. And this isn't just a business meeting.

It's a setup.

CHAPTER THIRTY-NINE

Deanna

After a few minutes of small talk, Jake and Lexi join. They say goodbye quickly and go off to some other restaurant in Palm Springs. Willa leaves for her room. It's been a long day. She's done with business. Whatever.

The Wilder siblings whisper about something, then Xavier reintroduces himself, and he leads me to the restaurant.

It's a perfect spot for a date. A wide-open room with round, linen-covered, candlelit tables. A romantic atmosphere, scored by classical music and quiet conversation.

He's a perfect gentleman every step of the way. He pulls out my chair, he lays his napkin on his lap, he suggests a dish but doesn't press when I order something else.

He smiles with the perfect amount of warmth. Enough to invite me. Not so much as to overwhelm me.

Practically speaking, the guy is doing all the right things. He's putting in effort for a medium-stakes situation. He's well dressed and groomed, friendly and flirty without overdoing it. He's asking questions and taking my one-word turned one-sentence responses and running with them.

And I'm sitting here, empty and numb and utterly unable to latch onto a single word.

He's from California, too. San Diego. How nice. It is warm there, too. And the beaches are also beautiful. And the food here is good. Sure, I barely taste my white fish and grilled vegetables, and I barely smell his Bolognese, and I don't think about the taste of wine on his lips, or the hint of lime on mine.

I order a gin and tonic. Because it's too hot, even in the air conditioning. Because I need the bitter quinine and the sugar to balance it. Because I don't have that sort of balance myself.

He's my perfect match.

He's handsome, successful, polite.

And I feel nothing.

Through every bite of dinner, every sip of gin and tonic, the last ice cube, I feel nothing.

"Deanna?" Xavier finishes his glass of wine. His second glass. A reasonable amount of alcohol for a first date.

A drink or two helps ease awkwardness. Any more and people start crossing boundaries, inviting closeness that feels wrong, or sleeping together early.

Sometimes, that works. Usually, it doesn't. Of course, we don't know if that's correlation or causation. It might be that people who want casual relationships sleep together quickly. It's probably that.

What would happen if I slept with Xavier? Maybe it would nail down our funding. But I can't stomach the thought. Even though he's handsome and polite, I don't want him to touch me.

That must be wrong. After all, he's a 95 percent match, and the algo works for everyone else, and I'm unattached now. I guess.

I should want him.

"Are you all right?" His voice pulls me into the moment. That, too, is just right: the perfect mix of soft and firm. He's concerned, but he's casual about it.

"That's a big question." I reach for my gin and tonic, but there's nothing left. "I'd be better if I had another drink."

He studies me carefully. I see it again—the concern in his

dark eyes. For a split second, I feel flattered. Then I remember the concern in River's dark eyes, and I feel sick.

A double maybe. Lexi drinks her way to fun. I can do it, too.

"Okay." Xavier nods and hails the server. The guy nearly runs to the table, takes our drink orders, and disappears.

He does own the hotel. But what hotel magnate gets into the start-up business? Start-ups are actively trying to destroy the hotel business.

Maybe that's his move. Maybe he wants to acquire the next Airbnb before it takes over the world.

Or maybe he's interested in money, wherever it comes from, or he wants to diversify his portfolio, or he always wanted a hotel for some reason.

If he is my perfect match, he has a reason. A good reason, but I can't bring myself to ask. I just don't care.

I force a smile. "I'm sorry I'm not a great date." Under the table, I press my palms together. Something to steady me. "I didn't know this was—"

"A setup? Yeah, I had a feeling." He smiles, that same warm, friendly smile, only with a little more knowledge. "My sister does this all the time."

"Oh? Is MeetCute not working for you?"

"Will you take offense if I say I don't use it?"

A few weeks ago, maybe. Right now, I see his point. "No."

"It's not personal." His voice stays soft and clear. "It's not the app and it's not you."

"You don't believe we're meant to be as a ninety-five percent match?" It's a really high number, especially for me.

"No, I do," he says. "You're a smart, ambitious woman. You're beautiful. I could see the two of us enjoying time together, spending days working and nights playing games. But it wouldn't matter if you were the world's best match. If you are the world's best match for me. I'm not ready."

I don't know what to say to that. It should be an insult, since he's supposed to want me. It should be a relief, since I'm not feeling this, either.

Is it really that simple?

He's not ready.

I'm not ready.

The stars don't align.

Thankfully, the server saves me from a response. He sets our drinks on the table, turns, and leaves us in awkward silence.

Well, awkward silence and Bach.

Dad's favorite.

He holds up his glass of wine to toast. "Can I tell you something?"

"Why not?"

"She asked me to vet the app by testing it, even though I told her I wouldn't, I couldn't. I did ask a friend to look at the code, though. He said it's brilliant."

"Thank you."

"Whatever happens, I'll tell her this was a fabulous date. I'll insist we sign."

"Can you do that?"

"We're fifty/fifty partners," he says. "But she'll agree. She likes you. She sees herself in you."

"But she still set us up?"

His laugh is hearty and honest. Exactly the way someone should act on a date. "It is strange. I think she blames herself."

"For what?"

"My divorce."

He's divorced. That's a bad sign, statistically speaking. People who are divorced are more likely to divorce again. But then men who were married are more likely to make another lifelong commitment.

Otherwise, he's perfect on paper.

He's perfect on paper—according to *my* criteria—and I can't bring myself to feel anything.

Maybe I could if things were different, if I had access to my heart.

"My ex-wife confided in her," he says. "About her feelings for someone else. She knew things were over before I did."

"I'm sorry."

"Don't be," he says. "We didn't belong together."

"We do." I swallow another sip, but the mix of lime and sugar and quinine and gin fails to steady me. "According to the algo."

"Is it always right?" he asks.

"Not exactly," I say. There are factors we can't measure yet. Maybe there are factors we'll never be able to measure. It's not as if any one match is guaranteed to work. It's more that a person who has ten great matches is extremely likely to find a stable relationship with at least one of them. "Statistically, it's likely we could have a great long-term relationship. There's a very high chance. But there's no such thing as a sure thing. That's what the data says."

"What if there's more than data?" he asks.

"You sound like my"—whatever I call him—"like someone I know."

"I probably shouldn't admit it, if I'm going to be in the dating app business." His voice shifts to a tone I recognize, a tone I know. Logic. "But there's only so much we can do with an algorithm."

I almost believe him.

No, I do believe him. Just not all the way. Not yet.

"There's a lot we can't explain," he says. "The chemistry we feel when we look at someone. The way their scent affects us. The heat from their touch. The joy of their laugh. We can't quantify that."

"Not yet."

"We can't explain chemistry," he says. "Two people could be a perfect match and feel nothing. Maybe they could feel something, under different circumstances—"

"But circumstances aren't different." I'm not ready. He's not ready, either.

He nods. "The app pairs people who are likely to go together. That's not destiny. It's a possibility. And it's not perfect. There must be people with low matches who work together well."

Maybe. I don't have any data that contradicts the claim. And, really, even if we're 99 percent accurate, that means we're wrong one out of a hundred times.

If we're only 95 percent accurate—and that's really accurate— that still leaves a lot of people who are supposedly not meant to be who work together.

Maybe there's more to love than algorithms.

"There's only so much we can do with logic," he says.

"Is that how you want to sell the app?" I ask.

"Yes." He takes a long sip. "I want to be honest with people. But I agree with what my sister said. I'm not investing because I want to launch MeetCute. I'm investing because I want to be in the Deanna Huntington business."

"She said that?"

"You're like Steve Jobs, only less of an asshole." He smiles. "Exact quote."

"It is not."

"It is," he says. "And it will be easier to work together, now that we know we're not interested in a relationship."

My laugh eases the tension in my chest. It's not enough. I need more. I need someone who makes me laugh. Someone who challenges me. Someone who sees the world as a place of magic.

But even if I put aside the likelihood of failure, the logic doesn't fit.

He belongs there. He has a job in the arts. A job that works best when he's at the cultural epicenter of the country.

He has friends and a life.

And I have the same here. I have Lexi here. I belong here.

I can't be the one holding him back. Now, I get it, why his grandma is so adamant about not wanting him to stay. Because it hurts, knowing you're in someone's way.

That's love.

Wanting the best for someone, even if it doesn't involve you.

It doesn't make sense. It doesn't follow the normal rules of human psychology, but that's what makes it love.

Love isn't logical.

Love makes us stupid in the best and worst ways.

CHAPTER FORTY

River

All night, I toss and turn. Grandma is right. This isn't where I fit. Not anymore. My bed is too small, too soft, too confining. But it isn't just the bed.

When the sun streaks through my windows, I rise. I run at the park. I shower. I fix breakfast and tea, and I lock myself in my room with a stack of graphic novels.

All my old favorites. *Watchmen* and *I Kill Giants* and even my old *Archie* comics. The classics of the genre and the adaptations that inspired my current gig. The mix of Grandma's influence and mine. She's a fixture in my life. And, as much as I hate it, she knows what I need, most of the time.

She's right again.

She always is.

My sisters knock on my door, but I stay inside. Grandma, too. They give me space. Wait until I emerge.

It's late afternoon, but the sun is still high in the blue sky. The house is still warm and bright. It feels like home, in a way it didn't when I was younger. But just like when I was younger, I have that same sense that I don't belong here.

Even though I want to be here, with Grandma.

That doesn't mean I'm leaving tomorrow. But it means I'm

accepting her wishes, too. Accepting her wisdom.

With caveats.

Major caveats.

I step into the kitchen.

Fern and North look up from their spot at the kitchen table. They're playing Five Hundred Rummy and, as usual, North is losing. Fern is a shark.

Grandma is at the counter, fixing a pot of tea.

Everyone is shocked I'm here.

"River, sweetheart, have a seat." Grandma motions to the small table. "Help North win a few rounds."

"Hey!" North pouts, but she still stands and pulls me into a hug. "You look like shit."

"Worse, actually," Fern says. "How was Palm Springs?"

"It was obviously bad," North says. "Look at him."

"Are you okay, sweetheart?" Grandma asks.

"Deanna ended things," I say.

The room falls silent. Everyone guessed that, maybe, but guessing is different from knowing.

I sit. I let Grandma fix me a cup of tea. I let my sisters offer generic condolences for a few minutes. Then a few more. Long enough to drink the entire mug of milky English Breakfast and request another.

Then I launch my counterattack. "We have a deal, Grandma."

She sits across from me and folds her hands in her lap. In her silk blouse and wide-leg pants, she looks like an executive in a Nancy Meyers movie. "Did you try your best?"

"I think so, but you can send her a questionnaire if you'd like proof." I take another sip as I consider my argument. "You're not supposed to argue if I stay."

She nods *that is the deal*.

"And I will stay, through your first round of treatment," I say. "That's nonnegotiable."

Fern and North share a look, but they don't say anything.

"After that, if you're doing well, if Fern and North believe they have this covered, I'll go back to New York," I say.

Grandma doesn't manage to hide her smile. "Great."

"With conditions," I say.

"Of course." She motions for me to continue.

"Three visits a year," I say. "At least one here and one there, if you can manage the trip."

She nods. "Doable."

"Complete honesty about your treatment," I say.

"Sure," she says.

"And you invest in my new company," I say. "My own press."

Grandma lights up.

See, that's the trick. She wants this more than I do.

"Of course," she says. "But I have a condition of my own."

"You're not in a position to make demands," I say.

"Come on, River, you'd really deny a sick woman?" Fern asks.

"That's messed up," North agrees.

This is how it always works. Three against one.

"Do you love Deanna?" Grandma asks.

"Obviously he loves her!" North motions to my face. "Look at him. He looks like he got hit by a truck."

"Three trucks," Fern says.

"I really appreciate your support," I deadpan.

They both smile.

"You need to fight for her," Grandma says.

"I'm not a fighter."

"You are, though," she says. "You fight me about staying here. You fight your sisters about…everything. You fight for what you want, you just do it differently."

"Yeah, did you tell her you love her?" North asks, as if it's that simple.

"I did. But we have different ideas of what love means."

North and Fern share a knowing look.

"What?" I ask.

"You've grown up so much, River," Fern says. "You don't have the same naive view of the world. You've even let go of certain old fixations."

She means Lexi. We all know it without her saying it.

"But you're as starry-eyed about love as Fern was," North says. "You want to run away, because she has doubts."

Deanna's doubts hurt, yes, but it's not that simple. "We're adults. I respect her choices," I say.

"Do you, though?" Fern asks. "Do you really agree with her reasons? Her logic? I'm sure she came at you with logic. It's not like she said, sorry, River, we can't work out because you didn't send me enough roses."

No. I don't agree with her logic. "So, what, I need to drop my naive ideas of romance to commit to a grand gesture? That's growth?"

"Not a River kind of gesture. You're not going to run to the airport," Fern says.

"Or write her name in the sky," North says.

"Actually, that would be sweet," Fern says.

North motions *see what I mean*. She's right. Fern is like me. She still holds onto a lot of her romantic ideas.

"You need to let go of things going your way. You need to let go of your need for perfect, pure, doubt-free love. You can't expect that from someone else. You can't expect them to feel the way you do. You need to stop arguing with your heart and start using your brain," North says.

"Cold, hard facts. That's what Deanna respects." North looks to Grandma. "Right, Grandma?"

"It's a smart plan, but it's River's choice," Grandma says. "We need to respect his choices, even when he makes them incorrectly."

That's unfair, but I know better than to argue. The women in my life double down when met with any debate.

It's better to act disinterested or let them believe they're right. But this time...

Maybe they are right. Maybe I need to let go of my idea of love, too. Maybe I need to meet Deanna halfway.

"What do you propose?" I ask. "An essay on my feelings?"

"Ugh, artists." Fern throws her hands in the air. "An essay? Come on. Use your brain."

"Use logic," North says.

"Convince her I love her with logic?" I ask.

Fern nods. "A slide deck maybe. Bullet points. 'Why We Belong Together.' Face it, she's totally a New Yorker. She would love the city as much as you do."

I can see her there, but I don't know if she would go there. Deanna wants to stay near her family. I respect that.

"You just need to explain it in terms she understands," Fern says. "A business proposal. Come on. Let's start now." She stands and offers her hand. "I know exactly how to do this."

CHAPTER FORTY-ONE

Deanna

In the morning, I wake to a notification on my phone. A Google Cal invite.

Meeting with River Beau re: business proposal.

We need to discuss the terms of our bet.
Monday. Three p.m. MeetCute conference room.
Your assistant says you're free.
Until then.

Sincerely,
Mr. River Beau

CHAPTER FORTY-TWO

Deanna

All day, the wheels in my head turn. What the hell is River doing? I have no idea. I pack in a blitz, I drive too fast, I toss and turn all night, I run for too long, I shower and dress and arrive at work early.

Our office is a rented space in a big building. Pink walls, white desks, room for a dozen people, even though it's usually the two of us, our assistant, and Lexi's marketing trainee, plus any contractors we have on hand.

There's the conference room, too, which we share with another start-up, one in the health space. They do some sort of sleep tracking. I'm not really sure.

Neither of us uses the conference room.

All day, I try to work, but I keep staring at the room. The glass walls, the long desk, the projector, the expensive ergonomic chairs.

When I try to shift my gaze to the view—the mountains in one direction, the ocean in another, all blue sky everywhere—I only manage to hold it for a minute or two. My thoughts keep returning to River.

Then it's two, and I'm frozen in anticipation. Nothing distracts me. There isn't a single thing in the world more important than this.

At ten to three, the elevator dings. River steps into the lobby in a sleek black suit and a pink tie. With his ink covered, he looks the part of the tech investor or maybe tech CEO. He's not too tall or too built or too meek. He's just right.

Lexi greets him with a hug, gushes over how well his tie matches the walls, leads him into the room. They set up something. A computer.

A computer with a…slide deck.

Is he seriously using slides?

But he's an artist. A creative. He doesn't make arguments with slides. He doesn't make arguments, period.

What the hell is happening?

Lexi bounces to me. She knocks on my door once, then she pulls it open. "Your meeting, Ms. Huntington."

"You're being weirder than normal," I say.

"I love you." She pulls me into a hug.

It feels good. Safe.

"And I'll love you wherever you are. You know that, right?" She squeezes me again. "Whether you're here or in San Francisco or New York City or London. We'll still see each other all the time. I promise."

"Why would I be somewhere else?"

She doesn't respond. She releases me with a smile and leads me to the conference room.

She motions for me to sit at the head of the table. "Ms. Huntington, this is Mr. River Beau." She smiles warmly. "Your three o'clock. He has a proposal for you."

"Unfinished business," he says.

His voice sounds the same. Not too deep, not too high, sincere and musical, with that strange mix of firmness and wonder.

He knows there's magic in the world.

He knows enough he convinced me.

"It's lovely to see you, Ms. Huntington." He nods goodbye to Lexi. Then, when she leaves and we're alone, he looks to me. "And you, too, Ms. Huntington."

There's joy in his dark eyes. Joy and mischief.

"I believe we made a deal," he says.

"A few."

He smiles. "You held up your end of the bargain on some. But not others. No. There's one major issue in the air." He taps something, the button for advancing the slide.

And it appears on the screen:

Wager: Is love solely a chemical reaction in the brain or is there more to it? Is there a certain magic? A self-sacrifice?

River's stance: Magic, everywhere

Deanna's stance: All logic

Terms: if River wins, Deanna allows him to pursue Lexi. If Deanna wins, River backs off. Of course, at the moment, Lexi is happy with Jake, so the original terms are moot. But there is a second portion.

The other terms: if I lose, you get my right arm. If I win, I get your left.

He taps the button and the screen advances to the next slide, a screenshot of our text.

"I believe you're familiar with this negotiation?" he asks.

"I am," I say.

"Do you debate the situation?" He looks me in the eyes.

I can see he's hurt. I won't argue with that. But calling it heartbreak? I'm not sure that's fair. "I ended things because they made sense."

"You deny my feelings?"

"We've only been dating a few weeks," I say.

He changes tack. "It didn't hurt you, ending things?"

"It hurt me, yes. But you let me."

"We agreed to the honor system, didn't we?"

"Yes," I admit.

"I asked if you have feelings. Did you lie?"

"Maybe a little," I admit.

"I should have argued more. Forced you to admit the full extent. But a part of me knew you weren't ready. And I wasn't ready. Not yet. I needed to think. I needed to look at the logic myself." River's eyes bore into mine. "You were right. There was logic I needed to see. But I was right, too."

"You were?"

"You lied about your feelings. Why?" he asks. "If there's only logic, why lie?"

"I didn't know how else to convince you."

"But that's not the only reason, is it." His eyes meet mine. "There's more."

There is. "I didn't want to hurt you." It occurs to me all at once. "I wanted to keep you closer, but I didn't want to hurt you. And I didn't want to hurt more later. I told myself that was logic, but…" I'm as illogical as everyone else. Sometimes, at least.

"So your left arm belongs to me."

What is he getting at? "Is there a tattoo artist waiting in the office?"

"No." He smiles. "I didn't specify a tattoo."

That's true.

"I believe there's a traditional use for the left arm. Well, the left hand." He pulls something from his pocket, a velvet ring box.

No.

He wouldn't.

That's crazy.

Too crazy, even for him.

He doesn't drop to one knee, but he does open the box and advance the slide, which reads *Marriage* in big, pink letters.

"I believe this would be fair, under the terms of our agreement," he says.

"If you want to be technical."

"And I know you do."

I do. I can't help but smile. "Are you asking?"

"Asking? No. You've already agreed. And it's a little early for a marriage proposal. But since I could force the issue, I believe I have the upper hand."

He does. Damn, he's good.

"I have a counter proposal." He taps the screen again.

A picture of the New York City skyline appears on screen.

"Come back with me."

"To New York?"

"You'd love it," he says. "Give it six months. If you hate it, leave, no questions asked. I won't fight you on it. Or insist I still control your left arm."

"Generous."

"If you love it." He looks me in the eyes. "You stay for a while. Maybe not forever. But for a while."

"Why would I do that?"

"Besides honoring your agreement?" He smiles. "I'm glad you asked." He taps the button to the next slide.

Reasons Why Deanna Huntington and River Beau Belong Together

1) *Neighbors already know how to coexist*

2) *Deanna's fierce logic complements River's artistic impulses*

3) *She's a great dancer and he needs training*

4) *They respect each other*

5) *They're in love*

All my breath leaves my body at once.
This is absurd and perfect and sweet.
Then he advances to the next slide.

<u>Reasons Why Deanna Huntington Belongs in New York City</u>

1) *The most powerful woman in the world should be in the center of the universe*

2) *She looks great in black*

3) *NYC weather allows for boots far more often than California weather*

4) *There are more jazz clubs in NYC*

5) *The Huntingtons are yet to conquer the East Coast*

"I find the arguments persuasive, but I understand I'm asking a lot," he says.

"You're asking me to leave my sister," I say.

He nods. "For six months. If, after six months, you don't enjoy New York, I'm willing to come back to California for six months."

"You'd stay here?" I ask. "You hate it here."

"It would be different, if I was here with someone I loved."

Oh. I swallow hard.

"I have one last proposal."

I don't know what to say, so I murmur an "Oh?"

"I'll be here for another six weeks. To finish up with the LA office. And help my grandmother—there's a lot I have to explain there—then I'm going back to the city. I've already talked to a friend who needs to sublease their apartment. It's a two-bedroom in the Village, a few blocks from a jazz club. Perfect for you." He looks into my eyes. "If you're still game in six weeks, you come with me and give us, and the city, a shot."

"Okay," I hear myself say.

"Do you have any questions?"

"Yes." I motion one minute, pull up my cell phone, navigate to the relevant site. He watches as I do what I need to do. "Is first class too bourgeois for you?" I flash him the screen. Two first-class tickets from SNA to JFK in six and a half weeks.

"Yes." He smiles. "But I'm willing to make an exception this time."

He stands, moves around the table.

My heartbeat picks up as he comes closer. Then he's there, two feet away, and I want him so much I can't breathe.

I'm not sure what it is: love or lust or logic, but I know I need it. I really, really need it.

He offers his hand. "We have a deal."

I shake.

When he releases me, he pulls me into a slow, deep kiss.

His lips melt into mine.

My entire body melts into his. "I have a counter proposal." I kiss him again, a little harder. "We go back to my office right now and have sex on my desk."

"What are the terms?"

"Well." I find some hint of sense. "I'm going to my office, and I'm taking off my dress. You can join me. Or you can stay here."

"A shrewd negotiation."

"Always."

EPILOGUE

Deanna

Home, sweet home. Finally. The flight itself was fast. Only six hours to travel three thousand miles. But the four cancelled flights, three days of waiting for snow to clear, and an icy cab ride to the airport? That felt like four thousand years.

Right now, it's hard to believe a blizzard wrecked the eastern seaboard. It's hard to believe the city is only *just* recovering from the four feet of snow. Right now, it's hard to believe there's any place in the world that isn't sunshine and blue skies.

A few years ago, it felt normal, like home. Of course it's sunny almost every day. Of course, the sky is blue and cloudless on Christmas. Sure, it's technically December 26, but the Xmas spirit is in the air. Dad hung the white string lights and the pine wreath. The Huntington Hills Christmas tradition. That and all the usual indoor things: hot chocolate, evergreens, presents with big red bows.

Like so many Christmases, like home. But not the way it used to feel like home. For the first time, I don't ache with homesickness. I don't feel overwhelmed with relief. I'm glad to be here—as happy as I've ever been—and I'm glad to leave in two weeks, too.

This isn't where I belong anymore.

Right on cue, the front door swings open, and Lexi rushes outside. Even now, seven months pregnant, she's wearing a silk slip nightgown (pink of course), and she's the picture of California girl charisma. Well, now it's more like California MILF perfection (her words).

She runs down the stairs and throws her arms around me.

"I missed you." She squeezes me so tightly I can't breathe. "I got you the best Christmas present." She leans in to whisper in my ear. "It's a vibrator shaped like the Empire State Building."

"Form and function," I say.

"Well, yeah." She laughs. "Since you'll never have a bachelorette."

"I'm not even engaged," I say. "And you'd buy me something even more perverse for a bachelorette." Lexi doesn't need a reason to turn the subject to sex (not in private), but she does celebrate the rare occasion the focus is more socially acceptable.

"True. Oh, I saw just the thing. River would love it." She says it without a hint of interest in her voice.

And I don't feel a single pang of jealousy. Not just because Lexi is head over heels in love with Jake. Not just because she relishes in tales of third-trimester horniness and her husband's desire to fill them. *He says I look even more beautiful like this. Can you believe it? I think it's because my boobs are massive now.* Not just because she's excited about impending motherhood in a way I can't imagine.

Because I love and trust my boyfriend and he never, and I mean never, shows interest in other women. It's freaky, really. Like he's above human biology. And New York City is full of beautiful, well-dressed, artistic women. New York City is full of beautiful women of every shape, size, age, and personality.

I look at them. I look at men. I look at everyone. It feels good to live somewhere with dynamic surroundings. Even if the weather is totally miserable half the year. Most of the year. There are two good weeks in fall and two in spring. The rest is...an adventure.

"I'm going to get you back one day," I say. "Maybe I'll buy you a sex toy for your baby shower."

"Oh, Dee." She laughs. "You think the women I'm inviting stopped enjoying sex toys because they're moms?"

"No. I think they'll be embarrassed because they live in Orange County," I say.

"Moms are still women," she says. "And we're still horny. Sometimes, we're really horny."

"Too much information."

"You asked for it." She releases me a tiny bit and she launches into a long, detailed story about how she finally took Jake to her old sex spot and had her way with him. Twice.

River waits patiently at the side of our rental car. Technically, it's his rental car. My Tesla is parked in the garage. Dad likes driving it when he's meeting people who care about the environment.

Initially, I insisted River rent a car, so he could have the best possible impression of life in Orange County. Initially, I thought, *This two-week trip is my chance to show him he loves it here.* And how could anyone love the suburbs without a car and a driver's license?

But I don't feel that pull anymore. I love it here, I do, but I don't want to live here anymore. I would move back in a second if Lexi or Dad asked, and he'd move with me.

But they wouldn't. They want me to have space to soar on my own. And I want that for them, too.

Finally, Lexi finishes with her dirty details (for now), releases me, greets my boyfriend with a friendly hug. He hugs back without any desire or embarrassment, then he follows us into the house and says hello to Jake and Dad.

After a catch-up session here, we unpack in the apartment (now officially a guest apartment, since Lexi and Jake have their own house in Newport Beach).

"What do you think?" River pulls me into the backyard and

motions to the big blue sky, the clean-cut grass, the sparkling azure water of the pool. "Are you tempted to move home?"

No, but I want to let him sweat it. "In some ways."

"Deanna Huntington." He smiles. "You're trying to play me."

"Play you? No. Never." I wrap my arms around him, too. "Use fair and valid negotiating tactics?"

"Always." He presses his lips to mine. It's a tired, messy kiss. That sort of *I'm too exhausted to do this with my best technique but I love you and I want to be close to you* kind of kiss. He's worn out, too. From the weather, the travel, the stress of juggling contract gigs with running a burgeoning small press. But he's here, with me. All of him is with me.

I kiss back with even less technique. After a long week at work debating our latest buyout offer (eventually we decided no, we can get more money) and our cancelled flight adventure, I'm something beyond exhausted. But his affection wakes me the way it always does. It reminds me I'm aware and alive. It reminds me the world is a beautiful place, whether it's blue skies and sunshine, or blizzards and storm clouds.

I haven't totally adopted his romantic predisposition, but I appreciate it more these days. I proudly display the roses he sends me and I devour the dark chocolate. He doesn't try to convince me *Before Sunrise* is the most romantic movie of all time (seriously, how illogical is it to not exchange phone numbers?) and I don't argue *Casablanca* is about duty and commitment, not passion (the text speaks for itself).

We're not perfect. We frustrate each other sometimes. We argue sometimes. But, usually, it's the sort of banter you see in an old movie. We respect each other's point of view and the way it enriches our own.

We are who we are, just together.

After another kiss, he leads me to his grandma's house, and we catch up with her. As usual, she's living large, dancing three times a week, playing bridge with friends, and, of course, writing a new erotic novel. This one is about a dominant woman. Which means way too many knowing glances from River.

Thankfully, in the middle of a story about her lunch with a publisher, River breaks to make us tea and Ida leads me to her backyard. The space where our worlds used to meet.

Ida looks at the succulents lining the white fence and shakes her head. "Fern and North love the cacti, but I miss the drama of the roses."

"These are better for the environment and easier to keep alive," I say.

She smiles. "And you like the look of them better?"

"I prefer them, yes." They're prickly, tough, hardy. It's easy to love a soft, feminine rose. It's a lot harder to adore a spiky cactus.

"That would be a way to do it. Put the ring on a cactus. Can you even keep them alive in the city? It's so cold there."

"It's a struggle." Wait a second. "What ring?"

Ida smiles in that impish way of hers. "He asked your father for his blessing."

"He did not," I say.

Ida nods. "Of course, he did. And of course, your father said, 'Good luck convincing my daughter of anything.' I told him the same thing, of course. He needs to wait until you're ready."

"But you still gave him your ring?" I ask.

She shrugs. "I couldn't help myself."

"Is he planning to do it while we're here?" I ask.

"No. I don't think so," she says. "Would you say yes?"

Technically, my left arm belongs to him, but he'd never hold me to that. He's still far too romantic to marry someone who doesn't actually want to marry him. "It's what makes sense." But I don't see love that way anymore. I don't believe we need to follow a certain set of steps. Dating, living together, marriage. I'm happy exploring the wide world of non-matrimonial partnership. If I stay in the dating app business, marriage is the smart career move. It says I believe in the mission.

And I do. I believe in our new message: trust the science and trust yourself.

That's what I do now. I trust the logic and I try to listen to my instincts. They say yes. One day, I want to marry River. But not today. Not yet.

For the first time in my life, I want to have fun with something. Not too much fun. A Deanna sort of amount. A few months. A year max.

Then, I'll be ready.

It won't be the image in my head or the one in his. It will be better, because it's ours, because we built it together.

ACKNOWLEDGMENTS

As always, my first thanks goes to my father, for encouraging me to follow my dreams, introducing me to film (including the works of Billy Wilder), and taking me to the bookstore when I was supposed to be grounded. I'd also like to thank my mother, for always encouraging my love of reading, and telling everyone what a great writer I was, as soon as I could hold a pen.

This was my first experience in the traditional publishing world and, wow, it's been a ride working with so many people! I have a much longer list than normal. Thank you to everyone at Bower for championing my vision of *The Neighbor Wager*, especially to my agents Aimee Ashcraft and Jess Dallow. Thanks to the team at Entangled, especially to Jessica Turner for believing in the project, to my editor Lydia Sharp for working day and night to get me feedback, and to Elizabeth Turner Strokes for capturing the characters in her adorable cover.

A special thanks to my husband, for putting up with my ridiculous schedule during my last round of edits, and to my long-time sounding boards, Dusty and Imma, for listening to my woes when I just couldn't deal with River and Dee's inability to get their shit together.

Fans of Christina Lauren and Tessa Bailey will adore this witty and unforgettable rom-com about skyways, highways, and all the perfectly wrong ways to fall in love.

PLANES, TRAINS, AND ALL THE FEELS

livy hart

As the black sheep of the family, choreographer Cassidy Bliss vowed she'd do anything to get home in time to help with her sister's wedding and avoid family disappointment...*again*. She just never expected "anything" would involve sharing the last rental car with the jerk who cut her off in line at the airport this morning. But horrible times apparently call for here-goes-nothing measures.

Driving across the country with Luke "life can be solved with a spreadsheet" Carlisle must be a penance for some crime she committed. Because the second he opens his mouth, it's all she can do to not maim him with her carry-on. But somewhere between his surprisingly thoughtful snack sharing and his uncanny ability to see straight to the core of her, her feelings go unchecked.

Suddenly, their crackling chemistry is just one more thing they have to navigate—and it couldn't come at a worse time. But after a lifetime of letting the expectations and needs of others drive her life, Cassidy must decide if she's ready to take the wheel once and for all.

Opposites don't attract. They swap lives...

EMILY DUVALL

From the outside looking in, socialite Lexi North's life looks decadently perfect, right down to her diamond-dusted nails. But you know what they say about glass houses... When one night goes horribly wrong—with the whole world watching—she's challenged to swap lives with the salty, albeit gorgeous, man she rear-ends with her car.

For mechanic Evan Bailey, life is definitely *not* a party. There's no "daddy's credit card" for fixing up his family's auto shop, raising his too-precocious-for-anyone's-good niece, and getting his accounts from deep in the red to black. Which is precisely when opportunity—and celebutante Lexi North—smashes into his life.

But what should have been an easy bet gets a whole lot harder with the inexplicably hot chemistry between them. Now the only way for either of them to get what they want is to go for broke...

*Don't miss the exciting new books
Entangled has to offer.*

Follow us!

AMARA
an imprint of Entangled Publishing LLC